TRASHED

TRASHED

Best wishes from

Norman Townsend

NORMAN TOWNSEND

Matador
9 Priory Business Park,
Wistow Road, Kibworth Beauchamp,
Leicestershire. LE8 0RX
Tel: 0116 279 2299
Email: books@troubador.co.uk
Web: www.troubador.co.uk/matador
Twitter: @matadorbooks

ISBN 978 1789015 096

British Library Cataloguing in Publication Data.
A catalogue record for this book is available from the British Library.

Printed and bound in Great Britain by 4edge Limited
Typeset in 11pt Adobe Garamond Pro by Troubador Publishing Ltd, Leicester, UK

Matador is an imprint of Troubador Publishing Ltd

FOR AMY K. TOWNSEND

Thanks to Jenny and Amy for constant support above and beyond! Thanks to Rex, Paul, Jill and Dylan for help and support for what must have felt like an awfully long year.
And a big thank you to Richard Barnfather for extra art work and publicity pictures as well as moral support.

CHAPTER 1

P aul Stafford turned his ancient Volvo estate on to the A331, heading out of Farnborough towards an auction house in Camberley. He liked the fact that the old car said "near poverty" to his tip and auction punters. He felt it showed he wasn't profiteering from them. And he liked that it fitted his six-foot-one-inch frame adequately. At just before eight the traffic was heavy as always at this time of a weekday morning. A Cream CD was in the player. A Victorian Canterbury and a reproduction Davenport desk were in the back. These had arrived damaged in one of his tips and had been rescued and repaired ready for auction.

Thirty-nine-year-old Stafford had spent more than twenty years in the military. It was this experience that enabled him to recognise the "crump" of a distant explosion, even from the confines of his car. Curious, he pulled his car into the nearest parking space and climbed out. The sky behind was almost black with vast amounts of debris, plastic bags, newspaper and a myriad of other unsavoury items wafting slowly down. He guessed the explosion was at or near the tip and U-turned as quickly as traffic would allow.

Since taking over the tips at Farnborough and before that at Aldershot, Stafford had experienced low-level vandalism at both sites. The previous managers had left both sites strewn with rubbish and all the Roll on-Roll off bins overflowing with trash. Red graffiti had been sprayed on the Portakabins declaring "You owe us major."

This explosion, he suspected, was further torment, designed to pay him back for taking away their very lucrative tips.

Racing towards the Farnborough site, his mobile phone rang. He saw it was from Garfield Lewis, and accepted the call.

'You need to get here...' The line went dead. Stafford hit the speed dial button, alternately trying the tip's land line and Lewis's mobile. He drove as fast as he dared. Getting no response on his mobile, he turned his attention to cursing the other drivers for not moving out of his way fast enough.

———————————————— ‖ ————————————————

The bomb blew at precisely 7.55a.m. Why that time nobody knew, not even the people who planted it. They didn't care, it had done its job. They knew Paul Stafford would get their message. From the front gates to the back wall the football pitch-sized Farnborough Waste Transfer Station was ankle-deep in household waste. The bomb had blasted its way through the massive metal roller shutters, taking with it the mountains of waste stored ready to be loaded and shipped to landfill.

Six members of staff had been preparing to open the site to start their day's work. The site manager had started to walk the thirty yards or so to open the large double gates. The weighbridge operator was at her desk turning on the computer, absentmindedly looking out of the office window, waiting for the first Ro-Ro bin lorry to arrive and tip its load. The yard foreman did what he'd done this time of the morning every working day for the last twelve years; he unlocked the side door to the huge warehouse waste storage area to press the buttons that operated the front roller shutters. As he put his key in the lock, he was thrown upwards, backwards, forcefully into oblivion by an invisible shock wave. Unconscious, he crashed to the ground twenty feet away, where he lay motionless, traumatised. Barely breathing and with eyes rolling back into their sockets he disappeared under the mass of waste descending from the heavens.

The driver of the hook loader lorry had been walking alongside the JCB operator to their machines ready to start their day's work. The lorry driver was nearest to the roller shutter when the blast ripped it apart, blowing them off their feet. Jagged shards of metal hit them at lightning speed. The lorry driver was lucky: he took the brunt of the blast and died instantly. The left side of his head and face disappeared, sheared off, covering his colleague with a spray, red with blood and snot and bone. Another shard hit with such force it sliced through his gut and carried on to do damage to his friend.

Shards hit and sliced through meat and bone alike. A final jagged shard severed the JCB operator's left hand. The power of the blast dumped it some ten feet away. Torn apart in milliseconds, they hadn't stood a chance. They crashed to the ground, landing one on top of the other. Fountains of blood pooled and mixed around them.

Screaming in agony, the JCB driver took longer to die, but the fountains of blood didn't last long. Within minutes they were covered in the household waste that still rained from the sky.

For just a few seconds the silence was absolute. The stench of rotting household waste hung in the air. Then sound began to break through. The weighbridge operator ran into the yard and screamed, tears streaming down her face. The site manager was slumped trembling against the unopened gates, mouth opening and closing like a stranded fish, shock and fear in control. The yard man who had been in the mess when the blast happened, shuffled aimlessly through piles of waste, mouth open, eyes wide, not believing what they were seeing.

Moments later Paul Stafford's crew from the adjoining household waste recycling centre chased down the concrete steps linking the two sites. They were led by Jamaican-born Garfield Lewis, the recycling centre manager. He realised the surviving transfer station staff were too traumatised to act rationally. Bringing his military expertise to bear, he took over. He ran towards the weighbridge operator, put his arm around her shoulders and guided her back to the office. Sitting her down he handed her the phone. 'C'mon now, love,' he said, 'we've got to get things sorted'. I need you to dial 999, tell 'em what's happened. They'll know what to do.' She nodded, wiped away the tears, and with trembling hands dialled the emergency number. Garfield quickly checked the day book that every waste site is required to have, noted six persons on site, then ripping a first aid kit from the office wall, he dashed back into the yard thinking the first aid kit would probably be a waste of time... it was.

——————————— ‖ ———————————

From seemingly all directions sirens were wailing and he could see the occasional blue and red flash in the distance as police and emergency vehicles raced towards the site of the explosion. The old Volvo screeched on to Templar Avenue, a road wide enough for him to overtake at high speed, well, the highest the Volvo could muster. Sliding around Elles Road roundabout the tyres fought to hold the tarmac. He saw two ambulances, sirens blaring, lights flashing, picking a hazardous pathway through morning traffic on the other side of the road. As he reached the Arrow Road roundabout, gridlocked traffic blocked his way. He decided to run the last half mile or so and eased his car into the car park of a company on the corner of a nearby road.

Even in his physical condition running was difficult and became more like a slalom as he dodged cars parked on the pavements, cars with doors left open, and abandoned hook loader lorries. Stafford dodged this way and that, trying to avoid the occupants as they craned to get a better view of what was going on. As he ran he realised he was running ankle-deep in household waste. Closer to the site he could see through the crowd of onlookers, five or six police cars parked haphazardly around the entrance gates to the transfer station and recycling centre. Police officers tried desperately to set up safety zones, pushing people trying to get to work further away from the danger area.

Making his way through the crowd, Stafford could see bomb squad vehicles parked inside the transfer station gates. Army personnel, forensic experts, police, and he presumed, Special Branch, were busy, carefully working their way through piles of rubbish.

As he approached the gates to the tip, two police officers barred his way. The younger PC spoke first, 'Sorry, sir, I'm afraid you're not allowed on site.'

Stafford showed the officers his ID and said, 'Yeah, I realise you have a major problem here, but this site's my responsibility. My men will have been here at 7:30 waiting to open up. I need to check who's here and if they are OK.'

Taking Stafford's credentials, the more senior officer walked over to the transfer station's weighbridge office that they were using as a temporary base. Stafford asked the young constable, 'So what's happened here? Is anyone hurt? Do you know what caused the explosion?'

'Yeah, there's at least four casualties that I saw, one's dead. Another probably won't make it,' said the young copper with trembling lips, voice hoarse with emotion.

The other officer returned carrying a clipboard. He glanced at the ashen-faced PC, then looked at Stafford and raised an eyebrow acknowledging that he knew the young man was struggling to hold it together. He handed back Stafford's ID and said, 'I thought as you're the contractor for the tip, my governor would want a word with you, but apparently not. So if you'll just sign here Major Stafford, you can go on through.' He shrugged and handed the clipboard to Stafford, who signed the form.

Opening the gate the officer said, 'I think all the casualties were transfer station staff.'

Stafford stopped as though stunned; he knew all the people who worked there. He took a deep breath and continued, his feelings of relief tinged with guilt... and grief. 'Thanks,' was all he managed to say.

With a wry smile at the officers and a pounding heart, he chased up the trash-covered drive-in slope to his tip. Reaching the flat parking area at the top, he could clearly see the damage caused by the blast. The massive metal roller shutters on the front of the transfer station's covered area had been completely destroyed. The explosion had obviously occurred in the mountain of waste stored in the warehouse-style loading area. Stafford guessed that shards from the roller shutter had been the cause of the casualties, as the household waste, though deep and spread over a huge area, was neither solid enough nor heavy enough to cause much harm.

Garfield Lewis and three of his staff were already beginning to clear up the debris. He walked across the car park to them and asked, 'What're we looking at, lads? Everyone OK?' Getting four nods in response he continued, 'Tell you what, let's grab some chairs in the sales shed and tell me what you know?' It took a few moments shifting items of furniture around as they created space to make themselves relatively comfortable.

'So come on, Garfield, tell me what the fuck happened here,' he said.

Lewis, more renowned for his Kanye West-like appearance and military skills than his conversational ability started, 'Well, Majo… Staf, not a lot to tell really, I was standing over there in the car park looking down at the graffiti, when the whole frigging front of the building blew out at me. Next I remember flying back across the yard, landing on my frigging arse and laying there being totally covered in shit, man. Totally covered, total shit, man, know what I mean?' The poorly suppressed chuckles did a lot to relieve the tension.

Stafford smiled, 'So what time did you unlock?'

'I got here at 7:30 or thereabouts, and everything looked OK, y'know, like normal. I left the gate closed but not locked, for the others to get in,'… Lewis gathered his thoughts then continued, 'I saw some writing on the ground, but didn't take much notice as I was goin' round opening up the place, y'know, office, mess, sales shed an' that.'

Stafford discovered that the other men had arrived soon after 7:30, and they all had commented on the new graffiti sprayed in red paint on the car park floor. The men had then gone into the Portakabin mess to change into their work boots and gear, and get a cup of tea before starting work. Whilst in the mess they had spoken to Lewis about the graffiti and he had gone out into the yard to see it for himself. He had been standing looking at it at precisely five minutes to eight when the bomb exploded. He had been protected from the metal shards by the rail fences at the front of each bin, primarily there to stop members of the public being injured by flying debris when the bin contents were crushed by the sites JCB digger in order to get more waste into each bin. These fences also stopped the frontal "attack" of household waste, but couldn't stop the torrent of waste that rained down from on high.

The men said nothing for a couple of minutes as they realised how lucky Lewis had been. Stafford told them to take a break, or go for a cigarette before continuing with the clear up. Lewis stayed sitting down with Stafford.

'Look, Staf,' he said, 'after the blast, me and the lads went down the steps into the transfer station. The guys down there were panickin' a bit, so I got them to call the emergency services. Then, we tried to find the lads that they said were missing.' He shuddered. 'But whatever that jumped up little DI says, I think this was a bomb of sorts and it was meant for us, not the transfer station.'

'He doesn't think it was a bomb then?'

'No, he was saying some shit about a gas cylinder blowing up. But when I looked in the storage area down there, the blast seems to have come right from the front near the roller shutter. Now the hook loader lorry driver came up here at around 5:30 yesterday afternoon and asked if I wanted him to pull out a waste bin that was nearly full, to save him doing it first thing this morning. I said yeah, so we chucked a couple of mattresses on the back end, you know, just to fill it up some more. So when he emptied the bin they would have been off first. They're still in the storage area, but not a lot else in front.'

'So you reckon the bomb could have been in our bin?'

'Looks that way to me. This bomb was aimed at us, boss. Mark my words, this is Runihura's doing. He's gotta pay, boss. He's gotta fucking pay for this.'

'Hmm, well, rumour has it that he's a tough nut, a hard man, but I never had him down for a fuckin' psycho,' said Stafford.

'But he's crossed the line here, Staf, he's killing innocents, man.' Stafford had no problem accepting Lewis's word. Sergeant Garfield Lewis and Captain Ryan Peters, now at the Aldershot tip, had been members of Major Paul Stafford's SIS and MI6 training teams at their last military posting at Fort Monckton in Gosport. They had worked many missions together and trusted each other implicitly.

'So tell me about the graffiti,' Stafford said as he stepped out of the sales shed. Lewis called over two of his men and asked them to clear the area where the new graffiti had been sprayed. The warning was exactly the same as at the Aldershot tip some weeks earlier, "YOU OWE US MAJOR."

They walked to the office and Stafford sat in a leather swivel chair. Lewis took the only other seat in the tiny metal shed. Stafford said, 'So the police have been up here then?'

'Yeah, they arrived on site about ten minutes after the blast. They secured the place and interviewed us all down there. Then the forensic team came up here, had a shufti round, thought everything was OK. Or at least after a few minutes poking around in the rubbish, said there was nothing of use to them up here and went back down to the transfer station.'

'So I guess the DI thinks he's covered all the bases and doesn't need to talk to me. Did they see or did you tell them about the new graffiti?'

'No, boss, I think most of us were too wound up, we just never thought about it.'

Stafford glanced at his watch. It was 10:15.

'Have you managed to contact Ryan over at Aldershot to tell him what's happened?' he asked as he picked up the landline receiver. The line was still dead. He replaced the receiver rather harder than he'd intended. Lewis showed Stafford his mobile. There was no signal there either.

Lewis was back helping his crew with the clear up when Stafford walked over to them.

'OK, lads, I really appreciate your efforts down at the transfer station. That took guts, so well done... Look, I need to talk to the police now, so I'll catch up with you all later.'

He walked down the slope to the entrance and exit gates. As Stafford came near, the older policeman swung the gate open for him, and tried to close it again, but Stafford stopped him and said, 'If you've got a moment I think there's something you should see up there in our parking area.'

The policeman hesitated for the merest fraction before turning to his sidekick and saying 'I shouldn't be too long, you'll be all right,' then closed the gate behind him.

As they walked together up the slope the constable offered his hand and said, 'Constable Gibson, Lee Gibson.' Shaking hands Stafford said, 'Yeah, and I'm Paul.' He then described the graffiti and vandalism that had occurred earlier at the Aldershot tip just after he had taken it over. He explained how his fledgling company, Andover Recycling, had initially been offered just the two sites by HCC and how the two original managers' contracts had been torn up for not reaching performance targets.

The level surface of the parking area had been cleared of rubbish and the red graffiti, large and garish, was startlingly obvious. The copper's face was grim as he said to Stafford, 'I think you're probably right. Looks to me like you, or the tip were the targets, not the transfer station.'

Stafford and Gibson walked back down to the gates and they left the site. Stafford gave the constable a business card, and said, 'I'd be grateful if you'd keep me updated on this.' Gibson nodded, put the card in his pocket, pulled out his notebook.

'Out of interest, what were the names of those two managers?'

Stafford thought for a second or two then said, 'The one here was Matis Bockus and at Aldershot it was Ayman Runihura.' Stafford checked the spelling with him, then left, saying to call at any time. He jogged back down to his unlocked car, climbed in, slid the nearest CD into the player and headed for Camberley, The Travelling Wilburys his travel companions.

CHAPTER 2

One man who did care about the timing of the explosion was Ayman Runihura. He didn't care about the deaths, that was just collateral damage. He was angry; his men had fucked up.

'Fuck, it was supposed to be so easy,' he said out loud as he bashed the Mercedes' steering wheel with his fist. His instructions to them had been quite clear. "Put the explosives in the household waste bin just before the tip closes," he had told them.

Runihura parked the black Mercedes X-Class pickup outside the Aldershot flat he occasionally shared with his team. No women lived there. The syndicate provided female company when they needed, though his tanned and pockmarked features repelled as many women as it attracted. Grim faced, he dashed up the iron staircase, burst through the front door and shouted, 'Matis, Matis, where the fuck are you? Get in here now.' One of the doors leading off the main room opened and a bleary-eyed Matis Bockus peered around it.

'Jeez, man, what your problem?' he said, his English heavily accented.

'My problem is that your fucking bomb blew up the

transfer station, not the fucking tip. You were just supposed to show him if he didn't work with us we'd hurt him,' he said, dragging Bockus into the room.

'Well, he get that message sure,' said Bockus regaining his balance and shrugging his shoulders.

'Yeah, and now we got police, special branch and MI5 sniffing around for Christ's sake. We don't fuckin' need it.' Runihura's dark eyes were ablaze with anger. It was the first time Bockus had seen this giant of a man lose control. He said nothing for a moment, then shrugged again and said, 'Anyway, ain't we gotta go sailin' today?'

Runihura shook his head in mock despair, and began to calm down. His men had managed to place the device in the bin at the HWRC twenty minutes before the site was due to close. They weren't to know that the hook loader driver would decide to clear one last bin before they locked up. And how could they know that he would then empty the load and give the tip a fresh bin to start the next morning? Runihura had told them, "Over night, I want the explosion to blast crap all over Stafford's site. I want it to rip the bin apart. And spray the message large. I want him to know if he won't work with us, we can hurt him any time we want."

Well, the bomb had done its job, reasoned Runihura, and surely put the fear of God into Stafford and his men. But they'd created a major incident and he knew he had to limit the level of retribution… somehow.

He'd worked long and hard to help build a massive money-making empire. He earned a great deal of money, but took all the risks. The tips had proved ideal for moving merchandise from the other businesses he controlled. They'd doubled their turnover in the whole alphabet of drugs. And the franchise operation had almost doubled it again with DVDs as well as drugs. He had made a lot of money for the syndicate and now they were in danger of losing it.

For many months he had passed bulky brown envelopes of cash to George Saunders, a senior executive at Hampshire County Council. Saunders's department ran their twenty-six household waste recycling centres. He received the money after promising he could place Runihura's men, with all the right paper qualifications, into managing the lucrative Hampshire tips. Money had been paid, and now George's promises had fallen apart.

HCC had uncovered George's money-making venture and further discovered that he had been extorting money from company bosses bidding for the valuable waste contracts.

Rather than open up to public scrutiny, HCC had forced Saunders to resign.

The council had first offered Stafford's little recycling company two sites, Aldershot and Farnborough. Now Major Paul bloody Stafford had won a contract for five, and was pushing all syndicate men off the sites. Runihura was determined to ensure George understood the error of double-crossing his paymasters. His new priority was to have a chat with George.

CHAPTER 3

PC Gibson told the young copper what he had seen and that he needed to go into the transfer station to talk to DI Fisher.

The public had all but dispersed. All that remained were reporters and photographers from local and national newspapers and a couple of TV trucks with their crews and presenters hoping for further details. As PC Gibson approached the gates to the transfer station, a diminutive, middle-aged and chubby man, with a small entourage came out of the office and walked towards the gates. The group stopped a few yards from the entrance. The chubby man moved forward alone and stopped a pace or two from the gates.

'I'm Detective Inspector Gerry Fisher and I'm the officer in charge of this investigation,' he said. Cameras clicked and whirred as he paused, tilting his head up to hide his double chin. 'The situation is now under control,' he continued.

'As you can see,' he said and waved a chubby arm in the direction of the space where the roller shutters had been, 'there was an explosion, however I am of the belief that this wasn't a bomb or an IED, but merely a tragic accident caused by an LPG bottle being left in the wrong place. The bomb squad have almost finished their search and investigation, I believe they will concur, and we can then begin the process of clearing up.' Fisher took a breath and looked at his notes. The crowd of reporters shouted questions. 'What about casualties? You haven't mentioned the casualties,' said one. 'What caused the gas bottle to explode?' asked another. 'Why was there no fire?'

DI Fisher raised his left arm and called for quiet, 'Yes, there were three casualties including one fatality, three are traumatised but OK and we will notify you of their names when the next of kin have been informed. That's it for now. Thank you.' The DI turned and headed back towards the office.

Constable Gibson faced the reporters and said loudly 'Our thoughts and condolences are with the families of those involved.' He squeezed through the media throng, let himself in through the transfer station's gates and walked to the door at the rear of the office. He knocked once, took off his helmet and walked in. Gibson realised by the hostile glare that DI Fisher was not best pleased with the intrusion inside the office or out.

'And what do you want, Constable?' asked the DI, making the word constable sound like something unpalatable.

'Constable Gibson, sir,' said the forty-year-old PC nervously smoothing down his short black hair. 'We need to talk about this attack.'

'Talk about this attack? We don't need to talk about this attack, we don't need to talk about anything, because there was no attack. Just a plain old gas cylinder blowing up,' said the DI as he turned back to the desk.

'Sir, I know some of our lads went up to the recycling centre earlier to have a look around, but I really think you should have a word with the contractor, Major Stafford,' started Gibson, couching his comments carefully as he knew Fisher had been the lead officer.

'And we found nothing wrong apart from piles of steaming shite, so if it's OK with you, I won't be talking to him,' said the DI looking around the room with a smile on his pudgy face, as if waiting for some response to his repartee. There were few sniggers.

'Well, that's because they didn't see the parking area when it was cleared of rubbish. There's graffiti on the ground that matches graffiti found earlier this year at the Aldershot tip and quite recently on the office wall of the tip up there,' said Gibson pointing out of the window to the raised concrete area that housed the tip.

'And that just means the kids have got back in again. They're always doing it. They're a bloody nuisance on all the sites, as you well know,' said the DI and waved the constable away.

Gibson walked back to his post at the site's entrance, pulled out his mobile and was pleased to see a signal. He called Stafford. Gibson told him the DI was not interested in discussing the theory that this was an attack on Stafford and his men. He preferred to believe it was a tragic accident. Gibson assured him that he would try to convince the DI by delving into the background of all the men previously employed at the two sites to see if anything in their background would throw light on it. Stafford suggested they meet to give him the employment details that he had. He explained that he would need to get the previous manager's details from the company left running the twenty-one sites that he didn't control. They agreed to meet at the Thatched Cottage pub in Farnborough at eight o'clock that evening. Stafford thanked Gibson and ended the call.

─────────────── **II** ───────────────

After offloading the two items of furniture at the auction house, Stafford decided, in readiness for the meeting tonight, he would sort out his manager's details. He headed for home.

Home, a detached, run-down, five-bedroomed Victorian house, was in a quiet suburb of Farnborough. He had bought the house some years earlier and was gradually restoring it to its former glory. The plot in which it stood wasn't massive, but it boasted a number of mature trees and shrubs in both back and front gardens. Some ten yards to the right of the house was a brick-built garage, where he stored and restored interesting items rescued from the tips. The house was just far enough away from his neighbours for him to be able to play his music as loud as it needed to be played. Stafford parked on the paved driveway in front of the garage and walked the few yards to his front door. Taking the three steps in one stride he let himself into the quiet and spacious hall. The rooms in the house were large, with tall windows and high ceilings. The kitchen was huge, far too big for his pathetic culinary skills. He used half of it as an office, complete with antique desk, computer and modern, but extremely large and comfortable black leather swivel and rocking chair.

He kept the details of his five site managers and their employees' records in a four-drawer filing cabinet. He opened the relevant drawer and selected the files.

The five managers were contracted to him, not actually employed by him. They employed their own staff and kept their own employee details. The files contained CVs, tax details, VAT forms, contract and qualification details presented and signed prior to him taking over the running of the five sites. In each file was a list of the managers' employees, their addresses and contact details. Knowing Aldershot and Farnborough's details were up to date he photocopied details of the other three sites.

He had met these three managers and some of their staff on a number of occasions, including when they signed their contracts and handed over the various necessary documents, including certificates outlining their waste management qualifications.

To manage a waste facility in Hampshire the council determined that a qualification known as a WAMITAB level four was a minimum requirement. This certificate meant that the recipient had undergone rigorous training and passed the Waste Management Industry Training & Advisory Board (WAMITAB) examinations.

As these three sites were staffed and functioning, albeit badly, Stafford had concentrated on getting Aldershot and Farnborough up and running properly.

Stafford spread out the three waste certificates in front of him. He could see nothing amiss, so called their HQ in Northampton.

'Hi, I'm Paul Stafford and I run a company called Andover Recycling in Hampshire, I need to follow up on the training history of three of my new managers.' The receptionist transferred him to the relevant department, and he explained what he needed.

'No problem, sir, can you give me their details?' Stafford reeled off their names. No one spoke for a second or two, then he heard the gentle sound of breathing and keys tapping as she typed in their names.

'Right, Mr Stafford, I'll give you the details if you are ready?' She paused for a moment then, 'Certificate numbers WM77326 and WM92147 are level two and certificate number WM64215 is level four. I hope that helps… Is there anything else I can do for you?'

He hesitated for a second or two, 'Thank you, no, that's all I need for now, but I may need to talk to you again,' he said and ended the call.

He looked again at the certificates spread out in front of him. All three showed level four qualifications. Only Basingstoke's it seemed was kosher. He cursed under his breath, 'Why the fuck didn't I check before?'

Barry Allen had run the Basingstoke site for just over two years, with a team of ten men. Five or six on site at any one time. He had achieved his waste qualification two and a half years earlier. HCC monthly figures showed that the site performed well to start with, but had slipped considerably over the last few months. Deciding it was time for a visit, Stafford picked up the three photocopied files and went out to his car.

As he headed for the M3 motorway he slipped a CD into the player and blasted his mind into cruise with Pink Floyd's "One Of These Days" at full volume.

Though traffic was fairly light, roadworks on the ring road turned the twenty-five-minute journey into forty-five minutes. Arriving at the site, he parked the car and picked up the Basingstoke folder. He found Barry Allen in the sales shed extracting a fiver from a punter buying a painted set of bookshelves. Stafford wandered around the sales area waiting for the transaction to end.

'Bloody hell, Staf,' said Allen as he reached out his hand. 'Am I glad to see you, I've been trying your number on an' off since we heard about the bang. What's occurring there?'

'Yeah, sorry about that, I ended up ignoring the phone; getting too many calls. To be honest, no one's sure what's going on. The explosion was in the transfer station, but we're going to be closed for a few days as well, so I am glad to see you're still making some money,' he said with a grin as he shook Barry's outstretched hand, then added, 'If you've got a few minutes let's have a stroll round the site, see how it looks and discuss any problems as we go.'

As they walked Stafford spotted a couple of new faces amongst the staff and mentioned this to Allen.

'Yeah, staff's quite a problem round here. No unemployment really, so it's fuckin' hard to find someone who wants to work in shite,' he said and chuckled. Stafford noted that neither of the new men approached the public to offer help. In fact they didn't appear keen on working at all, preferring to just lean on the rails beside the bins. As they continued round, Allen noticed a couple of black plastic sacks in the garden waste bin. He cursed and wandered over to empty them. Further on he pulled out plastic and polystyrene from the cardboard bin.

Stafford asked, 'Why didn't you call your lads over to sort that stuff out?'

'Well, you know how it is, sometimes it's quicker and easier to do it yourself.'

They completed the circuit and apart from some messy areas here and there the site was pretty much up together.

When they adjourned to Barry's office, Stafford had a little grin as he noticed a number of sporting items tucked into a corner. Weekends particularly can generate a lot of cash on the tips. Many managers kept by the side of their desk a little bit of insurance, usually in the form of a baseball bat or the shorter rounders bat. Unsure if this was legal, they also kept the odd tennis racquet, cricket bat and stumps and often a catcher's mitt and ball, to claim it was innocent sports gear for sale. Stafford asked a number of tricky questions regarding procedures for certain types of hazardous wastes. Getting detailed and accurate answers confirmed for him that Barry Allen's WAMITAB level 4 was kosher.

'These new guys, do they appear in my file?' asked Stafford looking at Barry and holding up his folder. Barry Allen's eyes looked everywhere except at Stafford.

'No, sorry, boss, I ain't got round to it yet.'

'OK… have you got their details handy? I can just add them in the file now.' Allen shuffled his feet, then moved some papers around his desk,

'Sorry, Staf, but I haven't really got any of their details yet, except their names.'

'So how long have they worked here?'

'Only about a month,' said Allen, sheepishly.

'What? A month, a whole month and all you've got is their names? Come on, Barry, get a grip.'

'Yeah, I know, but it's been bloody tough the last few months getting staff and you know I need at least five on site every day.'

'So what? You take on anyone who walks through the gate?'

'Pretty much, boss, yeah. But these guys came sort of recommended.'

Stafford asked for the names of the new men and added them to his list.

'Hmm,' he mused, 'I think you'd better tell me the whole story.'

CHAPTER 4

After resigning, George Saunders cleared his office of everything that could possibly incriminate him or link him to criminal activity. Two senior members of HCC's security team shadowed his every move, then assisted him in carting three storage boxes of files, laptop and personal items out to his Aintree Green Range Rover Evoque.

It was only a twenty-five-minute drive from the Winchester HCC offices to Saunders's eight-bedroomed detached home in leafy Chandlers Ford. Storming into the house, he took all three boxes into his study, threw them to the floor and slumped into the chair at his desk. Knuckles white, he gripped the arms of his antique office chair, stared blankly into space, desperately trying to think of his next move.

Eileen, his wife of twenty-five years, surprised by his sudden arrival, burst into the study and said, 'I didn't expect you home so early. Are you all right? You're not ill, are you?'

George was not in the mood to talk. Catching his breath he said, 'Just some trouble at the office I need to sort out, nothing for you to bother about. I'll be out in a while so just leave me to it.' Slowly he pushed himself out of the chair, guided her by the elbow back out of his study and closed the door behind her. He pulled out a briefcase from underneath the desk, laid it on top and checked the contents. There was still a few grand in there. Leaving it open he hunted through the desk until he found his passport and registration documents for the Range Rover. *You never know, if I run out of cash at least I can flog that,* he thought as he threw them into his briefcase and closed it.

---------- **II** ----------

Eileen knew better than to argue when George was in a mood. It was more than twenty-four hours before he came out of the study. She had knocked on the door numerous times offering tea or coffee and she'd asked if he wanted to eat or if he was coming to bed. Getting only grunts, and the occasional "Leave me alone," she left him alone.

He came out looking haggard and dishevelled. Hearing him come out of the study, she went to him to see if she could help. George wasn't a big or powerful man but he pushed roughly past her and staggered up stairs, carrying the briefcase. He dashed into their bedroom, reached into one of the wardrobes and grabbed the nearest suitcase. He stuffed a couple of clean shirts and some underwear into it and ran back down the stairs almost knocking Eileen over as he charged past.

'George, George, what's happening? What is it?' she said, tears leaving pink trails in her make-up 'Tell me, tell me what's going on, please, George! Why won't you bloody tell me?'

George turned to her as he reached the front door.

'I've got to get away for a couple of days, stuff I need to sort out. I'll phone soon, but I need to go.' He ran out of the house.

Eileen's still lovely face was streaked with mascara. Tears flowed and her head rocked from side to side as she watched him throw the suitcase and briefcase into his car and drive away from her, gravel spinning up behind him.

II

As he turned out of the drive, a black Mercedes X-Class Concept pick up pulled out some 200 yards behind him. It was still behind him as he joined the M3 motorway.

George was exhausted; he hadn't slept or eaten for two nights. He was heading towards London. He realised he was driving erratically. Exhaustion took over, his eyes started to close and he struggled to keep them open. He was fighting fatigue, his head lolling from side to side. Battling, willing his eyelids to stay open, George hit the button to open the car's front windows. The blast of air and the foul smell of diesel hit him like a slap in the face with a damp, oily rag. Partly revived, he panicked as he realised his near side wheels were on the hard shoulder. He jerked the steering wheel and pulled the car back into the carriageway. He realised how close he had been to falling asleep; the jolt of adrenaline had scared him awake. He was approaching junction one. He knew he desperately needed to get his head down. To rest, to sleep if he could. He was heading for the Travelodge Hotel, just by the motorway exit.

Smiling now, pleased that he hadn't missed his turn off, he recalled how he and Eileen stayed there one night when their holiday flight from Heathrow had been delayed. Instantly he dismissed the thought and pulled off the motorway, happier now, as he thought about getting some rest.

At the roundabout he took the exit for the A308 and quickly found the hotel. He parked the Range Rover, smoothed down his lank greying hair and climbed out. He grabbed his suitcase and briefcase off the back seat and locked the car. As he walked towards the reception area, a black Mercedes X-Class pickup pulled slowly into the parking area. As he drew near to the Mercedes two men slid out, one from the rear, one from the passenger's seat next to the driver.

II

'Going on holiday, George?' asked Ayman Runihura. Startled, George took a pace backwards, dropped his suitcase and made to run. As he realised these men would catch him before he got anywhere near his car he turned back to them and said, with a nervous smile, 'No, no, it's not like that, Ayman, just a bit of business I need to attend to.'

'Well, I think we should sort out our business first, George, so come and join me please. My colleague Matis will drive your car,' he said holding out his hand for the key. Although the weather was chilly, George was bathed with sweat, the stench of fear rising from him like steam.

'But, Ayman, can't we do this later? I'm meeting...' The sentence was never finished. Runihura, with incredible speed, backhanded George across the face. George staggered back a couple of paces. Blood seeping from split lips, he shaped up as though to swing his briefcase at Runihura.

'George, George, for fuck's sake, don't try to play the hard man, you know you can't win here.' George's shoulders drooped, he put his left hand in his trouser pocket, pulled out the key to the Evoque and gave it to Runihura.

'Good choice, George, now get in the back of the Merc.'

Saunders did as he was told, then slid across the seat to the far side and put his briefcase between him and the door. As he straightened up he realised there was a third man he didn't recognise in the driver's seat. George pulled out a handkerchief and cautiously dabbed his lips, feeling if any of his teeth were loose. Runihura gave the key to Matis Bockus, the ex-Farnborough manager, who only now did George recognise. Bockus walked towards George's Evoque and picked up the suitcase on the way.

'Stay behind us just in case of any problems,' said Runihura. Bockus nodded, put the suitcase on the rear seats and climbed into the Evoque. Runihura climbed in next to Saunders. As he settled in, he told George to pass him the briefcase and he did without a word. Runihura placed it between him and the door.

'Now put your seat belt on and put your hands together in front.' George did so without complaint. Runihura reached into the pocket at the back of the front seat, pulled out two industrial cable ties and expertly bound George's hands tightly together.

'OK, drive,' said Runihura. The two cars turned back to the M3 and headed south. Runihura reached into the inside pocket of his jacket and took out a small syringe. Carefully he removed the needle cover and without a word, plunged it into George's ample left thigh. Slowly and none to gently he pushed in the plunger. The diazepam gradually disappeared into George's leg. George started to scream and tried to push himself off the seat. He sank back, looking plump, almost contented now the fear and stress had drained from his face. His pupils rolled up into his head as his eyes closed. He sighed quietly, smiled and pissed himself.

'Fuck,' said Runihura, 'wanker's pissed himself.' The smell of urine filled the car. Floyd Winstone, the driver, opened all the windows an inch. Runihura opened George's briefcase.

CHAPTER 5

Stafford drove out of the Basingstoke tip, head spinning, and needing a musical fix. He slammed in the first CD he laid his hands on and headed home with Roxy Music playing "A Song for Europe".

He went through to his sitting room. This room, though restored and well decorated, was filled with mismatched furniture mostly rescued from the tips. They were simply convenient and useable space fillers, just waiting to be replaced by items he promised himself he would buy soon… eventually.

Sitting down on one of the three sizeable sofas he began to develop a plan of action. He knew that he needed to get rid of the Andover and Winchester managers. He guessed all their staff would go as well, one way or another. Hard or soft, the choice would be theirs. It seemed obvious that whichever site he went to first, they would notify the other manager.

Stafford's first instinct was to call his old army buddy, Ryan Peters, at the Aldershot site and discuss it with him. The time on the 1960s starburst clock hanging over the mantle piece was showing just after 6:15 p.m. Realising that the sites closed at six, he decided to postpone phoning anyone till later in the evening. Settling down he began to think about his conversation earlier with Barry Allen. It transpired that Barry knew Ayman Runihura, the deposed manager of the Aldershot site. Not as drinking buddies or anything cosy like that. Merely as fellow managers contracted to the same company. They bumped into each other once or twice at various managers' meetings; occasionally talked on the phone about HCC memos or contract edicts. One time, Barry recalled he had mentioned his difficulty in getting and retaining staff. Runihura boasted that he always had plenty of staff and only rarely had a problem with them leaving. After Runihura was dismissed, Barry assumed he wouldn't hear from him again. Wrongly as it happened. Five or six weeks later he had turned up at the Basingstoke tip offering Barry a deal. To a man struggling to keep the site open, let alone up together through lack of staff, the deal seemed pretty good. Runihura had said that since leaving the Aldershot site he had set up his own business recycling scrap electronic items. He had premises in the Andover area where they were now repairing and reselling computers, vacuum cleaners, hi-fi equipment, DVD players and the like. He produced a T11 document, rubber stamped by the correct looking official rubber stamps. This proved, he said, that he had the premises, trained workforce and health and safety systems in place to work on these items.

His problem? No, he, Runihura, didn't have a problem, Barry Allen had the problem... not enough staff. Runihura's deal would solve that, no worries. Ayman Runihura, would arrange for two of his men to work five days a week on Barry's site and he, Runihura would continue to pay their wages and keep them on his books. All Barry had to do was provide a truckload of electronic gear every week. Allen worked out the sums, it seemed like an excellent deal and the two shook hands on it. On a site the size of Basingstoke, Barry Allen thought he had a great deal.

Before he'd left the site Stafford had promised he would help sort out the staff problem in a way that HCC as well as Allen would find acceptable. He guessed Runihura wouldn't agree with any plan.

Stafford decided to wait until after his conversation with PC Gibson before he took his next step. Ensuring he had the three files with him Stafford left the house. It was only a fifteen-minute drive to the Thatched Cottage pub. He got there a few moments before eight, but Gibson was already there, throwing darts at a board in the low-beamed rear bar. It took Stafford a minute or two before he realised the dart player was Lee Gibson, so different did he look in civvies,

'Hey, that's good throwing,' he said as he noticed the 140 score.

Gibson turned, grinned at Paul, reached out his hand and said, 'I did used to play for a pub team once, but y'know, the job gets in the way.'

Noting Gibson's glass was half empty, as they shook hands Stafford said, 'Good to see you again, can I get you another?' He ordered a half of Thatchers Cider for himself, and Gibson asked for a half of lager. Stafford paid the surly barman and they adjourned to a small table in a corner of the barroom. They sat down opposite each other and clinked glasses. 'Cheers' they said in unison.

'Well, I'm afraid the esteemed DI Fisher hasn't changed his views on the explosion,' said Gibson 'I can't understand why he's being so stubborn about it.'

'In that case, we'd best see what we can do to find out the truth then,' said Stafford opening the folders and passing the two fraudulent WAMITAB certificates across the table to Gibson. Stafford explained what he had discovered and said because they were fraudulent, he was going to get rid of both managers for contravening their contracts.

'I guess their crews will leave with them, but that will be their choice,' he said.

The names Floyd Winstone and Jan Kapusniak on the documents meant nothing to Gibson and he added them to his notebook for checking later. Stafford showed him the list of employees at the two sites, and added the list from Basingstoke. There were ten names and just eight addresses on the list.

'Along with the Basingstoke guys, I've already given you Matis Bockus, the previous manager of Farnborough, he's Lithuanian I think. Now I reckon Barry Allen's OK. But his new guys, they gotta be dodgy, ain't they?'

Again the names weren't familiar to Gibson, but as he read on he said, 'Hmm, that's interesting, loads of these blokes have given the same address. Maybe it's some sort of hostel. I'll follow up on that. Can I hang on to these?' he said waving the three sheets, then, 'So why d'you think the new guys are dodgy?'

'Yeah, keep 'em of course…Well, I don't know if what Barry told me is relevant, but Ayman Runihura, the guy who used to manage the Aldershot tip, had been to see him and offered him extra staff. Unbelievably he offered to keep them on his books and pay 'em. All Barry had to do was sort out a weekly truckload of electronic items for him.'

'Doesn't that sort of stuff get shipped out to Third World countries?'

'Yeah, it used to, but don't you remember the massive public outcry when they found kids as young as six or seven were being made to strip out the precious metals used in making the stuff? They were even using cyanide to strip stuff clean,' said Stafford, then added, 'Well, the Environmental Agency stepped in and banned the export of wastes deemed hazardous. Now to work on it, or even move it around the country, you need to meet extremely rigorous standards. I mean, the amount of, say, mercury in one item is negligible, but if you're sat mucking about with it on a mountain of the stuff, who knows what damage it could do?'

'But none of this seems to warrant chucking bombs about. I mean, what's so special about your waste business that makes you a target? I know you were in the military, but who did you upset so they'd want to bomb you?'

Stafford grinned, 'You've done a bit of homework then, but I don't think this is about revenge, I reckon it's got to be about money or maybe a terror thing.'

'When I saw you were a major in the security forces, I was sure that would be enough to convince my sergeant and the DI because of the graffiti thing. But no, they still think the graffiti is down to kids with bad grammar.' He chuckled, then said, 'I don't see a terror angle though, and is there really enough money in waste to start killing people over?'

'As a contractor to the council it's early days for me, but the deal I got was pretty big, and some site managers have made a mill, or two. But bombs? I just don't get it,' said Stafford.

'Christ, a million or two, I'm definitely in the wrong job then. Anyway, I'll follow up on these names and addresses, including Messrs Runihura and Bockus. What about you? What's your next move?' he asked as he folded the papers and tucked them into his jacket pocket.

'I've gotta sort out those two sites pronto, before they bring me down. So I'm gonna use tomorrow to talk to my crews. I need to organise staff and buy at least a dozen new security padlocks. Then on Saturday we'll turn up at the Winchester site just before closing, sort that out, then head for Andover, do the same there.'

'Saturday, aye? Well, I've got rest days, Saturday till Tuesday, so if you want, I'd be happy to join you,' said Gibson adding, 'in an unofficial capacity of course.'

'Yeah, it'll be good to have you along, though I'm hoping to keep it pretty low key.'

'Good, count me in then,' said Lee getting up and going to the bar.

They finished their drinks and wandered out to the car park. Shaking hands Stafford said, 'Right, I'll give you a bell tomorrow sometime to let you know about Saturday.'

Stafford drove the short distance home in thoughtful silence.

CHAPTER 6

A t seven the following morning, Stafford was shaved and dressed in his usual jeans and open-necked shirt. His light brown hair was still wet from the shower as he waited, receiver to his ear, for his call to be answered. It rang for a moment or two before he heard a little voice ask politely, 'Good morning, who is this?'

'Oh hi, Ben, can you tell your dad it's Paul?'

The little voice said, 'Yeah, hi Mr Stafford, I'll give him a shout.' With no warning the little voice yelled, 'DAAAAD, it's Mr Stafford for you,' and dropped the receiver loudly on the table. Stafford held the phone a foot away from his ear, but he still heard the thudding as tiny feet dashed to more important business. Garfield Lewis picked up the receiver, and after apologies and greetings, said they couldn't open the tip again till the coming Saturday and that he had told his staff they could have the day off.

'That's fine, in fact that works quite well. Now there's stuff I need to talk to you and Ryan about, so can you meet me at the Aldershot site at 9:30 this morning?'

'Yeah, course, no problem,' said Garfield.

'Should only take an hour or so, so you can still get a bit of a day off.'

Stafford had just asked Garfield about his older son, when Marva, his wife, came on the line. 'So when are you coming over for dinner, Staf?' I hear you've managed to find another battle to fight, so I guess you're not feeding yourself properly.' Stafford laughed and promised as soon as things settled down a little he would arrange a dinner date. Ending the call, he walked into the kitchen, made a cup of tea and poured himself a bowl of cornflakes. He sniffed the bottle before adding the milk. Sitting down at the kitchen table he started to eat his breakfast, thoughtfully.

It had occurred to him as he drove home the previous evening that there could be a third, more frightening scenario concerning the bomb. *What*, he mused, spooning his cornflakes in, *if the bomb or IED had been loaded into one of the forty-foot transfer lorries? Could that have been the plan?* If that happened and the bomb had blown up on a road to landfill, the resulting carnage and chaos would have been devastating. He shook his head at the thought.

'Jesus H Christ,' he muttered, 'doesn't bear thinking about.'

Finishing his breakfast he added the spoon, bowl and mug into the pile already in the sink, and silently promised to wash up later. He picked up his jacket and walked through the house to the front door and out to the car. The dashboard clock showed a few minutes past 09:00 hours. Having missed, he hoped, the morning rush-hour traffic, the drive should take no more than twenty-five minutes. Sliding a Sparks CD into the player he turned up the volume on their "This Town Ain't Big Enough for the Both of Us". He pulled out of his drive and headed for the Aldershot tip. Arriving at the site he parked on the road outside.

The tip was smaller than Stafford's other four sites and different to them, as all the bins were on ground level, with stepped metal gantries between them providing access.

Ryan Peters had already been joined by Garfield Lewis. Whilst they sorted out chair space in the tiny Portakabin office, Stafford wandered around talking to some of the men working there. Going into the office he smiled to himself as he noticed there was no sports equipment here. Peters, he knew from experience, wouldn't need weapons. Tall and slim, Peters didn't look like a fighting man; people often underestimated him, to their cost.

Shaking hands with his two managers they made themselves as comfortable as they could in the small office.

'I reckon you know we have a problem,' said Stafford. 'Neither the police nor Security Forces seem to know what's going on, so we are just going to press on as best we can.' He went on to explain about the two managers and their fraudulent qualifications.

'You know Tommy and Mariusz are desperate for sites of their own,' said Peters. 'I hate to lose Tom and I guess it's the same for Lew' with Mariusz, but they've both got the qualifications.' Stafford looked at Lewis who nodded in agreement,

'Yeah, Mariusz will jump at the chance.'

'Good, I was hoping you'd say that,' said Stafford, 'and that'll be fun when we make the changes, letting HCC know. Now George Saunders has left, I've no idea who's running the show down there.' For the next fifteen minutes or so they discussed how to deploy their current staff to cover both the Winchester and Andover sites temporarily.

'So what's the timescale on this?' asked the blonde-haired, blue-eyed Peters innocently, a look of mild amusement on his face.

Stafford said, grinning, 'You need to talk to your men today and tomorrow and set this up to happen 07:30 hours Sunday.'

'Oh, so no rush then,' said Garfield, and he chuckled ruefully.

'Meanwhile, tomorrow at 16:30 hours we'll meet up in Farnborough. I'll phone Lee Gibson and tell him, then we'll go and pay Mr Winstone a visit at the Winchester tip. Depending how that goes, we will probably head to deepest, darkest Andover and sort that out too,' said Stafford.

CHAPTER 7

Eileen Saunders decided enough was enough. George had been gone too long and she had, she told herself, to phone the police. She must face the fact that his problems, whatever they were, were much worse than "problems at work" as he'd said when he hid himself in his study. She knew, well, she thought she knew, it probably wasn't another woman, or surely he would have taken more clothes at least. And he certainly wouldn't have gone looking as dire as he did. Besides, having been with him for twenty years, she would have known if there was another woman, wouldn't she?

Eileen had been sitting by the phone, twiddling strands of her long blonde hair, contemplating calling for half an hour or so. She had done this on numerous occasions over the last two days. She grabbed the receiver and started to dial a number, then aborted the call as she had done on numerous occasions already. She didn't really know what number to call. She had phoned his office, but no one had seen him or knew of his whereabouts. And she got the distinct impression that everyone she spoke to, when she said her name, had something more important to attend to. Perhaps if she actually went into his place of work she could find out more; talk to his secretary at least, she thought. Then she found out that George's secretary, Stephanie Turnbull, was off work, apparently sick, and that definitely gave her pause for thought.

Her hands shook as she clutched the receiver to her chest and tears streamed down her drawn but still bonny face. Sitting on a tall stainless-steel, leather-topped stool, she leaned her elbows on the granite worktop of the central island in her huge kitchen and wondered what to do next. She just couldn't bring herself to make the call; that would be admitting there really was a problem. Surely he would come home soon, or at least phone to let her know he was all right.

CHAPTER 8

PC Lee Gibson spent part of the Friday following his meeting with Stafford checking out the names he had been given. A number of the few English names on the lists had triggered responses. Mainly minor drug-related offences, selling or being caught with small quantities of class C and A drugs. These were dealt with by getting cautions and a slap on the wrist. There was one case of GBH, where the guy had apparently belted his drug dealer who he said, was trying to cheat him. He got two years and served thirteen months. His checks on the names of the foreign nationals came up with nothing. This surprised him; there is often a point at which the law and non-English people meet. Not necessarily for nefarious reasons, many would need to register within seven days of arriving in the UK. Then work related, visa or racial reasons tended to crop up. The addresses, however, were false and did not register anywhere. The one name that did register a hit or two was that of Ayman Runihura. His bio showed he was a British citizen with a British passport. He had vanished from the UK aged sixteen and turned up a month or two later in Egypt, the place of his birth. He appeared back in the UK some twelve years later. Details were sketchy, but showed that both MI5 and 6 had taken an interest in him. Apparently his time in Egypt had been spent in the military and it seemed he returned to the UK only when they cut him loose. A DI Fisher from Aldershot had carried out surveillance at the behest of MI5, eventually writing it off as a waste of time. Runihura had been stopped and searched in the UK and found to be carrying a quantity of cocaine. A smart lawyer, had argued it was an unwarranted stop and the cocaine was for personal use only. The judge had agreed and Runihura was given a two-year suspended sentence and fined £150 plus costs. Mr Bockus appeared not to exist. Rather than phoning Stafford with this limited information he decided to wait until their meeting the next day. He also decided to keep the information about DI Fisher and Special Branch to himself, at least for the time being.

At 16:30 hours on Saturday, Stafford, Peters and Lewis met up with Lee Gibson at the Farnborough tip. Three were dressed in jeans, orange hi-viz bomber jackets and work boots; Gibson in jeans, copper's boots and a brown leather bomber jacket. Stafford introduced Lee Gibson to Peters and explained his involvement. Then said, 'I see Mariusz is here. Is he up for the site?'

'Oh yeah, he's really up for it, says he'd prefer Winchester of the two sites though.'

'What about Tomasz, Ry', is he up for Andover?'

'Yeah, and he's got friends in Andover who'll work for him, so no problem there at all,' said Peters.

'Both got enough staff to cover?'

Lewis said, 'Yep, Mariusz is taking two of mine and one of his mates to start off with.'

Stafford looked towards Peters who nodded and said, 'Tom's taking two of mine, and to make up the numbers he's got a girl, well, a woman who will do sales. And he thinks at least two of his mates will work with him.'

'Good, well done for getting that sorted so quickly. I'll have a word with Mariusz before we go, then I think we are all set. Unless you've anything else to discuss?'

Gibson brought them up to date with his selected findings from yesterday. They discussed the details concerning Runihura, Bockus and the others. And decided that Gibson should check further into their backgrounds and look at known associates, particularly of the two previous managers.

'Anything else?' asked Stafford. Stafford watched as three blank faces looked at each other and shook their heads.

'Right, pile into the Volvo and I'll be with you in a mo',' he said. He stepped out of the mess hut and found Mariusz Wandoch; easy to do with the thirty-one-year-old Pole's imposing six-foot nine-inch frame. Stafford reached out his hand to Mariusz who ignored it completely, and pulled him into a bear hug. 'Thank you, Mr Stafford. I won't let you down for this chance.'

'I know you won't, you've worked hard for this and from tomorrow you start working for you and yours,' said Stafford stepping back somewhat breathless, 'but any worries or problems, phone me or Lew' any time. So, good luck and I'll catch up with you soon,' he said as he walked towards his car.

'Thank you, Mr Stafford,' said Mariusz, welling up, 'but I…,'

'It's no problem, Mariusz, and call me Staf,' shouted Stafford laughing, keen to avoid the tears.

Making sure he had the documents relating to the two sites and the dozen new high-security padlocks for the Portakabins and sales sheds, Stafford drove out of the site and headed towards the M3 motorway. There was little traffic this time on a Saturday afternoon. They reached the motorway in fifteen minutes and headed south. Traffic was fairly light. The old Volvo took a while to reach seventy, but when she did, she cruised comfortably. Stafford gave the dashboard a friendly pat and said, "Good girl," inwardly. They came off the M3 and reached the Bar End Industrial Estate at just before 5.50pm. Stafford pulled into a lay-by and parked up.

'We're two minutes away. I'll drop you and Lee off at the "in" gate,' said Stafford looking at Lewis. 'At 18:00 hours, you close and lock the gates then go across to the "out" gate and keep that open until I phone. Ryan and me will drive round and park in front of the office.' Stafford looked at each man to acknowledge. They nodded in agreement. Stafford pulled out of the lay-by, drove towards the site gates and stopped. Lewis and Gibson baled out, Stafford and Peters continued into the site.

Built in a huge circle that climbed up and around the bins, the road in made it difficult to see how many cars were parked in the recycling area. As they got close to the office, Stafford could see only two customers' cars. The punters looked as though they had finished dumping their rubbish and were preparing to drive out. There were just three staff members, all leaning against the rails of various bins. The only other vehicle, a black Mercedes X-Class Concept pickup, was parked close to the Portakabin office and sales area. Stafford pulled up next to it and they both climbed out of the Volvo. Stafford took the Winchester folder with him. Peters walked back to check on the progress of the two punters; both were driving out. As he returned to Stafford, he noted that the three workers had huddled together and were talking, casting furtive glances at them. He gave Stafford the thumbs up and Stafford phoned Lewis as the two customers drove past and headed out.

'Two coming out, mate, then close the gate,' said Stafford.

'Roger, rog,' said Lewis as he locked the gates.

The gate padlocks for all twenty-six of Hampshire's HWRCs were identical and provided by the council. This enabled lorry drivers to change bins out of hours at busy periods, weekends and bank holidays. As the tips became targets for youngsters nicking bikes, or mucking about on skateboards and even setting fire to waste bins, the council gave master keys to local police and fire stations.

Peters caught up to Stafford, who said, 'Go round to the mess hut, see if there's any more men.' Peters nodded and headed off. Stafford stepped up and in through the open office door. Glancing quickly around the small space, he was amused to see what could be a second-hand sports shop. Tennis racquets, cricket bats and stumps in abundance. The shaven-headed manager, Floyd Winstone, sitting at his desk, leaned back in his chair, and with arms folded across his barrel chest said, 'Mr Stafford, good to see you. What can I do for you at this late hour?'

'I am going to give you the opportunity to leave this site now, peacefully and quietly,' said Stafford taking the fraudulent WAMITAB certificate out of the folder and placing it on the desk. Winstone looked at the document, picked it up, glanced at it, threw it back down, and chuckled.

'Oh that. Come on, Staf, who's to know? We get the job done, don't we?'

'After a fashion, you do, but not well enough. It's pathetic you have to cheat about this,' said Stafford. 'It's hardly rocket science.'

'For fuck's sake, leave it, Staf, you don't know what you are dealing with here. You'd best be leaving things as they are.'

'You reckon? Well, maybe you'd better start telling me what I *am* dealing with then.'

'I'll do better than that, I'll fucking show you,' said Winstone leaping to his feet. He reached down the side of the desk to his left and pushed himself up with his meaty right hand on the leather-topped surface. Stafford's left hand shot out and pinned Winstone's hand to the desk top, his right hand already reaching for the anticipated rounders bat. Surprised by the instant response, Winstone lost momentum, Stafford ripped the bat from his hand, released Winstone's right hand and slammed the bat down across his knuckles. Winstone crashed back into his chair screaming, clutching his broken hand to his chest.

'Now get your stuff and get out before I bust the other one,' said Stafford.

Winstone's screaming brought his three men rushing to the office. Outside, Peters was leaning against the wall next to the open office door. Winstone yelled at his men to attack. Peters moved to the front of the open doorway. The first man to him threw a roundhouse right hand which Peters side-stepped easily. The guy tumbled forward, cracking his shins on the metal steps, he sprawled half inside the doorway. Expecting retaliation he frantically half turned, and raised his right arm to ward off the anticipated blow. Peters leaned forward with hand outstretched, an almost apologetic look on his face, offering the man a hand up. Relaxing somewhat, the man turned further and held out his hand towards Peters for assistance. Peters grabbed the man's thumb and with a sharp twist backwards, broke it. For a split second the guy stared wide-eyed at him, not believing what he'd just done. For good measure Peters flipped the man's arm sideways hitting the metal door frame with the injured hand. Peters screwed up his face, in a "Phew, that's gotta hurt," kind of way and said, 'Oops, what a bummer.' Stafford stepped over the now wailing guy in the doorway and joined Peters. Together they faced the other two men, who decided they were not up for the fight, much to Peters' disgust.

'Get these two out of here,' said Stafford, 'then get your gear together and get off the site.' The workers put Winstone and the other injured man into the crew cab of the Merc. They retrieved their belongings and equipment and loaded it into the back. Stafford phoned Lewis at the gate. 'Black Mercedes pickup coming out, and we'll be with you in a few minutes.'

With Winstone screaming a deathly vengeance on Stafford and his crew, the Mercedes headed out of the gates.

Stafford and Ryan used the new padlocks to secure the various Portakabins and sales shed, then drove down the slope to collect Gibson and Lewis. Sitting in the car, collecting their thoughts before setting off again, Peters said, 'Well, apart from a few breakages, that seemed to go pretty well.'

Stafford grinned and said, 'I suspect Jan Kapusniak already knows about this at the Andover site, so I think we may have a bigger reception there.'

'Maybe they'll put out bunting,' said Peters.

They headed back to the M3 and took the A34 towards Andover. Traffic was light; it took just half an hour to get to Andover's Scott Close roundabout. Taking the third exit and driving a few hundred yards up the hill towards the entrance they noticed the gates were open. The site should have closed at 18:00 hours. It was now almost 19:00 hours. Stafford pulled up ten yards short of the gate.

'No bunting then,' he said smiling. 'Lew', Lee, you get out here, lock these gates, then go down to the exit gate and keep them both shut till I phone.' He turned and readied to drive away.

'Sure you don't want us to stay till you see how the land lies?' asked Lewis, who despite his good looks, loved a good fight.

'We'll be OK. I don't really want to look as though we've come mob-handed,' Stafford said, then grinned and added. 'Anyway it's only about 200 metres from the gate to the office, should only take you about thirty seconds if we're in trouble.' Lewis and Lee climbed out of the Volvo smiling.

As Stafford turned left into the site he was surprised to see just one vehicle parked alongside the Portakabin office. He couldn't recall Jan Kapusniak owning a green Range Rover Evoque. Stafford parked alongside and they climbed out. Peering into the window of the Evoque, Stafford noted there was no one inside and said to Peters, 'Isn't this George Saunders's motor? What's he doing here?'

Ryan shrugged, 'Guess we'll soon find out.' They walked to the Portakabin office. Peters turned and stood outside as Stafford mounted the two metal steps and entered through the open doorway. An abundance of sporting gear again made him smile. Sitting in the chair at the manager's desk was the weather beaten bulk of the ex-Aldershot manager Ayman Runihura.

'Looks like you've done the job for me, Ayman. Did you tell Kapusniak and Co. their jobs were gone or did George scare 'em off?'

'That seems to be your speciality, Mr Stafford. I hear you've become quite the hatchet man lately,' replied Runihura.

'And you've no right to be here. So I would be grateful if you and George, wherever he's hiding, would leave the site now,' said Stafford quietly. Runihura's eyes narrowed as he contemplated Stafford for a moment. Stafford slowed his breathing, felt his muscles relax, preparing for action.

Runihura let out a long breath then said, 'I think you should hear me out first, Mr Stafford. Because I think your little hatchet is just not big enough for what you're getting into. You really have no idea what you're up against.' He slid open a desk drawer, pulled out a bulging brown envelope and placed it on the desk.

Stafford felt the threat subside and laughing without humour said, 'So everyone keeps telling me, but no one wants to tell me more.' Runihura picked up the envelope and handed it to Stafford. Stafford opened it. It was full of

£20 notes. He ran his thumb across the top of the notes, flicking them backwards and forwards, then threw the envelope dismissively back on to the desk. Runihura said, 'It really is very simple. This is just a down payment. All we want from you is a little cooperation; placing our men, on your sites, where we want them, as managers and workers.'

'Oh dear, Ayman, if you think that'll work with me, you've been very badly misled. Now do yourself a favour and get out before I throw you out.'

'You disappoint me, Paul, it worked very well when George was around. Now he's out of the way, we realise that being part of the company holding the contract will work even better.'

'Just a pity you don't have a contract company then,' said Stafford.

'We will have, Mr Stafford,' he said, then paused as he picked up the envelope. 'We will have yours.'

He got to his feet, brushed past Stafford and walked out of the office. He opened the Evoque's driver's door, then stopped as Stafford asked, 'So how come you've got George's car?'

Runihura smiled. 'Me and George came to an arrangement.'

'So is he the main man then, Ayman, you just the messenger boy? The main man too scared to do his own dirty work?... Aah, I can't be arsed. For fuck's sake piss off, before I really get mad.'

Grim faced, Runihura stepped into the Evoque. Closing the door, he wound the window down and said, 'I promise you, Paul, you're gonna regret you fucked with me.' Closing the window he drove down the incline to the exit gates.

Stafford made a mental note of the Evoque's registration number, then on his mobile said, 'Let the green Range Rover out, we'll be down in ten.' Using the new padlocks, Peters and Stafford secured the office and the other Portakabins before driving down the slope to pick up the others. Lewis secured the gates, then climbed into the Volvo. Stafford told Gibson the Evoque's registration number and asked him to check it out. They drove away, heading back, aiming for the A303.

This stretch of road has a swooping left-hand bend that goes on for at least half a mile, which was difficult to drive at over forty-five mph. As Stafford tried to negotiate the bend without slewing his passengers across to the driver's side of the car, he noticed in his rear-view mirror three cars in line some distance behind. The first car was a white pickup truck which he didn't recognise. He settled back and tried to accelerate enough to enter the A303 at a sensible speed. Checking the rear-view mirror again, he realised the other two cars were the black Mercedes X-Class pickup and Saunders's green Range Rover Evoque.

'Uh oh,' said Stafford, 'bandits at six o'clock.' In unison the other three turned to see who was behind. Accelerator now flat to the floor, Stafford urged the old Volvo on. The white pickup was travelling considerably faster than Stafford's sixty-five mph. As they reached the dual carriageway, the white pickup was right on his tail. Realising the driver was going to ram him from the rear, he flicked the steering wheel hard left, just enough for the pickup driver to miss. The pickup's brakes screamed as he pulled back behind the Volvo. The white motor tried again and this time managed to clip Stafford's-off side rear wing. The jolt pushed the Volvo's nearside wheels on to the rough grass verge. The car bucked and bounced almost out of control as Stafford slammed on the brakes. The pickup came alongside and Stafford recognised the driver as the long-haired, skinny, ex-Andover manager.

'Fuck, it's Jan bloody Kapusniak, bastard's only trying to run us off the road.'

Peters, holding grimly on to the roof handle grip, leaned over to look, confirmed it was Kapusniak and said, 'Fuck's sake, haven't these guys heard of industrial tribunals?'

Kapusniak drew marginally ahead and swung into them, trying to push the Volvo into the trees lining the grass verge. Pulling in front, the pickup managed to rip off the Volvo's front wing and bumper. Both skittered and bounced across the road causing Stafford to swerve violently to avoid them. In the rear-view mirror Stafford saw only the black Merc' X-Class and Range Rover on the otherwise empty road. He crunched the clutch to the floor and a split second later twitched the steering wheel right, instantly ripping on the handbrake. The Volvo's rear tyres screamed, acrid black smoke streamed from them as it lurched into an enforced high-speed U-turn. As soon as the vehicle was pointing towards the following cars, Stafford slammed into second gear, released the handbrake and powered headfirst at the black Mercedes. Startled and panicked the Mercedes driver swerved to his off side and slid sideways into the central metal Armco. The Armco crunched and scraped along the length of the car, sending a shower of sparks behind it like a comet's tail. Eventually regaining control, the driver roared off down the carriageway. The Range Rover raced past and into the distance.

With all three cars now past him Stafford did a rather more sedate U-turn, drove on to the grass verge and rolled to a stop. The engine noise drowned out the noise of the collective sigh. As they began to clamber out of the car, the sound of a motor roaring, howling, over-revving, seemed to be getting closer. Peters was the first to see it.

'Down, down, nearside now!' he yelled as he rugby tackled Gibson and they plunged further into the bushes. The reversing white pickup smashed into the front of the old Volvo. It revved hugely as Kapusniak struggled to get free from the Volvo's front end. Its wheels spun in the soft earth, then gripped, lurched forward and raced off down the dual carriageway.

Stafford and crew cursed loudly as they scrambled out of the bushes, dusted themselves down and found that apart from the odd bump and bruise no one had been seriously injured. Looking down the carriageway there was no sign of their pursuers. Stafford took out his mobile, selected a number and hit the call button. Walking away from the group, he spoke into the mobile explaining their situation. He ended the call and rejoined the others standing around the still steaming, clicking, cooling, battered Volvo. Twenty-five minutes later a grey Vauxhall Vectra SRi pulled on to the grass verge behind them. The driver switched on the hazards, took out the key and exited the car. Walking towards the group, he held out the key and said, 'There you go, Major Stafford, and worry not,' as he patted the Volvo, 'we'll get this old gal back to you in a few days, good as new.'

Stafford shook his hand, took the key and thanked him. As they piled into the Vectra, PC Gibson said, 'That's a mighty impressive roadside recovery insurance you've got there, Paul. Bet that don't come cheap.'

CHAPTER 9

Sunday morning just after 8:15a.m. Stafford's mobile vibrated and buzzed. He glanced at the caller's identity. It was Barry Allen, the Basingstoke tip manager. Stafford took the call, Allen told him that the two new men hadn't turned up to work and that he was one man short of the required number to stay open.

'Bloody hell, Barry, this can't be the first time. This is why you earn the big bucks; you're the manager, manage,' said Stafford, annoyed.

Allen was silent for a moment, then said, 'Well, I can normally borrow guys off Ryan or Lew', but all their lads are covering Andover and Winchester this weekend.' Stafford, realising that was his doing, relented a little and said, 'What about your missus. Won't she put on a hi-viz and do sales or something just to make up the numbers?'

'Nah, she can't get no one to look after the kids,' came the response.

Stafford thought for a second or two then said, 'OK, Barry, I'll get back to you.' Stafford sat down at the kitchen table and slowly turned the mobile over in his hands a few times, then punched in Lee Gibson's number. Gibson answered, 'Hi Paul, what can I do for you?'

'I need a favour, mate, any chance you could do a day's stint at the Basingstoke site?'

'What? Like working the bins and stuff?'

'Yes,' said Stafford sheepishly. 'The two Runihura guys didn't turn up, so I guess he pulled them after yesterday's fun and games.'

'Hmm, that's not a bad idea though. I might be able to get some info from the other lads. Y'know, to give us an insight to what's going on. So yeah, do you want me down there now?' said Gibson, sounding quite happy.

'If you're sure, that'd be great. I'll call Barry now and tell him you're coming,' then laughed, adding, 'I won't tell him you're a cop though.' Gibson laughed and said, 'I'll use, "I'm an old army mate" as a legend… See, I know the lingo, I've read the *Spider Shepherd* stories.' Gibson ended the call. Stafford was still smiling as he called Barry Allen.

———————— ▌▌ ————————

Later that evening Stafford's mobile rang, caller ID showing Lee Gibson. Stafford answered with a broad smile, 'So how did you enjoy your day with the rubbish dumping public then, mate?' For a moment he thought the line was dead, then,

'Fuck's sake, what a madhouse. It's like, I'm gonna dump my stuff or die in the attempt! Is it always like that?'

'You should try it on a bank holiday sometime, there's no let up at all then.'

'But you even have to explain why polystyrene packing doesn't go in the cardboard bin, it's quite amazing. But actually I enjoyed it, I can see how it can get into your blood, and some of the things they throw away I just can't believe. But I didn't call to talk about the rubbish, I called to say that Barry tells me the two guys Runihura put in pretty much kept themselves to themselves, and their English wasn't brilliant and they made no effort to make friends, or to work.'

'Yeah, when I was there they didn't even try'n look busy,' Stafford said as he wandered from his kitchen to the living room and made himself comfortable on one of the sofas.

Gibson continued, 'At first the other lads were pissed off with them, the newbies wouldn't even sit with them at tea breaks, but then they realised these guys had no money and most days had just a couple of slices of bread for lunch.'

'Hmm, I had a feeling things weren't right with them.' Stafford added, annoyed with himself for not asking more questions when he was there.

'Anyway, what I did discover, whilst not massive in itself, does give us a bit of a feel for the size of what's going on.'

'And what the bloody hell does that mean, Lee? Come on, man, spit it out, you're dying to tell me,' said Stafford feigning annoyance and laughing.

'Well, this truckload of electronic stuff that Runihura was getting weekly ain't your little Transit van or Luton truck stuff, it's a bloody great hook loader bin, and Runihura's driver comes in with an empty RoRo bin and simply exchanges it with the one being filled. So you know what that means? It means Runihura's got a decent size set-up behind him. At least, he's gotta have an operator's licence, and that means somewhere to park the lorry or lorries and the bins, and that don't come cheap.'

'I wonder where George Saunders fits into all this,' said Stafford half to himself.

'You remember the green Range Rover we let out of the Andover site? Well, that was George's, and Runihura said he was driving it because he had a deal or an arrangement with him. Makes me wonder if George is behind this, or at least involved somewhere.'

Gibson picked up the thread, 'Well, it gives me a good place to start digging when I get back to the factory on Tuesday.'

'Listen, mate, I appreciate what you did today and what you're doing, so let me know what you find.'

'I'm hooked now, I'm going back to work in Basingstoke tomorrow. Who knows, if I don't find out more about the set-up, I might find a Fabergé egg or something,' he said and ended the call.

CHAPTER 10

Eileen Saunders had reached the end of her tether. She realised there was no alternative but to call the police. Sitting on the stool in her kitchen she cradled the cordless phone and realised she had no idea what number to dial. She knew that she shouldn't dial 999, but what on earth was the number you're supposed to use she wondered. Thinking out loud and fuming she said, 'God, George, why do you make everything so bloody difficult?' Putting down the house phone she hunted in her handbag for her mobile and decided to google the nearest police station. It showed Eastleigh. Furious now with George, the police and Google she eventually arrived at a page that said, "For non emergencies dial 101".

'Hoo-fucking-ray, at last,' she said. She put the mobile back into her bag, picked up the cordless phone and dialled the number.

The control room call handler took some basic details then put Eileen on hold for a second or two whilst she switched the call through to a female PCSO. Having determined that Eileen was phoning from home, she checked the address and said that she, and a police constable would try to visit within the hour. They ended the call.

Eileen had no plans to go anywhere so she made a coffee and waited.

Twenty-five minutes later she heard the sound of tyres on the gravel drive. She walked into the hall and to the front door. Opening the door she was relieved to see a plain dark-grey vehicle, not a police patrol car, though the occupants, both female, were in uniform. The officers showed their IDs and introduced themselves. Eileen nervously invited them into the kitchen and they perched on the tall, white leather-topped kitchen stools surrounding the island. The two police officers exchanged glances that said simply "loadsa money". The WPC took out her notebook and asked questions regarding George's last movements. Eileen told them about George's behaviour before he left. They asked about his work and Eileen explained how he'd said that he had some problems there and he needed to sort them out. She said she didn't know what these problems were. After considerable questioning, the officers explained that they needed to search George's office. She walked them through the house to the study/office. The officers said that they would need to search not only the office, but the rest of the house, the garden, garage and any outbuildings as well. Eileen remonstrated a little at this, but was told this was normal practice to ensure nothing untoward had happened at home. The officers asked if she and George had separate bank accounts. Eileen said they each had an account and George paid a monthly allowance into hers. She said he also had a business account, though no details of that were found in his desk. The WPC asked why he had a business account and Eileen said, 'He liked to buy and sell things, so he kept that separate from our day to day stuff.'

'What did he buy and sell?' asked the WPC.

'I don't really know, but he did some deals on cars and ride-on mowers, stuff like that he mentioned once or twice.' The WPC made a note to follow up on this.

In one of the desk drawers, filed under a section labelled "vehicles", they found the registration and insurance documents for a VW Golf. Insurance certificates for a Range Rover Evoque were there, but no registration documents. The officers asked about this and Eileen said the Golf was hers and George owned a green Range Rover Evoque, but she had no idea why the registration documents weren't there. In another drawer they found half a dozen "WAMITAB" diplomas for level four Management of Sustainable Recycling Activities. There were no names on these certificates. When asked about this, Eileen responded with a shrug and said they must be something to do with George's work. The PCSO made a note of the certificate numbers, said nothing to Eileen, but decided to follow up by calling WAMITAB's HQ later. They asked about the three storage boxes dumped beside the desk. Eileen explained that George had brought them home from work. The officers looked through the boxes and found a laptop. The laptop was dead, but the charging lead was also in the box. The WPC plugged it in and fired it up. The screen-saver picture showed a moored, streamlined, ocean-going motor cruiser. She clicked various icons and found nothing other than work-related items. The officers found nothing else of interest or help in the office, and asked if they could look around the rest of the house. Eileen took them on the tour. They checked the downstairs rooms, then upstairs and the eight bedrooms, two with en suite bathrooms, two separate bathrooms, and various storage cupboards. They asked where the attic hatch was and were pleasantly surprised that it had easy access and electric lights. Again they found nothing untoward or of interest. Returning to the kitchen Eileen offered them tea or coffee and both officers accepted. As they sat down the WPC asked, 'What about his mobile phone, I guess you've tried his number?'

'Yes, I must have tried it a million times, but it just goes to voicemail.'

'Can you give me the number and the service provider?' Making a note of the details, they finished their tea, then searched the garage and garden but found nothing that would help them locate George. Eileen gave them a good description of the clothes he was wearing when he left, and the officers asked if she could find a recent photograph of him. She found a clear colour picture of him taken the previous year at their villa in the Algarve, looking like a slightly smug, overfed, successful businessman. As the officers left, they promised to update Eileen as they moved forward with their enquiries.

---------------- **II** ----------------

The officers drove back to the Eastleigh police station and spoke to their supervising officer. He thought the circumstances of Saunders's disappearance warranted a more in-depth enquiry and instructed them to scan George's photo, his description and that of the Range Rover into the Police National Database. He also instructed them to follow up with a visit to HCC offices in Winchester to find out what George's work-related problems were. The PCSO contacted WAMITAB in Northamptonshire and discovered that although the numbers were relevant, they had been issued as WAMITAB level two diplomas in various names of which she made a note.

Later they drove to Winchester, and parked in the multi-storey car park close to the HCC offices. At reception they asked to speak to George Saunders's boss, and were told it was a Mr Simon Peacock in the Waste, Planning and Environment Department. His secretary came down to reception and took them to his office.

Peacock was of medium height, slim, bespectacled and in his late thirties. He was dressed in a grey business suit. The officers showed him their ID and introduced themselves. He seemed nervous as he fussed around trying to arrange two chairs for them, before returning to his seat on the opposite side of his desk.

'Now can I get you anything before we start, tea, coffee … water?' he asked as he looked at the officers and smiled a nervous smile. Both declined and Peacock continued, clasping his hands together on the desk, 'So what can I help you er, ladi… officers with?'

The WPC took out her notebook and said, 'We're making enquiries about a George Saunders, and we understand that he worked for you until quite recently.'

'Yes, that's right, he worked in my department. Why?… Has anything, uh, happened to him? Is he all right?'

'That's what we are trying to ascertain, Mr Peacock. It seems he's taken his car and disappeared. Have you any idea why he would suddenly behave like that?'

Peacock struggled to find the right words. 'No, well, no, not at all, I mean after he uh, left uh, he…'

'Perhaps you could tell us why he left, Mr Peacock?' asked the PCSO.

Peacock looked nervously from one to the other and said, 'He cited personal reasons in his letter of resignation, but I didn't like to pry as to what they were.'

'Fine, could we see the letter? I guess you'll have it on file?'

Peacock hesitated momentarily, then said, 'Yes, no problem, I'll ask my secretary to hunt it out.' He picked up the desk phone receiver and punched in a number. After a second or so delay he said, 'Oh, hi, could you hunt out George Saunders's letter of resignation for me, please, and bring it on in? Thank you.' Peacock replaced the receiver and moments later the secretary walked in. She handed the letter to Peacock who gave it to the WPC.

'Did Mr Saunders have a secretary?' asked the WPC.

'Yes he did, a Miss Turnbull, Stephanie Turnbull. Actually, she still works for us but I think she's on leave at the moment.'

The WPC stood up, smiled at Peacock and said, 'In that case perhaps you could get her details for us, whilst we have a look through his office.'

'Uh, won't you need a warrant or something for that?' said Peacock.

The WPC fired a look at him with narrowed eyes and said, 'Mr Peacock, we do have a missing person here, so speed is of the essence. Your help in this would be appreciated.'

Peacock scrambled to get out of his chair and round the desk to get out of his office.

'Yes, yes, of course, sorry, no problem. I'll get my secretary to show you their office now.' He scuttled off in search of her. The police officers exchanged glances,

'Our Mr Peacock seems a mite nervous, what do you think that's all about?' said the WPC to her colleague

'Does seem rather odd,' said the PCSO thoughtfully. Moments later Peacock and his secretary returned.

'Here we are, now will you take these officers to George's office please, and perhaps hang on and bring them back down when they're finished?'

'Oh, and, Mr Peacock, should we find anything helpful in the office, I hope we will have your permission to remove it? We will of course give you receipts.'

Peacock nodded balefully.

'Thank you,' said the WPC.

The officers fell in line behind the secretary, who marched off glancing behind to make sure they were keeping up.

'It's up on the next floor, but it'll only take us a couple of moments to get there.'

As they walked the WPC caught up with her and drawing alongside, asked, 'Do you know Mr Saunders?'

She turned her head to look at the WPC and said, 'Yes, though not very well. I hope nothing bad has happened to him, he always seemed very nice to me.'

'So you can't think of any reason why he would suddenly disappear?'

Again she turned to look at the WPC, she almost stopped, then continued, 'No. Not working for him, I only sort of knew him to say hello to and stuff like that.'

'So you don't know if he had any problems?'

'Well, you know what it's like in a place like this, you hear all sorts of rumours.'

'Oh,' said the WPC and smiled like "we're all girls together", 'that sounds juicy.'

'I'd rather you didn't say anything to Mr Peacock,' she said in a whisper, 'but I heard he was asked to resign over some money issues.'

'What, Peacock asked him to resign?' asked the WPC.

'I think it may have gone further up the ladder, and Peacock did as he was told, I think. Stephanie could probably tell you more. I'll give you her details if you like when we get to their office.' Arriving at George's office she opened the unlocked door and held it for the two officers, she followed them in and closed the door.

The office, a fairly large, square room with a window on one wall, had two desks and size alone showed which one belonged to Saunders. There were a few items on Stephanie Turnbull's desk, the usual phone, leather blotter complete with blotting paper, a desk tidy with an assortment of biros, pencils and markers, and the obligatory computer, keyboard and monitor. A quick look through her desk drawers revealed nothing of interest. Behind Stephanie's desk stood a row of five, four-drawer filing cabinets. A cursory look through drawers at random revealed only routine recycling data. As the officers searched, Peacock's secretary sat at Stephanie's desk, picked up the phone and made a call. 'Yeah, hi, it's Mr Peacock's secretary, could you give me Stephanie Turnbull's address and mobile number? We need to contact her about some stuff Mr Saunders was working on.' She waited a few seconds, then asked, 'Do you know when she'll be back from holiday?' She was silent for a while, then said, 'Oh, she's off sick is she? Probably be at home then.' She wrote the details on the desk blotter then said, 'That's great, thank you,' and replaced the receiver. Nodding her thanks the WPC jotted down the details from the blotter into her notebook.

George's desk also had a phone and a computer, but nothing else on the top.

Switching on the computer revealed a screen-saver picture of the same boat as on his laptop. Calling the secretary over, the PCSO asked her if she knew anything about the motor boat. She walked round to study the picture.

'Well, I really hadn't taken much notice of it before, but George did talk about it, said he wanted to get one.'

'Ah, so it wasn't his then?'

'No, apparently it belongs to a friend of his.'

'Don't happen to remember the friend's name do you?'

'No, sorry, but again, maybe Stephanie will know.' The PCSO made a note to remind her to ask. All the desk drawers were empty, though stuck in the join between the base and rear of the righthand middle drawer the PCSO spotted a small piece of white paper, overprinted in red. She fiddled around with the drawer in place and couldn't get it out, so she removed the drawer completely. She was then able to see that it was the top quarter inch of a craft paper banknote wrapper. Carefully she eased it part way out with her fingernails. She could see that it was a band for £1000 in £20 notes. Pushing it back to where it was, she pulled out her mobile phone and took a picture of it in situe. She pulled out a small polythene bag from one of her uniform pockets, removed the paper band completely and slipped it into the bag, writing the details on the bag's little white panel. She jotted down in her notebook that there was no cashier's initial or rubber stamp in the space provided, just a brand new band. She showed it to her WPC colleague, who gave her a nod of appreciation,

'Nice one, girl, well spotted.' Neither the desk nor the

office revealed anything more of help or interest. They left the office and returned to the waiting Simon Peacock. He was sitting at his desk, a couple of papers in front of him to show that he had actually been working.

Sitting down, the WPC asked, 'Was handling money a big part of George's job, Mr Peacock?'

Peacock appeared completely flustered and said, 'Money? Money? Whatever makes you think he handled money?'

'It would be easier if it was just us asking the questions, Mr Peacock.'

'Yes, of course, sorry, but no, his job didn't involve him handling any money, in fact none of us in this department handles money. There's nothing we do here that involves mon...' Peacock didn't finish the sentence. He was too busy staring at the little polythene bag that the WPC held out for him to look at.

'So you wouldn't know why this was in his desk drawer then?' she said as she passed the bag to him.

Peacock took the bag and stared at the contents. He turned the bag over as he examined it. He shook his head as he handed it back and said, 'No, he wasn't dismissed over money.'

'Dismissed? I thought you said he resigned, you showed us the letter.'

Peacock, his face bright red, beads of sweat on his forehead and nose, said, 'Yes, yes, sorry, I'm getting confused, I meant, of course, when he resigned.'

'Come on, Simon, don't you think it's best if you tell us the truth now? You must realise it's bound to come out in the end,' said the WPC gently.

Peacock sighed, he leaned back in his chair, shoulders slumped and said, 'Yes, you're right, let's get it out of the way...We had to get rid of George. He had been taking large sums of money from various people, then doing all sorts of favours for them.'

'You mean he was taking bribes?'

'Yes,' said Peacock quietly, unable to look the WPC in the eyes.

'So, why don't you start at the beginning and tell us what happened,' said the WPC as she took out her notebook.

CHAPTER 11

The following Tuesday morning, Lee Gibson attended the usual start of shift briefing. Sergeant Tony Hawkins was conducting the meeting with his unique brand of old-school charm. At fifty-five, with cropped salt and pepper hair, Hawkins looked as though he'd been born a copper. Gibson was one of fifteen present.

'OK, listen up, got a bit to get through, so take note and concen-bloody-trate. First up, bit of bad news concerning the explosion at the waste transfer station. A second man has now died from his injuries.' He was silent for a moment then said, 'The bomb squad boys have confirmed it was an IED, not an LPG bottle as our precious DI had previously insisted. Special Branch and the Security Forces will now continue with that investigation.' A number of officers groaned; a major investigation had been taken away from them. The sergeant continued to talk about various incidents that had occurred overnight and issued instructions for each patrol to cover. Then, 'And finally, our friends down in uh, uh, Eastleigh as it happens, have bunged up details on the PNC of a MisPer in a green, hmmn, make that an Aintree Green, Range Rover Evoque. MisPer's name is George Saunders. You've got photos and registration details in the briefing notes. And that's your lot, lads, now try and catch some bad guys, please, that's what they pay us for.' The officers began to disperse, but Gibson collared the sergeant.

'Sar'nt, have you got a moment? I need to talk to you about the MisPer, George Saunders.'

'OK, Gibson, let's go back to my office.'

Sergeant Hawkins sat down at his desk. Gibson remained standing whilst he explained his Saturday evening at the Andover HWRC and of seeing the Evoque there being driven by Ayman Runihura.

'So what were you doing there?' asked the sergeant.

'Paul Stafford, who runs the site, is a mate of mine. We were just going out for a drink. Turns out he had a problem to sort out in Andover, so we went there first. And Runihura was there, in that car. The reg' number is definitely the same.'

'According to the DVLA, the car is still owned by Saunders, so we'd better find this Runi', what's is name, toot sweet and find out what's going on,' said Hawkins.

'Runihura used to run the Aldershot tip for the previous contractor, so I'll find out who they are and see if they have an address for him,' said Gibson.

Sergeant Hawkins looked at Gibson quizzically and said, 'I don't know what, or how you've done it, but you may get some serious brownie points out of this, despite your rather dubious excuse for being at the Andover tip. Anyway, I guess as you've just had four RDs (rest days) you've nothing much on at the moment, so stay with this, see where you can take it.'

'Thanks, Sar'nt, I'll keep you up to date.'

'OK, lad, press on,' said the sergeant. PC Gibson

returned to the squad room and sat down at his desk. He pulled out his mobile, found Stafford's number and used the office phone to call it. He told Stafford about the events in the briefing that morning then asked for the name of the company that held Runihura's previous contract. After making a note of the details he ended the call. Settling down at his desk he Googled the name of the waste management company. When he arrived at their website, he discovered the company was a massive international conglomerate with their HQ in France. Its UK HQ was situated in a small village just off junction 12 of the M3. They showed a series of divisional phone numbers and Gibson opted for the number adjacent to Human Resources. When the call was answered, Gibson introduced himself and said that he required personal information concerning a Mr Ayman Runihura, who used to run the Aldershot HWRC under contract to them. He explained further that this was a missing persons enquiry and needed a speedy response. The receptionist took his details saying she would talk to the manager of the department and call him back directly. Moments later she rang back and said to put his request on an officially headed police station email and send it to her boss, he would reply with the details immediately. That done, he received a reply that gave Runihura's address as a flat at number 10a. North Lane, Aldershot. Gibson googled the postcode and discovered that it was actually above a shop on the corner of North Lane and Queen Street.

Gibson dialled Stafford's mobile number. It was answered quickly. 'Hi Lee, what can I do for you?' Gibson told him what he'd learnt. Stafford said nothing for a moment, then, 'Look, Lee, when your sergeant told you that the bomb was definitely an IED, did he say that Special Branch were picking up the enquiry?'

'Yeah, actually he did, but I just assumed that's what they were doing anyway. Why you asking? It's got nothing to do with Runihura and Saunders's car has it?'

'Oh dear... listen, I'm gonna ask you to trust me here. Can you hang fire on following up on that address for a bit?'

'Why? What's up, mate? I thought you were keen to move on this.'

'Yeh, course I am, but before you go rushing off to confront Runihura, I need to fill you in on a bit more detail.'

'What, you got some more info?' asked Gibson.

'I guess you could say that. Look, have you got time to come round to mine? Then I can bring you up to date.'

'What's going on, Paul? You're not involved in this stuff are you?'

Stafford laughed and said, 'Not the way you're thinking. Look, mate, let's meet up and I'll tell all.'

'Well, I'm in uniform so it'd be odd going to a café or somewhere, so I'll come round to yours. D'you wanna give me the postcode?'

Stafford gave him the details and said, 'That's good, come round when you're ready.'

Gibson collected his necessary bits and pieces together and headed out of the squad room. As he passed Sergeant Hawkins's office the sergeant yelled out, 'Gibson! Come 'ere a minute.' Gibson walked through the open doorway. Hawkins was sitting at his desk and standing where Gibson had been earlier, was an attractive uniformed lady with WPC 1321 embroidered on her epaulettes. She held her cap in front of her, and looked directly at him. Gibson couldn't help but notice her dark brown hair had been cut in a very stylish bob. And even under the uniform he could tell she had a knockout bod. She appeared to be in her early thirties. Gibson gave her a shy and nervous little smile, then turned quickly to look at his boss. Sergeant Hawkins introduced the WPC as Nicole Martin. Gibson shook her outstretched hand.

'Nice to meet you, miss,' he said not making eye contact for more than a millisecond. She smiled at him and turned back to the sergeant as if expecting more.

On cue he said, 'Right, Gibson, Ms Martin has just passed her sergeant's course so she is now joining us for a while, waiting for a CID placement. I've decided to partner her with you. A. Because you are married, and B. because you tend to keep your nose clean.'

Gibson said, 'Great, Sar'nt, great,' but with little conviction.

'Now look after her and maybe do yourself a favour and listen to her, yeah? So where are you headed now?' he asked.

'I was… we're going to meet up with Paul Stafford, y'know, the tip boss I was telling you about, to follow up on this MisPer thing, Sar'nt.'

'OK, well, on your way, lad, and put your expensive training to some use for a change. Maybe Martin can show you what community policing is all about.'

'Yes, Sar'nt, thank you, Sar'nt,' they said in unison as they exited his office. They walked down the corridor to the stairs, Gibson managing to keep a few paces in front of WPC 1321. Descending two flights of stairs they reached the ground floor and a slightly breathless Gibson asked the desk sergeant for the key to a pool car that he'd been allocated. Together with Nicole Martin, and without speaking, Gibson walked out of the station, across the car park towards a two-door Ford Fiesta patrol car.

'Would you like me to drive?' she asked.

Gibson was not quite able to stop the involuntary flinch at the broken silence and produced a response a pitch or two higher than normal, 'No thanks, you're OK, girl, I'll drive, I know where we're going.'

'So what are we hoping to do?' she asked getting into the car. Gibson waited until they were both seated and strapped in.

'Well, this guy, Paul Stafford, runs five tips, and so far he's had a bomb blow up near one of them. That killed two people. Then loads of graffiti on three occasions and now a MisPers' car has been seen on his Andover site. To be honest, it's all getting a bit fishy. Then to cap it all, two of his managers had fraudulent qualifications so he had to sack them, and they smashed his car up on the 303!'

'What? You need qualifications to run a tip?'

Gibson drove to Stafford's house in silence.

CHAPTER 12

Ayman Runihura and Jan Kapusniak each carried two heavy, sealed black sacks out to the Range Rover parked in the Weyhill compound. The evening had gone better than Runihura had expected. They had all enjoyed the evening's entertainment, mostly due to George Saunders being the unwitting main attraction. But Runihura still found himself amazed at man's capacity to enjoy inflicting pain and humiliation on another human being. And he guessed that when Eric Potter, their jack of all trades, had finished editing it, some of the syndicate would sit and watch the DVD of the event over and over again.

Eventually George had been very cooperative, but only after they had lopped off his little finger with bolt cutters. Cooperative but noisy. Runihura chuckled at the memory. Kapusniak with a practised flick of his head, whipped hair from his eyes and looked at him with a questioning shrug.

'I not know what you were doing, why you ask George if he use right or left hand,' he said in his accented English. 'But it was so George wouldn't bleed over car document when he sign it. Fuckin' amazin',' he said laughing.

'Yeah, was unbelievable, prick even bought bank details and passport with him, must'a thought he was going on holiday or something,' said Runihura still chuckling. 'I almost felt sorry for him when we walked in and he saw the tarpaulin on the floor and the queue of men waiting in line. George liked to be liked, but I bet he never thought they were all waiting to have a turn on him. The dickless prick.'

'Yeah, I thought he was gonna lose that too,' said Kapusniak with a rueful laugh.

'Nah, after doing both bank transfers we went kind of easy on him.'

'You think this easy?' said Kapusniak raising the black sacks, a grin almost crossing his face.

'Well, whatever, we'd better go and dump this stuff at the Aldershot tip before they close,' said Runihura as he put a bag down and waved the remote in the direction of the Evoque's rear door.

'Too hot to keep meat in the car,' he said, grinning as the tailgate opened like a monster's mouth.

'Why we not take to Andover?'

'Too close to home, mate, and I want to implicate the wanker at the Aldershot tip.'

They placed the bags carefully in the back of the car and Runihura waved the remote again and the tailgate closed silently over its prey. They climbed in and headed to the Aldershot tip.

They dumped their sealed black sacks into the garden waste bin. Kapusniak used the pitchfork kept by the staff at the side of the bin, to cover the sacks with green waste, hiding the bags from view. As they drove out of the tip and turned left towards the town centre, Runihura said, 'Right,

I'll drop you back at the flat and tomorrow, make sure your motor is legal and drivable. Then get down to the boat. I'm coming with you on this trip, not Eric, so make sure there's enough fuel on board and that the batteries are well charged.'

'But collection isn't till day after is it?' whinged Kapusniak.

'Listen, just do as I say. I'm trying to make sure you lot don't fuck up again, so sort the fucking motor, then piss off to the boat. Make sure that's working, OK? Winstone will be down with the van the following morning if the stupid bastard can still drive it with a busted hand,' he said with a sneering laugh, 'so you might as well stay on board tomorrow night.'

'OK, boss,' said Kapusniak, not best pleased.

Runihura dropped him off at the Aldershot flat then headed back on the M3 towards Basingstoke and the World Citizen Hotel and Country Club. The crown jewel of the empire.

The hotel had an enviable reputation; it boasted an indoor swimming pool and a licensed casino. The customers were people like the owners, self-made, rich and ruthless; they didn't want designer food or pretentious wine lists. The restaurant offered a choice of the top three from England, France and Italy. Best quality well-cooked food. The wine list was adequate and the selection of whiskies went from the sublime to the even more sublime. It worked, the restaurant was packed most nights and you needed to book a table two or three weeks in advance. Their customers had plenty of disposable income, income many wanted to hide from HMRC and the management were ready and willing to help them dispose of it.

Most of the men involved with this organisation were white-collar criminals who liked to think of themselves as entrepreneurs. On the surface that's exactly what they were. Big country houses in villages far from the inner cities where they learned their trade. Their houses were filled with beautiful and expensive things, many of them antique. Most collected antiques as a way to hide and also invest money.

One investment Runihura liked to boast about, was the thirty-seven-foot-long Birchwood-Commando 370 offshore cruiser moored on the River Itchen. The boat was a constant source of income for the syndicate.

Runihura kept the empire safe. His background in military espionage proved invaluable on civvy street and the path he had chosen to tread. He hand-picked door staff for the hotel and the two nightclubs that were part of the empire. He wasn't interested in your actual thug, he wanted cool, hard pros. Men who knew how to obey an order, any order when the pay was right. It was his task to network throughout the empire. To spot targets, to stop competitors trying to muscle in, particularly in the area of brain-fucking entertainment. And it was his task to chastise casino customers, who gambled and lost; to ensure their debts were paid one way or another.

He rolled to a stop under the Grecian-style portico at the front steps of the hotel and got out of the car. A smartly dressed young man raced down the steps towards him.

'Mr Runihura, nice to see you,' he said as he took the proffered car key.

'Scratch it and you'll be limping to a new job.'

Runihura bounded up the steps and as he walked through the hotel he returned nods and greetings from staff and customer alike. He continued through into the casino, and was pleased to see, although early, a few punters were playing the dozen or so slot machines. Their hands waved frantically, touching screens where lights flashed and buzzers buzzed.

This was the money-laundering hub of the empire. Money from drugs, prostitution, blackmail, porn and snuff DVDs, poured in one end and came out of the system much cleaner than when it went in.

Even the separate room for the serious poker players had a steady flow of punters in and out, all wanting to play or watch the three different forms of the game currently underway. Runihura tapped loudly on the office door. It was opened seconds later by another smartly dressed young man, just a little too bulky to be wiry. He looked to be around late twenties and had a badge on the right-hand lapel of his dark-grey suit that read, "WORLD CITIZEN SECURITY".

'Good evening, Mr Runihura,' he said locking the door behind them. Runihura grunted a response.

The office was around thirty feet by twenty feet. Along the front wall was a run of four workstations, each manned by an operative viewing six monitors that showed real time CCTV colour pictures from discreetly placed cameras above the gaming tables. Each station had a keyboard and joystick enabling them to zoom in on selected players or dealers. The centre of the office was dominated by an island with a double bank of four monitors. One bank showed pictures from the cashier's cage, the reception area, front entrance and various other places inside the hotel.

The second bank monitored pictures from cameras placed strategically around the outside of the hotel.

To a casual observer the far wall looked normal, but at the touch of a button it slid back to reveal a bank of eight monitors used to show pictures from selected guest rooms. There was a door in this wall that opened on to a corridor in the body of the hotel, so the punters couldn't see the number of staff being used to spy on them.

Runihura sat in a vacant chair and looked around at the working monitors. This room was his handiwork and he was proud of it. It had earned the syndicate a great deal of money. The young man with the badge wandered over and sat down next to him.

'He's hit ten grand. The account's on hold.' He picked up a DVD, slipped it into a case and said with a grin, 'This is a compilation of his night-time activities. When you get a chance, watch it, it's a great laugh to see our boys in blue, in blue action.' Runihura nodded, put the DVD into his jacket pocket and left.

CHAPTER 13

The first lorry to arrive at Little Bushey Warren garden waste composting plant turned up at just after 09:00 hours on Tuesday. It was carrying a bin the driver had pulled out of the Aldershot tip some forty-five minutes earlier. Driving the lorry through the open double gates, the driver stopped on the weighbridge, jumped out of his cab and took his transfer note to the weighbridge operator. He said a quick hello and walked back to his lorry. She weighed the lorry and gave him a thumbs up. The driver climbed back into the cab and as he drove further into the facility, a yard man directed him to the area where he wanted the load deposited. He drove a huge U-turn under direction from the yard man and then reversed the vehicle to the base of a stack of garden waste, stopping the vehicle on command. The yard man walked behind the lorry and slid open the large bolts on each side of the "cat flap" style bin door. He moved away and made sure he was visible in the lorry driver's huge wing mirrors. He signalled the OK to start tipping.

The driver pushed the lever that rolled the covering mesh net back. Then the levers that made the huge bin slide back and rise from just behind the driver's cab. Trying to stay perpendicular, the cat flap swung gently backwards and forwards and then as the five or six tonnes of waste slowly began to pick up momentum the driver eased the lorry forward so the cat flap wouldn't bind in the waste. As the hook hauled the bin to its fulcrum the yard man shouted in annoyance, 'Stop! Stop!' The driver slammed everything to a halt and climbed out of the cab to see what was wrong.

'Fucking arseholes, black bloody sacks, always the bloody same with the Aldershot bins,' said the yard man pointing to three or four half-buried black sacks.

The lorry driver laughed and said, 'I'll have a word with Peters when I get back, tell him his men need to be more on the ball.'

'That's something I've never worked out; Peters seems too frigging posh to work in the tips,' said the yard man as they climbed over the piles of steaming wet grass cuttings, branches and leaves to retrieve the black sacks.

'Yeah, I know what you mean, but he's all right. Seems to have plenty of dosh though, and they say he's got a share in a helicopter,' said the driver.

'How the fuck can a tip manager afford a bloody helicopter?' asked the yard man.

The driver shrugged and said, 'I think he does other stuff on the side.' They picked up two bags apiece and placed them to one side.

After brushing green waste from his boots and trousers, the driver climbed back into his cab. Checking for safety in his wing mirror he saw the yard man bend almost double, turning quickly away from one of the now open black sacks. The driver watched as the yard man retched, then spewed up violently into the garden waste. The man crashed down on to his knees and the retching continued. Thinking maybe a bad pint or two last night, the driver with a rueful smile clambered back out of his cab to check on him.

Gasping for breath and unable to speak, the yard man waved a pointing hand in the direction of the sacks. The driver walked to the sack and opened it further. Instantly he recoiled in horror as he recognised a human foot attached to a calf and knee joint.

Struggling against the urge to throw up, he grabbed the yard man under the shoulders, helped him upright and walked him as fast as he could back to the weighbridge office. Bursting in through the door he shouted at the girl to dial 999 and ask for the police. She stared at him wide-eyed and open-mouthed, 'Why, what's happening?'

'Just dial, I'll talk to them,' he said as he plonked the yard man into the nearest chair. She dialled 999 and handed him the phone.

'Police,' he said into the receiver, 'I'm at Little Bushey Warren composting plant, we've got a dead body in a bag in our waste.' Silence for a moment, then, 'I'm a truck driver and yes, of course it's bloody human; well, it's a leg, we've got three more bags that I haven't looked into and I ain't going to.' He replaced the receiver with a shaking hand. The weighbridge operator was transfixed, both hands to her mouth.

'A real dead body?' she asked her voice quavering.

'Well, I only saw a leg, and it looked real enough to me..and it was definitely dead…Well, it's your office, girl, and now I gotta sit here and wait for the law. How's about a cuppa tea?'

It took twelve minutes for the police to arrive. The first car contained two very young PCs who proceeded, with a reel of plastic police tape, to cordon off the area around the lorry and its load. The second car to arrive was a white Mondeo, driven by Detective Inspector Gerry Fisher.

CHAPTER 14

Gibson parked in the driveway next to the Vectra. Stafford opened the door and took them through to the kitchen-cum-office. Lee Gibson made the introductions, and Stafford was delighted to meet the lovely WPC 1321. Sitting his visitors around the kitchen table he said, 'I'm not really sure where to start, but, well, I was in the military for twenty years, and I ended up with the rank of major. My final posting was to Fort Monckton down in Gosport and I worked there with Ryan and Lew',' he paused for a moment, looked at Nicole and said, 'I guess Lee has told you about those two?'

'Nope, I know nothing about your set-up, I only met PC Gibson for the first time about an hour ago, but it intrigues me that you went from the army to the tips?'

'Hang on,' said Gibson, 'Fort Monckton? Isn't that where they train SIS and SBS in all sorts of unbelievable hand-to-hand and other stuff?' Stafford held up his hand as if in surrender.

'Slow down, folks, we're all on the same side here, you know.' Then he continued, 'I suppose it does seem a bit odd, but the tip stuff started when I bought this place.' Stafford laughed and waved an arm around to indicate the house.

'This place was in really poor condition when I moved in, so I was taking a lot of stuff to the tip. I became fascinated by the whole recycling thing. Especially when I saw some of the great stuff people throw away. Anyway, I got involved, took the exams and started up Andover Recycling.'

―――――――――― ‖ ――――――――――

Gibson, keen to find out why Stafford had asked them to come over in the first place, opened his mouth to remonstrate, when his mobile rang. Looking at the caller ID he said, 'Sorry, I'd better take this. All right if I go out in the hall?' Stafford nodded.

Gibson wandered out closing the door behind him.

As Stafford continued to talk to Martin about his transition from major to tip boss, he couldn't shake the feeling that her unusually large, but beautiful brown eyes were penetrating his thoughts. Seconds later his mobile buzzed and vibrated. It was a blink or two before it registered. Slightly embarrassed, he felt his cheeks going red as he picked it up and saw it was Ryan Peters. He listened in silence as Peters told him that George Saunders had been found. And the police had collected Peters from the Aldershot tip and taken him to the police station for questioning.

Stafford said, 'Right, I'll see what I can find out and catch up shortly.' He was contemplating his next move when Gibson returned.

―――――――――― ‖ ――――――――――

'Hmmn, that was interesting,' said Gibson, 'it seems that George Saunders has been found. That was my sergeant, telling me that DI Fisher wants me to get you to come back to the station with us. Apparently Mr Peters is on his way there now.' WPC Martin looked from one to the other, but said nothing. Stafford looked at Gibson, puzzled.

'Is that all he said? He didn't say if George was OK, or where he was?'

'No, not a word, just wanted us to get back pronto.'

'Fine, no problem, just need to make one phone call,' said Stafford as he selected a speed dial button. The call was answered in seconds.

'It seems me and Captain Peters are required at...' Stafford looked quizzically at Gibson, who caught on immediately.

'Aldershot Police Station,' he said.

Stafford repeated that, then said, 'Will you bring them up to speed on this, and maybe get the two uniforms I'm with now out of the frame for a while. Yeah, Martin and Gibson, yeah, that's good, thanks.'

'What was all that about?' said Gibson. 'What d'you mean take us out of the frame? What the fuck's going on?'

'Lee, Lee, just trust me on this for a bit. You still want to be involved in this I'm guessing, so trust me here, all right?'

Standing up, Gibson glared at him and silently motioned Martin and Stafford to walk out of the house. Stafford stood, picked up his keys and mobile. Out on the drive Gibson opened the passenger door of the Fiesta, tilted the front seat forward and signalled for Stafford to clamber into the back, then said, 'Best we go in this car, mate.'

'Roger, rog',' said Stafford as he climbed in the back.

———————————— **II** ————————————

Arriving at the Aldershot police station, the three of them were directed to DI Gerry Fisher's office. He was seated behind his desk. Also in the room was Sergeant Hawkins. There was no sign of Ryan Peters. Realising that five people in the office was going to be a bit of a crush, Fisher sent Gibson to see if there was an interview room free. In the state of silent limbo that followed, WPC Martin decided to make the introductions. Stafford shook hands with the DI and the sergeant, then asked, 'So how is George? Where did he turn up?'

'We'll get to that shortly, Mr Stafford,' said Fisher curtly, not looking up from his desk.

Gibson returned and said, 'Sorry it took a while, but Interview Room Three's available and I've organised a few more chairs.' The DI picked up a folder from his desk and they all followed Gibson crocodile-fashion to Interview Room Three. Gibson opened the door and stepped aside to let them in. The room had been recently painted a very pale green, the smell of paint overriding any other smells. A six-by-four Formica-topped table stood in the centre of the room, its steel legs bolted to the uncarpeted, brown painted concrete floor. DI Fisher took the lead, grabbed two chairs, placed them on the far side of the table and indicated for Sergeant Hawkins to sit alongside him. PC Gibson placed two chairs opposite the DI and one at the table's left-hand end. Indicating WPC Martin to sit there, he sat opposite his sergeant, leaving Stafford only one option, which he took. The Detective Inspector placed his folder on the table, looked at Stafford and said, 'As I understand it, George Saunders's car was seen on your Andover site last Saturday evening.' Stafford looked directly at the DI, a slightly puzzled look on his face, but said nothing.

'Well?' demanded the DI.

'Was that a question?' asked Stafford.

'Oh, so that's how it's going to be. Yes, was it there or not?'

'Yes, it was there.'

'And what was it doing there? I understand it was after hours?'

'Well, apparently the driver wanted to see me.'

'Why didn't he come during opening hours? Or phone you to meet at your office?'

'I don't know why he just decided to turn up there; I guess he had heard I'd been to Winchester and that I was going on to Andover, but surely you should ask him that?'

'Why was the site still open after six o'clock?'

'Again I really don't know, but I assume that Ayman Runihura, the guy driving George's car, had told the staff to bugger off.'

'And why would he do that, Mr Stafford?'

'Why are you asking me this stuff. Shouldn't you be asking Runihura?'

'Well, why was Runihura driving Mr. Saunders's car?'

'Good grief, man, how on earth am I supposed to know that ?'

'Are you always this obstructive, Mr Stafford, or is there something you don't want us to find out?'

'I've had enough of your stupid questions, Sergeant Fisher. As I am not under arrest I'll take my leave,' said Stafford standing up and pushing his chair back.

DI Fisher jumped to his feet, leant forwards, hands on the table and said, 'It's Detective Inspector Fisher, not, sergeant, and sit back down Stafford.' Stafford stopped and turned back to Fisher.

'Sorry, another one of my bad traits is forward thinking,' he said as he moved towards the door. Fisher sat back down trying to work out if he had just been insulted or not. Sergeant Hawkins and Co. desperately tried to suppress their sniggers.

As Stafford reached the door, there was a double knock, and it opened almost immediately.

'Sorry, sir,' said the desk sergeant addressing Fisher, 'there's an urgent call for you.' Red faced, the DI walked around the table, he carefully avoided Stafford and followed the sergeant out. Almost immediately he rushed back in, scooped up his folder from the table and dashed back out again. Stafford guessed the phone call might concern them, so returned to his chair. As he sat, the others couldn't help but quietly release their previously suppressed laughter.

Five minutes or so later the door opened and DI Fisher ushered in Ryan Peters. Standing in the open doorway, almost snarling, the grim-faced Detective Inspector said, 'He can fill you in.' Then slammed the door and stormed off.

Stafford stood and patted Peters on the shoulder. He introduced him to the sergeant and Martin, then said, 'Grab a seat, mate, and tell all.' Peters took the seat vacated by the DI.

───────────── **II** ─────────────

'Right, where to start? Though I can't believe the DI didn't bring you up to speed himself.' He shrugged and said, 'Anyway, in your briefing this morning, Sergeant, you included a bit about Special Branch taking over the investigation of the IED in Farnborough, well, now they've linked George Saunders's disappearance and subsequent murder...' The room erupted, everyone asking questions at the same time.

'Woah, Woah,' said Peters, his hands in the air. 'Let me finish first, then we'll get to the questions.' The noise subsided and he continued, 'George Saunders's badly mutilated body was found earlier this morning.' Once again pandemonium as questions were fired at him from all directions.

'Come on, folks, let me finish, or we'll be here all day,' he said. The room quietened.

'The DI seems to think it was something to do with me, that's why he brought me in for questioning.' Murmurs carried round the room as Peters's grim-faced audience waited for more.

'Now this is where it gets tricky,' he said, looking at Stafford. 'Do you want me to continue, or do you wanna take it from here?' Stafford indicated for him to continue.

'Right... Staf, me and Lew' all retired from the army at much the same time, Stafford quite innocently set up his own recycling company and invited us to come on board. It seems that George, working for HCC, had been accepting bribes from people who wanted the tips. Apparently MI5 and Special Branch had been investigating these people for some time, suspecting them of drug dealing, people trafficking, prostitution, slave labour and maybe some terrorist links. It seems they thought the diverse range of people in and out of the tips and the anonymity of the staff, made these places ideal for some of their criminal activities.' The room was strangely quiet. Everyone fascinated to hear what would come next.

'Now here's where it gets even trickier, my compadres.' He paused and looked towards Stafford, who nodded. Peters continued, 'Ex-military drift into all sorts of careers, mainly private security. Some with particularly unusual skills may be asked to continue to perform the occasional task for HMG, maybe MI5 or 6, or in our case the director of Special Forces. You've probably heard media rumours of clandestine military groups with names like Group 13, E Squadron or The Increment. The authorities never confirm or deny their existence. Well, I will confirm that the first and last are figments of an over-active media imagination,' he said with a hint of a smile.

---------------------- **II** ----------------------

'OK, Ryan, I'll take it from here,' said Stafford. 'Our bosses have asked that we continue this investigation, with carte blanche to do what we have to, in order to break their whole operation. Now, Lee, my phone call from home earlier was simply to get you on indefinite leave. And I apologise for this,' he said turning to Sergeant Hawkins, 'but I didn't have time to do it the right way. Anyway, Lee, I figured if you want to be part of this, it would be easier if you were taken out of your usual tasks. And if you were on leave then your governors could work around that.

Sergeant Hawkins jumped in and said, 'Hang on a sec, I'm not at all happy that WPC Martin is being dragged off to get involved with mayhem and bloody murder. It may be all right for you lot to be all gung-ho about this, you've been doing it for twenty years.'

'I hear what you're saying, Sergeant, and I promise you we won't put her into any situation where she could be hurt. But it's useful to have a female around when dealing with people trafficking and prostitution.'

'Don't we get a say in all this?' said Gibson, indicating himself and Martin. 'After all, it was me talking about Major Stafford that people started to look at this as being a recycling centre problem.' Stafford nodded in agreement.

'And that's why I want you on board. Nicole was a bit of a surprise, but I think you could both be an asset to us in this op.'

'Well, I definitely want on board,' said Nicole, 'I joined up to do something worthwhile, and I really want to get stuck in.'

Sergeant Hawkins shrugged and said, 'Well, as you two are apparently on official leave, there's not a lot I can do regarding your decision, but, Martin, as you'll be in plain clothes your acting DS role can kick in. And you bloody well better get some good results out of this, or your careers will be in shit street. Now do what you have to do and keep me informed.' Hawkins stood up, shook hands with Peters then Stafford, and looking at him straight in the eyes said quietly, 'Look after my people, Major Stafford, or I'll have you.' Stafford nodded his understanding, and thought, *that would be an interesting contest.* Sergeant Hawkins left them alone in the interview room.

'OK,' said Stafford looking at his watch, 'our governors have organised that we can use the facilities here at Wellington Avenue, but let's reconvene back at my place at say 16:00 hours, and I think it best if you were out of uniform.'

Acting Detective Sergeant Martin looked at him maybe a little longer than necessary. Stafford felt annoyed with himself as his cheeks started to redden. Gibson looked at Stafford and Peters, then shook his head in disbelief.

'Jesus Christ, so you two are spooks? The years I've been in the force the most exciting thing I've done so far is nick golf balls off the Queen's highway after a bloody RTA; Christ knows where we're gonna go now?' he said causing the rest of them to chuckle as they left Interview Room Three.

CHAPTER 15

Runihura was quite happy to pay for information. A score here, a pony there was usually pretty good value. But generally the bigger the debt or "offence" the better the information. Working nightclubs, casinos and a hotel with strategically placed CCTV cameras had given him unique opportunities to persuade people it would be in their best interest to share titbits of information when he deemed it necessary.

For some weeks a DI Gerry Fisher had been following him, apparently at the request of DCI Talbot, head of Hampshire's Special Branch based at Eastleigh. Runihura on numerous occasions visited Whitelines nightclub and the World Citizen Hotel. At first it seemed Fisher had thought Runihura a player, availing himself of the facilities on offer. Fisher couldn't flash his warrant card at the burly doormen, he'd paid the cover price to get into the nightclubs. Runihura was always just waved through, and once inside he rarely spent any time in the areas where the action took place unless he was drinking with the punters. He often used the third-floor facilities at the Whitelines club. The first time Fisher decided to follow him there, he was asked for a further £100. He paid the charge. His problems started when it became a regular occurrence. He began to go there regardless of Runihura and would try to cover the entrance fee and the extra £100 to use the third floor, by gambling in the casino. It worked a few times. Sometimes he would win at the roulette wheel, he might occasionally win at blackjack, but not often enough. Runihura had easily spotted his tail and was amazed that someone could achieve the rank of DI with such an apparent lack of surveillance skills.

Runihura told the house to offer Fisher an account. He took up the offer and continued to bet in the hope he would win big. Big enough to cover his losses. But he had lost. And lost again and again. Fisher decided on one last try; The World Citizen Hotel was the venue. As he asked for £50 worth of £5 chips, the cashier in the glass cage picked up the phone and dialled a three-figure number. He turned to Fisher and said, 'Thank you for waiting, Mr Fisher, there seems to be a problem with your account. The boss will be with you in a moment to explain.'

The house had pulled the plug at £10,000. Arriving on the gaming floor a few moments later, Ayman Runihura approached Fisher with an evil grin and an outstretched hand. Stunned, Fisher used what inner strength he possessed to stop shitting himself. He wiped his hands on his trousers and shook Runihura's hand.

'Well, Mr Fisher, Gerry, isn't it ?' he asked. Fisher nodded whilst wiping away the sweat running from his forehead into his eyes.

'Well, Gerry, it appears we have a considerable problem with your account. I think it was explained to you, that we don't ordinarily do accounts. But because you are one of our regulars we extended you the hand of friendship. But I see tonight you have come expecting to use *our* money in order to gamble in the hope you can repay *our* money. Is that right, Gerry?'

Fisher only managed, 'Er, well, yes, I suppose that's it really.'

'And that, DI Fisher, is taking the piss.' At the use of his rank, Fisher staggered a pace backwards as though he had been struck.

'What? Do you think we'd let you gamble up to ten grand without knowing who the fuck we're dealing with?... So I guess you are not in a position to pay this debt?'

Fisher shifted from one foot to the other. 'Well, no, I don't have that sort of money.'

Runihura sighed loudly, and said, 'Ah, Gerry, Gerry, that's such a shame. You know, I really liked you, what with us being so close an' all lately. And being one of our boys in blue, I thought you were bound to be trustworthy. Yet here you are trying to rip us off.'

'It's not like that, Mr Runihura, Ayman, I'm not trying to rip you off. I will pay you back, but I'm just going through a divorce and I'm having...' said Fisher.

'Enough, Gerry, enough,' Runihura said as he gripped the DI by the right arm and steered him to the bar. At the bar, he asked, 'What would you like to drink, Gerry?'

'I'll have a Scotch on the rocks, please,' said Fisher rubbing his sore right arm.

'I guess you'll need a double?' Fisher nodded.

'Now I am going to offer you a way out of this dilemma. But first I should perhaps mention that if you can't pay me today, like now, this time next week the debt will be £11,000, the following week £12,100, do you get the picture DI Fisher?' Fisher picked up his glass and looked nervously at Runihura. He guessed there was worse to come.

'Now, Gerry, I know that for some time you've been looking very hard at me, following me everywhere, even to the fucking bog. And this upsets me mightily. I should point out that it is not a good idea to upset me.'

'But hang on a minute, you're suspected...' started Fisher before being interrupted.

'I don't give a fuck what you suspect me of. I don't give a fuck why you are following me. I give a fuck that you are wasting your time following an innocent man. Wouldn't you agree that would be a waste of time, following an innocent man, DI Fisher?'

'Well, of course if he's innocent, then yes it would be a waste of time,' said the DI.

'And if you could convince the powers that be that you are wasting your time, you will find this could be the start of a change in fortune for you,' said Runihura as he pulled out a DVD case from his pocket and waved it, taunting Fisher, 'but if you are unable to stop this witch-hunt, then I will take further action on this debt. It would be such a shame if a copy of this DVD showing how you spend your hours on the third floor of Whitelines got into your superiors' hands. I guess they would be unhappy to see that you're claiming expenses for fuck... er, well, I will call what you seem to like to do, fucking whores. Am I making myself clear, DI Fisher?'

'Loud and clear, Ayman, loud and clear,' whispered Fisher, trembling, almost in tears.

Runihura got up from his stool, put the DVD back into his jacket pocket and walked towards the roulette table. He reached into his trouser pocket, pulled out a single £5 chip and flipped it to the DI. Reflexes caused Fisher to try and catch it; he failed badly.

'Try that, Gerry, you may find it's your lucky day after all,' Runihura said as he walked away, scratching his right cheek with three fingers, a prearranged sign to the roulette croupier.

CHAPTER 16

Stafford and Peters were in his kitchen-cum-office when the two police officers arrived dressed in civvies. Nicole Martin looked younger and prettier in tight jeans, white shirt and waisted brown tweed jacket. Stafford didn't notice what Gibson was wearing. Moments later Lewis arrived.

Once they were all sitting around the kitchen table, Gibson opened up his notebook and said, 'The way I see it, Runihura and Bockus are pissed off because they lost their sites to you. Then you win the contract and two more managers go. Graffiti and the bomb are warnings, George turns up dead and they meant us to find him. Christ, he was even delivered in a bin from Aldershot. They could have buried him, or chucked him in the waste bin, but no, an easy find. They are saying, "Mr Stafford, do as we want, because this is what we can do if you don't"; how am I doing so far?'

'Pretty good I think, but the main question is, who is the "we"? I don't see Runihura or Bockus as being bright enough to run a gig like this, they were even too stupid to see they needed to keep the sites running well, and got red-carded,' said Stafford. 'Having said that though, this geezer's got to be a dangerous bastard, cos you don't get chucked out of the Egyptian military for nothing.'

'But George was pretty bright,' said Peters.

'So why kill him?' asked Stafford.

'Well, this all started when Mr Stafford took over the tips, now three people are dead so far. This has got to be much, much bigger than, "oh, I've lost my job", surely,' said Nicole.

'You're right, call me Staf, by the way, it has to be way more than that. We know that Special Branch had been keeping tabs on Runihura, suspecting him of people trafficking, drug dealing and buying bomb-making stuff, so we need to find him and soon.'

During the thoughtful silence that followed, Nicole asked, 'So what *is* the "E Squad" all about? Are you all part of it?'

Lewis chuckled and said, 'Well, we could tell you, but then we'd have to recycle the pair of you alongside George.'

Stafford waited till the chuckles subsided and said, 'Hmm, sometimes there's a task HMG needs doing that's too small for say, the SAS, but too big for one operative.'

He was then interrupted by Nicole's question, 'For operative do we read spy?'

'Just let me finish, OK?' said Stafford with a smile. 'So they use ex-military with the skills necessary to complete the task, in this case we fit the bill exactly because we know rubbish.'

'Yeah, right,' said Nicole.

'Trouble is, this isn't the work of responsible criminals, these are psychos. They don't see a "them and us", they bomb innocents,' said Peters.

'Anyway, back to the matters in hand,' said Stafford, anxious to change the subject.

'There's not a lot we can achieve tonight, but I hope you guys have got plenty of cover on your sites for the next few days because we've got a lot to sort out.'

Lewis and Peters nodded in acknowledgment.

'Right, Nicole, Lew, tomorrow I want you to head down to Eastleigh and check with the coppers who took statements from Eileen Saunders and George's workplace. Follow up on anything they have. They may even have something new. Contact Mrs Saunders, see if you can get to talk to her. Lew, use our connections if you need to.'

Nicole and Lewis nodded their agreement. Nicole gave her mobile number to Lewis and said, 'Well, I live in Aldershot so it would make sense for me to come over to Farnborough and pick you up.'

'OK, good, I'll call you later to arrange,' said Lewis.

'Lee, Ryan, I want you to visit the last address we have for Runihura, and see if you can discover addresses for the other three managers, Bockus, Kapusniak and Winstone. Follow up on them because we need to find someone who can point us in the right direction.' Lee and Ryan already had each other's mobile numbers, they nodded their agreement.

Peters said, 'Yeah and we'll keep going through the names of the workers, see if any of them want to earn a few extra shekels by talking to us.'

'Meanwhile, I will talk to the DVLA about George's car, then find out what I can about fraudulent WAMITAB certificates. I'll check with the pathologist to see how George died. I've also got to catch up with the bomb squad and see what they can tell us about the IED in the waste,' said Stafford.

After they left, Stafford quietly cursed DI Gerry Fisher for losing them at least two days of the investigation, by trying to prove the explosion was accidental.

———————————— ‖ ————————————

Next morning, having washed up a sink full of crockery, Stafford was sitting at his desk tapping the desk phone's receiver thoughtfully against his left palm. He had just spoken to a woman at the WAMITAB HQ in Northamptonshire who confirmed that the qualification certificates held by Runihura and Bockus were false. To find out the extent of the fraud he asked if he gave her the site names and locations, would she then be able to find the name of the managers and their qualifications. She was hesitant at first, so Stafford suggested that if it was a problem, he could always produce a warrant, bring a squad in and do the search themselves. He gave her his email address and suggested she check out HCC's website for the sites he was interested in. He next phoned Sergeant Hawkins at Aldershot Police Station.

'Ah, morning, Sar'nt, it's Paul Stafford. I was hoping you'd have a file or two covering the recent happenings?'

'Well, yeah, course there's a file. What d'you need?'

'Frankly, as much as I can get, we're a bit behind the curve thanks to your DI,' said Stafford smiling, 'but specifically I wanted a copy of George Saunders's post-mortem report or at least the name of the pathologist who carried it out.'

'Right, well, we haven't yet had the full post-mortem

results, but the prelim states a massive heroin overdose, severe beating prior and mutilation after death. The doc is Professor Stuart McIntyre at Basingstoke and North Hants Hospital.'

'Thanks, that's great, look, if I give you my details will you send me copies of everything you have concerning the explosion, Saunders's disappearance and murder, you know, anything relevant really.'

'Not a problem, Major, give me half an hour or so and I'll wire some stuff to you, we've been fully briefed on your involvement, and what we have we share with you,' he added, 'including my office apparently.' A chuckling Stafford thanked him, gave him the details and ended the call.

Stafford was perturbed that since they had seen Runihura driving George's Evoque, not one of the UK's network of ANPR cameras on roads or in patrol vehicles had picked up the registration number as a vehicle of interest. It meant it was either parked up out of the way, or the number plates had been changed. But they needed to find out why George had parted with the motor. He phoned the DVLA and discovered that the Range Rover Evoque had been transferred to a Whitelines Entertainment holding company affiliated to a plethora of shell organisations in Reading, Berks.

It seemed unlikely to Stafford that George had been killed for his car; maybe, he mused, he'd been killed for the money he'd received for it. Confused, he determined to sift through the chaos surrounding Whitelines Entertainment Ltd, the holding organisations and numerous shell companies that appeared to be involved.

CHAPTER 17

A black Mercedes X-Class Concept pickup truck was in the residents' parking area behind the building. Noting the vehicle had considerable damage to the driver's side, from front to rear wing, Peters and Gibson climbed the iron staircase to the front door of Runihura's flat. There was no bell or knocker so Peters bashed the side of his fist against the sturdy black-painted door. Getting no response he continued to beat the door with a steady rhythm for eight or ten seconds. He dropped to one knee, tilted his head then lifted the letter-box flap and shouted through it, 'This is the police, open up or we'll break the door down.' Peters stood up, and they both moved each side of the door. They could hear movement from inside as though someone was scurrying around. Moments passed. Staying to the side, Gibson reached across and bashed the door again, the door swung inwards, opened by a grim-faced Matis Bockus. Gibson and Peters showed him their ID, and Gibson made to step inside. Bockus made no move to back up, but stood firm, tattooed arms folded, attempting to block their entry with his impressive five-foot nine-inch physique.

'You ain't police,' he said looking at Peters.

'No, I'm worse, as you're gonna find out if you don't move.' Bockus hesitated for a second then stood aside to let the two men in. As he closed the door, Peters realised it was reinforced with steel, various bolts and in a metal, not wooden, frame. It seemed nobody living there had thought to tell Bockus it would take a tank to burst through that door. As they walked through a dimly lit hallway, Gibson noted a number of expensive looking fishing rods and a Korum tackle box parked alongside a row of coat hooks. They passed doors on either side, leading into a living room furnished in much the same way as Stafford's. The room smelled of male occupation, sweat, cigarettes and beer.

'Is there anyone else in the house?' asked Gibson. Bockus shook his head.

'Does Ayman Runihura live here?'

The question received a cursory nod and, 'Sometimes,' in reply.

'What do you mean, sometimes?'

Bockus shrugged and said, 'He live other places.'

Peters turned to Gibson and said, 'You press on with the questions, I'll have a look around.' Bockus started to object, but after a withering look from Peters, slumped on to a sofa instead.

'So do you live here, Mr Bockus?' Another nod in reply.

'Can I see some ID, please?' Bockus reluctantly climbed to his feet, walked to a small sideboard and rooted around in the top drawer for a second or two, then pulled out a passport and handed it to Gibson, who flipped it open, and asked, 'So where is Runihura?' Bockus shrugged his shoulders.

'Listen, sunshine,' said Gibson, 'we're conducting a murder inquiry here, if you don't wanna talk to me here, we'll take you down to the police station.'

Bockus looked at him with venom, and said, 'I don't know nothing about murder, and I don't know where he go.'

Gibson made a note of the Lithuanian's passport number, then asked, 'Driving licence?' Bockus puffed out his cheeks, exhaled noisily and stood up again. He reached into the rear pocket of his jeans and pulled out his wallet, flipped through it and took out an international driving licence. He flopped back into the sofa and the look on his face reminded Gibson of the glare he got when he scolded his ten-year-old son. The PC made a note of the licence details; the date of birth put Bockus at thirty-five.

'Why is the address different?' he asked. Bockus made no response.

'I asked why the different address? You're doing yourself no favours by being like this. We'll find out the truth, one way or another.'

Peters came back into the room, holding out a clear polythene bag, half full of white powder. He stood in front of Bockus, waved the bag and shook his head.

'Is not mine,' said the Lithuanian.

Peters looked around the room, and said, 'Well, what a bummer, I can't see anyone else here.' Then to Gibson he said, 'OK, this is too much for own use, it's possession with intent, let's get him down to Wellington Avenue.' Gibson nodded, and read Bockus his rights. Bockus, head down, tried to dash past Peters. Peters flashed out his right hand at shoulder level and slammed pointed fingers into the side of Bockus's neck. Bockus's eyes closed instantly, he hung in the air for a second, then crumpled in an untidy heap to the floor. Gibson shook his head, mouth open in disbelief, not sure what just happened. His notebook and pen were still poised in his hand.

'Best add resisting arrest to the charges, Lee,' said Peters, nodding towards the notebook.

They attempted to bring the semiconscious Lithuanian back to his senses. Between them they helped the unsteady Bockus out of the flat, down the iron staircase and into their car. Before driving away, Peters pulled out his mobile and called Stafford to update him. The call went to voicemail. Ryan left a message,

'Hokus pokus we just arrested Bockus; with a load of white stuff. We're taking him to Aldershot nick. We'll keep you updated.'

Thirty seconds later, the mobile told him he had a text. It read, "Roger, rog". Peters drove out of the parking area and headed towards the police station.

CHAPTER 18

Nicole and Lewis were on their way to Eastleigh. They had arranged to meet the officers who had taken Eileen's statement. Parking in the nearby multistorey they walked the short distance to the police station. At the front desk they were met by the WPC who took them up to the first-floor squad room, where she introduced them to her colleague the female PCSO.

'You know of course that since this became a murder investigation we've had nothing more to do with it?' said the WPC without any trace of bitterness.

Lewis nodded and said, 'Yeah, sorry about that, but the decision was made above our heads too.'

'It would be good if you'll let us know how it progresses,' said the WPC.

'Of course. We know it was your initial PNC info that alerted us to this, and we'd appreciate a nod if you think of or find anything else that might help.' They discussed the moves made to date by the Eastleigh officers. George's secretary had apparently been on sick leave, but as she was never home when they tried to contact her, it was now a priority to talk to her. The duo had also set up an interview with Eileen Saunders and George's boss. They also handed over the bank note wrapper the PCSO had found in George's desk drawer. The four of them spent a moment or two checking details, then Nicole and Lewis headed back out to the car.

Deciding to have their chat with Simon Peacock before talking to Eileen Saunders, they drove to the HCC offices in Winchester.

The receptionist pushed a button on her console and after a short delay, said into her headset, 'Ah yes, Mr Peacock, your visitors are here,' then to Lewis and Nicole, 'If you'd like to sit over there, his secretary will come to collect you.'

Minutes later a woman walked into the reception area and introduced herself as Peacock's secretary. She took them to his office, where, handshakes over, Lewis said, 'Why didn't you prosecute Mr Saunders when this was such an open and shut case?'

'I…I…I… it wasn't my decision, a senior executive offered him a way out, so the council wouldn't be embarrassed by a public inquiry.'

'And if he'd done the right thing, Mr Saunders might still be alive,' said Lewis.

Peacock slumped in his chair and offered no response.

'OK, we need to see his office, we'll be taking his computer and maybe other stuff for further investigation. You'll get a receipt,' said Lewis. Peacock called for his secretary, who took them to Saunders's office and fired up the two computers. Nicole asked the secretary if she'd had any more thoughts about George's disappearance and death.

'I guess we can all understand why he'd want to disappear for a while, but to kill him like that was unbelievable. What on earth could warrant that?'

'That's exactly what we're going to find out,' Nicole said sitting down to look at Stephanie Turnbull's computer. Lewis settled himself behind George Saunders's desk. Initially all he was aware of on the monitor were the numerous icons to do with George's work. Scanning through them offered him no immediate clues. But as he got used to the screen he realised the screen saver showed a picture of a streamlined motor launch moored close to other expensive looking sea-going craft. Calling Peacock's secretary over, he asked about the boat.

'Yeah, the other officers mentioned that, but I don't really know anything about it. I think he kept the picture to remind him, y'know, sort of a goal.'

'So it wasn't his then?' said Lewis as he zoomed in on the picture trying to find the boats' name or a clue to its mooring. 'At least I can make out the name, it's called *Whitelines*.'

'Yeah, George said the name was a sort of joke. Apparently it belonged to a friend who had a nightclub or something. He told me he'd been out on it a few times.'

'Any idea who the friend was?'

'No, just someone he knew from his job, I think, but Steph would probably know.'

'Well, there's nothing obvious here, so if we can disconnect this thing, we'll take it with us. One of our boffins may be able to find something useful,' said Lewis as he pulled out the scart and keyboard leads. The girl bent down and pulled out the power lead. Nicole wrote a receipt and handed it to her. They headed back to Peacock's office, Lewis carrying the computer. He stood in the doorway and holding out the computer, said, 'For now, we'll take this and concentrate on finding George's killer, but there may be some follow up on your governor's decision not to prosecute.' Simon Peacock nodded silently.

Back at their car, Lewis put the computer in the boot and wrapped it in a travel rug left there for that purpose. Using her mobile's sat nav, Nicole guided them to the address they had for Stephanie Turnbull. They were only a few minutes' drive away. They had been told they were looking for a Victorian terraced house in Bar End Road. Nicole spotted the house, but as it faced directly on to the road, directed Lewis to a residents' car park a couple of hundred yards away. Parked up, they walked the short distance to the house.

The houses on this long stretch of road had no front gardens, but a low wall about two feet from the front of the house gave enough room to park a push bike or two. Standing on the steps to the front door, Martin could see a little panel to the left with two buttons and cards that showed Flat No. 2: S. Turnbull. She pressed the button. Moments later, about to ring again, the door was opened by an attractive, but dishevelled blonde-haired lady whose age could have been anywhere between thirty-five and forty-five. She took a cigarette out of her mouth as she said, 'Sorry, I must look a mess, but I haven't slept much since I heard about George.'

'So I guess you're Miss Turnbull, Stephanie Turnbull?' asked Nicole as she held out her ID.

'Yeah, yes, that's me, come on up,' she said as she walked along a short, dimly lit hallway to the stairs to her flat. They followed her up the steep stairs and were ushered into a large living room, with two closed doors on the left-hand wall, and an opening to a kitchen-dining area on the right-hand wall. One tall sash window to the front and a high ceiling with an off-centre ornate ceiling rose the only remnants of a more salubrious past. Stephanie motioned for them to sit, waving an arm in a "wherever you like" gesture.

'I hope you're feeling better now, nothing too serious I hope?' Nicole said as she settled back into a two-seater settee with a colourful crocheted throw across the back. Stephanie hovered by the opening to the kitchen, ignored the question and asked, 'Would you like a drink? I've just opened a bottle of wine, but I can do tea or coffee.'

Both declined. Lewis sat down in an old wing-backed armchair and asked, 'So what was the trouble then, Miss Turnbull?' Again she ignored the question and moved unsteadily into the room to sit in the matching wing-backed chair. She balanced her glass on the arm.

'I don't normally drink at this time of the day, but since I heard about George...' Unable to continue, she stubbed her cigarette out in an overflowing ashtray. Her lips trembled as she grabbed a nearby box of tissues, nearly knocking over her wine glass. Pulling out a handful, she pushed aside her long, straggly hair and dabbed her eyes.

'We realise this must have been a massive shock to you, but we really do need to see if you can shed any light on the circumstances leading up to this,' said Nicole.

'Not sure I can, I knew George was no angel, but he was lovely. I really don't know why he was killed, or even who would want to kill him.' The tears began to flow again.

'You do seem extremely upset by this. Were you and George close, outside of work, if you know what I mean?' asked Lewis. Stephanie looked daggers at him for a second, then lit up another cigarette.

'Huh! Not like you mean, we'd been out for lunch a few times, that's all. Christ, he was my boss, he was at least fifty-five,' she said dabbing at her tears again, looking everywhere except at Lewis.

'Did you know he was accepting bribes to place unqualified men as managers in the tips?' he asked.

'I didn't know they were unqualified,' she said taking a large sip of her wine.

'But you did know that George was taking bribes?'

'No, not bribes. I saw him with money. It's just, well, once or twice I came back in from lunch, and he was at his desk with his briefcase open, slipping bands around bundles of notes. He said he just sold his wife's car, or once he said he'd sold a ride-on mower.'

'What can you tell us about the boat picture he's got as a screen saver?' asked Nicole.

'Oh, the boat, God, he loved that boat. Kept the picture to sort of motivate himself. You know, like a goal to aim for, he wanted to get one, said he'd take me out on it when he did,' she sniffed, head bowed.

'Do you know whose boat it is?'

'No, not really, George said he'd been out on it a few times, with a friend who I think he said owned it. I think he said the guy was called Eamonn.'

'So you don't know who this Eamonn character is then? You didn't meet him?'

'No, he never came in the office, George just said he knew him because of work.'

'One of the site managers was called Ayman, do you think it could have been him?' asked Nicole.

'It's likely, I suppose. George had to visit the sites quite often, so he knew all the managers,' she said, once again pushing long hairs away from her face.

'Any idea where this Eamonn moored the boat?' asked Lewis.

'Didn't really take a lot of notice. I'm not much for the sea and stuff like that, but I think George said it was somewhere on the Itchen… wherever that is.'

Feeling they had all they were going to get, Nicole and Lewis thanked her and left.

Walking to their car, Nicole told Lewis she thought Stephanie Turnbull had been having an affair with Saunders. Lewis nodded in agreement. They headed to Eileen Saunders's home.

—————————— ▮▮ ——————————

Eileen Saunders checked their IDs at the door. She did a double take when she saw Lewis's Security Forces ID card, but said nothing. Inside, she took them through to the kitchen and they settled around the central island.

'So sorry to disturb you, Mrs Saunders, but we really do need to ask you some questions, if you feel up to it,' said Lewis.

Taking tissues from a box, Eileen said, 'I'm not sure I can tell you any more than I told the others.'

'Eileen, you have our deepest sympathy, and we'll be out of your hair as soon as we can,' said Nicole, 'but we need to talk about George's bank account and credit cards. We also think that the boat picture on his work computer and apparently on his laptop may be of interest to us.'

Eileen slipped off her stool and disappeared into the hallway, half closing the door behind her. Moments later she returned carrying a laptop and charger. Plugging it into to the sockets on the worktop she slid it across to Lewis who opened it and powered it up. Nicole moved so that she could see the screen. Behind the various icons and apps was a screen-saver picture of the same expensive looking motor launch.

'So what can you tell us about this, Eileen?' said Nicole gently as she turned the laptop towards her.

Hesitating for just a moment, Eileen replied, 'All I know is that George had been out on it a number of times with the man who owned it. He loved it, he loved going out on it.'

'Do you remember the owners' name?' asked Nicole.

'No, sorry, I know George wanted one, he even joked about putting it on his bucket ......' Eileen stopped talking as the tears began to flow. She grabbed some tissues and dabbed her eyes. It took a moment or two before she composed herself.

'Sorry, sorry, it just comes over me.'

'No need to be sorry Eileen, we understand, but I think we'd best take the laptop with us for further checks. We'll give you a receipt of course,' said Nicole. Eileen nodded.

'Did George ever say where the boat was moored?' asked Lewis.

'The River Itchen, I think. A couple of times he said he'd been fishing there, so I assume it was moored there.'

'Ah, that's good,' said Lewis encouragingly, 'the other things we need to follow up on are George's bank account and mobile phone. Did he take his mobile with him?'

'He must have taken his phone and all his bank stuff with him, because I haven't found anything here. I know his current account was with Barclays, same as me, but I've no idea who his business account was with.'

'Do you use the branch in Chandlers Ford, and what about debit or credit cards?' asked Martin.

'Yes, we use the local bank, and he's definitely taken his cards, because they aren't here. I have to say I haven't checked with my bank yet, I just haven't been up to going out.'

'Just one more thing, Eileen, then we'll leave you in peace. Can you remember what service provider George's mobile was with?' asked Martin.

'Yes, he was with 02.'

Thanking her for her help, Lewis unplugged the laptop. Nicole wrote a receipt, thanked Eileen, gave her a gentle hug and said, 'We'll get it back to you as soon as possible, take care, Eileen.' They made their way out to the car. Nicole took out her mobile and called Stafford.

'Hi Staf, it's Nicole, we've finished at Eileen Saunders and the only lead we have is the boat. It's named *Whitelines*, and it's thought to be moored on the River Itchen. Now we're only a few miles away, could you check out marinas on the Itchen and see if any of them has a boat registered with that name?'

'Yep, I can do that, might take a while though because the Itchen's a pretty big river. Do you have a name of the owner?'

'Apparently it belongs to a friend called Eamonn, which we thought was an interesting coincidence.'

'Hmmn, that *is* interesting. Well, I'll tack on the name Runihura, and see what happens.'

'There's one other thing you can do for us; George was with 02; could you check out his phone records? One other thought from Lew and me is that George was having it off with his secretary, Stephanie Turnbull. I think we may have to talk to her again.'

'Right, I'll sort out the phone records, but that's interesting about Turnbull, it's definitely worth looking into. Thanks for that, I'll get back to you soonest,' said Stafford as he ended the call.

II

There was a small queue of customers waiting to use the DIY banking facility. A woman wearing the bank's uniform was hovering in case assistance was required. Lewis approached her, took out his wallet, removed his warrant card and said quietly to her, 'My name is Garfield Lewis and this is Acting DS Martin, we need to talk to the branch manager, please.'

'He's on a busy schedule at the moment, but I'll see what he says,' she said.

'Perhaps you would take my warrant card, and explain that we're from the Security Forces and we will actually create a gap in his busy schedule if this becomes necessary,' said Lewis with a friendly smile. Looking slightly startled, she scuttled off.

Moments later she returned, handed back Lewis's warrant card and said, 'Follow, me please.'

She led them upstairs to the first floor where there was a little seating area.

'If you'll wait here, he has someone with him now, but should only be a few minutes,' she said. Lewis sat down, made himself comfortable. Martin thanked the young lady and joined him on the banquette.

The manager's office door opened and a middle-aged man in a grey business suit ushered out a stern looking forty-something lady dressed in what she must have felt was an alluring style. Judging by her face and attitude, the manager had not succumbed to the allure. They didn't shake hands; she stormed away flashing a frowning, pouting glance at him. Unperturbed, the man approached Lewis with a smile and offered his hand saying, 'Mr Lewis?' Lewis shook hands and introduced Martin.

Holding out his right arm the manager said, 'Please, come in, take a seat.' Closing the door behind him, he took his seat at a neat, tidy, modern desk.

'So, Security Forces, aye? That sounds interesting. What can I do to help you folks?'

'We're investigating the murder of a Mr George Saunders and we believe he had at least one bank account with you,' said Lewis taking out his notebook. 'His wife banks here and apparently, every month, he transferred money into her account. We have an account number for her, but not for him.'

'A murder? Goodness, what on earth happened? Where was that?' asked the manager.

'He'd been missing for a while, then his body was discovered a day or so ago,' said Nicole.

'George Saunders you say? That name does ring a bell,' he said as he looked at his monitor and clicked buttons on his keyboard. 'What address did you say?' Lewis, checked his notebook and read out the address.

'Now this is where I should tell you you'll need a warrant for me to say any more, but now I see the details, I know who you are talking about,' he said, still looking at the monitor, 'and there's definitely something very wrong here. Mr Saunders has two accounts, as you intimated, a current account and a business account.' He turned the monitor around so that Lewis and Martin could see the screen.

'As you can see, both accounts now have the minimum £1 balance.'

'Woah,' said Lewis, 'what was the previous balance?' Turning the screen back, he clicked a few more keys, then turned the screen back again. It read, "Business account no. 179425. Balance. £156,000.00, current account no. 326745. Balance. £85,000.00".

'So just under a quarter million has been removed in four days,' said the manager.

'Can you see where the money has gone to?' asked Martin.

Working the keyboard again, the manager said, 'It seems they were online transfers, apparently by Mr Saunders. All I've got here are numbers, no names of any recipients, however the money seems to have been transferred to the Channel Islands... Mind you, it's probably been moved from there by now, likely to the Cayman Islands. It'll take a while to follow that journey.'

'Can you find out the name of the account holder?' asked Lewis.

'I doubt if they'd be that obvious. I can find out the banks involved, but the money will undoubtedly have passed through numerous shell companies and banks. And that, I'm afraid, may well take a forensic accountant to sort out.'

'Will you print out details of both accounts for the previous six months for us to take away, please?' asked Nicole.

'Under the circumstances I will, but I do need a warrant or something official to cover mine and the bank's arses,' said the manager with a smile.

'I can organise that now,' said Lewis taking out his phone. 'What's your email address?' he asked. Getting up and walking into a corner of the office he selected a speed dial button and spoke quietly into the phone.

The computer emitted a ping, denoting an email had been received. Checking it, he nodded at Lewis and said, 'Thanks for that.'

He pressed a couple of keys and a printer hidden under his desk began to chunter away.

Moments later Martin and Lewis headed for the car park carrying a bundle of A4 paper. They got back to their car and dumped the papers on the back seat.

'So what's our next move?' asked Nicole.

'I think we give Staf a bell and tell him we're gonna need a pro accountant to plough through this lot. See if he can line someone up.'

'Yeah, we'll do that anyway, but what do you think about driving down to the Itchen as we're so close? You never know, we might get a bit of luck and spot the boat.'

'Go on then, you phone him, I'll head for the M3.' Lewis fired up the engine and pulled away.

'I've checked out the Itchen on Google Maps. I don't think they'd moor up at Ocean Village, that's gotta be way too busy; too many people around to do anything naughty. So I think the best place to start would be Shamrock Quay.

That looks pretty spread out, so you could end up being quite anonymous there. Shall we try that?'

'Sounds like a plan.'

Nicole hit the speed dial button on her mobile and set the phone to speaker. Stafford picked up, 'How's it going?'

'Seems George did have two bank accounts, both with Barclays and both with £1 balances, would you believe?'

'Hmmn… I'd have thought he was better at business than that. How much do you reckon he lost?'

'Looks like they emptied just under a quarter mill. But it's all been paid into various accounts, the bank manager thinks in the Channel Islands and beyond. Says it'll take a hell of a lot to untangle its movements.'

'I can't believe that three people are dead for just a quarter of a million; gotta be more to it than that,' said Stafford. 'Anyway, we've probably got someone on board who can sort it, if we need to.'

'Well, the bank manager's gonna try, and we've got print outs anyway.'

'So what are you doing now?' asked Stafford.

'We're on our way down to the Itchen, to see if we can get a feel for where they might park a boat,'

'I can give you half a dozen places where they haven't parked it,' said Stafford, 'just give me a mo.' They heard him scrabbling around in the papers on his desk as he tried to find the relevant one. 'Sadly there's no DVLA equivalent for boats in the UK apparently, ah, here we go, got a pen?' He reeled off the names of seven marinas, none of them Shamrock Quay.

'Hey, that's great, we said we're gonna start at Shamrock Quay, it looks big enough, so you could be pretty autonomous there.'

'Well, good luck with that and keep me informed,' said Stafford as he ended the call.

'So that could be a pretty good guess then, Miss Smarty Pants,' said Lewis grinning at her.

'See, I'm not just a pretty face.' She switched her mobile to sat nav and directed him to Shamrock Quay.

Southampton traffic was a nightmare, but after forty-five minutes of stop start, stop start, they eventually found the street where they turned right on to the quay. As they drove in, a sign showed directions to a car park with arrows pointing to pontoons A to D and in the opposite direction, E to G. Lewis, with a sigh of relief, drove into one of the few remaining spaces and parked up.

'Right,' said Nicole showing Lewis her mobile, 'Google satellite shows three, maybe four walkways on to the pontoons. Shall I start with A to D and you go down to E to G?' Pointing her finger to show the left-hand end on the screen.

Lewis studied it for a second or two, then said, 'Yeah, that'll save a bit of time. I mean, there must be at least 200 boats here.'

'And Staf would have phoned if he had located our one.'

'Fair enough, you press on to the right, and I'll wander over to the office. I know it's closed, but they might put up an out-of-hours number. For Christ's sake, girl, be careful, don't fall in, God knows what diseases you could catch in there,' he said looking at the murky brown water with a grin.

'Gotta keep in touch,' she said waving her mobile at him. 'See ya, last one back to the car's a cissy.' Lewis walked away, turned, smiled at her and waved his mobile.

CHAPTER 19

The Beautiful Butties Café in Aldershot. Stafford was ordering a mug of coffee when Ryan Peters and Lee Gibson joined him.

'Make that two more coffees then, Staf,' said Ryan as he and Lee settled down in a booth for four at the far end of the greasy spoon caff.

'Either of you want a bacon butty?' Staf enquired.

'Yeah, why not, if you're buying,' said Ryan, and Lee added, 'Yeah, I'll go for one then, Staf.'

Taking the order and the money, the young lady said, 'I'll bring 'em over when they're ready sir, thank you.' Stafford nodded his thanks and walked towards the booth.

'So where are we with Mr Bockus,' he asked, sitting down.

'We booked him in with the custody sergeant, emptied his pockets; not much there. Just his wallet with a driving licence and £60 in notes, eighty pence in change, no cards, and of course the mobile phone. Then we just parked him in an interview room. Thought we'd let him stew for a bit, then have a little chat when you got here,' said Lee.

They stayed silent as the waitress placed their butties and coffees on the table. As they ate, they brought Stafford up to date with the possible charges Bockus faced.

'Has he asked for a phone call yet? Or a solicitor?' asked Stafford.

'No, not yet, I guess we'd better make him aware of both,' said Gibson.

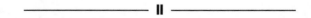

Back at Aldershot Police Station, Stafford asked, 'So how long has he been locked up for now?'

Gibson looked at his watch and said, 'About an hour and twenty.'

'Good, just nice time for a chat then.'

The custody sergeant led them to Interview Room Two, unlocked the door and set up the recording machine, loading in two new tapes.

Matis Bockus was leaning back on two legs of his metal chair, fingers interlaced behind his head. In front of him was a metal-legged table with a Formica top. Two metal chairs faced the table. Stafford took one of these and indicated for Gibson to take the other. Peters stood with his back to the door. Gibson turned, looked at both red lights in the corners of the ceiling and nodded, satisfied that both cameras were operational. He hit the record button and stated the date, time and his name. He indicated for Peters and Stafford to state their names. Realising that it was Paul Stafford in the room, Bockus dropped the chair back down on four legs and crashed his hands down on the table.

'You're not the police,' he sneered in accented English.

'When you start planting bombs, Matis, you attract more attention than just the police,' said Stafford.

'I don't know nothin' about no bombs, and I'm supposed to be somewhere, I need to make a phone call,' said Bockus wrapping his arms around his chest as he spoke.

'You can make your phone call in a minute and you may want to make that to a solicitor, because you've been arrested for some pretty serious stuff. You were found with half a kilo of cocaine. Now, you can get six years in prison for having that sort of quantity.'

'I told him it wasn't mine,' he said pointing to Peters.

'Oh, so that's all right then,' laughed Stafford. 'Look, Matis, I am trying to help you here. Even just the wrong address on your driver's licence can cost you £1000 fine.'

'What? Only moved a week ago, ain't got round to it yet.'

'What's got into you, Matis? A few months ago you were getting along OK in the waste business, you could have built a good life for yourself. Now, well, two people are dead because of a bomb in the waste. That's life in prison. Twenty-five years, Matis, why did you get involved with that? We won't stop till we find who did it, you know.' Matis rested his elbows on his knees and looked at the floor. Stafford stood up and beckoned for Gibson and Peters to follow him out. Stepping into the corridor, Stafford approached the custody sergeant.

'Can you let him make his phone call, then bung him in a cell for an hour or two, give him time to think about his future?'

CHAPTER 20

Lewis walked towards the chandlery. On the door a sign showed opening times 8 a.m. to 6:30 p.m. He cursed mildly to himself as he noted it was just ten minutes past closing. He turned and started to walk between rows of parked cars. He squeezed between the sides of two cars that brought him to where just one row of cars separated him from the riverbank.

After a few paces he noticed a man, eighty yards or so away, loading a number of items into the back of a white pickup truck. Lewis stopped walking, and sidled up to the side of the nearest parked car. He could see that the pickup truck's rear end was badly damaged. The man half turned as he bent to pick up items from the tarmac. Instantly Lewis recognised the profile of the long-haired Jan Kapusniak. Ducking down between two cars he pulled out his cell phone and hit the speed dial button for Nicole's mobile. As Lewis waited for her to answer, Kapusniak began pulling the plastic cover over the rear of the truck. Realising he was getting ready to drive away, Lewis pocketed his mobile and ran towards Kapusniak, shouting, 'Jan, stop, Jan, stop!'

Kapusniak, about to climb into the cab, turned and stared. As recognition dawned on him, he jumped into the driver's seat and fired up the motor. Engine screaming, he sent the pickup truck into a reverse left-hand turn, slammed it into first gear and drove between the rows of cars, headlong at Lewis. The truck screeched to a stop a few yards away. Kapusniak leant out of the window and yelled in heavily accented English, 'Get out fucking way or I kill you!'

'Come on, Jan, it needn't be like this, we just wanna talk to you.'

Kapusniak reached across to his passenger seat with his right hand and brought out what looked like a bright orange toy pistol. He shouted, 'Out of my way or I shoot you.'

For a split second Lewis started to laugh; the orange pistol looked like a toy, the sort of toy his boys would play with.

Kapusniak pulled the trigger. The Orion distress flare hurtled towards Lewis. Too late for him to react, the twelve-gauge flare slammed into his right upper torso. He staggered backwards and crashed writhing to the ground as it buried itself some two inches into his chest. Lewis screamed in agony and tore at the flare. The searing red heat flash blasted out its full 16,000 candela light force, inches from his face. Neck, face, eyes and hair were on fire. Desperately he tried to rip the flare from his chest. His internal organs were burning, his jacket was on fire, the skin on his hands blistered and burned in the two-and-a-half-thousand-degree inferno.

Blindly he scrambled to the water's edge, stumbled over the low wooden guard rail and plunged headlong into the river.

It took just seven seconds for him to die.

Kapusniak's eyes streamed from the searing red flash. Though unable to see clearly through the billowing red smoke, he gunned the pickup's throttle. His wheels spun madly. As his tyres screeched, trying for traction, he smashed into a couple of parked cars before making his high-speed exit.

Nicole felt her mobile vibrate and pulled it out of her pocket. She saw it was from Lew and accepted the call. With the phone to her ear she stood still, not comprehending what she was hearing. She could hear the sound of a car engine, very muffled, but revving loudly. The noise covered up what she thought were distant voices. As she contemplated this, a huge bright red flash caused her to duck and flinch. The flash lasted no more than a few seconds, but acrid red smoke billowed around distant cars. She dashed towards it, desperately trying Lewis's mobile number. When she got closer, greyish pink smoke billowed around her making it difficult to get her bearings. Her eyes streamed, her nose was running. The acrid smoke caused her to heave and she struggled for breath. She heard a vehicle travelling at high speed in her direction. She was rooted to the spot for a split second, then sighed with relief as she realised it was two rows of cars away.

She ran forward again and shouted for Lewis. Apart from the parked cars, the place appeared deserted. She walked slowly, searching between the cars to her right and left. She saw a narrow plume of greyish pink smoke rising from the river. She walked to the concrete edge of the river, and there between the bank and the wooden pontoon, floated Lewis, face down in the bubbling, murky brown water. Taking out her mobile she dialled 999, requested ambulance and police. Her eyes still streamed as she phoned Stafford.

The tears that streamed down her face now, were tears of sorrow.

Stafford, Peters and Gibson were sitting around a table in the squad room at the Aldershot police station. Stafford took a call from Nicole. Peters knew immediately from Stafford's body language that the call was not good news.

'OK, Nicole,' he said sternly, 'this is not your fault. Go back to the car and wait there till the police arrive. We'll be there in forty-five minutes.' He ended the call and with shoulders slumped, gazed at the mobile's blank screen as if in a trance.

'God, what's she gone an...' started Gibson, but Peters silenced him with a raised hand and a look. Stafford, head bowed, was deep in thought. After a moment or two he snapped out of his reverie and sprang to his feet.

'Right, into the car. Lee, sat nav Shamrock Quay, fastest route. I'll explain as we go,' he said as they dashed from the squad room. He climbed into the Vectras' driver's seat and shouted, 'Hold on tight, we'll be using the blues and twos.' He hit the switch for the grill's blue lights and siren as he turned out of the car park heading for the M3 south.

Traffic was busy and he raced down the outside lane as vehicles moved aside.

'There's no easy way to tell you this… but Garfield is dead.'

Stunned into silence, Peters and Gibson listened as Stafford continued, 'Not really sure what happened, but Nicole and Lew split up to search the quay.' Voice hoarse with emotion Stafford told them what Nicole had said. As they raced down the motorway and the blues and twos cleared their passage, not a word was spoken, their quiet reflection interrupted only by the incongruous voice of the sat nav.

Shamrock Quay was heaving with police personnel and police cars. Two patrol cars blocked their way. Getting out of the Vectra, the three of them walked towards two uniformed policemen, IDs at the ready.

'Ah, Major Stafford, yes, Acting DS Martin said you were on your way. You'll find her through the car park around pontoon "F".' They lifted up the blue and white police tape and the three of them ducked under and entered the marina.

Nicole, along with four other uniformed PCs were walking slowly, in a line, heads bowed. They were looking intently at the ground immediately ahead of them, searching for anything that could help pinpoint what had happened there. Two other men, both in dark grey suits, were standing near the chandlery, notebooks out, talking to a ruddy-faced, blonde-haired man.

Stafford, headed for Nicole, called out her name. She turned, saw her three colleagues and said something to the constables on either side of her. As she walked to meet them, the officers moved closer together to cover her area. With head bowed, she walked towards them. Rushing forward the last few steps she grabbed Stafford in a bear hug. She put her head on his chest and cried, huge sobs racking her body.

'I'm sorry, Staf, I'm sorry.' Stafford put his left arm around her shoulders and motioned with his right arm for Peters and Gibson to join them. Arms around each other, they stood silent, heads bowed and touching, a quiet homage to Garfield "Lew" Lewis.

Moments passed. Stafford took a step away and said quietly, 'So tell us what you know, Nic'.' She dried her tears with the sleeve of her jacket.

'When we got here and saw how big this place was, we decided to each start at one end and meet in the middle.' As she talked she started to walk towards the low wooden guard rail by the concrete bank of the river. Stopping at the riverside, she told them about Lewis's strange phone call, the huge red flash, the roar of a fast-moving vehicle and how she had then found him floating in the river where they were now standing. She said when the paramedics had pulled him out of the water, she could see he had been horrifically burned by the orange flare that had been protruding from his chest. Tears streamed uncontrolled as she described how Lewis's hands, face, neck and hair had been destroyed. Turned into an unrecognisable, charred and blackened mass.

Lewis's body, after being searched and examined by the forensic crime scene investigators, had been taken to the mortuary at Southampton General Hospital.

Indicating the two men in suits, Nicole said that these were the DC and DS from the Southampton Police Station and the man they were interviewing was the manager of the chandlery. As they walked over to the plain clothes policemen, she told how the forensic investigators had videoed the whole area, and she showed them where white paint fragments had been collected from two parked cars, damaged possibly by the perpetrator's vehicle exiting the marina. The forensic team had also photographed and measured skid marks on the tarmac close to the damaged cars in the area Nicole had pointed out, where the smoke had been the most dense. But they all knew that without either a confession or an eyewitness, this provided only speculation not evidence.

Stafford, noticing the officers had finished talking to the chandlery manager, walked across to them and introduced himself and his colleagues. PC Gibson decided that he and Nicole could be more useful elsewhere and returned to the other uniformed officers to join in the search.

Stafford realised by the detectives' body language they were not happy. Understandable, he thought; no sooner had they been handed what would likely become a high-profile murder case, it was snatched away again by arseholes from the Security Forces.

'Please tell me they've got CCTV in there, and out on the marina,' said Stafford.

'Looking for the easy way out already, Major?' asked the DS, sneering the word Major. 'Well, the most notable thing we found when we pulled the stiff out of...' Before he could finish the sentence, Stafford smacked his open hand around the detective sergeant's neck and slammed him up against the chandlery wall.

'His name was Garfield Lewis, and he was one of the good guys; you talk about him with respect.' He loosened his grip, pushed his hand upwards and away, causing the left side of the sergeant's face to collide with the wall.

Peters noticed the DC start to make a move to help his governor, and held up his hand in the classic stop sign. The detective looked Peters in the eyes for a millisecond and stood down. The sergeant, eyes screwed tight in obvious pain, rubbed his neck and said, 'Fuck you, Stafford, you mad bastard, there was no need for that.'

Bending forward, hands on knees, after a long intake of breath and a short laugh, he said, 'Yes, there was, Major, you're right, sorry about that.' He stretched out his hand and said, 'Let's start again.' With a nod and a hint of a smile, Stafford shook the man's hand.

'OK... when Mr Lewis was pulled from the river, we could see about an inch or so of the flare that hit him protruding from his chest. We showed a close-up picture of it to the guy who runs the chandlery. He tells us he thinks it is an American twelve-gauge flare, made for use with flare launchers or pistols. But he doesn't sell them and thinks they are unavailable in the UK. It seems legislation is a bit confusing about the use of flare pistols, so most UK suppliers sell only hand-held flares.'

'Let's bring him back over and have another chat with him,' said Stafford. The detective constable wandered off to find him.

'So did he remember who his last few customers were?'

'As it happens, he only had one latish one. Around quarter past six. A young foreign guy. Apparently he'd been in a few times before, he bought Calor gas bottles, a couple of five-litre bottles of water and a twenty-litre jerry can, always paid cash,' said the DS referring to his notebook.

The DC returned with the manager and introduced him to Stafford and Peters.

'Can you go over this last customer's description again? I want to try and get a picture of him.' asked Stafford.

'To be honest I didn't take a lot of notice, I just wanted him to piss off so I could cash up and go home,' said the manager, 'but I have seen him before, so I'd say he's about six-foot to six-foot-two inches tall. He's slim and got long, curly hair. I guess he's around thirty to thirty-three and he's not English, he talks it with a heavy accent. I think he's probably Polish. Definitely Eastern European.'

'If we got a police sketch artist to come down, do you think you could remember enough about his look, to guide him?' asked Stafford.

'Yeah, probably could, I'll give it a go anyway.'

'And you say you don't know what he was driving, or if he has a boat moored here?'

'I've no idea what he was driving and he definitely doesn't have a boat moored here, sorry.' Stafford said he would get a sketch artist to visit tomorrow, thanked him for his help, and walked with Peters across the car park to Nicole and Gibson.

They discussed what little information they had. Stafford pointed out that if the unknown foreign gentleman bought this type of product fairly frequently, then it's probable that he drove a van or a pickup of some sort. Now adding white paint scrapings and a heavily accented, possibly Eastern European, long-haired driver, and maybe, just maybe, three out of the four of them had recently had a run-in with such a vehicle and driver.

'I guess finding Jan Kapusniak has just become our number one priority,' said Peters.

With his team together, Stafford said, 'I don't think there's a lot more we can do or learn here, so Lee, you and Ryan take the Vectra and go back and see Stephanie Turnbull. Nicole and Lew thought she was holding back about her relationship with George. So push her, we really need a break here, push her as hard as you have to.'

'Peacock, George's boss, gave us the impression she was on holiday, but actually she was off sick. When we arrived in the morning she looked a state, and was already halfway through a bottle of wine. We thought she was too upset for just a boss/secretary relationship,' said Nicole to Lee and Ryan.

'Me and Nicole'll head back to Farnborough and see Marva, Lew's wife,' said Stafford looking forlorn.

Peters and Gibson took the Vectra and headed back to Winchester. Stafford and Nicole walked across to the two detectives, Stafford gave the DS his card and said, 'I need you to keep me updated. Anything, anything at all that will help us catch the bastard who did this.'

'You got it, Major, I'll do all I can down this end, this was a fuckin' awful way to die.'

'Well, the sketch artist should be down here first thing in the morning. I've asked him to email me the results immediately and you'll get a copy too. I don't think there's any more we can do here now, so we're going to go back and talk to the widow.'

'Hmm, good luck with that then,' said the DS as they shook hands.

Returning to the car, Stafford asked Nicole to drive.

As they pulled out of Shamrock Quay, Stafford decided he would break the news to Mariusz, who for some years had been mentored by Lewis, face to face. They headed to the M3 in silence.

CHAPTER 21

Kapusniak called Runihura. The call was answered quickly,

'Well?' said Runihura.

'Don't go near chandlery, go to boat, when you come, come to boat,' said Kapusniak, a trace of excitement in his heavily accented voice.

'What the fuck have you done now?' but the line was already dead.

Jan Kapusniak was less than half a mile from Shamrock Quay. He had driven through Saxon Wharf to the little used side gate of Southampton Metal Recycling Ltd (SMR Ltd). Stopping outside the gates, he unloaded the newly purchased items on to the tarmac, then carried them carefully down the uneven grassy footpath alongside the outer fence of the scrapyard to the motor cruiser, moored between the scrapyard and Southampton Yacht Services.

When all items were on board, he walked back to the yard gates, unlocked the padlock and parked the vehicle inside. He left the site, pulled the gates closed behind him, slid the bolt across and put the padlock back on, but didn't lock it. He walked back to the boat and climbed on board. The flare pistol he locked in the waterproof security cabinet, then he coupled a gas bottle to the built-in stove, grabbed a bottle of vodka and settled in for the night.

The following day, as Ayman Runihura drove the Range Rover Evoque with new plates towards Southampton, he was thinking about their task this evening. As long as Kapusniak hadn't caused another major problem, tonight's collection should go like clockwork. Floyd Winstone had assured him that he could drive the van with a broken hand and would meet as arranged at the boat's mooring place. Runihura had already received the GPS coordinates on his cell phone, so all he had to do was keep the boat pointed in the direction of the flashing red dot and as they got close to the incoming craft a yellow flashing dot would appear. Collection would take place when the two dots were close to overlapping. They'd done it many times before, it should be a piece of piss, he assured himself. But no matter how much he tried, he couldn't help but feel nervous. Kapusniak had obviously encountered a problem at Shamrock Quay; he must have sorted it or surely he would have been in contact to change the plan.

Knowing they had to cruise past the quay on their way out to Southampton Water, he had taken the precaution of getting two new name plates made up. From today, the motor boat *Whitelines* would be called *Cleopatra*. It would be dark when they set out, but if people were looking for a specific boat, a name change could maybe give them an edge. They just had to stick to the plan. People's lives depended on doing this; most importantly, thought Runihura, his own.

When he arrived at Southampton Metal Recycling's side gate, Winstone's and Kapusniak's vehicles were already parked up. He pulled in alongside Kapusniak's battered white Nissan truck.

Picking up a powerful torch and the new name plates from the passenger seat, he climbed out of the car. Padlocking the scrapyard's gates behind him, he picked his way carefully down the narrow footpath to the boat. He found them in the dinette, each with a beer in hand. Runihura stowed the torch in the underseat cabinet and slapped the two name plates down on the table. They exchanged fist bumps and greetings all round. Runihura pulled a can of beer from the depleted six-pack on the table, sat down and said, 'So what shit have you brought on us now, Jan?'

Kapusniak hesitated for just a moment, then said, 'Wasn't my fault, Ayman. Just loading stuff on truck and black guy from Farnborough was shouting at me to stop.'

'What? Lewis, the man who took Matis's job?'

'Yeah, that one. I get in truck, he want me to stop. I get flare pistol, he laugh. I shoot him and he fall in water. I go before anyone see.'

'So did you kill him?'

'I don't know, I just drove, but I hit cars on way out,' he said sheepishly.

'Fuck,' said Runihura, 'did you see anyone with him?'

'No, I see only him, whole place empty, I see no one.'

'Now listen, yesterday I had a phone call from Matis. He's been arrested. They found him with half a kilo of coke. Serve the little wanker right, 'cause he must have nicked it from Weyhill. Anyway, with the copper who arrested him was that other prat from Aldershot, Ryan fucking Peters and when they interviewed him, Paul bloody Stafford turned up. I just hope Matis keeps his mouth shut, or he'll fuckin' regret it.' He paused for thought, then continued. 'Seems they're Special Branch or Security Forces. They gotta be working with the cops, trying to find who caused the bang or what happened to George, so I don't want any more fuck-ups, comprenday?'

'If Lewis was down here they must know about the boat and think maybe George had been hiding out in it,' said Floyd Winstone.

'Even if they do find this boat, there's nothing to link George to it. Anyway, Jan, you can get out there and change these fuckin' name plates over,' said Runihura, sliding them across the table at him.

'OK, boss,' said Kapusniak not best pleased.

'And we'll get rid of that motor of yours, at least it's in the right place for that. I'll phone Frank and get it sorted.' Runihura took out his cell phone and punched in a number,

'It's Ayman, when you get in tomorrow, there's a white Nissan pickup over by the side gate, needs getting rid of, take care of it for me, will you?'

'Yeah, that's great, I owe you one, cheers Frank,' he said and ended the call.

As daylight turned to evening, the three of them sat in the plush leather seats of the open cockpit, getting their eyes acclimatised to the growing twilight.

Not wanting to advertise their position, Runihura had yet to turn on the navigation lights necessary for night sailing. He'd set up the broadband radar system that would show any hazard looming out of darkness on the busy river. He would also post Winstone as lookout down at the sharp end, where he could hold on to the bow grab rail and operate the headlight and searchlights when needed.

Kapusniak had checked and rechecked their equipment, ensuring they had everything they needed for a sea fishing trip. Runihura had taught and tested his shipmates and others before them, the fine arts of fishing in the English Channel. Even in his broken English, Kapusniak could explain to a customs officer why you would use a mackerel feather, or what a twelve-inch, twenty-pound braid leader was used for, and he'd never put a fishing line in the water. Winstone actually enjoyed sea fishing, though on these trips he never got the chance. But he had selected the rods, including some of his own. Even the tackle box and contents looked the part and he could bore the most vigilant of customs men into submission by extolling the virtues of a fixed-spool spinning rod for fishing bream or bass. By now all his friends knew never to say the words "wreck fishing" in his earshot. *Yep*, thought Runihura with a chuckle, *we really could be going fishing.*

From previous experience, Runihura knew that if they didn't encounter too much marine traffic whilst leaving the Itchen for Southampton Water, the crossing to the rendezvous point would take about three and a half to four hours. Limited to six knots per hour until they were south of Hythe Pier, they would pick up speed as they hit the Western Approaches and out into the English Channel. The main danger would be crossing the East Cowes ferry's shipping lanes, but once through there, he was confident it would be plain sailing to the RVP, some fifteen miles off the French coast. There, he knew, they'd need to avoid the Irish ferries going to and from Cherbourg.

He called the two men to the cockpit, to give them final instructions.

'Listen, Floyd, use the safety line on the bow rail, it could get rough out there and your busted hand ain't gonna help. The both of you, I need your eyes and ears everywhere, I don't want a collision before we even get out to sea. Now get ready to cast off.' Kapusniak, having heard it all before, looked bored.

Winstone said sarcastically, 'Aye, aye, Captain,' and headed off to the sharp end. Runihura fired up the twin Volvo engines, checked all gauges and systems were live, then turned on the navigation lights.

'All set? Then cast off,' he shouted.

Winstone fore, Kapusniak aft, cast off. Runihura gently throttled up and eased the cruiser out into the River Itchen.

CHAPTER 22

Peters and Gibson arrived at Stephanie Turnbull's Winchester flat. Though only mid evening, she answered the door bleary-eyed and wearing a dressing gown. Gibson showed her his ID.

'Stephanie Turnbull? Sorry to call this late, but there's been a further development concerning George Saunders's disappearance and murder. We have some follow-up questions we need to ask you.' At first Stephanie was reluctant to allow them into the flat. Gibson explained there had been another murder close to the River Itchen and that it was probably connected to the boat George liked to use in that area. Shrugging her shoulders in a "whatever" gesture, she turned and unsteadily led them up the steep stairs to her flat. She ushered them into an untidy living room, slumped into a wing-back chair and picked up a three quarters full glass of wine. Airily she waved her arm and said, 'Have a sheat, fellas, have a sheat.' Then, 'Whoops,' she said with a giggle, as wine sloshed over her dressing gown.

'We won't keep you long, Miss Turnbull,' said Gibson. 'The two officers who were here earlier went down to the River Itchen to see if they could find the boat George used. Unfortunately they became involved in a major incident, another murder in fact.' Stephanie's hands went to her mouth in horror.

'But I've been here all day,' she said. She grabbed a packet of cigarettes, pulled one out and with trembling hands tried unsuccessfully to light it.

Gibson took the lighter from her, flicked back the top, and spun the wheel till it lit. He held it to her cigarette and said, smiling, 'It's all right, Stephanie, don't worry, we know you weren't involved. We just need you to think back to when you were last in contact with George and explain how things were between you then. There could just be a snippet of information that would help us to find George's killer.'

Stephanie moved a couple of empty wine bottles on the coffee table, reached for her tissues, looked at him defiantly and said, 'I'll tell you somethin' now, if I ever find out who killed my lovely George, I'd bloody shoot 'em myself.' She stopped, thought for a moment, giggled and said, 'But I ain't got a blinkin' gun.'

'Stephanie, listen; we've got George's phone records, we'll be sifting through all the numbers that George called during his last few days. If your mobile number turns up, your next interview will be at the police station,' said Gibson staring at her while taking out his notebook. *Even half pissed she was one sexy woman*, he thought.

She dabbed her tearless eyes with a bunch of tissues. Then settling back in her chair, she crossed her legs, revealing perhaps a little more inner thigh than she'd intended. Gibson was transfixed for a split second. Stephanie's almost imperceptible smile suggested she was, maybe, only a quarter pissed.

'OK,' she said eventually, 'so I fucked him a few times. That's not a crime, is it?'

'No, Steph, it's not, but I think you'd best tell us what happened with you and George.' Now the tears were real as she dabbed her eyes.

'I liked him, I liked him a lot, he was a lovely guy,' she sobbed. 'At first we just used to go out for lunch, and he would buy me presents. You know, perfume and jewellery and stuff.' She stopped to wipe her nose, and clear the straggly hair that had fallen across her face.

'I saw him with money in the office a few times, quite a lot of it really, but he always had a good reason for having it. Then we went out a few times in the evening for a drink or a meal and we'd end up back here. And well, you know, after a couple of drinks,' she finished with a shrug. Gibson and Peters remained silent, waiting for her to continue.

'Poor George, he wanted us to be together. I liked being with him. He was good, you know, in bed, but he was old enough to be my dad; he couldn't see that it was just a bit of fun. No, that's wrong, it was more than than, I loved him in a way, you know? Anyway, one day, I'd been off sick and he phoned me at home to say he'd resigned and walked out. He said he needed to talk to me and that he'd booked a room in a hotel near the M3 and would I go up and meet him. He sounded so stressed, almost panicking, so I thought I'd go and cheer him up a bit. But he never turned up. He booked the room in my name and paid for one night, so I stayed the night, but he never came,' she said, and began to cry again.

'I kept trying his mobile but he never responded. I left him voicemails, I even thought about calling his home, but I didn't. First I was really angry, bloody furious actually, then I started to worry, you know; why did he resign? Was it to do with the money? I got really ill, ill with worry. I couldn't face going to work, so I phoned in sick again.' She slumped forward in her chair, head in hands and sobbed, 'Poor George, poor George.' Gibson waited a moment or two, then moved across and sat on the arm of her chair. He put an arm around her shoulders and said quietly 'It's all right, girl, just take it steady. Would you like me to make you a tea or a coffee?' She nodded.

'Hmm, yeh, coffee please, black.'

Peters signalled to Gibson that he would make the drinks. When Peters was out in the kitchen, Gibson handed Stephanie a card, and said quietly, 'If you think of anything, anything at all, give me a ring, night or day, doesn't matter.' Peters returned a few moments later with three black coffees, plus a milk carton and sugar bowl on a tray,

'There you go, Steph,' he said as he placed the tray on the coffee table. Stephanie pushed straggly blonde hairs away from her face and nodded her thanks.

'So can you remember the name of the hotel and where it is?' asked Gibson.

Stephanie took a sip of her coffee.

'Yeah, it was a Travelodge, just off junction 1 of the M3.'

'So what time was it when you arrived there?'

'I guess it must have been around 3:30 p.m when I checked in.'

'And this was the day after George had resigned?' Stephanie nodded.

'Just two more questions, then we'll be out of your hair: what car do you drive, and do you remember the reg. number?'

'I've got a little dark blue Ford Ka. Uh, it's number is... oh, I don't know. But you'll see it in the car park when you go.'

Gibson put his notebook away and finished his coffee. Peters too, drained his mug and as they got up to leave Gibson said, 'Look, Steph, this has been really helpful, I can't see that any of this needs to be made public, so my advice for what it's worth, is get back to work as quick as possible and put all this behind you, all right?' Stephanie nodded, then dabbed her eyes with the tissues.

'You never told me who it was got killed,' she said. Peters looked at Gibson and nodded.

'It was the black officer who came to see you earlier today, Sergeant Garfield Lewis, I'm afraid, so if you think of anything that may help, ring me, OK?' said Gibson as he reached and patted her shoulder. Tears shone in her eyes as she clasped her hands to her face.

Heading back to the car Peters said, 'Well done, mate, that was really good, I thought with two blokes she'd get really spooked, but you handled it well.' The two men bumped fists.

'To be honest I felt a bit sorry for her. I mean, unless you count fucking George, she's done nothing wrong. And let's face it, you can't blame George, she's fucking gorgeous. Let's just hope this hotel has got CCTV, and maybe we can make some headway.' Before driving away they found Stephanie's little motor and noted the registration number.

CHAPTER 23

Nicole and Stafford were in the car heading for the M3. Stafford had already made a number of phone calls. He looked across at Nicole. She seemed extremely distraught, struggling to hold it together.

'You sure you're OK driving?'

She didn't reply for a moment or two, then said 'Yeah, sorry…I'll be all right…Just wish I had stayed with Garfield, I might have been able to do something.'

'Now listen, you can't dwell on that, you both did what was best at the time. There's no way you could have known what was gonna happen.' She nodded, but said nothing. Several miles passed in silence.

'Do you know his wife well?'

'Yeah, she's lovely, we've met lots of times over the years, mainly at some military function or other. And we've been to each other's houses and out for meals, but since they've had kids it's been less frequent.'

'Oh my God, Lew had kids?'

'Yeah, couple of boys, must be around eight and ten now, so this is going to be pretty traumatic, I'm afraid.' They continued in silence until they approached the Farnborough turn-off.

'So you know where they live?' Stafford nodded and directed her to a modest brick-built semi-detached house with a small, neat and tidy front garden. A 62-plate Vauxhall Zafira sat in the driveway. Stafford told her where to pull up.

Curtains were closed, but little slivers of light could be seen between the downstairs drapes. They sat in the car silently for a long moment. Stafford could see a moving blue light through the gap in the curtains. His mind was all over the place; he'd hoped Marva had maybe seen or heard about it on the local news channel.

Now he felt guilty.

'Would you like me to come in with you?'

'Please, I need all the help I can get, I'm not very good at this sort of thing.'

They got out of the car. Stafford led the way past the Zafira into the little storm porch. He steeled himself, before ringing the bell. Taking a pace backwards he noticed a shadow cross the spyglass in the solid wooden door. The door was opened by Marva Lewis.

'Stafford,' she said, 'you'd better come in.' She stood aside and held the door open for them. Stafford and Nicole stepped inside the beautifully decorated hallway. Stafford took Marva into his arms and they joined together in a wordless hug. Marva's shoulders shook as she pressed her face into his chest. Moments passed, she stepped away and wiped the tears from her face with trembling hands. She took them through to the living room. Stafford introduced Nicole, who opened her arms, a hug she needed as much as Marva. As they parted, Nicole said, 'Would you like me to make a cup of tea or something, while you have a word with Staf?' Marva nodded to her and said, 'Tea would be good.' Nicole found the kitchen and busied herself with the drinks.

Stafford took Marva's hands and guided her gently to the three-seater settee. Sitting down, she said haltingly between sobs and with tears streaming, 'I've sort of been expecting you. I caught the news earlier and they talked about an incident by the River Itchen. Garfield told me about a beautiful boat you were trying to trace down there, so when they said someone had been killed at the marina there, I feared the worst.' Stafford could only nod. He felt guilty now. He almost wanted to be more than just the messenger boy, but sometimes this job took him too far into the inner workings of other peoples lives. A place he felt he had no right to be.

'Yes, I'm so sorry, Marva, but I'm afraid it was Garfield.'

'So where is he now?' she sobbed.

'They've taken him to Southampton General Hospital, for a post-mortem. I'm so sorry, Marva.'

The door opened and Nicole came in carrying the tea. She set it down on the coffee table and sat on the sofa's arm next to Marva. Putting her arm around Marva's shoulders she asked, 'How do you like your tea?'

Marva seemed not to hear and helped herself to milk and sugar then said, 'When will I be able to see him?' Nicole looked over Marva's head towards Stafford and shook her head. Stafford nodded his understanding.

'Marva,' he said, gently taking her hand, 'Garfield was killed by a marine distress flare, it set fire to his clothes and he was badly burned, it's best that you don't see him now, but...' Marva slumped against Stafford, her shoulders heaving. Eventually she sat upright, wiped her face with her hands and reached for her tea. The tea slopped over the sides of the mug as she continued to be racked with grief. Stafford asked, 'Is there anyone we can call, y'know, to come and stay with you for a while?' Marva shook her head.

Nicole said, as she used tissues to mop up the tea spills, 'If you'd like me to stay with you tonight, I'm perfectly happy to stay and help with whatever you need to do in the morning.'

Again Marva shook her head, and with the semblance of a smile through tears and sniffles said, 'No, no. It's OK, and I thank you for your offer, but as a military wife you kind of get ready for a day like this and I need to be strong for the kids.' Stafford marvelled at her composure. Marva was a beautiful woman; seeing her in tears, seeing her vulnerability, he felt totally out of his depth. He wanted her to know he would be there whenever she needed. He wanted to say something profound, something deep and meaningful. He said only, 'Well, Marva, the offer is always there. I'll come over in the next few days to see how you and the boys are doing. Now if there is any way we can help, or anything you need, just call, day or night, doesn't matter, just call. We are here if you need us.'

They let themselves out, and drove in silence to his home. Nicole pulled into the driveway and circled around to face the exit.

'Would you like to come in for a coffee or something stronger?'

She gave him a baleful look and said, 'On any other occasion I would, but tonight, well, I'm just about holding myself together. I need a soak in a nice hot bath and maybe down a bottle of Pinot Grigio, then try to get some sleep.'

'Yeah, reckon I'll do much the same. Anyway, you gonna be all right for the morning?'

'I'll be fine. I'll get here for about eight o'clock if that's OK?'

'Good… Look, I'm sorry you had to go through all of that today… Y'know, if you need some time away, I understand.' Nicole leaned across the handbrake and kissed him lightly on the cheek. The delicate touch surprised him. He turned to look at her. She looked both fragile and desirable in the soft light. Instantly, he turned and began to fumble, searching for the door handle.

'I'll be fine… goodnight, Staf, I hope you get some sleep.' Stafford, unable to speak as he struggled to hold it together, nodded his appreciation and made a scrambled exit from the car. He stood on his front door steps and watched as she drove away. As he entered his house, the day's events began to take their toll. He wandered through the hallway to his living room. He sat in the dark on the edge of a sofa. He couldn't help but think about Marva and her boys.

II

Death and destruction were nothing new to Stafford. He had joined the military at sixteen to escape his mother's evangelical fervour. By the time he was eighteen, he had seen that religions around the world were the cause of more evil than good. The God concept, he believed, damaged people, countries and continents.

'Jesus Christ,' he said to himself. 'Somehow I'm gonna find the fucker who did this, and one day soon, I'll make him fucking pay.' It was the nearest thing he had to a prayer.

He was suddenly very glad he was alone.

CHAPTER 24

Peters and Gibson stayed on the M3 and headed for the Sunbury Travelodge Hotel, in order to confirm Stephanie's story and maybe retrieve some CCTV footage of her visit. Traffic was light and they made good time. It was getting on for 10 p.m., but they hoped they would find someone useful at the hotel.

The car park was about two-thirds full and Peters parked as close as he could to the front entrance. Both men got their IDs ready as they approached the neatly dressed, shaven-headed young man behind the reception desk. He examined their warrant cards carefully, handed them back and said with a smile, 'So what can I do for you gentlemen this evening?'

'Well, first off, do you have CCTV in this area and the car park?' asked Gibson.

'Yeah, we do, yeah, we have a couple of cameras in the parking area. One covering the front entrance and one here at reception,' he said and pointed to what looked like a normal light-fitting above his head.

'So how long do you store the images for, and is it on tape or DVD?'

'Gotta tell you it's a pretty old system now, but we store pictures in the unit for thirty-one days before they're erased.

And we can burn the images to DVD, so they can be played on a normal DVD player.'

'That sounds brilliant, we need to look at footage from last Friday, about 2.30 in the afternoon and onwards,' said Gibson.

'I'm going to need my line manager or the security manager to sanction that.'

'I should tell you, mate, this is a multiple murder investigation, so speed really is important. Is there any way you can reach either one of them now?' asked Gibson.

'Well, I can't promise anything, but give me a mo and I'll see what I can do,' he said picking up the reception phone. He pushed a couple of buttons on the console and after a few moments he began to explain what was needed to the person at the other end. He offered the handset to Peters and said, 'It's my boss, he wants to talk to you, wants to know why Security Forces are involved.'

Peters took the handset and said, 'Good evening, sir, sorry for such a late call. I'm Captain Peters of SF. We're working with Hampshire police, investigating four violent deaths, two caused by an explosion, hence SF involvement. The other two deaths seem to be linked, and today we found that one of the victims was due to meet someone here last Friday. We need to look at the CCTV footage urgently. Can you get over here now to set it up, please? We can pick you up if need be.' Peters listened for a moment then said in a low growl, 'Well, there's always the hard way, but I'm trying to avoid that.' Another pause, then, 'Thank you, sir, we look forward to seeing you in about fifteen minutes,' he said.

'Playing hard to get was he? Christ, it's not that late, and he only lives around the bloody corner.'

'Oh well, he's on his way, so we'll sit over there and wait for him,' said Peters pointing to a little seating area. Sitting down, they began to idly flick through the range of brochures advertising various venues and events taking place in the surrounding area.

Peters had been debating with himself whether to phone Stafford and update him, or leave it until the morning. He decided that Stafford would appreciate a call, any call, just to stop him dwelling on Lewis's demise. He hit the speed dial button on his mobile phone. Stafford answered, 'Hiya, mate, where are you? You home yet?'

'No, not yet, we're up at the Sunbury Travelodge Hotel. We found out from Stephanie Turnbull that she was supposed to meet George up here the day he disappeared. She says he never showed, so we're here waiting for the manager to come in and run the CCTV films. George apparently booked a room in her name and paid by card for one night. So we could also verify it on his phone log and bank statements if we need to.'

'So Lew and Nicole were right about them having an affair.'

'Yeah, seems like it. I knew I wouldn't be able to sleep much, so we came straight up here. Anyway, how are you doing? Do you want me to come on over when I've dropped Lee off?'

'No, you're all right, just come here around eight in the morning and we'll suss out where we go from here.'

'OK, Staf, Roger that, now take it easy and get some rest, mate, we'll see you in the morning.' Peters ended the call and settled down to wait for the manager.

Just as it seemed he was going to be a no-show, a short, tubby man wearing an open-neck white shirt, grey trousers and trainers came bustling through the entrance.

'Good evening, Gov,' said the check-in clerk loudly, for the benefit of Peters and Gibson.

With his right arm on the reception desk and head down, the manager puffed and panted, trying to catch his breath. When he was able, he looked around and said, 'So where are these geezers…?' The clerk pointed to the guests' seating area; the manager bustled over to them, both hands outstretched.

'Sorry, sorry, bloody dog got out and I had to chase the little fucker to catch him. Anyway, I'm here now,' he said, sitting down heavily in one of the guests' chairs.

Peters and Gibson leaned across to him, right hands outstretched and introduced themselves. His hand was damp and squidgy; afterwards, both the officers resisted the urge to wipe their hands on their jeans.

'So you want to find some CCTV footage then? What date is it you want?'

'We need to start from around 2:30 p.m. last Friday,' said Peters.

'Right, let's go through to the control room,' he said getting up and pointing in the direction of the reception area. As they walked towards the reception desk, the clerk raised the hinged top and opened the half door below to allow them access to the room directly behind his work area. They wandered into a room that seemed to double or treble as a staff locker room, tea-making area and CCTV control centre. Pushed up against the rear wall was a long, narrow bench. A large flat-screen TV was mounted on the wall and showed six different pictures from various areas in and around the hotel. On the bench, a keyboard, mouse and joystick. There was one comfortable-looking high-backed leather chair in front of the screen and the manager planted himself in it.

'Grab yourselves a couple of those chairs, and bring 'em over here,' he said waving an arm to indicate a number of metal and plastic dining chairs littered around a table that the staff obviously used for their meal breaks. They grabbed a couple and settled one on either side of him. At lightning speed he hit a few keys and the screen changed to show a menu. Deftly he navigated around the screen hunting for the day and time they wanted to see.

'Right, so here we have last Friday. Now what time did you say?' he asked.

CHAPTER 25

After a fitful night's sleep, at 6 a.m. Stafford decided he might as well be up and working. He printed out the information Sergeant Hawkins had sent. With this and George's bank statements, he sat at his kitchen table and began ploughing through it. He found a recent payment by debit card to the Sunbury-on-Thames Travelodge Hotel which tied in nicely with their thoughts of George's likely intention to meet Stephanie Turnbull. There were a number of payments also by debit card, to The World Citizen Hotel near Basingstoke. *Why would he pay to stay in a hotel while less than a hour away from his home?* Thought Stafford. *Must have had too much to drink*, he concluded, but determined to follow it up. Deciding to get his command centre's help in untangling the final money transfers in the accounts, he put them to one side and started on the phone records.

George had made a considerable number of calls to Stephanie Turnbull's mobile and The World Citizen Hotel. One to the Travelodge Hotel, and four or five numbers that each time Stafford dialled, no one answered.

‖

Nicole Martin was first to arrive, followed by Gibson and Peters, who both appeared to be particularly buoyed up. They piled into the kitchen and settled down around the table. Stafford began by talking about the visit to Marva, then said, 'Now listen, this may seem callous, but we can't let our feelings about Garfield drag us down. We have to redouble our efforts to find whoever did this. It's obvious they'll stop at nothing to get their way, so we have to finish it, and finish it before anyone else gets hurt.' They nodded. No one spoke for a moment or two. Then Stafford said, 'We've now got a copy of George Saunders's post-mortem report... Hmm, I thought it was pretty bad before and yeah, Professor McIntyre confirmed George died from a massive overdose of heroin. He goes on to say that before death he had been tortured and abused pretty badly.'

'Christ,' said Gibson, 'we're dealing with a really sick bunch here. What does he mean by "abused"?'

'Apparently his left-hand little finger had been cut off and has not been recovered.'

'D'you think they've kept it for a souvenir?' Nicole asked.

'We've got no answer to that at the moment,' said Stafford, 'but even worse, there's evidence that he was sexually abused. The prof says raped multiple times, perhaps as many as twenty-five or thirty times.'

'Jesus, that's unbelievable, totally, totally shocking,' said Nicole shaking her head.

'Poor old George, what a bummer,' said Peters.

The others turned and looked at him in stunned silence.

'What?' he said. 'What?' He looked at each of them, completely unaware of his faux pas. Then the four of them, heads down, unable to look at each other, allowed themselves wry smiles. Taking a moment to compose himself Stafford continued,

'The professor believes this was to humiliate him completely before delivering the *coup de grâce*, a beheading, probably two blows with an axe, he thinks. The limbs were then separated with a thinner-bladed weapon, he says most likely a machete.'

Stafford continued, 'Professor McIntyre added that he feels the gratuitous violence should be regarded as a message, a warning that these people are prepared to go to any lengths to achieve their goals.'

Stafford's mobile phone buzzed. The sound, amplified by the pine kitchen table, broke the silence. He looked at the screen and saw it was SF Command. He picked it up, excused himself and wandered into the living room to take the call.

'Bloody hell,' said Gibson to no one in particular, 'these geezers are seriously twisted.'

'I think the prof is right; they've gone overboard with the violence to put the fear of God into us. But how can he estimate multiple rape like that?' said Nicole.

Peters stared at her for a moment or two. Then, decision made, said, 'Check out the 1970s rock band, 10cc, why they chose that name, that'll give you a clue. But it won't work, we'll find the bastards. And they are gonna pay.'

Whilst Stafford was out of the room, the laptop on his desk pinged, announcing the receipt of an email. Peters wandered over to it, opened it up and navigated the cursor to the email icon. It was from the Southampton Police sketch artist. Clicking on to the attachment showed a head and shoulders colour picture of a man probably in his early thirties. The "subject" said, "the final customer of Shamrock Quay Chandlery."

'Hey you guys, get over here, have a look at this,' said Peters. The other two pushed their chairs back and joined him.

At that moment Stafford came back into the room and walked over to them, he looked over their shoulders and said, 'Well, that's a good a match as you will ever see... Nicole, Lee, meet Jan Kapusniak.'

'I guess we anticipated it was him,' said Peters, 'but it's still a hell of a shock, seeing it confirmed like that.'

'Right, we'll get this info up on the PNC along with everything else we know about him, his car reg. and so on. Also add the picture to the Police National Database and we need to notify all ports and airports to be on the lookout for him.'

Peters reached into his inside jacket pocket, pulled out a plastic DVD case and taking out the disc, gave it to Stafford and said, 'Yeah, no problem, and while I'm doing that, bung this into the DVD player. Lee can talk you through it.'

Leaving Peters to it, the others adjourned to the living room. Nicole and Lee settled down on one of the sofas while Stafford turned the fifty-inch flat-screen television on and slid in the DVD.

'There is no sound to this,' said Gibson, 'but you can see the date and time shown in the bottom right-hand corner. So this is definitely the Friday George left home. Now this is the view coming into the hotel car park. At 15:12, see the little dark blue Ford Ka comes in. The reg. number, WM09DVJ, is definitely Stephanie Turnbull's. Sadly because of the angle of the windscreen and sun you can't really see if it's her driving, but we could get it enhanced if we need to.' There was a pause and the screen went blank. Gibson continued the commentary, 'Now we're changing to the camera inside, actually pointing at the front entrance. Look, here she comes through the doors carrying a large shoulder bag. As you can see, it's definitely her.' Stephanie walked towards the reception desk and she disappeared under the sight line of the camera. The screen was blank for a second or two, then she could be seen talking to the desk clerk, obviously checking in.

'Right, you can see why George fancied her, she's a real looker, isn't she? I wonder if that long blonde hair is real?' he said almost to himself. Nicole and Stafford glanced at each other and grinned. Gibson continued, 'Now there's a gap for some time, actually three hours and eight minutes, before the next action, which I think you'll find extremely interesting,' he said with a bit of a smile.

The screen opened up to what appeared to be the original view, but the time in the bottom right-hand corner showed it was now 18:18. The vehicle turning into the hotel car park was a green Range Rover Evoque. The windscreen and the sun's angles were helpful this time and the driver was obviously George Saunders. Stafford turned to Nicole and said, 'Jesus, that is George, so the dirty old bastard did turn up to meet her then.'

'Shh, keep watching,' said Gibson with a grin. A moment later, in through the car park entrance, travelling very slowly, came a black Mercedes X-Class Concept pickup, driven by Floyd Winstone. Clearly visible in the passenger seat was Ayman Runihura. The shape of a third person, though not identifiable, was visible in the rear of the car. Another blank on the screen as the camera view changed to the second one in the car park. This showed the black Mercedes pulling up and parking. Runihura and the man in the rear seats exited the car. The man was Matis Bockus. The men met and walked together for two or three paces, then stopped as though waiting for someone. George Saunders, head down and looking dishevelled, walked into the picture carrying a briefcase and a suitcase. He looked up, dropped the suitcase and made to run back to his car. He stopped, shrugged his shoulders and walked towards Runihura. Words were exchanged. And George seemed to stumble.

'Fuck,' said Stafford, 'did Runihura just hit him? It happened so fast, I couldn't really tell.'

'Yeah, we've watched it a dozen times and he definitely gives George a back hander,' said Gibson. Back on screen, George put his hand in his pocket, pulled something out and gave it to Runihura, who gave it to Bockus. Bockus walked a pace or two forward, picked up George's suitcase and walked out of picture.

'Looks like George gave them his car keys, and Bockus has gone to get the Range Rover,' said Nicole.

'Well, keep on watching,' said Gibson as George and Runihura climbed into the black Mercedes. The Mercedes reversed out of the parking space and headed out of the hotel car park, seconds later George's Range Rover followed. The screen went blank. A few heartbeats went by before anyone spoke again.

—————————— ❙❙ ——————————

'Well,' said Stafford, 'that's bloody brilliant, well done you two. But it makes my little bit of news pale into total insignificance. That phone call I just had was Command telling me they are returning my Volvo today. So I'm chuffed about that. Oh, and we're also keeping the Vectra.'

Then turning to Gibson he said, 'Having seen that, I think you and Ryan should go back to the Aldershot nick and have further words with our friend, Mr Bockus. I reckon we're going to have to threaten him with being charged as an accessory to George's murder, as well as the drugs and licence problem. Anyway, you know the score; try and make him talk to us with the offer of a better deal. Get an interpreter if you think it might help.'

'I think before we do that, we'll pay another visit to his flat; you never know, maybe Kapusniak or Runihura will be stupid enough to go there again,' said Gibson.

'Yeah, good idea, but we'll nip back to my place first though, and pick up a tracker or two. We can bung one on the black Mercedes if it's still outside the flat. That might lead us to one or other of 'em,' said Peters, picking up the Matis Bockus file. The two men bumped fists.

'I'll catch up with you later then,' said Stafford.

As the two men departed, he turned to Nicole and said, 'I'm going to leave you here for a while. I need to see Mariusz and Tomasz to talk to them about Lew.'

'Jeez, I don't envy you that conversation.'

Stafford gave her a wry grin, shrugged and said, 'Anyway, what I'd like you to do is try and find out if there is any substance in the talk of Special Branch or MI5 investigating

Runihura and his mob. Find out if it's true, what they found and if they've stopped. Then put something together that we can bung out to the media. We need to get that picture of Kapusniak out there in the papers and on TV. You may be able to get a picture of Runihura, even if it is only a mug shot. Oh, and it'd be good if you're here when they bring the Volvo back.' Nicole nodded acknowledgement to him as he walked through the kitchen to the front door, then blew a kiss at his departing back.

Half an hour later Stafford was on the M3, headed towards Andover. There he told the story to Tomasz, who through his friendship with Mariusz, was also friends with Garfield and his family. Next he drove to the Winchester recycling centre. He knew that this would be the most difficult of meetings. Lewis had mentored Mariusz from the day he had ventured into the Farnborough tip asking, in very broken English, for a job. Mariusz worked hard, learnt quick. The two men had become close friends. Garfield and Marva had helped him improve his English and encouraged him to work towards getting his own site. With their help, Mariusz had the opportunity to create a rewarding career and life for himself in the UK. Stafford didn't relish this meeting at all.

CHAPTER 26

Runihura was totally at ease at the helm of the newly named *Cleopatra*. He, Tony Amos and Eric Potter, from their Weyhill factory, took turns to do this trip. They had done it dozens of times and never yet encountered a problem they couldn't overcome.

Tonight was to be rather different to the usual trip. On other nights Runihura insisted that someone film the transfer; he thought it would help if they were hauled over by the coastguards or coastal patrols. Tonight there would be no filming.

II

So far the River Itchen had been as smooth as the proverbial mill pond, but that changed as they powered through Southampton Water and on towards Calshot Reach.

Runihura grinned to himself as he battled to keep on course, the *Cleopatra* seemingly fighting him as she hit the more turbulent waters. He wasn't worried, he knew he'd win.

Around his neck, he carried a mini night scope. This gave him an almost daylight-bright image of his surroundings, albeit with a green hue.

On his starboard side, as Calshot Castle came into view, he shouted, 'Floyd, stay awake now, keep your eyes peeled, we're gonna be turning to starboard across the ferry routes.'

'Aye, aye, Cap'n,' came the sarcastic response from the bow.

Runihura throttled the twin engines up, then struggling to keep his balance he manoeuvred the *Cleopatra*, rocking and rolling into the Solent. He headed towards the Needles at the bottom right-hand corner of the Isle of Wight. Past there, he throttled the engines up again, to power through the open water of the English Channel and on to their RVP some fifty miles away.

The sky was absolute black, perforated by a billion stars. Waves crashed against the boat. She bucked and bounced, spray and wind whipped across her bow and the cockpit windscreen wipers were in overdrive. The roar of the massive diesel engines competed with the crashing waves and created a deafening cacophony of sound. Runihura, the ship's master, was in total control of the rollercoaster ride.

What a great night for a fishing trip, he thought, *what a pity people are gonna die.*

The boat's GPS system showed they were approaching the RVP. Runihura took out his mobile phone and flicked on to the GPS app. He saw a constant red dot, the *Cleopatra*. Half an inch or so above it, a yellow dot flashed, the incoming craft. He throttled the engines back and steered the boat whilst he studied the mobile. The dots moved closer together. Runihura yelled, 'Jan, Floyd, get up here to the cockpit now.' After a moment or two they joined him. Floyd took out his mobile and set it to video mode.

'Put it away, Floyd, we won't be doing any videoing tonight,' said Runihura.

'I thought we always film it? We do when Eric's on board, so if we get stopped by coastguards, it proves that we'd just rescued these poor immigrants from their sinking dinghy.'

'Yeah? I know full well why we fuckin' film it, Floyd. And Eric ain't here, so just do as I fuckin' say,' said Runihura as he took off his night scope and handed it to Winstone. 'Tonight ain't gonna be the same as normal, so take this and look out for the inflatable.' Winstone did as he was told.

'According to the sat nav, we're pretty close now,' said Runihura throttling the engines back.

'Yep, yeah! I've spotted them, over on the right han... sorry, boss, starboard side,' said Winstone. Runihura turned on the remotely operated red searchlight mounted on the starboard grab rail. He flicked the switch on and off rapidly, hoping the incoming craft would see it. Getting closer, he could see there were a dozen or so people all wearing tatty clothes and tattier life jackets, huddled together in an ancient inflatable dinghy. The assembled immigrants waved excitedly, Runihura could hear muffled cheers, and an odd one or two "Allahu Akbar's" not quite drowned out by the sound of the crashing sea and boat's engines. He did a quick head count; *yep, a dozen, all present and correct and paid for*, he thought.

Even though the sea was fairly calm, it was still hard to draw close to the inflatable. This was always the hardest part, bringing people on board, but this time there would be fewer than usual.

When they were ten or twelve feet apart, Runihura switched on the searchlight and shouted across, 'Anyone speak English?'

A male voice said, 'Yes, a little, enough, OK?'

'OK, good, can you see an orange rope hanging into the water?'

'Yes,' came the reply.

'Good, now pull it out of the water,' he said as though talking to a bunch of children. As the *Cleopatra* rose on the crest of a wave, the inflatable was lost from view. As she settled back down, Runihura could see two men hauling on a rope at the rear of their craft. When they pulled the rope clear of the water, a package the size of a microwave, wrapped in blue, plastic emerged and was dragged on to the floor of the inflatable. This was four or five inches deep in water. Runihura gently eased the boats closer together.

'Now untie the rope from the boat and throw it to me.' He caught the rope and handed it to Kapusniak, who, unable to keep his feet as the ship lurched, draped his arms over the grab rail, then supported under his arm pits, and with legs outstretched behind him, hauled the package aboard. Carefully he got to his feet, clutched the rail and dragged the package down the steps into the cabins. Runihura shouted across to the inflatable, 'Get the women over to this side, we'll get them on board first.' Even this simple request created havoc, with men shouting, women screaming as they shuffled around trying to change places without falling into the sea. As the inflatable rose and fell, they desperately clung on to the looped grab ropes on the side walls, determined to survive. Eventually just three women sat on the outer tube wall. Runihura threw the rope across to the woman on the left, and shouted, 'Tie this around your waist, then jump, we'll pull you aboard.' Despite the rise and fall of both boats she deftly caught the rope and wrapped it twice around her waist. A man reached behind her and tied the rope tight. He gave her a hug, kissed her cheek, helped her move forward then steadied her as she jumped into the sea. Kapusniak, now back in the cockpit, and Runihura, hauled her aboard. Winstone took her below deck. Runihura, rope in hand, pointed to the younger of the two women.

'You next,' and threw her the rope. She caught it on the second attempt, and wrapped it around her. Another man tied a secure knot, and kissed her. She screamed in terror as she was helped over the side. Again, Runihura and Kapusniak hauled her aboard. Runihura told Kapusniak to take the helm.

Kapusniak stared at him then pointed at the inflatable, and asked, 'Not her? Them?'

Runihura shrugged and said, 'Too old, too fat. We can't whore fat, ugly Arabs.' He moved back to the cockpit's starboard side, looked at Kapusniak and signalled for him to throttle slowly forward, then signalled stop. The ten people that remained on the inflatable were silent for a second, then seemed to realise Runihura's intentions. They began to shout, to cry and scream. Runihura slipped his hand under his life jacket, into his waterproof coat's pocket and pulled out a pistol. Some of the men dived headlong into the sea, swimming away under water for as long as they could. Runihura waited for the *Cleopatra* to ride the crest of a wave, then as it started to bottom out, took aim and fired three times into the inflatable craft. One or two of the immigrants managed to reach the rope still dangling over the motor boat's side. It was useless, not attached to anything.

At the sound of the gunshots, the two women, panic-stricken, clambered back up the steps into the cockpit. One of the women looked over the side at the half-submerged inflatable. She saw two men swimming close by and screamed at Runihura in a foreign language. She rushed at him, arms flailing, beating him, tears streaming down her face.

'Husband! Husband!' she screamed. Runihura was tempted to throw her back to her husband, but instead he threw her down the stairs, then shouted at Winstone, 'Get them below, get their passports, then put the lock on the bloody door.' He peered over the side, spotted the two swimmers, raised the pistol and fired at each of them. He stopped only when they floated, not moving, in the red swirling sea. He slipped the pistol back into his coat pocket and moved back to the helm. Seated in the pilot's chair, he throttled up, powered the boat in a huge semicircle and headed towards Southampton. Above the roar of the engines, and the crashing of the waves, he could just hear the screams and shouts of the doomed immigrants. But that soon ended.

Kapusniak settled in the plush leather seats at the rear of the cockpit, looked up at the heavens and fell asleep.

II

Winstone, having got the screaming, soaking wet and shivering women into a cabin below deck, held out his good left hand and said, 'Passport, give me passports.' The women shrugged, shook their heads, in a, "Passports? We don't know what you mean," kind of way. Winstone sighed loudly, half turned as if to walk away, then without hesitation swung his left arm, and hit the nearest woman full in the face with the back of his hand. She staggered back and collapsed on to a bunk. Blood poured from her nose. She looked across at her companion who nodded. Both women reached into their sodden jackets, took out a polythene bag which they handed to Winstone. Winstone withdrew from the cabin and locked the door behind him.

Cursing loudly as the boat lurched from side to side, he staggered on the steps and hit his damaged right hand as he tried to stop himself from falling. He handed the passports to Runihura, who put them in the helm's chart drawer. As Winstone started to make his way back to the sharp end, Runihura shouted at him, 'Scope!' Winstone looked puzzled for a moment then realised he was still wearing the night scope. He handed it to Runihura then made the precarious journey back to the bow, fastened the safety line to his belt and continued to keep a lookout for the Dublin ferry.

―――――――――― **II** ――――――――――

The return trip was almost uneventful, with just a couple of hairy moments as they went past the Needles and back into Southampton Water. Runihura steered the *Cleopatra* through the slalom-like waters of the River Itchen to their moorings alongside Southampton Metal Recycling without further incident.

Kapusniak leapt ashore and tied up fore and aft. Runihura had given their passengers a couple of bottles of water and apart from the subsequent toilet breaks, they had caused no trouble. The women, exhausted, wet and shivering had spent most of the journey in fitful sleep.

Runihura knew better than to drive to the "factory" in a van during the early hours of morning. They would wait until the relative safety of the morning rush hour, to move their merchandise.

Once moored up, they erected the cockpit cover, then he and Kapusniak unwrapped the package they had pulled aboard. Taking off the last layer of thick blue polythene revealed four, one-kilo bricks, individually wrapped in a transparent film. When this was removed, each brick was wrapped in waxed brown paper. The two men unfolded the paper from one end of the nine-inch-long blocks. When all four blocks had been opened, Runihura was satisfied that once again their supplier had delivered exactly what had been paid for. Two one-kilo blocks of pure compressed cocaine and two one-kilo blocks of compressed heroin. Street value as delivered, £250,000, value when cut and bagged in the "factory" for franchise and retail sales, £1 mill. plus. Runihura knew that the four blocks had only cost around sixty grand. He felt certain that losing a potential workforce of ten, who had each paid £6000 for the crossing, was a better deal than having them around, doing sod all. The fact was, losing the tips meant losing what had been a fairly safe drug distribution network and a huge reduction in scrap electronics coming into the factory. The ten extra workers would have had bugger all to do. He desperately needed to push Stafford into working with them.

The women weren't such a problem; if they were reasonably attractive and with a decent pair of tits, they could be put to work making movies. They could work in the nightclubs as hostesses or whores. The fat, old and ugly ones they had brought in on previous trips were used as chambermaids, cooks or cleaners in the hotel. Or for cooking crack, cutting and bagging the drugs in the factory. Or even just bagging up the porn and snuff DVDs ready for sale.

Runihura was pissed off, he knew they couldn't keep bringing in dead weight. OK, they'd managed to get George Saunders in their pocket, and dreamt up this scheme. But, thought Runihura, *it wasn't my fault George got found out and binned. So it's not my fault we're in this shit, I'm just doing my best to get us out of it.*

The chances of getting another George at HCC were remote. And there was no way they could force the international company running the other twenty-one sites into submission, so their best, probably only, hope, was to break Paul bloody Stafford.

It had been a great idea, using the tips as a base to sell drugs. It was like having retail and wholesale outlets in each town, and for that business alone, he was determined to do whatever was necessary to get Stafford and his pissball company on side.

Runihura looked at the passports of the two women. They were both shown as twenty-seven years old and even in the passport pictures, they looked reasonably attractive. Assessing the women further would wait until he had them cleaned up and made presentable, away from the confines of the boat. He would determine their future later.

Having done all they could for now, two of them snatched a few, hours sleep; the third man, in this case Kapusniak, sat on watch in the cockpit.

Before sun up, Kapusniak roused Runihura and Winstone. They loaded the fishing gear, bottled water and all the other mundane items into the van. Runihura packed the night scope, and other small items used on the trip into a portable waterproof lock box, and gave it to Kapusniak to put into the metal storage cabinet fixed to the van's bulkhead.

'And make sure you padlock it securely,' he said. He got a raised eyebrow response from Kapusniak for that. Runihura opened the door to the women's cabin and walked in. Both women were sitting on the lower berth. Pleased, now that he could see them clearly, both women were at least as attractive as their passport pictures. Both, still in wet clothes and shivering, looked frightened and they watched his every move. He grabbed one girl by her arm and hauled her to her feet. He turned her around, wrenched both arms behind her back and bound her hands together with cable ties. The second girl stood, turned to face the cabin wall and meekly put her hands behind her back. Runihura, with a satisfied smirk, bound her hands too, though this time, not quite so tight.

He shouted up the steps, 'Floyd, come and take one of these up to the van, and send Jan back down for the other one.' Runihura turned to the women.

'Do you speak English?' He asked. He got blank looks as a response.

'No matter,' he said pulling a hypodermic syringe out of his inside coat pocket.

The women shrank back in alarm. Both ended up sitting on the edge of the bottom berth, wide-eyed, frightened.

'We're putting you in van, now. We don't leave for two and half hours,' he said. He put his hand over his mouth, then over one of the girl's mouths, 'Any noise, any shouts or screams, I give you this,' he said taking his hand away and waving the syringe close to their faces.

'Any noise, you get this, understand? Comprenday?' he said loudly, as is customary to non-English speakers. The women nodded frantically in response.

'And Jan, don't forget to lock the bloody van,' he shouted as they climbed the steps to the cockpit.

When the two men returned, Runihura said, 'Jan, you've got two and a half hours to get your head down; Winstone, you're on watch. We start back at 8:30 a.m. and we're all going in the van. I'm leaving the Range Rover here for Frank to change a few things on, before we sell it.' He packed the drug bricks into a canvas shoulder bag and put his pistol into the bag between the drugs. Set his mobile phone alarm for 08:15 and lay down on the bottom berth. He fancied he could smell the not unpleasant odour of the previous occupant. After a while he slept.

CHAPTER 27

Having collected the magnetic tracking devices, Peters and Gibson went to North Lane in Aldershot. They rolled to a halt in the residents' parking area. The black Mercedes pickup was there. They baled out and walked over to the Merc. The driver's side had been repaired and looked as good as new. Peters reached under the offside rear-wheel arch and attached a magnetic tracker. They went over to the iron staircase and climbed it as quietly as they could. Gibson bashed on the door. After a few moments he bashed again. No response. He knelt and peered through the letter box. He could see into the unlit hallway, but could hear only silence from inside. He bashed the door again and shouted into the letter box, 'Police, open up, this is the police.' Again, no response. Gibson stood up, looked at Peters and shrugged, 'Well, it was worth a try.'

They returned to their car and Gibson took the driver's seat. As Peters strapped himself in, he caught a glimpse of a white Ford Mondeo pulling away from the opposite kerb.

Before heading to the Aldershot nick, Peters pulled out his mobile and switched to the app that indicated the position of the tracker. On the screen a stationary little red dot flashed. With thumb and forefinger he enlarged the image. It enabled him to read North Lane and Queen Street adjacent to the dot. Satisfied, he closed the app and put the mobile in his pocket. Now Gibson headed to the nick.

Peters picked up the Bockus file from the back seat. Gibson parked in the police station car park and they walked across to the nick's rear door. Peters saw a white Ford Mondeo parked in the bays reserved for senior officers, he walked across and put his hand on the centre of the Mondeo's bonnet. It was warm. Gibson stopped and waited.

'What's up?' he asked.

'Well, I saw a white Mondeo drive away when we were at North Lane; this one's still warm.'

'That's DI Fisher's motor.'

'Hmm, wonder if that was him at North Lane? Why would he be checking us out?'

'He was the one who started this investigation, if you remember. Maybe he's just interested.'

Peters nodded and said, 'Yeah, OK, maybe.'

They walked through the doors and approached the custody officer.

'Morning, Sergeant, you know Captain Peters from the Security Force, don't you?' Gibson asked. Peters and the sergeant shook hands.

'Yeah, we met when DI Fisher had you brought in,' said the sergeant with a laugh.

'Now we need to interview Matis Bockus again,' said Gibson.

'No worries. Interview Room Two is free, so if you set up in there, I'll bring the dick… suspect up to you.'

In the interview room, Gibson checked the two cameras and cassette recorder. Satisfied they were working, he unwrapped two brand new tapes. Peters placed the Bockus file on the table and Gibson took out his notebook and pen. They used the chairs on the far side of the table. The custody officer brought in the handcuffed Matis Bockus and pointed him to the chair opposite Gibson. As Bockus sat, a look as dark as his five o'clock shadow crossed his face. He gripped both knees with his manacled hands as if trying to stop his legs from bouncing up and down.

Peters nodded his thanks to the departing custody officer. Gibson placed the two cassette tapes into the recorder and set it to record. He stated the date and time, followed by his name and rank. Peters followed suit, and Gibson stated for the tape that they were interviewing Matis Bockus.

'Right, Matis, you've had plenty of time to think. Are you sure you don't want a solicitor present? We can delay this interview and get one here for you. It's free, and it's in your interest to have one,' said Gibson.

'Fuck you,' said Bockus, 'just let me go out of here.'

'We're trying to help you here, Matis, would you like us to get you an interpreter?'

'Fuck you,' said Bockus, knees bouncing at pace.

'Is that what you do, Matis, fuck men?' said Peters. Bockus made to spring from his chair, then perhaps noticing the half smile on Peters's face, dropped back down again.

'So, Matis, do you have a girlfriend, or is it a boyfriend?' Bockus stared at Peters, face twisted with anger, then looked at the floor.

'Do you not understand, Matis? You are not just going to walk away from this. You will be going to prison; how long may depend on whether you help us here. If you go to prison you will be deported, sent back to Lithuania when you've done your time,' said Gibson gently. 'If you help us now, we may be able to help you.'

'What can you tell us about George Saunders's disappearance, Matis? We know you were driving his car on the day he disappeared. Did you kill him for his car? Or did you kill him after having sex with him?' asked Peters. 'Is that why you went to the hotel, to have sex with him; is that it, did he pay you for sex?'

Bockus jumped to his feet and shouted at Peters, 'No, no, not like that, I not like that, I not kill him, I just drive car.'

'Why don't you just start at the beginning and tell us what happened?' said Gibson.

'You help me? If I tell you, you help me?'

'We will do whatever we can, we will do our best for you, but you will still have to go to court and answer these charges,' said Gibson as he tapped the charge sheets.

Bockus shrugged his shoulders, sighed and said, 'OK, day I drive George's car, Ayman come to flat, tell me to go with him.' Peters put his hand up.

'Hold on a minute, you said Ayman came to the flat; Ayman who?'

'He have funny name, like Runihurry I think,' said Bockus with a slight smile.

'So why does he tell you what to do?' asked Peters.

'He boss, we work, he pay.'

'So he wanted you to go with him; what happened next?' asked Gibson.

'We go out to car. Floyd driving. Ayman got in front, I get in back,' said Bockus.

'What car was this?' asked Peters .

'Black Mercedes pickup.'

'And you say Floyd was driving; Floyd who?'

'Floyd Win-stone, then we go to George's house. Ayman see his car in drive. Say we wait. We wait maybe one hour and half. Then he drive out.'

Peters stopped him again and asked, 'What was George driving?'

'OK, George driving green Range Rover.'

'Right, carry on,' said Peters.

'We follow him to hotel.'

'That's it? Just straight up the motorway?' Peters again.

'Yeah, we come off near end motorway, follow to Travel hotel.'

'Travel hotel?' asked Peters.

'Yeah, something like that, Travel something, maybe Travel log?'

'Well, I think we'll take a break there, Matis,' said Gibson as he got to his feet. 'Do you want something to drink; tea, coffee or water maybe?' Peters removed the cassettes from the tape recorder and put them in his pocket. Bockus asked for a coffee. They exited the room, found the custody sergeant who promised to find a constable to make a coffee and take it in to Bockus.

Taking a time-out gave Peters and Gibson a chance to discuss what they had learnt, and where to take it next. Sitting down in the squad room, Peters said, 'I think we've got a bit more to learn from Mr Bockus. He's acting pretty strung out. If he's been used to drugs on tap, it's been quite a while since his last hit. I think if we push him a bit more he's gonna crack.'

'Yeah, you're right, and we really need to find out where they took George, and if Bockus followed them all the way to their destination. And then, what did he do with the Range Rover?'

'Yes, of course, and, where is it now? And we haven't even asked him about the boat yet.'

'I guess there's only one way to find out,' said Gibson and with a weary grin, he stood up.

'Yep, no rest for the wicked, or the righteous, it would appear.'

They walked back to Interview Room Two. Matis Bockus had finished his coffee and was slumped in the chair looking pretty fed up. PC Gibson checked that the little red lights in two corners of the ceiling were on. Satisfied, he held out his hand to Peters who gave him the tapes, Gibson slotted them in and set the machine running. Preliminaries over, Gibson said, 'OK, Matis, tell us what happened when you followed the black Mercedes out of the hotel car park.'

'I just follow to where Floyd drive,' said Bockus looking puzzled.

'Well, yes, but in which direction. Was it on to the M3 to London or the M3 to Southampton?' asked Gibson.

'Yes, we drive M3 south, but not Southampton. After maybe forty minutes Ayman come off M3 to other road and near small town.'

'Matis, think carefully now, can your remember the name of the town or road you were on?' asked Gibson. Bockus shook his head.

'No, no, busy not to lose Floyd. We went past small town to little, little village.'

'Do you think if we drove with you on the M3 again, you could show us?' asked Gibson.

'Maybe, yes maybe,' said Bockus who seemed to perk up a little at the prospect of going out.

'Let's see how we go here first,' said Peters.

'So tell me, Matis, where do you like to go fishing?' asked Gibson. Peters and Bockus looked at him in surprise.

'How you know I like to fish?' asked Bockus with a hint of a smile.

'I saw the Korum tackle box and rods in your hall. Only a keen fisherman would have kit that good,' said Gibson with a smile.

'Yes, it's good. Me and Floyd, we go fishing when we have time off.'

'So where do you like to fish best?' asked Gibson.

'We do some on river, but sea best. Bigger fish,' said Bockus almost smiling.

'Yeah, I like to fish in the River Hamble,' said Gibson.

'Nah, we fish in Itchen.' Bockus said nothing for a moment, then leapt from his chair. His eyes blazed and growling like an animal he tried to clear the table to reach Gibson. He screamed and shouted abuse in Lithuanian, with more than the occasional English expletive.

'Fuck you! Fuck you! Wanker! Wanker,' he yelled as he tried to grab Gibson around the neck. Gibson shot out of his chair and sent it crashing behind him.

As Bockus half knelt and scrabbled across the table, Peters raised his right arm and slammed his pointed fingers into the side of Bockus's neck. Bockus crashed on top of the table, rolled off, and hit the floor, spark out.

'What a bummer. Shame really, as you were getting on so well,' said Peters as he turned off the tape recorder. The custody sergeant burst into the room as Peters and Gibson, with one arm each, tried to get the now semi-conscious Bockus back into his chair. The sergeant looked up at the two red lights in the corners of the ceiling. He appeared relieved to see that they were still on.

'I'd better retrieve that DVD now and check out what it shows,' he said.

'Don't worry, Sar'nt,' said Peters with a grin, 'it was self defence.' The sergeant looked at him and grinned back.

'Yeah, I've heard about your defence systems,' he said. Bockus was now beginning to come round.

'We'll give you a hand getting him back to the cell,' said Gibson as he collected the two cassette tapes. Peters held his right arm and Gibson his left as they pulled him out of the chair and half-dragged, half-walked him through the police station. The sergeant opened the cell door. They half-carried Bockus across to the wooden bench with a two-inch foam mattress that pretended to be a bed and sat him down. They stepped out of the cell and the sergeant locked it behind them.

As they walked back through the station to the front office he said, 'They're sending over a vehicle from Winchester Prison later. That's where they're going to remand him till he comes up for trial. So next time you want to talk to him you're going to have to arrange it with them.' He then phoned the on-call doctor and asked him to get in as quickly as possible, saying he wanted the prisoner checked over before being transferred to prison.

'He really will need a solicitor next time we talk to him,' said Gibson. The sergeant nodded agreement.

'Stupid boy should have lawyered up straight away,' he said. 'Right, let's go and look at the movie.' They wandered through the corridors to the control room. As they rounded a corner the sergeant almost bumped into DI Gerry Fisher, who seemed extremely anxious to be elsewhere. Fisher gave the sergeant an impatient nod as they sidestepped each other.

They entered the control room and saw three blank monitors and one "live" one which showed a picture of an empty Interview Room Two. The monitors stood on a long bench fitted to the far wall. The sergeant expressed surprise that the one monitor was actually switched on. Peters and Gibson exchanged glances. 'Fisher,' mouthed Peters. Gibson, stern-faced, nodded agreement. The sergeant walked to the control unit, pressed a few buttons then pressed play. The screen showing the empty room suddenly burst into life, busy with Peters, Gibson, Bockus and the sergeant preparing for the interview. He fast-forwarded the video until they came to where Bockus launched himself at Gibson.

'Stupid, stupid boy,' said the sergeant. The three of them winced in unison as Bockus crashed to the floor.

'How do you do that?' Gibson asked Peters.

'Practice, my boy, practice,' said Peters.

'But how do you practise?' asked Gibson.

'On people, dear boy, on people. Oh, can you get us a copy of that, sergeant?'

'Already done, I set it up while we watched it. I'll get it out of the machine for you,' he said. He bent over the control unit, pressed a button and out slid a pristine DVD.

'I'll even put it in a case for you.'

Gibson and Peters walked out to their car. Peters got into the driving seat. Both men settled in, then Peters said, 'Why can't we find these geezers? There's a guy called Eamonn who seems to own a boat somewhere on the Itchen. There's a Jan Kapusniak lookalike who buys stuff on a marina near the Itchen. Then there's Mr bloody Bockus who blows a fuse when he realises he let on he fishes in the River Itchen. What say you and me go and rent a boat and spend some time cruising up and down the River Itchen?'

'That, Ry, sounds like a very, very good idea. It definitely sounds like a plan to me.'

Peters fired up the motor 'You call Staf, see where he is, tell him we're on our way to his.'

CHAPTER 28

M*I5, Special Branch and the E Squad, aye? Well I guess I didn't expect to be involved in all that stuff when I applied to be a WPC,* thought Nicole with a wry smile. *But how on earth do I find out why SB were following Runihura? And what they found out about him?*

'Thank you, Major Stafford, for dumping this on me,' she said out loud, with a smile that was even more wry.

She knew that each regional police force had a Special Branch. It would be sensible, therefore, she thought, for a local station to have a link man. So all she needed to do was to find Aldershot's. *Yay, simples,* she thought.

Picking up the landline phone, she dialled Aldershot Police Station, said who she was, and asked to be put through to Sergeant Hawkins. Seconds later he answered, 'Ready to return to the fold yet, Acting DS Martin?'

'No, not yet, Sar'nt, anyway, good morning. Look, I understand we have a link man to the head of Special Branch at our...'

'Hey, hey, hang on a minute, Martin, just you hang on a mo. I know you're officially on leave, but I've heard about the incident at the marina; you sure you still want to be part of Stafford's set up?'

'Yeah, OMG yes, in fact more than ever now. I, well, we all want to find whoever killed Garfield Lewis.'

'Well, my girl, that could just as easily have been you. So just you take care. I'm still not happy about this you know.'

'I know, Sar'nt, but I'm OK, and well up for it, so don't worry, I'll take care,' she said, then continued, 'Anyway, can you help me here? I need to talk to someone who can tell me what Special Branch found out about some people we're trying to find.'

'Your Major Stafford dumped you in it with this one, girl, 'cause the link this end is his favourite DI, DI Gerry Fisher.'

'Ah,' said Martin.

'Yes, ah indeed, but if he plays silly buggers with you, the HSB would usually report to the head of CID, and in this case it's a DCI Talbot down at Eastleigh. If you go that route, just chuck in Major Stafford's name and give them his mobile number so they'll know you're privy to it. And tell them to phone him to verify you're OK.'

'Brilliant, Sar'nt, thanks for that and I guess we'll talk soon.'

'You take care, girl, don't let that major of yours take liberties. Now I'll put you through to DI Fisher.'

After a couple of clicks and some buzzing, next thing she heard was, 'DI Fisher.'

She introduced herself and told him what she needed.

'Oh, Ayman Runihura, yes, he came across my radar some while ago. Something to do with drugs as I remember. Yeah, we looked at him for a bit, then decided that running dumps was just about right for his skill level, so we stopped looking.'

She felt herself bristle with indignation,

'Well, actually you need a degree level qual… no, never mind, so what made you look at him in the first place?'

'There was talk about people smuggling, associating with known terrorists as well as the drugs. But we found nothing. In the end I told my contact at Eastleigh I thought it was a waste of time, so we ended the surveillance.'

'Could you tell me who your SB contact at Eastleigh was, so I can talk to them to see what prompted their inquiry in the first place?'

'Look, Martin, if I gave out his number to any Tom, Dick or Harry, it wouldn't be very special would it?'

'But I'm not any Tom…' she started to say before she realised the line was dead.

'Well, thank you for your help, DI fuckin' Fisher,' she said into the dead receiver.

She had just about settled down enough to phone Eastleigh, when the doorbell rang. She walked through to the hall and opened the front door. On the doorstep stood a smartly dressed, blonde-haired young man, maybe in his early thirties, holding out a set of car keys. He smiled broadly and said, 'Ah, I'm guessing you're not Major Paul Stafford.'

'How very astute of you,' she replied, also with a smile. 'No, I'm Nicole Martin and I am working with him.'

'Good to meet you, Miss Martin. Well, I've brought his old Volvo back, fully repaired, restored and with a couple of added extras,' he said and waved his arm in the general direction of the driveway. Nicole walked down the steps and on to the drive. Next to her car sat an elderly green Volvo V40 estate car that looked in pristine condition.

'Wow!' she said, as she walked around it, 'he's gonna love that, it looks brand new. I heard it had been pretty badly smashed up. Major Stafford's going to be so chuffed with this. Is there anything I need to sign?'

'No, nothing, no paperwork whatsoever,' said the young man.

'Well, can I call you a taxi, or take you somewhere,' she said, then felt herself blush.

The blonde-haired young man fairly preened at that, but said with another broad smile, 'No, you're all right, I have a lift waiting out on the road, but thank you. Maybe next time, aye?' He turned and walked down the drive. Before exiting the garden, he paused, turned, gave her a big grin and a little wave. Nicole checked that the Volvo was locked and returned to the house.

Sitting down at the kitchen table, she put down the Volvo keys and began to hunt for her mobile in the depths of her handbag. Finding it, she googled the number for the Eastleigh HQ of Hampshire's police force, then used the landline to call the number. She asked to speak to DCI Talbot. The call handler asked for a few details before she said, 'Putting you through now.'

An extremely deep voice answered, 'DCI Talbot, how can I help you, Ms Martin?'

'Yes, hi, good morning, sir. I'm working an investigation in Farnborough with Major Paul Stafford and Captain Peters of the Security Forces. A name came up that we heard you were interested in recently. We need to know if you in CID or Special Branch have any recent intel on this character?'

'Well, Ms Martin, why don't you give me the name?' Feeling slightly stupid, she said, 'Yes, good idea. It's an Ayman, and that's spelt Ay...'

'Yes, Ayman Runihura? Is that the one? Yes, I remember the name. You're right, we were looking at him. I seem to recall he was flagged up for buying some materials that could be used for bomb making, or at least IEDs. Ah yes, it's sort of coming back to me. He first came on our radar when a high-powered lawyer stepped in to help him get off on a fairly mundane drug bust.'

Talbot hesitated for so long, Nicole thought the connection had been lost, then he spoke again, 'Look, Ms Martin, we've not met and I know nothing about you. But I'll tell you this for what it's worth. We, and that includes SB, thought he was well worth watching. You must have heard how strapped we are for cash and personnel; anyway, we put a local, local to you that is, DI on it. Well, he spent some months checking it out and came back with nothing. He felt it was a waste of time to continue. Anyhow, before we pulled the plug, we put up a bit of intel on the SB's version of the PND. Tell Major Stafford, if he had clearance to use the National Special Branch Intelligence System that was up some years back, he should now be able to access NSBIS2 using his security code and his old password. This is supposed to be the all-new singing and dancing version. Runihura is listed there.'

'OK, sir, that's great, I really appreciate your help... Hmm, maybe I shouldn't say this, but more help than I got from a local DI.'

'Thank you for that, Ms Martin. I wish you well with your investigation. Please feel free to talk to me again. But certainly let me know how it goes,' said the DCI as he ended the call. She would definitely keep him in the loop, she thought.

II

She heard the letter box rattle and a light thud from the hallway. Walking into the hall she saw a small pile of letters by the front door. She picked them up and noted amongst the usual junk mail and brown envelopes was a small brown, padded Jiffy bag, with a neat computer printed address label. She took the mail through to the kitchen and dumped it on the table for Stafford to sort later.

Picking up the folder that contained the e-fit picture of Jan Kapusniak she started to write a report for the media. After two or three false starts, she felt she had created a media-friendly document that when published and aired on TV, would help in their search for Runihura and Kapusniak. All that was missing was a decent picture of Runihura. She had managed to get a print from the hotel DVD footage, but it was far from satisfactory. She hoped they would be able to get a better one from one of the police's or SB's databases. Putting that to one side, she used Stafford's laptop to google and list all local newspapers and TV stations' email addresses. She had just finished sending out the media info packs when Stafford walked in.

'Christ, I feel a bit shallow now,' he said. 'I arrived home feeling sad and low, turn into the drive, see the car and it's brilliant! I walk in the house happy.'

'Oh, so it's not me then?' said Nicole with a grin. Stafford looked at her as though slightly puzzled, then laughed again.

'Well, of course… it's great to have someone make me a coffee when I walk in the door.'

'Your coffee will be ready forthwith, sir,' she said with a false pout and a curtsy.

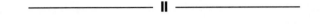

Stafford smiled at her, sat down at the table and picked up his mail. He got up, wandered around the kitchen table, picked out the junk mail and dumped it into his recycling bin. The more important looking brown envelopes he put to one side to deal with later. Opening the cutlery drawer he pulled out a kitchen knife, sat down at the table and held up the Jiffy bag.

Brown packaging tape had been wrapped around the opening, three or four layers of it. Carefully he slid the blade under the little ridge that denoted where it had been folded over before being sealed. Gently he moved the blade across its width, then slit up the sides before pulling up the flap and opening it. He peered inside. It was packed with what looked like absorbent kitchen paper. He felt rather than heard alarm bells. He turned to Nicole and asked, 'Do you have any forensic gloves?'

'Yeah, I think so, somewhere in the bottom of my bag. Why, what do you think it is?' she said as she started to route around in her handbag.

'Put it this way, it ain't that someone would send me a nice present. And I've not ordered anything online for months, so your guess is as good as mine, but I don't think it's going to be good.'

Nicole, after a few minutes of frantic searching, found a small pack of latex gloves which she handed to Stafford, who chuckled and said, 'Christ, it always amazes me what women carry about in their bags, but thanks anyway.'

'Huh, well, it's like my mum always used to say; "Nicole," she'd say, "you never know when you might have to touch the beastly thing".

There was a moment of silence. She blushed furiously. Stafford noticed, and with a smirk, turned back to his task. He pulled out two gloves and snapped them on, expertly. He held the package in his left hand then brought it closer to his face and peered in and around it.

'I can't see any electronics or wires, so I guess that's good, but it feels like maybe a .410 shotgun cartridge.' With the thumb and forefinger of his right hand he gently removed a pad of folded absorbent kitchen paper and laid it carefully on the table. He picked up the Jiffy bag and peered inside. It was empty. He steeled himself to continue.

Nicole had walked around the table and was standing behind him, both hands on the back of his chair. Stafford resisted the temptation to shout "bang" very loudly, and leap out of his seat. Instead he began to slowly unfold the absorbent paper sheets. He removed four sheets... nothing happened. He hoped the next one would be the last. It was. As he unfolded it, it revealed an ordinary small brown paper envelope, this with an empty half, folded over a half with a small cylindrical bulge.

'Hmm, it's smaller than I first thought.' The envelope wasn't sealed, he unfolded it, opened it and out slid a small resealable polythene bag. Stafford held it closer to examine the contents better. Nicole screwed up her eyes trying to focus on the item.

'I guess this'll be George Saunders's final message to us.'

Stafford held the bag up over his shoulder to show Nicole. She stared at it for a few seconds, then realised she was looking at a human little finger. Eyes shut tight, as though to un-see it, she whispered, 'Jesus H Christ, we really are dealing with some sicko bastards.'

'And it seems they're not gonna stop till we play it their way.' Stafford shook his head sadly as he placed the poly bag back on to the absorbent paper.

'Right, we'd better get this stuff over to Scientific Services Dept. down in Cosham. I don't suppose they'll get much from it, but at least they'll be able to confirm if it's George's finger or not.'

They were silent for a while. Then Stafford said, 'Did your mum really say that?'

--------------- **II** ---------------

Peters and Gibson arrived back at Stafford's place and parked alongside the resurrected Volvo. They couldn't resist walking around it, pleased to see it looked better than ever. Inside the house they found Stafford and Nicole seated at the kitchen table. Peters and Gibson brought them up to date with the Bockus interview and histrionics. Stafford mulled over the information for a moment or two then said, 'There's certainly a real significance to this river, it's definitely linked to this boat.'

'Yes, that's what we thought, but unfortunately Bockus wasn't well enough at the end to expand on that particular theory,' said Peters with a grin.

'Hmmm, was that the hand of God or the hand of Ryan intervening?' asked Stafford.

'I'm afraid it was the hand of Ryan,' he said as he passed over the DVD of the interview. 'It's all on there, Staf, view it at your leisure.'

'Anyway, he's been remanded to Winchester Prison. So that's where we'll need to interview him next,' said Gibson.

'We thought what we'd do next, is rent a boat and spend some time cruising up and down the Itchen. See if we can locate the boat. If there's no one aboard we could maybe bug it and watch it for a while. See what occurs,' said Peters.

'Trouble is, I don't see where the boat figures. So George liked it and wanted one... oh, by the way, they sent us his little finger,' said Stafford.

Stunned silence broke out amongst the others, then Peters yelled, 'What? When? And why didn't you tell us before?'

'Where is it now?' asked Gibson.

'Hold on, we'll get to that in a minute, let us just consider this boat; so George wanted one, but what's that got to do with the explosion and George's death? And if it was Kapusniak who killed Garfield, would he be so stupid as to go there again so soon?' asked Stafford.

'When you first talked to me about all this, Staf, you gave me a list of people Runihura, Bockus and your Barry Allen, were employing. If we think back to those names, they were mostly foreign nationals and except for 10a North Lane, the addresses didn't exist. So maybe the boat is used for people smuggling,' said Gibson.

'And that's why Runihura was able to offer Barry Allen a seemingly unending supply of cheap labour,' said Stafford. 'Bloody hell, mate, I reckon you could be right. There was mention early on about illegal immigrants, but Special Branch seemed to dismiss it. I think we'll just hang fire on the boat till we've had another chat with Bockus.'

'But it was Fisher who persuaded SB to dismiss it, remember,' said Nicole.

'OK, boss, well, we have a tracker on the black Mercedes parked outside 10a, so if they use that, we could get an indication of their whereabouts,' said Peters.

'What I can't get my head around is the size of their set-up. I mean, if they aren't staying at the flat, they must be living somewhere. And as we said before they're using hook loader lorries. They've gotta park them somewhere. So who's paying, and how are they paying for all this? Runihura had, what, eight men on his books? Bockus, another eight, two were working for Barry Allen and then there's Kapusniak and Winstone. How the hell do they all get paid? Runihura told Barry he had premises, be good to find that,' said Nicole.

'With that size workforce, they can't all have gone to ground, they've got to be out there somewhere making money to keep themselves afloat, if you'll excuse the nautical pun,' said Stafford. 'So anyway, Nicole has put together and sent out a media pack to all local and national TV stations and newspapers with details and pictures of Runihura and the e-fit of Kapusniak. She's shown why we've linked all the events together, so hopefully we'll get some feedback from that.' Stafford finished off the update by explaining they were now able to access the National Special Branch Intelligence System 2 on their computer. He explained that they had discovered Runihura had been under scrutiny, initially by MI5, then by Special Branch. He had originally been suspected of buying bomb-making materials, but apart from the drug bust, he hadn't raised his head above the parapet for some months. This led the SB link man for north Hampshire, one DI Fisher, to report that, after considerable time and effort had been spent tailing and watching Runihura, he became convinced it was a waste of time and effort. Fisher had offered the few months of inactivity as proof.

'However,' said Stafford, 'there were a number of pictures of Runihura taken during surveillance that Nicole was able to use for the media pack.'

Nicole showed Peters and Gibson the pictures she had taken of George's finger and the pack and packaging it had been sent in. She explained the items had already been sent by courier to the police forensic labs in Cosham.

'I think George's problem was, he got too greedy, had his fingers in too many pies,' said Peters.

They wrapped it up for the day.

CHAPTER 29

Runihura's alarm woke him at precisely 8:15 a.m. Sleepily, he wandered through to the head. Had a piss. Splashed cold water on to his face and smoothed his jet black hair into a slightly tidier shape. Ablutions completed, he checked on the other two. Winstone had already roused Kapusniak, and mumbling and groaning they finished their rudimentary ablutions. Runihura told them to take a look around the boat to make sure they left nothing of importance behind. That done, they went to the van, checked the women were OK and waited in the cab for him. Runihura ensured everything was secure below deck and locked the access door behind him. He checked he had the two women's passports, then hoisted the canvas bag to his shoulder, padlocked the cockpit canopy, and stepped carefully across to the grassy pathway.

Winstone, who had driven the van to the gates of the metal recycling compound, leaned out of the window and gave the padlock to Runihura who closed and locked the gates behind them. He climbed into the van alongside Jan Kapusniak and placed the canvas bag under the seat.

'They all right back there?' he asked.

'They were sitting up and moving, if that's what you mean,' said Winstone laughing.

'Good enough then,' said Runihura. Winstone slowly edged his way through the morning traffic to the M3. The traffic was bad as always at this time of the morning. *Good, that should deter the cops from stopping people at random,* thought Runihura. As they headed north towards Winchester, the traffic in the near-side and middle lanes slowed to a crawl. Winstone took the near-side lane and began the stop start, stop start climb up the incline to the roundabout. Once through the roundabout the traffic was less and Winstone was able to cruise at a steady fifty-five mph towards Andover. They cruised past Andover, through a little hamlet to the west and at a mini roundabout Winstone headed down a deserted and now almost unused road. Runihura pulled out one of his many mobile phones and selected a speed dial button. Seconds later he said, 'Five minutes, Eric,' and put the phone away.

A mile further, on the right-hand side of the road they came to a long row of high, mature hedges and trees. They obscured everything behind from view. A large pair of wooden gates divided a twelve-foot-high hedge that stretched for about 200 yards. Winstone drove through the gates on to the drive of a large, brick bungalow.

Looking from the road through the gates, all that could be seen was the driveway running down to a brick wall at the rear of the property. Winstone drove past the building and rear garden towards the wall, then turned at right angles. In the wall fifty yards further on, was a small wooden door, two feet from that, another pair of huge wooden gates. The gates opened as Winstone rolled up. He drove through into an area the size of a football pitch. On his right he passed eight caravans in various states of decay, though obviously still in use. He came to a halt at the rear of the site, alongside two double residential mobile homes. They climbed out of the van and stretched. The gates had already been closed behind them.

Runihura held the canvas bag on his shoulder. Digging in it he pulled out his pistol and slipped it into his inside jacket pocket. He gave the canvas bag to Eric Potter who had opened and closed the gates then walked up to join them. Eric was white and appeared to be around thirty years old. He wore a faded black tee shirt with a "SAXON" logo, jeans and Nike trainers. He grinned at Runihura and pushed out his fist.

'Ayman, my man, how ya doin'?'

Runihura bumped fists, and handed him the bag,

'This needs to be sorted pretty quick, so mind you take care of it,' said Runihura ignoring the question.

'Never fear, Ayman, my man, we're just finishin' de weed,' he said stretching the double ee. 'Done 300 sandwich bags, loads of Louis', Henry's and de Hunks, man. It all looking good. All de rest in one pound bales,' he continued with his terrible attempt at a Jamaican yardie patois.

'What, you want a pat on the back now?' said Runihura with a grin. 'We'll get the van emptied, then over to the lab to load up. You can get the magnetic signs and stick them on the van. Looks a bit more kosher having it sign written.'

'Well, can't see anyone wanting to do a stop and search with those signs on the sides,' said Eric laughing.

'They want the load up in Basingstoke this afternoon, so let's get it moving,' said Runihura as he wandered over to where Jan Kapusniak and Winstone were chatting. He pulled a key out of his pocket and gave it to Kapusniak.

'Jan, get the women out of the motor and over to my place. Show them where the food is and the bathroom. Tell them to get cleaned up. Make sure you lock the door and bring the key back to me. I'll be over by the warehouse. Floyd, you go with Eric and put the signs on the van.'

'Ah, fuck, boss, am I gonna be driving it with them signs on it again?' said Winstone.

'Yep, that's exactly what you're gonna be doing,' said Runihura and laughed, 'but this time I'm coming with you.'

Kapusniak unlocked the back of the van and dragged out the two women. They were even more frightened and dishevelled. Both squeezed their eyes shut at the sudden glare of daylight.

'Don't cut their ties till you've got them inside, and don't you fucking touch them,' shouted Runihura after him. Kapusniak turned round with a sneer on his face.

'With stinking Arab? No fuckin' chance,' he shouted back.

'Hey, Jan, remember they're all pink inside like white ladies,' he shouted as he walked towards the warehouse. He paused by the dog pound and patted the three German Shepherd dogs that bounded up to him. He spoke to them for a moment then continued on.

At the front of the warehouse, beneath a covered area, was a hook loader lorry, a twenty-foot-long bin on the back. The driver had just tipped a meagre load of electronic waste on to the concrete floor. A group of eight or ten men slowly picked the stuff up and were taking it into the warehouse-cum-factory where they placed the items on to racks or into large metal stillages. The rear end of the warehouse was fitted out with floor to roof pallet racking; some racks held double-stacked stillages. In the central area were two rows of metal work benches, with men using various small tools and chemicals, busy working on the broken items. On the benches in front of them were stacks of circuit boards and plastic trays that contained slivers of various coloured precious metals.

Two more of Runihura's trusted men, Tony Amos and Mark Whitlock, who seemed to think that shouting and whipping people with cable ripped from electrical appliances was motivational, were in charge.

---- **II** ----

The wounds caused by the cable were visible on many of the workers' arms and faces. But the motivation to work was already within this workforce. They knew if they did what they were told, exactly what they were told, they would be rewarded. It wouldn't be money or time off, it would be the next desperately needed hit of crack, pipe of crystal meths or rock of MDMA. They weren't the fastest workers in the world but, by Christ, they were loyal. It's unlikely to appear in any handbook on management, but a crack-addicted workforce is as motivated and loyal as you could hope to get. They didn't have to go out stealing, they didn't have to buy food and they had a roof over their head. So when they were told to stand in a line and kick the shit out of someone, anyone, or arse fuck a bound man or woman, or bury a worker who'd o'deed, they did it, and maybe, just maybe, they got a bonus smoke as well. The workforce looked terrified and as broken as the items they worked on. Terrified their reward would be withheld.

———————————— **II** ————————————

Runihura and the lorry driver bumped fists. Runihura looked at the load on the floor.

'All right, Brandon?' he asked by way of a greeting. Brandon Miller was one of Runihura's trusted "lieutenants", another disenfranchised military man. Lorry driving was a minor part of his skill set.

'Was that it?' Runihura asked and pointed at the dumped load.

'Yep, wasn't even a full load. Frank, down at the metal recyclers, wanted some readies, so I paid him according to the weight on my inboard scales. Just 3.5 tonnes worth. So you owe me for that, boss. Mind you, I left one of our bins down there, 'cos he's going to try and get more of this stuff for us, so he says.'

'Fuck, that's good then, 'cause we need it, he's the only supply of electronics we've got now. Mind you, if he needs extra cash, flogging gear from our chemical division could help,' said Runihura with a grin.

'OK, so when I'm down there later, I'll get him to give you a ring about it. He's always complaining that all these new laws make it difficult to do cash deals, so he could well be interested.'

'Yeah, good, park up then come over to my place. I'll square you up with the cash and give you some details about the gear on offer,' said Runihura. Miller climbed in his cab, drove alongside the warehouse and parked between another hook loader lorry complete with bin and a line of five spare twenty-foot bins. Runihura winced as he walked past the bins, remembering they had so recently been used on the five sites Paul Stafford now operated.

The mobile unit that Runihura currently thought of as home was nearest to the site's right-hand wall. Jan Kapusniak was sitting on the step outside waiting to return the key.

'I'm starved, boss, OK if I go to cook, see if he do me a sandwich?'

'Yep, do that, and I'll shout when I need you,' said Runihura as he unlocked the door and stepped inside. He turned, locked the door behind him and put the key into his jacket pocket. Then walked through the short hallway and opened the door to the bathroom. He closed the door and turned on the in-bath shower. Moving to the end of the bath, he eased the panel aside and reached in and underneath. He felt around until he found a thick polythene bag, then took the gun out of his pocket, put it inside, sealed it and put it back underneath the bath, then replaced the bath panel.

He stripped off his clothes, dumped them in a pile on the floor, stepped into the bath and under the shower. Five minutes later he turned the shower off and dried himself. Putting on his boxer shorts he thought, *now for a bit of staff training*. He opened the door to the main bedroom. The two women, still wearing the clothes they had been picked up in, minus their coats, were perched on the edge of the double bed. He frowned, shook his head, opened a door to the built-in wardrobes and pulled out two dressing gowns. He threw one on to the bed and tucked the other one over his arm. Grabbing the nearest girl by the arm, he pulled her into the kitchen and pointed to the washing machine. His face screwed up as he tugged at her shirt and said, 'These stink.' He held his nose as if to prove the point. Then threw the dressing gown at her. 'Put this on and clothes in there,' he said louder now so she would understand. He put his hand on her shoulder, turned her around and pushed her back in the direction of the bedroom. He returned to the bathroom and picked up his clothes. In the kitchen, he draped his jacket over the back of a chair and pulled out the two women's passports; both were Syrian. One of them walked through with their dirty clothes. He got up and opened the washing machine's door and she fed in the washing. He showed her where the powder was kept, and watched as she set the machine in motion.

When the washing was underway, he grabbed her wrist and returned to his seat pulling her with him. As she stood in front of him, he untied the cord of the dressing gown. The gown fell open and revealed a two-inch-wide strip of smooth olive-coloured skin from her neck to her black curly pubes. Runihura looked up at her expecting to see fear. He saw only defiance. *I guess they don't get this far by being meek,* he thought. He slipped his left hand inside the gap of the gown and grasped her right butt cheek. He pulled her close and with his mouth on her right nipple, let go of her wrist and put his right hand between her legs. Pushing her legs apart, he roughly thrust his fingers inside her. After a moment or two, he took his right hand away and forced her to kneel. He took out his erect penis and pushed her head down towards it. Her closed mouth touched it. With both hands entwined in her short black hair, he forced her head down again,

'*Mrtoo ao mitoo sharmoota*,' he hissed in her ear, trusting he'd correctly remembered one of the few Syrian phrases he'd bothered to learn: "suck it, bitch."

She didn't move. Runihura put his right hand around her throat, thumb at the front and squeezed. Now she sucked; but after a few moments, stopped. Runihura grabbed her head with both hands and started to force it down when he realised someone was bashing on the front door, shouting, 'Ayman! Ayman! Come on, man, I gotta go.'

Runihura slumped back in the chair, penis flaccid. The woman took the opportunity and escaped to the bedroom, but not before she turned and said defiantly, '*Ras ai-air.*' She certainly knew the Syrian for "dickhead."

Runihura straightened his boxers, opened the front door and said, 'Fuck you, Miller, you arsehole, you do pick your moments. Stay there and I'll get you your fuckin' money.' He went into the living room and removed a box hidden behind a Velcro seam in the back of the sofa and pulled out a bundle of £20 notes. He counted out fifteen of them, and replaced the box. He returned to the front door and handed them over to Miller, who smiled broadly and said, 'Sorry if I picked a bad time, boss, but you did tell me to come over.'

Runihura ignored the comment and said, 'There's 300, that'll cover you for going down to SMR again. Yeah?'

' Yeah, that's fine, Ayman. I'll see a bit less of you later, I guess.'

He chuckled as he walked quickly away, stuffing the cash into his pocket. Runihura was about to close the door when Winstone appeared and shouted, 'Come on, Ayman. We're all loaded up. I thought this stuff had to be in Basingstoke this after'.

Runihura peered round the door and waved him off. He muttered to himself as he closed and locked the door, 'Fucking hell, can't even get a blow job in peace.' He wandered back inside and went into his bedroom where both girls were. He beckoned to them and walked back out. They followed and he opened the door to the second bedroom, stood to one side and unceremoniously pushed them in. He locked the door and took out the key. Back in his bedroom he put the key on his bedside cabinet and dressed in fresh clothes. He stood still for a few seconds, then picked up the bedroom key again, he went to the kitchen, opened a cupboard under the sink and took out a yellow plastic bucket. Then walked back to the second bedroom, unlocked the door and smiled to himself as he placed the bucket inside without a word.

Clean, but still mightily pissed off, he let himself out and locked the door behind him. He walked over to the lab where the van was parked.

'I've changed my mind, Floyd. I'm not coming with you. I'm taking a pool car,' he said pointing to a group of three black Mercedes pickups. 'I need to find out what's happening with Matis. I just hope he's not opened his big gob, so I'll maybe see you in Basingstoke later.' Winstone did not look happy, but just shrugged, fired up the van and drove towards the gates. Kapusniak pushed them open and closed them after him, before they drove away.

Runihura's mood lifted as he watched the van disappear. Surely they could see that a van with, Southern Washroom Services, Female Hygiene Disposal Units, Discreet Hygienic Service, emblazoned on each side and Experts in Hygiene, W/C & Urinal Sanitisers, on the back doors was excellent cover? *Maybe I'll get some, "Ask The Driver For Details" decals for the front doors*, he mused.

Moments later, in one of the black Mercedes pickups he left the compound.

CHAPTER 30

Winstone, as Southern Washroom Services, had only three deliveries to make and none of them to do with feminine hygiene. Losing the recycling centres to Paul Stafford had changed their weekly drug run from an all-day job a couple of times a week, to just a morning run out.

'Stafford's really fucked this for us,' said Winstone.

Jan Kapusniak thought for a moment then said, 'Maybe a little, big problem is keeping men in factory workin'.' Winstone turned to look at him, a puzzled look on his face.

'Drugs and DVDs were good without tips, but tips made it better, but then syndicate hear about gold, silver, platinum in electronics. Need more men. Now need all time more electronics. They fuck it up with electronics,' he said in his heavily accented English.

'Well, Ayman says he's got a plan to get Stafford begging to work with us, said he'd tell us about it later.'

They were silent as they drove in through the gates of The World Citizen Hotel. Winstone travelled through the car park and rolled to a stop outside the double doors marked "goods inwards". Kapusniak climbed out of the van and bashed on the doors. Winstone opened the rear doors to the van. He climbed in, unclipped the strap that held bins in place and dragged forward an orange-lidded, yellow five-litre "sharps" bin followed by bins labelled "feminine hygiene", "Clinical waste", and "nappy bin". He jumped off the van and took one of the bins to the opened goods inwards doorway. The guy in charge of goods in, pushed out his fist and Winstone bumped it in greeting. He picked up an identical but empty bin and returned to the rear of the van. Kapusniak picked up two of the full bins and exchanged them for two empties. Winstone managed the fourth and last bin. Both men bumped fists again with Mr Goods Inwards and climbed back in the cab.

II

Winstone turned the vehicle around and headed out to Whitelines, a nightclub in the centre of Basingstoke. This had once been a big-name department store. Having been bought at a bargain price in the early part of the recession, the syndicate had turned it into the hottest entertainment venue in town. This was partly due to good management, getting some of the best up and coming bands, entertainers and DJs around. And partly due to the somewhat unique services available to those able to afford it.

The nightclub itself happened in the huge basement. The ground floor consisted of a wine bar-cum-restaurant decorated in an Art Deco style, and offered great food. Admission was officially members only, but this was loosely interpreted. A £50 note would often act as a temporary membership card.

Access to the third floor was strictly controlled and only via a lift from the ground floor or basement. There were stairs, but these were cordoned off, emergency exit only. There was a cover charge of £100 to use the lift; it was mainly used by men. The cover charge included a bottle of house wine, a pick'n'mix selection from an A to Z of designer drugs, and a no questions asked hour with a woman of your choice from the scantily clad selection on offer. Depending on how busy they were, there would be eight or twelve women, sitting on high stools around the bar. Or lounging on settees, trying their best to look sexy, ready to suck or fuck your balls off. Often difficult to do, unless the punter had a penchant for glazed eyes and tramp tatts. A further six or eight girls would be working in the dozen or so rooms available. The unspoken house philosophy was, you want it, you pay, you get it.

The girls were mainly foreign nationals, and came from Africa, Afghanistan, Pakistan, Libya, Lithuania, Syria and other troubled countries. They were all there courtesy of the newly christened motor launch, *Cleopatra*. Each girl had paid around £6,000 for the privilege of getting to the UK with a guaranteed job. The operation worked well, six nights a week. From 10 p.m. till 2 a.m., the basement rocked, the ground floor dined and the top floor sucked and fucked to your wildest fantasy.

At the rear doors of these premises, Southern Washroom Services delivered mind-blowing chemical entertainment and DVDs that, in some circles, were enjoyed to the max.

II

Staff discounts were available and Winstone and Kapusniak would often, on a night off, check in with Third-Floor Sheila, and avail themselves of the services on offer. More to their taste though, for a proper lads night out was their last port of call, Hurricanes. Hurricanes was a nightclub for the young. It was accessed via a dingy back street in one of the more downtrodden areas of Basingstoke. It was open from 10 p.m. till 3 a.m. and offered the cheapest booze in town. A tenner got you in with a ticket for a free drink. The club was right on point. A direct hit at the clientele for which it was opened. It was one of the very few clubs in the south of England that could boast a queue to get in on Friday and Saturday nights. It was no frills, no red carpet, no VIP area. Just a great intimate vibe, with the music on song, be it drum'n'bass, jungle and dubstep or bashment and trap.

Booze and boogie brought the crowds, B-Bombs brought the profit. Even without the tips to deliver to, Southern Washroom Services provided massive profits. Their products were franchised widely to other clubs whose bosses knew better than to enter into competition. Winstone and Kapusniak completed their final delivery and headed back to the factory.

CHAPTER 31

Runihura took the M3 as he headed back towards the factory. Traffic was sparse. As he drove he mulled over the meeting. It hadn't been a good one. He had fought his corner, but he knew if he didn't produce the results he would be gone. Annihilated. He would cease to exist.

He couldn't get over the fact that before they had George in their pocket, before they had the tips, the syndicate was a beautifully simple set-up. Just had to tap a few buttons via the Internet and social media. Then bring in a boatload of women and drugs. Put the women to work, sell the drugs, make a few DVDs, easy. And since they'd been making their own crack and MDMA, profits had soared. Why did they want the tips? Why the fuck did they think the future was in "urban mining" as they insisted in calling stripping crap electronics?

'This guy Stafford is a threat to everything we've built. We need him with us or dead,' they'd said. Runihura had argued the point,

'Forget the tips, forget urban fucking mining, let's just stick to what we do best. Stick to what we know,' he'd said.

But they came back at him, 'And where are the women? You said you brought two back, where the fuck are they?

We know you like to play with them first, but now you fucking get them up here today, do you hear?'

The temperature in the room seemed to drop as the silence continued. They were first to break it.

'This guy is bloody Special Branch or Special bloody forces or some such bloody thing. Your man just killed his oppo; do you think he's just gonna walk away?'

Then, 'Ayman, Ayman, we are where we are. There is no going back. Get the bastard on side or kill him, or we'll get someone with balls enough to sort it.'

Runihura knew that if he'd had his gun he would have shot them dead then and there. But he also knew if he didn't resolve this, he would end up in black sacks in a landfill somewhere.

Then they fucking changed tack. 'Ayman, let's not fight about this. We have some information and an idea that will get Stafford on side. There's too much invested in this syndicate to lose it now. We are never going to get into these sites unless Stafford is on side. We need his company.'

Runihura knew he didn't have a choice, he knew he would be killed if he tried to walk away, so he listened as they laid out the new information and plan. He came out of the meeting thinking that it might just work. And even he had to admit he was impressed their contacts had given him such useful information. For a start they had discovered that Matis Bockus had been sent to Winchester Prison on remand. They had arranged for a lawyer to visit him soonest. Runihura knew that the solicitor would find out how much Bockus had told the police about their operation. They also told him that Bockus had been knocked out by that psycho Peters. They knew too, that the solicitor would have applied for copies of any tapes, audio and video, of any and all of his interviews.

However, what had lightened Runihura's mood the most was that twat, Ryan Peters, had been spotted putting a tracker on the Mercedes pickup at 10a North Lane. Runihura had detoured via the flat and found the device. This was now attached to a black cab he had spotted parked outside the Beautiful Butties Café.

Runihura had argued that even if they scared Stafford into complying, he could easily fuck up the whole operation from the inside; they had an answer. So that was not the only detour he had made. He had detoured to take photographs of two houses. The first address was Nicole Martin's. They explained that she was the WPC now working with Stafford. The second was that of Marva Lewis. And there he couldn't believe his luck; Marva had come out of the house with her two children. And he'd got a good picture of her strapping them into the Vauxhall Zafira. The memory stick in his pocket would shortly be delivered to Paul Stafford. *Yes*, he thought, *this really could work. Step out of line, Mr Stafford, and we won't fuck you, we'll fuck your friends and their kids.*

------------------ **II** ------------------

Runihura drove into the Weyhill compound. Getting out of his vehicle he walked across to the dog pound and searching in his pocket pulled out some loose dog treats. As he approached the pound, the three German Shepherds bounded silently across to him, tails wagging furiously. He patted all three, spoke to them for a few minutes then threw in the treats. He left the dogs, went into the second mobile home and through to the living room. Jan Kapusniak and Floyd Winstone were there, drinking cans of beer. Runihura pulled out a can, popped the tab, sat down and said, 'You all right to drive, Floyd?'

Floyd lifted the can with his good left hand and said, 'Yeah, this is the first one.'

'Is the van empty?'

'Yep, we cleared it out. And I took the bloody signs off,' said Winstone with a grin.

'Good, I need you both to take the two women up to Whitelines and hand 'em over to Third-Floor Sheila to sort out,' said Runihura.

'Aw fuck! I was gonna have a go on them tonight,' said Winstone.

'Well, the only way that'll happen, is if you tell Sheila you want to start their training when you get up there. They might as well start earning their keep with a tiddler and work their way up to the bigger fish,' said Runihura. Winstone gave him the finger.

'Anyway, I need you both to go because I want you, Jan, to pick up the motor over at the flat. That twat Peters had put a tracker on it, but I found the fucker, so it's fine. I want it back here for the job tomorrow,' he said as he rooted around in his pocket trying to locate the memory stick.

'Then I want you to get round to Stafford's house and stick this through his letter box,' said Runihura.

'Why, what is that then?' asked Kapusniak.

'I took pictures of two houses, one belongs to the black guy's widow. The other to that new female cop they've got working with them; that should focus his mind a bit,' said Runihura with a grin.

Kapusniak looked at him, nodded and said, 'Nice idea, could work.'

'Why do you want pictures of their houses?' asked Winstone.

Runihura groaned, looked at Kapusniak, and said, 'Explain it to him on the way up, will you?' Kapusniak laughed, nodded and took a swig of his beer.

'Then when you get back, come over to my place. We need to talk about the job for tomorrow. So now, bring up the van, get the women secure and in the back. I'll put this memory stick in a Jiffy bag, with a phone number and we're all set,' said Runihura as he finished his beer.

Later that evening they reconvened in the living room of his mobile home. Kapusniak had brought back the black Mercedes pickup and they'd all had a good laugh at the thought of Stafford and his crew chasing around London and north Hampshire after a tracking device fixed to an unsuspecting cabbie's taxi.

The atmosphere changed when Runihura outlined the job for the next day. He had selected from his hidden cache a Beretta 93R, an elderly Italian machine pistol. Both Kapusniak and Runihura had used the weapon before.

'Well, Floyd, looks like with your busted hand, you're going be driving again. There's no way you could handle this little beauty yet,' said Runihura sliding the loaded box magazine into the Beretta as though he were making love to it.

'No, this one's down to you again, Jan, if you want it,' said Runihura as he slipped the magazine back out and passed the weapon to Kapusniak.

'You know me, boss, always ready to work,' said Kapusniak as he moved the slider gently backwards and forwards.

'I want to do this in one pass,' said Runihura.

'Fuck, boss, I good. Not sure I can do in one burst.'

'Yeah, I know it's tricky on the move. And I really do wanna hit Wandoch. Stafford and him are big buddies, so I wanna show Stafford we can fuck with his head at any time.' Kapusniak nodded his understanding and said, 'Maybe do first, one looking drive through.'

'Yeah, that's possible. All depends how busy it is, we don't want to get slowed down getting out.'

'I really wanna get this fucker, so I'd say a slow drive through first would be best,' said Winstone, 'then I could get an idea of how fast I need to be going to get us out of there. I mean, I don't wanna get stuck with the bastard under my wheels.'

'OK, so, Floyd, try a run through first, power up the hill at about twenty (mph). Then cruise the flat section at about twelve to fifteen (mph). Don't look for the target, just keep your eyes on the road, then if you hear the gunshots, get us the fuck out of there. And straight down the M3 to the Itchen. No gunshots, cruise round again. Yeah?'

'Sounds good to me, boss,' said Winstone. Kapusniak nodded.

'Right, we'll set off from here about midday tomorrow. Stafford will have had the whole night to think about the pictures we sent him,' said Runihura.

CHAPTER 32

The first visitor Matis Bockus had at Winchester Prison was his new solicitor, Howard Neilson. Neilson's first task was not to determine if Bockus was guilty or innocent, or whether they could reasonably defend the charges. His task was to discover how much damage Bockus had done and could do to the syndicate who owned and paid them both. Neilson was already in the small interview room, sitting at the table watching the door opposite, waiting for it to open. The room smelled of stale sweat and old trainers. Neilson was used to it. He'd been in this situation, in fact, in this very room more times than he could ever remember. He leaned back in the chair, crossed his legs and adjusted the creases in his grey suit trousers.

The door opposite opened and a guard ushered in a dejected looking Matis Bockus. The guard pointed Bockus to the only other chair in the room, looked at Neilson and said, 'Just ring the buzzer at the side of the table when you're done. OK?'

Neilson nodded. He stood, leaned across the table and with outstretched hand said, 'Hi, Matis, my name is Neilson, Howard Neilson. I'm here to see how I can help you get out of this mess.' Bockus ignored the outstretched hand and slumped back in his chair, arms folded across his chest.

'Gotta tell you, Matis, that stupid son of a bitch attitude will get you nowhere. You may think you're a tough guy now, but a few days out of remand and into prison proper, you'll realise there's always someone tougher. Now me, me-e, I don't give a shit what happens to you. I'm here to protect the syndicate's interests. If you can't help me do that, then I'm out of here.' Bockus shuffled about in his chair, then he nodded.

'Good, well, I've been through your statements and I don't see you've got any choice but to plead guilty to possession of a class A drug with intent. I don't see any choice but to plead guilty to resisting arrest.'

Bockus's chin was on his chest, arms folded again.

'Now first offence, that's gonna get you about four to six years, reduced to maybe two and a half to three if you behave. But at the end of that they're gonna want to deport you, send you back home, do you understand?'

Bockus jumped to his feet, waved his arms and shouted, 'I not go back. Can't go back, what I need do stay here?'

Neilson positioned his hand over the buzzer and said, 'Calm down, Matis, cool it, can't you see, jumping about like that doesn't do you any good. In fact it's got you knocked out twice already.' Bockus returned to his seat. Neilson removed his hand from the buzzer.

'OK, OK, I calm now, tell me what I must do.'

'The good news is, they can't charge you with George Saunder's murder. They have no evidence. But you jumping up and having a go at that PC made everybody wonder what was so terrible about you saying you liked fishing in the River Itchen. They can't wait until the doctor clears you for the next interview, that's what they're gonna be asking.' Bockus looked puzzled.

'Well, I nearly say about boat; if they find boat, they find what we do.'

'No, Matis, they find boat, they find boat. Doesn't mean you do anything wrong, does it? But because you jumped up and had a go at the policeman they think you do bad stuff, do you see now?' Bockus slumped down in his chair again.

'Now, you've got two choices here. First, tell them nothing, and do the time. At the end of that you may be deported, but the syndicate would help you fight it. Second, if you can't face going back at the end of your prison time, you may be able to do a deal, by talking about what you do in the boat and whatever you know about George Saunders's death. They might cut you a deal, if you cooperate.' Bockus looked puzzled again.

'Cut you a deal, what is this?'

'It means that they may give you a shorter time in prison and they may help you stay in this country.' Bockus brightened up considerably.

'You think they let me stay,' he said with a smile. Neilson returned the smile.

'I think they probably would, Matis; in fact if you help them, you'd probably never have to leave.'

'I think we do that then please, Mr Neilson,' he said holding out his right hand. Neilson shook Bockus's hand and got up to leave.

'Before I go, Matis, I've organised for them to put you in "A" wing. I told them you're depressed and possibly suicidal. Now, if you need anything … You know what I'm saying? If you need anything to take the edge off, find Terry, he'll sort you out, understand?' Bockus nodded. Neilson pressed the buzzer, the guard entered from the door behind him and escorted him to the exit.

Neilson walked to his car thinking, *Fucking hell, why do they do it? They think they're so bloody clever, but it's hard enough committing crime in your own language.* Before he drove away he pulled out his mobile and hit a speed dial button. The call was answered on the second ring.

'It's got to be plan "B", I'm afraid, but it's in motion,' said Neilson to Ayman Runihura.

CHAPTER 33

Despite their best efforts, Stafford's crew had made little in the way of progress.

Stafford had been ready to wrap it up for the day and start afresh in the morning, when the letter box clattered, followed by the flump of something landing on the floor. Knowing the postman had already been Stafford dashed into the hall, saw the Jiffy bag, ripped open the front door and leapt down the steps on to the drive. He saw no one, walked to the gateway and looked both ways. There wasn't a moving vehicle in sight. He turned and walked back to the house. Peters and Gibson were on the doorstep. Stafford said, 'Nah, no sign of anyone.'

As he stepped into the hall he picked up the Jiffy bag and walked back to the kitchen with the others. Nicole had already found her pack of forensic gloves and grinned as she handed it to Stafford. Stafford placed the Jiffy bag on the table and snapped on the gloves. He got out a sharp kitchen knife and began to slit the brown packaging tape across the front of the bag.

'I bet it's the middle finger this time,' said Peters.

'It's not very big, whatever it is,' said Stafford, 'it certainly isn't a finger. In fact it feels almost empty.' The other three sat on the edge of their chairs in total silence. No one, it seemed, was breathing. Stafford slit up the two sides and slowly folded back the flap. He opened it and peered inside.

'Well, the good news is, there are no wires again, just the same folded kitchen paper.' Stafford eased out the wad of absorbent paper, set it on the table in front of him, then sat down.

'Aw, com'on, the tension's killing us,' said Gibson. Stafford grinned at them, interlaced his fingers and with palms forward, pushed his arms out and cracked his knuckles. He unlaced his fingers and began to unfold the kitchen paper. After four layers, he stopped. The other three groaned in unison.

'Thinks he's bloody Dynamo,' said Peters as he grabbed the item. He pulled off the last sheet and a memory stick dropped on to the table. Peters smoothed out the sheet of kitchen paper, revealing what appeared to be a mobile phone number written on it.

'Hey, Nicky, pass the laptop over,' said Stafford. She slid the laptop across the table and Stafford pushed the memory stick into the relevant socket. The others left their chairs and crowded behind him. He pressed a couple of keys and an image of a pleasant suburban semi-detached house appeared. On the drive outside the house, Marva Lewis was preparing to put her two children into the car. A second picture brought a sharp intake of breath from Nicole as she recognised her own home, a modern apartment in a development of four apartment blocks close to Aldershot town centre. A third picture showed a piece of paper with the word "BOOM" scrawled across it in red.

It was Stafford who broke the silence as he said, 'Bastards, bastards, that message is pretty bloody clear.' He slumped in his chair and shook his head.

'Yeah, right. They need our five sites and they need you, because you're in the council's good books. But even if you do work with them, step out of line and they'll fuck your friends,' said Peters.

'Right, so we've gotta get Marva, the kids and you, Nicole, safe and out of the firing line,' said Stafford. 'Trouble is, Marva can be so bloody stubborn, it'll be a fight just doing that. I think the only way we'll convince her of the urgency is to just arrive at her front door, then refuse to take no for an answer. So, Ryan, get on the phone to command, we need a safe house… like right now.'

Peters pulled out his mobile phone and nodded to Stafford, 'Already on it.'

Peters finished his call, 'OK, we're all set. They've got a four-bedroomed detached place in Portsmouth. They're sending someone down there to open up with some basic supplies and stuff. They'll wait till we arrive to see what else we need. They'll text you the postcode shortly.'

'Good… now, Lee, print off those pictures for us to take to Marva's, then photograph the package and the memory stick and organise a courier to take the bits to Cosham SSD. After that, just hold the fort here till we get back.'

'You got it, boss,' said Gibson.

'Ry', use your motor to get to Marva's, me and Nic will go in the Volvo. I reckon we'll leave Marva's car on her drive.' Stafford put the prints in an A4 folder, and as they walked to the cars Stafford said to Peters, 'I guess you're gonna get there before us, so park up a bit away from the house and wait for us. Yeah?' Peters nodded, jumped in the Vectra and headed for Marva's home.

As they settled into the Volvo, Nicole turned to him and said, 'You look worried. You all right?'

'I am worried, girl. I said ages ago that Runihura and Kapusniak hadn't got the brains to run something like this, but let's face it, they're way ahead of us. They're running rings around us. We've got nothing, absolutely bugger all.'

Stafford fired up the motor and rolled out to the street. They were silent for a moment or two, then he said, 'All we've got is an e-fit picture of the last customer at the marina and a DVD showing Runihura and Bockus with George just before he disappeared. Could be he sold the car, took the money and ran. At the moment we can't prove anything. So, girl, too right I'm worried.'

'Seems to me, like we'd better get and talk to our Mr Bockus again. He's the only real connection we've got.' Stafford nodded and gunned the old Volvo.

———————— ‖ ————————

They pulled up to where Peters had parked, some 250 yards from Marva's house. All the houses in the street had off-road parking. Seeing nothing or no one suspicious, Stafford led the way to Marva's driveway and edged past the Zafira. He stepped into the storm porch and rang the bell. Marva, looking shattered and surprised, opened the door and gave Stafford a quick hug. Marva took them through to the living room. Nicole and Stafford settled at each end of a sofa, Peters sat between them. Marva sat in an armchair whilst Stafford, tapping the brown A4 folder nervously on his knee said, 'Sorry to descend on you mob-handed like this, but it's important that we talk.'

'Yes, I guessed it wasn't a social call,' said Marva.

'Hmm, difficult to know where to start. But look, we think that Garfield's death and a number of other killings are the work of a group who want to run our five sites.'

'Why do they want your sites so badly?'

'Gotta tell you, we're not sure. But we think it's to do with illegal, cheap, or maybe even slave labour, stripping out precious metals from scrap electronics.'

'And there's enough money in that to warrant killing people?'

'Like I say, we really don't know, but there may also be a drug link here.' Marva shook her head in dismay.

'A drug link? In what way?'

'We think they smuggle the stuff into the country by boat, then network it through the tips,' said Peters.

'But most important at the moment, we need to talk to you about this,' said Stafford opening the folder and giving the prints to Marva. Stafford continued,

'These people are responsible for at least four deaths up to now. Today we received a memory stick and these were on it.' Marva studied them silently.

'The threat is obvious, don't you agree?' asked Stafford. Marva nodded and looked at him, as if expecting more. Stafford found it difficult to meet her gaze. Peters explained that the apartment block in the picture was where Nicole lived.

'These people are ruthless. We think the only way we can protect you is to get you into a safe house,' said Peters. No one spoke, all waiting for a response from Marva.

'Well, to be honest, I'm too exhausted to think straight

let alone fight. And the kids are off school, so I guess it's fine by me,' she said.

'Brilliant, Marva, phew, that's a relief,' said Stafford.

'How long is this going to be for, do you think?'

'There's no way of telling, it just gives us a bit of peace of mind knowing that you're safe while we keep looking for the bad guys.'

'So, Nicole, what about you?' Stafford asked.

She hesitated for a moment then said, 'I think it's got to be the best thing for Marva and the boys.'

'Good, well, that's all settled then. Marva, will you put some bits and pieces into a couple of cases for you and the kids. You know, enough to last for a week or so. Nicky, we'll get you down there first and sort some stuff out for you later,' said Stafford. Marva nodded and got to her feet.

'I'll go tell the boys. They're on their X-boxes in the bedroom,' she said.

As she made her way upstairs, Nicole hissed at Stafford, 'Listen, Staf, I'm not the victim here. I'm not staying at the safe house, I'm gonna continue working the case, there's no way you're cutting me out now.' Stafford raised both his hands as if to ward off an attack.

'Woah, woah, point taken. We'll sort something out,' he said.

'Yeah, you bet we will,' she said.

Stafford's phone buzzed letting him know he had a text. It was the postcode for the safe house.

Fifteen minutes later they were in the cars heading for Portsmouth. Marva and her two children were in the Volvo with Paul, Ryan and Nicole in the Vectra.

—————————————— ‖ ——————————————

Peters noticed a white Mondeo pull out some 200 yards behind them as they drove away. He opened his mouth to say something about it, when Nicole snapped, 'For Christ's sake, don't you start! Listen, once and for all. I'm gonna help with this investigation till we catch these bastards.'

'Bloody hell, girl, don't have a go at me, I think you're safer with us. But I do think it's dangerous you staying at yours though,' said Peters and he laughed.

Slightly embarrassed, she said smiling but with no humour, 'Yeah sorry, don't worry, we'll figure something out.'

Peters, feeling the tension subside, concentrated on driving. And he began to get more preoccupied as every so often he caught a glimpse of a white car some distance behind. Sometimes he saw it in the wing mirrors, sometimes in the rear-view mirror. He mentioned it to Martin, who spotted it a number of times, though it was always five or six cars behind and too far away to identify. The white car seemed to disappear just after they left the M3.

It took over an hour to reach the safe house. The driveway was big enough for both cars to stay out of sight behind a tall hedge that bordered the front garden. It was a typical 1920s-style middle-class, middle-management detached house. As they busied themselves getting the children and suitcases out of the car, Peters again noticed a white Mondeo, this time, slowing down as it drove past the house.

—————————————— ‖ ——————————————

Stafford carried the two cases to the front door, it opened and two young men with short, gelled hair, both wearing jeans and bomber jackets came out.

'Good afternoon, Major, family's grown since I last saw you,' said the tallest of the two with a grin. Stafford recognised him as one of his Fort Monckton trainees.

'Well, it's you that's gonna be doing the baby sitting for me.'

'My pleasure, sir,' said the agent as he took the suitcases and went back into the house.

As Nicole approached the front door, she said quietly to Marva, 'Hmm, maybe I will change my mind and stay with you after all.'

'You should, at least you'd be safe here,' said Marva seriously, completely missing Nicole's lascivious smile and attempt at levity.

As they all piled into the living room, Stafford shook hands with the two agents, who introduced themselves to the others. Marva's two boys dashed upstairs to choose bedrooms. Marva followed at a more sedate pace.

'Nicole, look, are you sure you wouldn't rather stay here?' asked Stafford.

'Well, it's a lovely house, and there's a couple of things that make it really tempting. But no, unless Marva wants me to stay, I'm continuing to help with this investigation. OK?'

'OK,' he conceded.

Peters and one of the agents walked around the house and garden checking for any areas where they might be vulnerable to attack. Peters mentioned to the agent that he had seen a white Ford Mondeo behind them on the journey down, and again, when it seemed to slow as it drove past the house. He said he didn't know if it meant anything or if he was being paranoid, but suggested they kept an eye out for it just in case.

The house itself looked like an ordinary 1920s middle-class home. But it was full of the latest protection and surveillance devices linked to a monitoring set up in the attic and the command HQ in Fort Monckton.

Having done as much as possible to ensure the safety of Marva and her kids, Stafford and crew headed out to their cars.

Peters jumped into the Vectra and with a wave drove away. Stafford said, 'Before I set off, I'll ask you one mor…'

'No need to ask, I've already given you the answer. I want to carry on with this investigation,' she said curtly. Stafford shrugged, fired up the old Volvo and headed for the M3.

'I don't think you should stay at your place though, I think we should head up there now, collect what you need for a week or so. Then stay at mine. There's a couple of bedrooms you can choose from and I think you'll be safer under my roof.'

'Sounds like a plan, if you're all right with it.'

'Well, it is my fault you're in this situation.'

'Yeah, that's true, so do I get overtime pay for this then?' she asked with a grin.

'I'll tell you what I'll do. When we've collected your stuff, guide me to a decent restaurant in Aldershot and I'll buy you dinner.'

'That's a deal, boss.'

——————————————— ▌▌ ———————————————

She chose an Indian restaurant. It was obvious from the reception they got that she was a regular. The restaurant wasn't busy and they were shown to a dimly lit table for two in an alcove at the far end of the dining area.

'As you seem to know your way around this place, what would you recommend?'

'Depends really, do you like hot or mild curry?'

'Hmm, I tend to stick with mild. I don't understand the point of eating red-hot spicy food.'

'Then I have no hesitation in suggesting you try the chicken or mutton rezala. It's a white curry with yoghurt, poppy seeds and cashews, and it's delicious. I'm gonna have the mutton myself with a chunk of naan bread,' she said. They both ordered a Cobra beer to accompany their meal. The food arrived and as they began to eat, for once Stafford had no choice but to look at, as well as talk to, his colleague. For the first time since they met he realised that Nicole was not just an attractive girl, but a very beautiful woman. He found himself staring for one long moment into her large brown eyes, almost oblivious of what she had just said. Somewhat embarrassed, he said, 'Sorry, Nicole, I seem to have missed that.'

'Oh, it was nothing important. I was just wondering if Lee would still be around when we get back to your place.'

'I could phone him I suppose, but that seems a bit like checking up on him. So I'll wait till we get there.'

For the rest of the meal he avoided eye contact as much as he could without, he hoped, appearing rude. Stafford complimented her on her excellent recommendation and assured her they would come back again. He paid the bill and they returned to his Farnborough home.

Gibson's car was still in the driveway and Stafford rolled the Volvo to a halt alongside it. He lugged Nicole's suitcase into the hallway and they wandered through to the kitchen.

Gibson was going through George Saunders's and Matis Bockus's phone records.

'Hiya guys. Hah, I'm surprised to see you back here, Nic,' he said.

'Hah, you ain't getting rid of me that easy, sunshine,' she said with a grin, 'as I keep bloody saying, I'm gonna continue working this investigation. Anyway, Stafford suggested I stay here for a day or two, and at least this way the other people in my block won't be in any danger.'

'Right, yeah, good thought that. We'll get you sorted out with a bedroom, then Lee can tell us what's new,' said Stafford. He walked into the hall, picked up her case and switched on the upstairs light. She followed him up. The landing led to a long corridor with doors on either side. Stafford stopped at the first door on the left.

'This is your first choice,' he said as he stepped inside and turned on the light, 'the second choice is the next door down on the left, so if you want to look in there just help yourself. You know where the bathroom is, don't you? So I'll leave you to get settled in.' He walked thoughtfully back down the stairs to the kitchen.

When Nicole rejoined them, Gibson said, 'First off, I've organised another interview with our Mr Bockus at 11.30 a.m. tomorrow at Winchester Prison. Apparently, they're keeping him in "A" wing, the induction and supervision unit rather than the remand wing. They're a bit concerned, it seems he's been showing signs of agitation and they can keep a closer eye on him there. But he's allowed pretty much free association.'

'You happy to do that with Ryan then, as you've been his main contact?' asked Stafford.

'Yeah, of course, can't wait to see what he finds so special at the River Itchen,' said Gibson with a grin.

'Anything interesting turn up in the phone records, like the number on the kitchen paper?' asked Stafford pointing to the pile of papers in front of Gibson.

'Well, yeah, it's sort of interesting, but no, not that number. And nothing very helpful. I mean Bockus and Saunders have a few numbers in common that they've called over the last six months. So there's obviously a link between 'em, but I think they've been using cheap burner phones, 'cause I get no response from those numbers at all.' Then Gibson continued, 'Oh yeah, we had an email from forensics saying that the white paint scrapings we collected from the marina are from a 2005-2008, Nissan Navara D40, utility vehicle. Or in other words, a white Nissan pickup. And we know that's what Kapusniak was driving when he rammed us. Sadly though it doesn't prove he was driving it at the marina or even if it was his motor.' As he said it he passed the email to Stafford.

'Hmm, so where is the bloody thing? It's so frustrating that we've had no ANPR sightings of it at all, anywhere,' said Stafford.

'And just one more piece of probably useless info to chuck into the mix. Did you know that the red phosphorus used in distress and road flares is also used to make ice? And I mean ice, as in crystal meths,' said Gibson. 'I chuck that in because if the chandlery also sells battery acid, alkaline batteries, starter fluid, liquid camping stove fuel, that's about a third of the ingredients you need to cook up crystal meths.'

'Woah!, said Nicole, 'that's a big leap you've made there Lee.'

'Yeah, I know, but if you look at the American and Aussie drug scene, that's the way it's going. This stuff's easy to get, cheap to buy and easyish to make. And with a huge profit margin.'

'Good God, Gibbo, you have been busy, haven't you?' said Stafford.

'Sadly, it gives us a lot to think about, but not much help catching these bastards,' said Gibson as he stood up and made his way to the door. 'Well, goodnight, folks, I'll meet up with Ryan in the a.m. and catch up with you later,' he said as he disappeared into the night.

'Y'know, I'm gonna have to start pushing Gibson into going home at a sensible hour. I know he's keen, but he does have a family to get home to.'

'Yeah, but it's the same with all of us. It's so bloody difficult to make any progress, we just think if we keep looking harder something will break for us.'

'Hmm, well, anyway, I'm going to have a mug of tea before I head off to bed. Do you want a mug while I'm at it?'

'Yeah, go on then. Then is it OK if I have a shower?'

'Of course, don't have to ask, just make yourself at home.'

CHAPTER 34

Matis Bockus wouldn't have called himself a drug addict. A drug user maybe.

The bag of coke he was found with, the police had classified as "possession of a class A drug with intent to supply", but it was his and he had no intention of selling it or sharing it with anybody. He thought of it as a perk of the job. But he'd been without a hit of any sort for hours and he was beginning to feel stressed.

Agitated and jumpy after his meeting with Neilson, he was returned, not to the remand unit, but to "A" wing. The guard who removed the handcuffs informed him that this wing was the induction and supervision wing and he would be better looked after here. Bockus simply nodded. The guard walked him around the wing, showed him the free association area where he could make tea or coffee, watch a large-screen TV and mingle and chat with other inmates. After the relative peace of the remand unit and the interview room, the noise in the large open area was overwhelming to Bockus. Even the smallest sound reverberated throughout the open landings of the four-storey Victorian building. The guard showed him the shower block, where the library was and explained how he could contact the chaplain if he felt

the need. Bockus put his hands over his ears in an attempt
to block out the noise.

'Cell,' he said, 'show me cell.' The guard explained there
was still time left on the afternoon free association session,
but Bockus was adamant. 'No, take me to cell.' The guard
shrugged and did as asked. Bockus entered and sat down on
the metal bed, chin on his chest. He gripped his knees in an
effort to stop them shaking.

The guard watched for a few moments then put his
hand on Bockus's shoulder and asked, 'You ill? You need a
doctor or anything?'

Bockus was still for a second then shrugged off the
guard's hand and shook his head, 'No, I OK,' he said. The
guard paused again, then walked out of the cell. Bockus
lay down on the bed, but couldn't settle; the background
noise was too much. He got up, had a pee, drank some
water and tried to settle on the bed again, but to no avail.
He hadn't had a hit of anything in days, he was stressed
and getting depressed. Agitated, he wandered out into the
free association area. A few lags were still there, a number
of them watched as two others played pool, cheering or
jeering loudly at each and every shot. A couple played table
tennis. They ignored him.

He sat down to watch the large-screen TV, some
childish game show was in progress. He got up and returned
to his cell. He sat on the edge of the bed. His knees were
bouncing non stop. He lay down on the bed, face to the
wall. Moments later, just as he had managed to calm his
twitching legs, he began to feel uncomfortable, as though
somehow vulnerable. He felt as though he was being
watched. He half turned then told himself he was being

irrational and tried to settle down. Then he heard, 'Ah, so you are awake then, me old mucka?' Startled, Bockus whipped his legs round to the floor and jumped to his feet. The quick movement made him feel dizzy, he stood still for a second then sat down and gazed at his visitor, a shaven-headed young man in grey tracky bottoms, orange trainers and a black tee shirt, leaning against the door jamb.

'Meolmucka? What is this?' asked Bockus. The visitor laughed.

'It means "mate, friend",' he said as he walked into the cell with right hand outstretched. 'My name is Terry, pleased to meet you, mate.' Bockus shook the offered hand, then his head.

'English, you English, why say meolmucka, when you need only say mate?'

'Well, never mind that, mate, I'm told you're in need of something to take the edge off,' then checking his watch, 'fuck, it's nearly the end of free association, here, take this.' And with sleight of hand a magician would be proud of, he slipped two pinkish-grey crystals much smaller than peas into Bockus's breast pocket. Bockus stood, put his hands in his trouser pockets and pulled them inside out.

'No money, can't pay, have no money.'

'Already paid for, me old mucka, already paid in full,' said Terry as he walked away. With the door to his cell closed, Bockus sat on the edge of his bed. He took one of the little crystal rocks and turned it slowly between thumb and forefinger. He recognised it as probably "pink champagne" or some form of MDMA or crystal meth. For all Bockus knew it could have been any one of half a dozen "fun" drugs. He didn't care, he just needed to escape for a while. He stuck the rock under his tongue, grimaced at the initial sour taste and leaned back against the wall. He closed his eyes and smiled as he recalled that pink champagne was supposed to be the "party drug". *Ah well, maybe he could party in his head for a while*, he thought. The next fifteen minutes seemed like an hour to him and still the party hadn't started. He took out the other little rock and slipped it under his tongue.

He thought he could hear music, quiet at first as though in the distance. He stood up and looked towards the sound, it was louder now. He heard the thudding beat. He felt the rhythm pounding in his head. His smile stretched from ear to ear. He called out for people to join his party, 'Come on, people, come, I have party, I have party,' he shouted. He banged on the cell door. No one came. He danced frantically in time with the music. Still no one came. He wrapped his arms around himself, he loved how sensual his touch felt. As he moved, his clothes felt sensational against his skin. He wanted to touch people, he wanted them to share his loving touch. His hands felt gentle and soft as he leaned on the sink and looked at himself in the metal mirror. He saw his face, unlined and beautiful. Skin so smooth… His eyes began to lose focus, he saw flashing pinpricks of piercing white light. His forehead was bathed in sweat. His skin felt clammy, damp. He was tired, exhausted, struggling to breathe. He felt faint, he started to panic; clutching his chest he crashed to the floor. His body convulsed as his arms and legs thrashed. He felt sick, stomach muscles screwed into an excruciating knot… He threw up, without warning, the party in his head was over.

II

It was half an hour before they found him. The screw who had taken him to his cell had realised it was his first time in any of Her Majesty's Prisons and decided, with another officer, to check on him. He peered through the little window in the cell door and could just see Bockus's left forearm and hand lying motionless on the floor. He immediately sent his colleague for the defibrillator and medical team. He entered the cell. Bockus was on his back and seemed to be unconscious, but his chest was heaving violently as he gasped for breath. The guard tilted Bockus's head back, flipped his jaw open, checking for obstructions and began CPR. The second guard dashed back in with the defibrillator and as they proceeded to apply the therapeutic electric shock, said, 'I've called for the medical team.'

The medics arrived and quickly assessed a cardiac arrest. They gave a radio shoutout for CODE BLUE then gave Bockus a hit of adrenaline and lifted him on to a gurney. They handcuffed his left wrist to the side bar and rushed him to the medical wing where they gave him oxygen and coupled him to a mobile monitor.

Code Blue automatically alerted the control room to call for an ambulance and notify the gate to prepare for its arrival. Control also arranged for prison officers to escort the prisoner to the hospital. The ambulance arrived and the paramedics rushed in. They checked the patient over and wheeled him to the waiting vehicle, where they were met by the two prison officer escorts. With blue lights flashing, they raced to the nearest hospital, where he was rushed to the ICU.

Back in the prison, the guard checked the information they held on Bockus and discovered that he had no next of kin listed in the UK. In fact no kith or kin appeared anywhere on his info sheets. He was due a visit from both his solicitor and the police at 11:30 a.m. the following day. The officer made a note of the details and decided to phone both parties first thing in the morning to notify them of the situation and cancel the interview indefinitely.

CHAPTER 35

At 7 a.m. the following morning, Stafford was awake, though still in bed. He was agitated and had no desire to get up, but his bladder had other ideas. With a huge sigh and wearing a pair of boxer shorts he flung off the duvet and wandered bleary-eyed to the bathroom. He peed and decided as he was now reasonably alert he might just as well shower and shave. A clean shave, no designer stubble for him. Ablutions complete, he slipped his boxers back on, opened the door and almost collided with the incoming Nicole Martin.

'Jesus H Christ,' he said as he fell back against the door jamb. 'You frightened the life outta me. I forgot you were here.' Nicole, wearing a pale yellow dressing gown, moved back a pace and studied him carefully. As if she'd pressed a button, Stafford's chest puffed out as he sucked his stomach in. Nicole grinned.

'Nice pecs, but you must tell me the stories behind the scars some time.' As she spoke, she gently put the tips of her index and middle finger on the ragged, almost star-shaped scar under his left collar bone. She slid her fingers down across an impressive six pack and touched livid scar tissue just above his left hip. Slowly she moved aside to let him pass.

He tried his best to look nonchalant as he walked back to his bedroom. But he felt his cheeks begin to burn at the effect her gentle touch had on him. Half an hour later, both now dressed and sitting at his kitchen table drinking mugs of coffee his cell phone rang. The call was from Gibson, Stafford listened for a few seconds then said, 'OK, Lee, we'll see you both shortly,' and ended the call. He sat quietly for a while and contemplated the call. Nicole waited silently.

'This can't be a coincidence, or an accident, this has to be them. How is it they are always so far ahead of us?' he said shaking his head in frustration.

'What's happened now?'

'Well, Lee and Ryan were due to see Bockus in Winchester this morning, but he's apparently had a cardiac arrest. Now he's in a coma in the ICU at Winchester Hospital.'

'What? That's incredible, he's only about thirty, isn't he?'

'Yeah, but the initial toxicology report indicates a drug overdose.'

Twenty minutes later Gibson arrived, followed by Peters. Each of them vented their frustration. Declaring in their view, it couldn't be an act of God, or a coincidence.

Bockus had represented their best hope of moving the investigation forward and now it seemed that hope had disappeared.

'Did they give any indication of if or when he might recover?' asked Stafford.

'No, the prison staff really didn't want to know, they referred me to the consultant at Winchester Hospital. I managed to talk to him this morning and he said, it's possible that he'll never come out of the coma. Even if he does he may well be brain-damaged,' said Gibson.

'What did the prison tell you about what happened?' asked Stafford.

'It seems Bockus had managed to get himself a hotshot lawyer, a guy called Howard Neilson. Seems this Neilson visited yesterday afternoon. They're absolutely adamant that the lawyer couldn't have smuggled any drugs in, because they searched him and his briefcase carefully before the interview took place, as they do all visitors.'

'So Bockus had either secreted the drugs about his person, which would be almost impossible, or he was given them by one of the other lags,' said Peters.

'Why was he on "A" wing and not kept on "B" wing with the other remand prisoners?' asked Stafford.

'Yeah, I asked that too. They were reluctant to tell me, but it seems our Mr Neilson came out of the meeting with Bockus and claimed that he was showing signs of being stressed, agitated and depressed. Said he was worried that he was contemplating suicide.'

'What, and they always do what a solicitor wants?' asked Stafford.

'Well, it seems that they've had a few run-ins with this guy before, and with the current media hooha about deaths in prison they tend to take the easy way out.'

'Hmm, not sure I like the sound of this guy. Who called him in?' asked Stafford. 'Because there's no way Bockus could ordinarily get access to a guy like that.'

'Good question, boss. It's got to start with the Aldershot nick, 'cause that's where we first held him. I'll talk to Hawkins, see if he knows,' said Gibson. 'Give me a minute,

I'll go out in the hall and chat to him,' and he started to walk into the hallway.

'Hey, before you disappear, Lee, can you ask him if DI Fisher is still working this case?' asked Peters.

'Yeah, sure, no problem,' said Gibson as he disappeared around the door.

'So what's that about then?' asked Stafford.

'Well, far be it from me to cast aspersions, but when we went down to Portsmouth yesterday, we registered a white car behind us every now and again, but if he was following us he was good, you know, never too obvious. Then when we unloaded the cars, I saw what I thought was a white Mondeo driving past quite slowly,' said Peters.

'You didn't say anything while we were down there,' said Stafford.

'I gotta say it was all a bit subliminal, if you know what I mean, but I did mention it to the young agent. At the time I thought I was just being paranoid because of the circumstances, but last night I was thinking about it and I'm sure the same car went past us when we put the tracker on that black Mercedes pickup at North Lane. Then when we got back to Aldershot nick there was a white Mondeo in the car park. And of course Fisher drives a white Mondeo. To much white Mondeo for coincidence, me thinks,' Peters said.

'Now that's a very interesting supposition, young Ryan. Do you reckon he's spying on us then, not investigating the case?' said Stafford, then, 'Fuck, doesn't that put stuff in a different light?'

'Hey yeah, and remember when I spoke to DCI Talbot, he definitely wasn't impressed with Fisher's performance,' said Nicole.

'It'll be interesting to see if either agent spotted the Mondeo again. And say Fisher did spot me attaching the tracker to the Mercedes, that'd explain why the bloody red light spends all its time in central London,' said Peters with a grin. Gibson came back into the room and sat down at the kitchen table.

'Well, that was quite an interesting conversation. It appears that Howard Neilson arrived on the scene some time ago; he was the geezer that represented Runihura. Seems Neilson and Fisher know each other pretty well, apparently Fisher's pushed for him to represent a number of people we've banged up in Aldershot and Farnborough. And they were mainly foreign nationals. Oh yeah, and Hawkins says Fisher is definitely not on this case.'

'That will be an enlightening area to investigate, by the sound of it,' said Nicole.

'You're right, I think maybe we should start to work out of the incident room at Aldershot nick a bit more. That way we could keep a close eye on the DI, see if we could flush him out,' said Stafford.

'It'll look a bit obvious if we all simply pile over there,' said Peters.

'OK, so, Lee, you get on all right with Hawkins, don't you? Well, phone him back, see if you can get him to meet us. Beautiful Butties perhaps, or here if he'd prefer. But tell him not to mention to anyone that he's meeting us,' said Stafford.

Gibson phoned and after a few awkward moments persuaded Hawkins to meet them at the café at 10:30a.m. Hawkins's parting words to Gibson were, 'This had better be good, sunshine, you'd better not be wasting my time.'

Gibson responded, 'I promise you, Sar'nt...' then realised the line was already dead. He related the details to his colleagues.

'Good, I think it best if me and Ryan talk to the sergeant. So you two head off down to Winchester Hospital and see what's occurring with Bockus. Then over to the prison to see if you can make sense of what happened there,' said Stafford. Gibson breathed a sigh of relief as a smiling Stafford continued, 'And that'll save you from trying to convince your sergeant that his DI is bent.'

Peters threw the Vectra keys to Gibson.

'You might as well take the Vectra, as I guess the major will want to drive the old Volvo,' said Peters with a grin.

When they'd gone, Stafford said to Peters, 'This is a real bastard, I can't help feeling we're missing something obvious.'

'Roger that, but it's not so easy when the cowardly bastards won't stand up and fight.'

'But we're nowhere, mate, absolutely no fucking where.'

'But we know it's being orchestrated by Runihura, and we do know that Bockus, Kapusniak and Winstone are involved. And now we might have Fisher to work on.'

'They're cannon fodder, expendables, like George and now probably Bockus. We need to find who's pulling their strings. We need to start fighting back,' said Stafford, 'and fast.' They parked close to the Beautiful Butties Café and walked in. Hawkins was already there. He had selected a booth towards the back of the greasy spoon. He was wearing a black macintosh over his uniform. Stafford and Peters ordered tea. Hawkins indicated that he had his drink. Stafford paid and they joined the sergeant.

'Thanks for coming, Sar'nt, there is no easy way of starting this, so let me ask you, what do you think of your DI?' he asked. The sergeant sat quietly for a while.

'Where's young Gibson? I thought since it was him who phoned me, he'd be here?'

'I thought it best we started this conversation without him. Because we think your DI is working against us, I thought it prudent to get Gibson concentrating on other things till we get your opinion,' said Stafford.

'So what gives you the idea that Fisher is bent?'

The waitress brought over their tea and placed it on the table. Stafford smiled his thanks. When she'd gone he said, 'I'm afraid we've nothing concrete at the moment, just a number of little events that occur and seem to hinder our investigation.'

'Are you sure you're not looking for a scapegoat for your own shortcomings, Major?'

Peters' immediate thought was to grab the sergeant by his throat, but Stafford, marginally ahead of him, placed a restraining hand on his arm and said, 'Steady, Ryan, we're just talking here.' Peters settled back down and Stafford continued, 'I can understand why you'd think that, but from the start he's not been helpful. First he tried hard for two days to convince everyone that the explosion was just an unfortunate accident. Then he wasted our time by pulling in me and Captain Peters for questioning over George Saunders's disappearance.'

'Perhaps he felt he had to explore every eventuality.'

'Yeah, I can accept that, but when Martin phoned him to discuss his surveillance of Ayman Runihura he was totally rude and unhelpful. We since found out that he told DCI Talbot it was a waste of time following Runihura because he saw no evidence of wrongdoing. But we easily found out that even his qualifications to work in the waste industry were fraudulent; surely that would raise most people's suspicions?' asked Stafford.

'I know he spent a month or two watching him, maybe he felt it was all minor stuff?'

'OK, fair enough, but when Bockus was nicked, Fisher had obviously been checking our interview on the monitors, and when Captain Peters put a tracker on their motor he spotted a white Mondeo lurking nearby.'

'Did you get the Mondeo's reg. number?' asked the sergeant.

'No, but late yesterday we had occasion to go to Portsmouth and we were followed by a white car, and a white Mondeo was again spotted cruising slowly past when we stopped. It just seems too much for coincidence when your DI drives a white Mondeo,' said Stafford.

'So you think that because you've seen a few white Mondeos between here and Portsmouth, that points to my senior officer being bent?'

'Yeah, I know it's tenuous, but now we hear that Matis Bockus has been visited by the solicitor, Howard Neilson. We now know that Fisher and Neilson are, well, maybe not friends, but associates at least. After Neilson's visit, Bockus was transferred from the remand wing to the supervision unit, apparently at Neilson's request, and is now in a coma in Winchester Hospital,' said Stafford.

'And this convinces you that the DI is corrupt?'

'It certainly gives me reasonable doubt, that's for sure,' said Stafford, 'but you've obviously worked with him for a while, what do you think?'

The sergeant picked up a tea-spoon, stirred his tea slowly and said, 'This is my senior officer we're talking about here, I've worked with him for a few years now.' He paused again, as if to regain his thoughts.

'And during that time I've found him to be an incompetent, bigoted, arrogant, lazy arsehole. It's a nightmare working with him, in fact it's embarrassing.'

Stafford and Peters looked at the sergeant, speechless. Then Peters said, as they started to laugh, 'You bloody wanker, Hawkins, you don't know how close you came to getting thumped then.' Hawkins looked at him and grinned.

'Oh yeah, you and whose army?... Ah, I forgot, you actually have got an army, haven't you? Anyway, moving on. As we all agree that the DI is probably working against us, how can we use that to our advantage?'

'With you working with us, we've got to feed him some sort of misdirection, see what action he takes,' said Stafford.

CHAPTER 36

Winstone had filled the tank of the Mercedes pickup. Kapusniak, knowing he would probably leave at least three cartridges behind at the tip, had emptied the Beretta's magazine. Wearing surgical gloves he had nicked from their drug lab, he wiped each bullet clean and reloaded the twenty jacketed, hollow-point rounds. He slid the magazine into the 93R's hand grip, then fitted and adjusted the extendable steel shoulder stock. This, he knew, would give him a little more control when he fired.

At exactly twelve o'clock midday, Runihura carried his canvas bag, Kapusniak carried the Beretta pistol in a tennis racquet bag and Winstone carried the car keys as they piled into the Mercedes. Runihura in the back and Kapusniak in the passenger seat, they headed towards Winchester. As they approached the recycling centre, Runihura said, 'Pull into the lay-by just before the tip.' Winstone turned in and rolled to a halt. Both men looked at Runihura. He handed them each a black woollen balaclava from his canvas bag.

'No, don't put it on yet, Floyd. We'll do a drive through first, but Jan, get your window down and if you see Wandoch as an easy shot, take it. If not, we'll try and spot him then go again. Right?' Both men nodded. Kapusniak lowered his window, unzipped the bag at his feet and held the Beretta on his lap, ready. Winstone pulled out on to the road, turned into the recycling centre and gunned the motor up the steep incline. At the top, in second gear, he cruised slowly around the long right-hand bend.

In unison Kapusniak and Runihura shouted, 'Fuck, fuck, drive through, drive through.'

Winstone, not sure what had happened, almost in panic, punched his foot to the floor and powered through. Once out and on to the road Runihura said, 'Fucking hell... Winstone, pull up in the lay-by again.' As he did, Kapusniak and Runihura fell about laughing. The adrenaline they'd been pumping needed an out, this was it for now. Winstone looked at them as though they were mad. Kapusniak and Runihura got out of the motor. Kapusniak walked around the front and got in behind Winstone. Runihura walked around the back and got into the passenger seat beside Winstone. Runihura said, 'OK, take two.' Winstone looked at him, mouth wide open.

'We forgot, Floyd, the access road in the tip turns right, like clockwise. We were set up for a left-hand turn, like anti-clockwise,' said Runihura. Winstone, mouth still open, suddenly got it. His mouth opened further as he roared with laughter.

'Now start the fucking engine and go again,' said Runihura no longer amused. Kapusniak opened his window as they turned and drove back into the recycling centre. The site was quiet, only five or six cars there. No one took any notice of them as they made their second pass. At first there was no sign of any orange-jacketed staff member. As they approached the sales area and shed, the imposing six-foot nine-inch figure of Mariusz Wandoch wandered across to talk to a punter there.

'Great,' said Runihura, 'quick, Floyd, straight out, then helmets on and back in again, go, go.'

Winstone drove out, slowed enough for them to put on their balaclavas, then powered back up the in slope. He hit the top deck at twenty mph then slowed, giving Kapusniak the chance to set his gun on the edge of the window. Holding a steady twelve mph he eased round the bend approaching the sales area.

Wandoch was still there, chatting. Kapusniak lined up the shot as best he could, the hi-viz orange jacket creating a massive target. Kapusniak squeezed the trigger. The noise in the car was deafening. Mariusz and the punter crashed to the ground.

Winstone gunned the Mercedes, it careered down the slope, screeched into a ninety degree left turn at the bottom and raced towards Southampton Metal Recycling Ltd.

'He not so fucking big now,' said Kapusniak in his heavily accented English.

CHAPTER 37

Nicole and Gibson had badged their way into the ICU at Winchester Hospital. They had seen Bockus and spoken to the doctor in charge of his case. He'd confirmed that it was a cardiac arrest caused by a massive overdose of the drug MDMA. He did not predict a speedy or satisfactory outcome for Bockus. He said Bockus had perhaps a thirty per cent chance of survival. And probably a ninety-five per cent chance of being severely brain-damaged if he did survive. In his final statistic, he said the chance of him coming out of the coma was only around thirty per cent. With that, he shook his head and disappeared into the ward.

———————————— ‖ ————————————

From the hospital they made their way towards the prison. Standing on the kerbside waiting to cross, Gibson said, 'I'm a bit worried about this you know, Nic. I thought we were doing the right thing getting involved with this high-profile lot, but we seem to be getting nowhere. And now we are actually accusing our DI of being a bent cop. If this investigation goes tits-up we can look forward to a future of directing this stuff.' He waved his arms to indicate the traffic on the busy road.

'Bloody hell, Lee,' said Nicole as they nipped through a gap in the traffic. 'Where did all that come from? I mean, you've done really well so far, coming up with various ideas and information that will help us bring these bad guys down.'

'I hope you're right, girl, I hope you're right,' he said as they approached the prison gates. Once inside they were introduced to two local police officers who had been called in to investigate how Bockus had acquired the drugs so soon after his return from the interview with his solicitor. They'd ruled out any idea of Neilson's involvement as he had been thoroughly searched prior to the meeting. And of course they got no help from the lags on the wing.

'See what I mean?' said Gibson as they made their way out, 'nowhere, absolutely no bloody where.'

Walking to the car park, they became aware of a distant cacophony of police sirens. So many, they stopped in their tracks for a moment or two, trying to pinpoint the direction the cars were racing in. The sounds were getting quieter, the cars obviously heading away from the town.

'Another motorway smash I guess,' said Gibson as they carried on to the car park.

CHAPTER 38

'They, whoever "they" are, obviously want Bockus out of the way. I guess he could hurt them badly if he tried to do a deal for a lighter sentence. Maybe we could use him; let it be known that he was starting to come out of the coma,' said the sergeant.

'Hmm, I don't think Fisher will be that gullible, he's bound to be suspicious,' said Stafford.

'But he may react just to be on the safe side,' said the sergeant.

'Problem is, if Bockus doesn't wake up, or if he dies, then Fisher will know we're on to him. No, I think something along the lines of, well, maybe us talking about a vehicle having been spotted behaving suspiciously down by the safe house and how we've now got to move them all again,' said Stafford.

'I think you should start using our incident room more, let him get used to you being there, then he might slip up by getting too nosy,' said Hawkins.

'Yep, I agree. Right, when you leave here and go back to the nick, we'll come by in about forty-five minutes. We'll come in to your office, then get back to work in the incident room, see if we can reel DI Fisher into our net,' said Stafford.

'Sounds like a plan, and I saw what you did there,

Staf, I saw what you did,' said Peters with a grin. Sergeant Hawkins left the café and headed back to his nick.

Stafford and Peters decided to have a bacon butty apiece before going to the police station.

They found Sergeant Hawkins in the incident room checking over the events listed in chronological order on the large white boards that took up most of one of the side walls. It showed every incident that could be linked to the recycling operation since the bomb had exploded in the transfer station. DI Fisher was alongside the sergeant explaining his latest theory. When Stafford and Peters entered, the conversation stopped abruptly.

Stafford said, 'Ah, good to see you both taking an interest. Any new suggestions or thoughts on how we can catch the bad guys?'

The DI strode out of the room and grunted, 'I thought that's what you were supposed to be working on.'

Hawkins said, 'Hiya, lads, here, come on down to the office. I'll bring you up to date with our DI's latest theories. I think you'll find them entertaining if not useful.' As they settled into the office, he closed the door behind them and said, 'Before I start, I gotta remind you this is my DI's theory, OK? ... Not that long ago, Staf, you left the military and started to work the tips. Soon after you aren't a worker anymore, you're a manager with your own site. Then two, then as if by magic, five.'

'And the DI thinks that's not right?'

'Our esteemed DI thinks you couldn't have come so far so quickly by being honest. He thinks your hands are dirty and that you've managed to start a gang war by taking the sites away from Runihura and Co.'

'Well, he's got a point, Staf,' said Peters laughing.

'Yeah, I suppose he has, I did take the sites from two incompetent bastards. But then I won the contract fair and square.'

'Apparently Fisher found out that no one else bid for the contract, so he thinks you greased palms to get them. Anyway, he tells me that he's going to do all he can to expose you as being corrupt, so be warned, Major, be warned,' said the sergeant with a wry smile.

'So he's not interested in finding out who's behind all this violence, he just wants to prove I'm a crook and get me out. Hmm, that's interesting, I wonder if that's because he wants the others back in,' said Stafford, as much to himself as the others.

'Anyway, while he was rabbiting on, I fed him the idea that the safe house had been compromised and we were thinking about moving them again,' said Hawkins. Stafford's mobile phone buzzed and vibrated, he pulled it out and excused himself. As he went into the corridor, Hawkins's desk phone rang. Stafford closed the door behind him and took his call. It was from the Hampshire Police HQ in Eastleigh. The caller explained that three members of the public had phoned from Winchester Recycling Centre in a state of panic, saying there had been a drive-through shooting. The PNC information showed Stafford as lead investigator on other recent incidents concerning crimes linked to recycling. Stafford said they were on their way and ended the call. Returning to Hawkins's office, it was obvious that his call had been about the same incident. Peters was already on his feet and with a cursory wave, they dashed out of the office and headed for the car. Peters hit the speed dial button on his cell phone. Gibson picked up almost immediately.

'Where are you Lee?' asked Peters.

'Just about to leave Winchester,' said Gibson.

'OK, now turn around and head back to the recycling centre, there's been a drive-through shooting there. Local police are attending, we're on our way, but about forty minutes out.'

'Roger, rog',' said Gibson as he fired up the Vectra, hit the blues and twos and raced out of the car park. It took Stafford and Peters nearer fifty minutes to reach the industrial estate where the tip was located. It was a no-through road and police had set up a roadblock. TV crews and other media vehicles were being allowed through to the front gates of the tip. Members of the public were being turned away. Traffic was heavy and chaotic with all types of vehicle trying to U-turn. Some drivers argued to be let through to their workplaces on the estate.

Peters asked Stafford for his warrant card, then jumped out of the car and ran past the queuing vehicles. The copper he spoke to radioed his senior officer who immediately instructed him to let them through. When they reached the front gates of the tip, uniformed policemen had secured both the in and out gates. Again they showed their warrant cards and were allowed in, and the officer told them to park on the lower deck.

They walked up the sloping semicircular perimeter road to where the public park to use the recycling bins. Three "civilian" cars were parked there. Alongside were two ambulances. The paramedics were in their ambulances and readying to drive away. As they did so, Stafford could see

Gibson and Martin standing in the sales area, talking to two grey-suited men; men Stafford recognised as the DS and DC they had encountered at Shamrock Quay. After handshakes and commiserations all round, the DS explained that there were two victims, both dead. The bodies were still on the ground where they fell. They had been covered with blue plastic sheets.

'The staff tell me that the victims are your manager, uh… Mariusz Wandoch and a member of the public, who was a regular buyer apparently,' said the DS.

Stafford felt physically sick. It seemed he'd promoted Mariusz to his death. Peters knew immediately what Stafford was thinking. Mariusz had worked with both men. Stafford, Peters and Garfield Lewis had all helped and mentored him. They had all been involved with the lanky Pole's development and had admired his attitude to people and a job that most regarded as the pits. Now he was dead and Stafford felt responsible. He knelt beside the blue cover and gently pulled it back. He could see Mariusz had been shot twice, one round hit him in the left shoulder. The second, probably the kill shot, had hit him some six inches to the right. Death would have been instant, thought Stafford. The other man was at least eight inches shorter than Mariusz, he had been hit in the throat. It would have taken him longer to die.

Stafford looked at the dead men for a moment or two, then pulled the cover back. Death was nothing new to Stafford, he'd seen it numerous times, first hand and up close. With Garfield, he had been able to compartmentalise his death. Garfield Lewis was military through and through. They'd faced death together side by side on many occasions. Garfield understood the battle and accepted the odds. But this was different; Mariusz's battle had been simple, to fight his way out of poverty, to give himself and his family to be, the chance of a better life. He was not a soldier or a military man, he was a hard-working young man aiming to better himself. His death was not the result of a fight for king and country, a noble struggle for life or death. Both these deaths were the result of a cowardly, anonymous attack on unarmed, innocent people. He promised Mariusz justice, some kind of justice.

As he stood, he realised that these shots, fired from a moving vehicle, were the work of a skilled shooter. Or a very lucky one.

According to the detective sergeant, Mariusz had four members of staff on site. It was they who had phoned the police and they had all been interviewed. The men were in the Portakabin mess hut and Stafford went in to talk to them. They were understandably shocked. They told Stafford that they had all been busy with other tasks around the site. One thing they all agreed on, was that they heard only one shot. It came as a surprise when they saw the victims had been shot three times.

Stafford guessed the shooter had used a machine pistol of some kind. That type of weapon would be able to fire 1100 or 1200 rounds per minute; or just a three-round burst. With the latter, most people would simply hear one very loud bang. This gave Stafford an indication of the make of weapon. A gun that fitted the bill and had proved itself as the weapon of choice for the military, police and crooks worldwide, was the Beretta machine pistol. It wasn't very accurate over twenty-five yards, but for close-quarter stuff it was ideal. And at under ten inches in length, was small enough to be easily concealed.

Two of the three brass casings had been collected in the gutter of the perimeter road by the forensic team. After a cursory look in the evidence bag, these, Stafford and Peters agreed, were probably 9 x 19mm parabellum, the same type used in the Beretta machine pistol. The three members of the public all stated that the vehicle in question was a black Mercedes pickup. Though none had managed to see the registration plate, they thought it was a fairly new model. Two of the three had seen the driver and the shooter, but said they were both wearing black balaclavas. These same two both commented on the driver's right hand. Apparently the hand had not been gripping the steering wheel, simply pushed against it, with the fingers described by one witness as "just two wide fingers in a grey glove." The other witness stated seeing "two thick fingers sticking out past the steering wheel, like in a bandage or plaster."

Stafford's immediate thoughts were that Floyd Winstone had taken revenge on Mariusz for taking over what had recently been his site.

Stafford asked Mariusz's assistant manager if he would take over the running of the site at least temporarily. He knew the ropes, having worked there for a year or so. He agreed and Stafford arranged to talk about making it permanent later in the week.

The forensic team had found little in the way of evidence and left, taking the empty brass casings with them, promising to contact Stafford should they reveal anything of interest. A plain black transit van from Southampton Hospital had collected both bodies and taken them for post-mortems.

Stafford and his crew left the site.

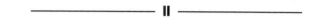

They were sitting in the incident room at the Aldershot nick. It was quiet, other officers out on different business. The mood was sombre.

'I can't help but think we're missing something here. It feels like when a word is on the tip of your tongue, but it won't come into your brain,' said Stafford.

'Have you tried the phone number that was on the paper wrapping the memory stick?' asked Nicole.

'I'm sort of leaving that as a last resort really. I guess it'll be an "are you ready to work with us now," kind of conversation,' said Stafford.

'Yeah, but it might lead to a meet where we could nab one of them,' she said.

'Hmm, I think they've shown us enough already, to know if we did that, our friends would be in real danger,' said Stafford.

'We've got files on Runihura, Kapusniak, Winstone and Bockus. We've got Saunders's phone and bank details and a great pile of stuff that the public have shipped in after Nicole contacted the media,' said Stafford.

'Yeah, that!' said Nicole. 'We've been ploughing our way through that and it's mainly just reiterating what we already know or smart-arse comments about the filth investigating the filth. We even had one that said, "What do you think of it so far?", y'know, the 1970s comedians Morecambe and Wise's catchphrase. The answer of course being…'

'RUBBISH,' they all shouted in response.

'Very droll,' said Stafford, 'however, moving on, let's divvy up these files and go through them again, including the statements from Stephanie Turnbull, Simon Peacock et al. See if we can't find something new, something we missed.'

Stafford pushed the files into the middle of the table and each in turn took a folder till the pile was gone. There was a scraping of chairs across the floor and a bit of banter as Peters and Nicole hunted for somewhere more comfortable to sit.

||

Gibson was first to speak. 'I'm gasping, I need a coffee, anyone else need one while I'm there?' he said.

Nicole got to her feet and said, 'Yeah, I need a caffeine hit, I'll give you a hand. Staf, Ry, want anything?' Both asked for coffee.

The silence was later broken, when Nicole said, 'I'm just reading about your visit to Barry Allen at the Basingstoke tip, Staf. What happened to the two guys Runihura got for him? Did they ever turn up again? Did you find out their names?' As Stafford thought about the question, Gibson said, 'I gotta say, I was only there for two days and I had a great time. If it all goes tits up here, I might well go and see him for a job.'

A moment or two passed then Stafford leapt to his feet.

'Fuck! Fuck! Fuck, why didn't I see it before?' he shouted

as he swept the folders and coffee cups on to the floor in frustration.

'What a bloody idiot, it's been staring me in the face for days. Well, since I was in Basingstoke. It's so fucking obvious, why didn't I see it before?' He sat down, hands flat on the table, shaking his head in disbelief. His colleagues looked at him wide-eyed, waiting for an explanation.

'Barry Allen,' he said. 'Barry Allen's got the key. I should have seen it straight away.' He took out his mobile phone to call the site, then realising it would be closed, put it down and said, 'Every service vehicle pulling bins out of the tips has to have a specific transfer note for the waste they are collecting. Runihura's lorry driver should have produced a transfer note to show the date and time the bin was removed. Not only that, it should show the address of the collecting company and crucially for us, where the stuff was being taken.' He shook his head with exasperation. The excitement in the room was palpable; it was the first move in a positive direction since arresting Bockus.

'Bugger. Sorry, Staf, but I should have seen that too, how on earth did we overlook that?' said Peters.

'Seems to me that we've been trying to work it from the emotional side, the killings, rather than the nuts and bolts of bin movements,' said Nicole. Stafford smiled his appreciation.

'Thanks for that, Nicky, but even more ironic is that those transfer notes will have been collated and filed in my office at home, waiting to be sent with the rest of the monthly figures to HCC. George Saunders's old department as it happens,' said Stafford.

'Look, there's nothing much more we can do here tonight, we'll call it a day and reconvene at mine in the morning,' he said as he began to pick up the mugs and folders he had swept to the floor. The others were preparing to leave when Stafford said, 'Just a thought before we go. Nicole, you're nearest, check the door for me, see if anyone's lurking.' Nicole walked across to the open door and peered out in both directions. Stafford and the others took their seats again.

'No, it's all clear, but I'll stay here and indicate if someone comes,' she said.

'Good, now, I think we can use this to bring a certain DI out into the open. What do you lot think about that?' said Stafford. There was a murmur of general agreement as they settled around the table again and began to throw ideas in for discussion.

'Maybe we should get Hawkins in on this,' said Gibson.

'Well, yeah, if he's around, he probably knows better than us what's likely to spook our man,' said Stafford. He picked up the office phone and dialled the internal number for the sergeant.

'Tony, it's Staf, any chance you could join us in the incident room?' Stafford was silent, listening, then said, 'Good, we'll see you in a moment or two,' and replaced the receiver.

'We need to convince Fisher that getting the details from these transfer notes would be the key to threatening their whole set-up,' said Peters.

'Yeah, but he isn't likely to try and steal them from Stafford's place,' said Nicole.

Hawkins walked into the room, grabbed a seat and said, 'Right, now what's all this about, I got a hot dinner waiting for me, so make it quick, yeah? Oh, sorry to hear about the shooting in Winchester, I understand you and the manager were good mates.'

'Thanks, Sar'nt, yeah, we all sort of mentored him and of course I promoted him. Poor kid only had the site for a few days.'

'Well, let's see if we can't catch these bastards then,' said the sergeant.

'We've got something we think will move us in the right direction for a change,' said Stafford and he outlined the details of the transfer notes.

'We reckon we can use this to flush out anyone working against us, and if we do that, they might open up if we offered a deal,' he continued.

'So what do you have in mind?' asked the sergeant.

'We need to act on this first thing in the morning whatever happens. So we have to try and get our suspect to act tonight,' said Stafford.

Hawkins said, 'This man isn't stupid. He's actually on shift tonight; due in shortly.' He looked at his watch, then said, 'Now these transfer notes, you say they came to you from the Basingstoke site. You do what you do with them, then bung them down to HCC, right?'

'Yeah, that's right,' said Stafford.

'And there would be more of these from other sites at HCC?'

'Yes, some from Andover, Winchester, Aldershot and Farnborough, but these would have been sent before I took over the sites and got rid of Runihura and his lot,' said Stafford.

'So to stop you finding out where this stuff was going,

these notes need to disappear from you or the HCC tonight, is that right?' said the sergeant.

'Yes, but if they are nicked from my office I can still find the details by going into the HCC,' said Stafford.

'But our man won't necessarily know that. He may think they just end up with you,' said Peters.

'Good point. So what if we let it be known that these notes are still at the Basingstoke tip and they would normally only be given to me at the end of the month to collate the figures,' said Stafford.

'But if we're going to collect them tomorrow, would that be enough time for our suspect to try and get them tonight? Would he know that the key you hold for the Aldershot and Farnborough sites also opens the Basingstoke tip?' asked Peters.

'Yeah, I'm sure he knows that, after all he started this investigation, so it's gotta be worth a shot,' said the sergeant.

'Yeah, and even if he doesn't bite, we'll still have our lead,' said Stafford.

Hawkins caught the new enthusiasm in the room and volunteered to hang around until the DI turned up for the late shift. Chairs scraped as they got up to leave, they picked up the files to take with them. Nicole collected the coffee cups to take back to the kitchen. As she reached the doorway she rattled the cups noisily, turned and mouthed the word "Fisher". As they walked out of the incident room into the corridor the sergeant said loudly, 'Well, at least you've made some progress today. Pity you can't get into the Basingstoke office tonight though, you'd have a clear run at it tomorrow then.' He headed towards his office. Stafford and crew followed. The DI was walking towards them. Stafford said to the sergeant, 'Yeah, but no real problem, we can't follow it up tonight anyway, so tomorrow will have to do.'

Fisher, walking in the middle of the corridor, moved to one side as they approached.

'Good evening, DI Fisher,' said the sergeant, slowing the whole group down, 'we've had a bit of luck with the waste investigation, I'll bring you up to date when you're ready.' Fisher paused and nodded.

'My office, Sergeant, ten minutes,' he said, Gibson and Martin's greetings went unanswered. Stafford and crew bade their farewells.

At the nick's front entrance Stafford said, 'At least you'll get an early finish tonight, Lee, you need to get home, spend some time with your family.'

They arranged to meet at Stafford's place in the morning, unless Hawkins messaged to say he thought the DI had taken the bait and was going to make a move, then they would immediately set up surveillance at the Basingstoke tip.

Nicole rode in the old Volvo with Stafford. He was out of the car almost before it rolled to a halt in his driveway. He dashed up the steps, fumbled the door open and ran into his makeshift office, Nicole just a pace or two behind. He selected the third filing cabinet in the row and opened the drawer labelled Basingstoke. There were just three transfer notes he was interested in and as he examined them he sank, cursing quietly into the nearest chair. He threw the transfer notes on the table in disgust.

'What's up? What's wrong?'

Stafford nodded towards the transfer notes without looking at her. She picked them up and saw the problem immediately.

'I wonder if that was accidental or if it was done on purpose so it would look OK at a casual glance?' she said. Slowly she went through them again, as if hoping that the black ink, smeared and totally illegible, rubber stamp marks in the address boxes, would somehow become legible. She placed a comforting hand on his shoulder and said, 'Maybe they were more complacent when they ran the sites and the earlier ones at HCC will be nice and clear.'

Stafford patted her hand and said, 'I hope so, Nic, I bloody hope so.'

They settled down and waited for Sergeant Hawkins to phone.

— ‖ —

Hawkins walked down the corridor to DI Fisher's office. The door was closed. He knocked once and walked in. The DI said, 'So what got you lot so excited?'

'We've just realised that Runihura pulled out a number of bins of electronics from the Basingstoke tip. Of course rules can be bent moving this sort of stuff, but it's likely they had legal looking documentation for each load in case they were pulled over. Either by us or the Environment Agency.'

Fisher said, 'And?'

'Yeah, well, up to now we've had no way of knowing where he's operating from. So anyway, Stafford's going down to Basingstoke tomorrow to get hold of the transfer notes, because they'll show where the company's base is and where they were taking the waste.'

'And what do they propose to do with these transfer notes?'

'They're used to collate monthly info for HCC, so it's only the addresses he's interested in. Once they have those, they'll be able to observe what's going on with the whole set-up.'

'Christ, is that it? Is that the sum total of their progress?'

'I know it doesn't seem like much, but once they have the details of where their lorries are based they should be able to figure out if it is Runihura who's running the show.'

'And you're telling me this because…?'

Hawkins screwed up his face, bemused by the question. Then said, 'You were in at the start of this investigation and when I told you earlier we were beginning to make progress, you said, "my office, ten minutes", so I thought you were interested.'

'That's all for now, sergeant,' said the DI curtly.

Hawkins returned to his office, closed the door and sat at his desk thinking about the DI's reaction to their conversation. He turned it over and over in his mind, got up and walked to the secure office behind the front reception desk. He checked the key press and located the position for the Aldershot/Farnborough HWRC gate key. The key wasn't there. Returning to his office, he closed the door, picked up the phone and called Stafford.

'Stafford? I told him what we'd agreed and his reaction was, "what you telling me for?", as if now he's off the case he wasn't interested.'

'So what's your feeling then?'

'I checked the key press, and the key's gone, so I believe he's hooked. He's up shit creek somehow and he's going to react. Me, if it were my decision, I'd be setting up surveillance.'

‖

Stafford, decision already made and about to punch in a new number, turned to Nicole and said, 'Do us a favour, organise us a couple of flasks of coffee, it looks like we're gonna have a long old night.' He dialled Peters number. He too, had been waiting by the phone and answered immediately.

'Meet us in the lay-by on Faraday Road. We'll be there in about forty minutes.'

'Roger rog',' said Peters.

Stafford and Nicole, with two flasks of coffee, headed for Basingstoke and Faraday Road.

CHAPTER 39

Fisher was sitting quietly at his desk. He got up and closed the door the sergeant had left open. He sat back down again. He toyed with the phone, picked up the receiver. Put it back down again. He took out the HWRC key from his pocket and put it on the desk top. He span it round and round with his index finger.

Making a decision, he grabbed the receiver and dialled. As he listened to the dialling tone he began to change his mind and readied to replace the handset. Then he heard, 'Yes,' from the earpiece. Startled, he said, 'Ayman?'

'Of course, and what can I do for you, Detective Inspector?' he asked, making the last two words sound weirdly pornographic.

'It seems we have a problem,' said the DI.

Receiving no response he blundered on, 'First off, this may be of use to you; Stafford has moved the black woman and her kids to a safe house in Portsmouth. If you've got a pen, I'll give you the postcode.'

Runihura took the details and said, 'So what's the problem?'

'It seems Stafford has found a way to discover your whereabouts, both your base and the factory.'

'And you're telling me this because you think a problem shared is a problem halved, is that right?' Fisher hesitated a moment.

Runihura continued, 'My friend, I should tell you that in this case, a problem shared is a problem doubled. If you don't resolve this problem, you'll have an even bigger one with me. So get it fucking sorted before it comes back on me. If that happens, DI fucking Fisher, you're done for, hook, line and fuckin' sinker!' Fisher sat in stunned silence, still holding the dead receiver to his ear. He gave an involuntary twitch and semblance of a smile as Runihura's brand of humour slowly dawned on him.

He replaced the handset gently, leaned back in his chair and began to churn the options over in his mind. He was still and silent for a very, very long moment when the answer came to him. He'd seen what they did to George Saunders. He knew if he didn't act now he would be Runihura's next victim. But he needed to sort it tonight, before his involvement was discovered by Stafford. As a disgraced DI, ending up in prison alongside people he'd banged up, he knew he wouldn't last six months.

He stood up, walked out of his office, through the station and out to his car. In his white Mondeo, he headed out of Aldershot to the M3.

———————————— ▐▌ ————————————

Lee Gibson hadn't gone home. It's not that he didn't love or want to be with his family. But they had been going through a bad patch, the job always getting in the way. For the last six weeks he'd been renting a run-down bedsit in

Aldershot's old town. It was dingy, cold and miserable. And besides, he couldn't relax when murderous bastards were out there threatening innocent people so close to home. He feared that Stafford wouldn't call him away if there was any action tonight. So he had driven out of the police station car park and positioned himself in a row of other motors where he could observe the to-ings and fro-ings of vehicles at the nick.

He recognised the white Mondeo and pulled out behind it, keeping a six to eight-car distance between them. It seemed to him that the DI was driving, maybe not erratically, but recklessly, overtaking every vehicle that got in his way. As they approached the complex road system leading on to the M3, he lost sight of the car. Feeling certain that the DI was heading for Basingstoke he joined the motorway and headed south.

Traffic was sparse, and a stretch of roadworks limited his speed to fifty mph for a couple of miles. He travelled in the outside lane and spotted the Mondeo half a mile ahead. Gibson pushed his foot to the floor and urged the motor on, but Fisher managed to stay well ahead of him. Gibson wasn't worried about losing him, he was convinced now that he was heading for the Basingstoke tip. He was sure he would meet up with him there, one way or another.

As he raced down the motorway, he couldn't get rid of the feeling that Fisher knew he was being followed. It seemed every time he got within six or eight cars of the Mondeo, it would just speed away, as though toying with any pursuers. Gibson settled in behind at a steady seventy mph. The Mondeo roared away again. It began to hit speeds of eighty, then eighty-five then ninety mph and more. Gibson, sure he'd been spotted, settled down in the nearside lane. They neared Fleet Services and the Scott Mills Bridge. It usually made him smile when he drove under this stupidly named structure.

Close enough to see lights in the windows of the covered motorway bridge, a huge blast of air rocked the car; so fierce, the steering wheel was almost wrenched from his hands. Milliseconds later a huge flash, followed by a thunderous bang, threw a fireball almost to the underside of the bridge. All around him traffic began to screech to a halt and he could hear the crunch, crunch as vehicle after vehicle began to concertina into each other. He became aware of other drivers fighting to keep their cars under control, as fragments of blazing metal flew into the road. As he neared the bridge he could see cars had stopped and drivers trying to help. Others videoed it, probably for later inclusion on social media, he thought. He pulled on to the hard shoulder, switched on his hazards and walked towards a scene of devastation.

People had phoned the emergency services. One or two had courageously tried to put out the raging fire with their in-car extinguishers, but it was too little too late. Gibson approached a man who had been driving the vehicle closest to the crash. He said the white Mondeo had hurtled past him at a speed, he estimated, of at least 110 mph. The vehicle had then swerved or steered directly at the massive concrete structure supporting the bridge. He said the driver appeared to brake at the last second, causing the rear end to fishtail and crash into the support, and the petrol tank had exploded in a fireball. The witness said it looked like the Mondeo driver was performing a stunt for a film.

There was not a hope in hell the driver could have survived.

Gibson realised he couldn't help the responding cops, as he hadn't actually witnessed the crash. Back in his car, he edged out into three lanes of slow-moving traffic heading south. This time he didn't smile as he drove under the bridge.

He turned off the motorway at the next junction and pulled into the nearest lay-by. Whilst he sat there he could hear the emergency services' sirens as they raced to the crash site. He pulled out his mobile and called Stafford.

Gibson had seen the aftermath of numerous road traffic accidents. He had dragged people out of burning wrecks, and cleared up body parts as well as debris from the roadsides. But this had shocked him badly. Not only was the dead driver one of his senior officers, but it seemed to him that DI Fisher had deliberately rammed the bridge hoping to kill himself. Gibson wondered how on earth Fisher could have found himself in such a dire situation. He took a few deep breaths to gather his thoughts. Stafford answered, 'Lee, where are you?'

'DI Fisher's dead, Staf,' he blurted out.

'WHAT? How the fuck did that happen? Where are you?'

'I'm in a lay-by just off junction 5. If you're at the tip I can be with you in about fifteen minutes.'

'We're in the lay-by on Faraday Road. Meet us there.' Gibson leaned back in his seat, took a couple more deep breaths, then fired up the motor.

As he neared the lay-by he could see Stafford and crew were all in the Volvo. He rolled up behind it and climbed into the nearside rear passenger seat. Gibson gratefully accepted the cup of coffee offered by Nicole.

'I thought you were supposed to be going home for an evening with your family, young Lee,' said Stafford.

'Yeah, I know, and I was,' he said sheepishly, 'but you know what it's like. Can't settle when bastards like these are out there threatening our families and stuff.'

'But you need to look after your family, mate, otherwise you're gonna regret it. Anyway, lecture over. Fill us in, what's been going on,' said Stafford. Gibson related the events that had occurred, starting with his parking up outside the Aldershot nick. The others listened in silence.

'So it's pretty definite he'd worked out we were on to him. I guess he thought he was fucked either way,' said Peters.

'Yeah, that's how I see it,' said Gibson, 'but how did he get in so deep with Runihura?'

'Well, there's not a lot we can do now tonight, so let's meet up at the Aldershot nick at 8 a.m. tomorrow. I've got an inkling of an idea how we can make the DI's demise work in our favour,' said Stafford. The journey home for all of them took longer than usual, DI Fisher's crash causing major delays on both sides of the motorway. Nicole hunted through Stafford's CDs and selected Leon Redbones's "Lazy River", knowing his gentle, gravelly voice would soothe their troubles momentarily.

'Good choice,' he said as they drove through the darkness.

———————— **‖** ————————

Gibson was last to leave the lay-by. When the others headed north and disappeared, he turned south and headed towards Winchester and, he hoped, the warm, comforting arms of Stephanie Turnbull.

CHAPTER 40

Runihura had a number of reasons for feeling pleased with himself. He had done a deal with Frank from the metal recycling company and now the green Range Rover Evoque and the black X-Class Mercedes pickup were in a container on their way to customers in Bosnia. He'd only pocketed a few grand for the two motors, but he knew the score well enough and had acquired a seven-year-old grey Mercedes Sprinter van as part of the deal. And on this latest trip across the English Channel they had picked up their usual supply of drugs and eight women. No men at all. Kapusniak had as usual holed the incoming inflatable craft and Winstone had this time been told to capture the "rescue" on video. Once again luck and the establishment's lack of resources were on their side. They had returned to their moorings on the Itchen without incident. Runihura, as usual, planned to stay on the boat until the morning rush hour was under way. They had raised the boat's cockpit canopy and secured the women in cabins below deck. Flipping through the women's passports, he was pleased to see that only one was over thirty. And they were all reasonably attractive, at least good enough for the clientele passing through Whitelines Nightclub.

---------------------- **II** ----------------------

The women were apparently fleeing the war in Syria, though three were from Libya. By the time they had made it halfway to France their money had run out and they were forced to sell their jewellery to survive. They spent many weeks travelling on foot, through country after country, sleeping where they could, but often sleeping rough. They competed with hundreds of other female refugees, who saw selling their bodies as the only way to earn enough money to pay ruthless traffickers for their passage to the UK, Germany or the Netherlands or any other country seen to offer a better way of life. Many perished on this journey. Some by their own hand. Those who got this far were made of stern stuff. If they were to be treated like a commodity they made sure they profited by it. It meant they stayed alive.

---------------------- **II** ----------------------

To Runihura, none of that mattered, all that mattered was that they had paid their £6,000 passage. It was a bonus if they were attractive enough to be put to work on the third floor of Whitelines. His verdict on his current passengers was, "seven out of eight ain't bad."

Once moored up, none of his crew was ever desperate enough to screw their women passengers. They'd been travelling for days, weeks even, trying to evade capture by European immigration authorities. They'd slept rough or with anyone prepared to give them a bed. They had eaten little and showered less in their quest to get through Europe to the promised land. Runihura and his men were willing to wait until the women had been showered and given clean clothes. He cursed as he realised that soon he would have to let some of the women out hunting through charity shops for more clothes. Thanks to Stafford, the stock pile they'd collected while operating the tips was rapidly running out.

Once the women were cleaned up, they would be shown the sort of work they would be doing in the promised land. This time, he promised himself, he would only take the women to Basingstoke and into Third-Floor Sheila's care, when he was ready, and had tried out at least some of the merchandise.

This night he'd acted as lookout. He wanted to get the women in the back of the van before daylight. At 5:30 a.m. he woke Kapusniak and Winstone and gave them each a bunch of heavy-duty cable ties. Unlocking the door to the berths below deck, they dragged the women from the bunks, pulled their arms behind their backs and cable-tied their wrists together. The women were compliant and quiet. Still half asleep, soaking wet, exhausted and hungry they offered no resistance.

Kapusniak picked up a torch and began to climb back into the cockpit. He turned and signalled for the women to follow. Winstone brought up the rear. Carefully they made their way along the narrow grassy footpath to the rear gate of the metal recycling compound. Kapusniak removed the padlock and led the women to the rear of the Mercedes van. He opened the back doors and ushered them in. Once inside he turned on the interior light and Winstone passed him a roll of gaffer tape. They made the women sit with their backs to the side walls, legs straight out in front. They used the tape to bind their legs together. Runihura handed

Kapusniak a length of rope with a "D" ring attached to one end. He clipped this on to a bracket just inside the left rear door. He took the other end and fed it behind the women's backs, between their arms until all eight women were linked together. He then fastened the rope to a bracket just inside the right rear door. Runihura stepped up into the van and brandishing a hypodermic syringe said, 'Any fucking noise out of you and you'll all get this. Comprenday?' He put his left hand over his mouth and waved the syringe in his right hand to ensure they got the message. He turned off the interior light, jumped out of the van and closed and locked the doors behind him. Winstone climbed into the driver's seat and reversed the van so that the rear doors were inches away from the fence. When Runihura was satisfied all was secure, the three of them returned to the boat. Runihura said, 'Jan, you're on watch, me and Floyd will get our heads down, we've got two and a half hours before we leave.'

CHAPTER 41

At eight the next morning Stafford and Co. met up in the incident room at the Aldershot nick. The mood was somber. Word of Fisher's death had permeated the place and top brass had put their own spin on things. Radio and television reports were telling about the hero cop, killed in a high-speed pursuit of bad guys. Burned to death in his car as it crashed and turned into a fireball, caused by a front tyre blowout.

Gibson had already spoken to Sergeant Hawkins and told him what the first witness had said. The sergeant said he hoped that during the course of the investigation they would find out the cause of the DI switching to the dark side.

Gibson promised to keep him updated.

***

Stafford called the group together and said, 'Me and Nicole are going to HCC's HQ in Winchester to go through their files and see if we can locate some of Runihura's transfer notes. What we find there might determine our next move, but if nothing else crops up I think we should start looking for the boat. Meanwhile, I want you two to go down to Winchester Hospital and check on Bockus's situation. We need a follow-up interview with him if at all possible. Then when you clear the hospital, check in with me, so we know what's going on. It may affect what we do next.' Ryan and Lee nodded their agreement.

'Before we go, what's this idea you were talking about last night? Any more thoughts on that?' asked Peters.

'Ah, yeah, I reckon we might be able to wind our Mr Runihura up a bit. Start making him think that his people are prepared to sacrifice them all to keep their names out of the frame.'

'So what you got in mind?' asked Gibson.

'I'm gonna have to make it up as I go along, but as soon as this bomb exploded, George gets killed, then Bockus is put out of commission and now poor old Fisher joins the list of bad guys coming to a sticky end. So I'm going to phone the number they left on that kitchen roll and just kind of poke him with a sharp stick.'

'What? Like, looks like your people are cleaning house, Ayman, two killed in action, one out of commission. Who's next, mate; Jan, Floyd or you?' said Peters.

'Yeah,' grinned Stafford, 'something like that.'

'Brilliant, it's gotta make him think about it, surely? Might just put him on the back foot for a while,' said Nicole.

'Good luck with that then, mate, we'll be in touch later,' said Peters.

When they had gone, Stafford made a few notes before he made the call. He wanted to score some hits, to goad Runihura. Psychological warfare wasn't his thing, but what the heck, he thought, it seemed to work for North Korea. He guessed that the call would go to voicemail or simply record his number as part of Runihura's control strategy. He wanted a few notes so that whenever Runihura returned the call he could stay cool and deliver a confident and cutting message, wherever he happened to be. He dialled the number; it went straight to voicemail, he said only his name and ended the call.

'Right, let's get down to HCC. I'll take my notes, you can drive, then I can give both barrels when he phones back,' he said, throwing the Volvo keys to Nicole.

The M3 was slow; volume of traffic rather than the aftermath of DI Fisher's crash. As they drove past the crash site, all that remained were a few chips in the reinforced concrete column and black scorch marks most of the way up it.

Sad how an event causing death and destruction could leave such a minor mark.

A man had died and life just carried on regardless; *doesn't seem right somehow*, he thought shaking his head.

She parked the car in the multistorey close to HCC HQ and they walked the short distance to the reception area. Stafford told the receptionist they were there to see Simon Peacock.

Peacock's secretary arrived and greeted them warmly. On their way to the office, Stafford said, 'Actually we don't need to see Mr Peacock, what we need are copies of transfer notes for the bin loads of waste electrical and electronic equipment Ayman Runihura pulled out of Basingstoke and other sites.'

'Ah, they're going to be in Mr Saunders's old office and Stephanie should be able to find you those, but we'll check in with Mr Peacock first, to let him know what we're doing.' She ushered them into Peacock's office. He rose from behind his desk, offered his hand and said, 'Please, take a seat.'

'No, that's all right, we only need a few copies of transfer notes from George Saunders's old office,' said Stafford.

'Well, that's no problem; take them up to Stephanie, would you? Let me know if you don't find what you need,' he said to his secretary.

They followed her to the next floor and into Saunders's old office. Nicole introduced Stafford to a rather tired looking Stephanie and he explained what they were looking for.

Sitting at her desk, she moved a few papers and selected a brown card folder labelled BAS. WEEE. As she handed it to Stafford she said, 'I hope this'll help you find the bastards who killed him, Major Stafford. And when you do, I wouldn't mind having a bloody go at him myself.' Stafford took the folder and said with a wry smile,

'You'll find yourself in a very long queue for that, I think, Miss Turnbull.'

He opened the folder and found exactly what he was looking for. He sat down at George's old desk and looked through the contents.

His mobile buzzed and vibrated. Pulling it from his pocket he checked the caller details. It was Ayman Runihura.

'Stephanie, would you mind giving us a few moments here, I need to take this call; perhaps you would make us copies of these, please,' he said and handed her four transfer notes. Stephanie nodded and left the office, closing the door behind her. Stafford accepted the call and put it on speaker.

'Ah, so you've decided to work with us then, Major,' said Runihura.

'What? And become another one in the row of sitting ducks,' said Stafford laughing. Runihura was silent for a moment.

'What you talking about? Sitting ducks?'

'Haven't you worked it out yet, Ayman? First you fuck up the contract and George gets killed. Then Bockus is arrested and is put out of commission and now your man on the inside, DI Fisher, has paid the price for fucking up.'

'What do you mean, Fisher's paid the price?'

'Oh, haven't you heard yet? He's dead, mate, dead. Your people are cleaning house. Who's gonna be next, Ayman, you? Kapusniak... or Winstone? My money's on you... Fuck, Ayman, I wouldn't wanna be working alongside you, mate, you're a dead man walking. You don't know where it's gonna come from, do you? Or who's gonna get to you first, me or your lot? You could be better off talking to me, mate,' said Stafford laughing as he ended the call. Stephanie came back in with the photocopies. Stafford looked at the top one and with a grin, handed it to Nicole.

'Would have liked two different addresses, but this is a good starting point.' Stephanie put the original transfer notes back in the folder and returned it to a filing cabinet in the row behind her desk.

Stafford and Nicole left the council offices and as they walked to the car, Nicole said, 'Stephanie surprised me today, she seemed a lot more ballsy than last time we spoke.'

'Yeah, I was a bit taken aback, Gibson sort of gave the impression she was a bit weepy, but she was really up for kicking the shit out of someone,' said Stafford laughing.

Nicole got into the driving seat and as she fired up the motor, turned to Stafford and with a quizzical look said, 'Did you notice where she got the Basingstoke folder from?' Stafford was preoccupied phoning Peters, 'Didn't notice, why?' ... Peters answered.

'Where are you now?' said Stafford.

'We're about to clear the hospital. There's been no change, he's still in a coma,' said Peters.

'Ah well, I guess that was always likely, so head on down to Shamrock Quay and we'll meet you there in about forty minutes, OK?'

'Roger, rog,' said Peters as he ended the call.

CHAPTER 42

I t was 8:15 a.m. when Runihura's mobile alarm woke him up. He roused Kapusniak and Winstone and told Winstone to check on their passengers and ensure the van was ready for the off. At 8:25 Runihura's "burner" phone received a call. He knew it would be Stafford and that it would go to voicemail. He tried to forget it for a while, but curiosity got the better of him. He picked it up and checked the voicemail. There was a one word message… 'Stafford.' Runihura decided to let him stew for an hour or so; he felt sure Stafford would see he'd got no alternative but to work with him.

Winstone returned a few minutes later, having opened the gates, turned the van around and found the women to be alive, if not kicking. Runihura had unwrapped the drugs and placed them in his canvas bag along with his pistol. Checking they had left nothing of value in the boat, they closed and padlocked the cockpit canopy then walked single file along the footpath to the van. Winstone clambered into the driver's seat and Runihura climbed in alongside him. Kapusniak closed and padlocked the gates behind the van as it drove out, then jumped in.

Winstone negotiated his way slowly northwards through heavy traffic to the M3. Runihura decided to leave calling Stafford for at least another half an hour. He didn't want to appear too keen. Winstone joined three lanes of slow-moving traffic on the motorway.

'Great, just what we need,' said Runihura. And he meant it. They crawled slowly to junction 10. Sitting in the queue Runihura decided that was long enough to keep Stafford waiting. He pulled out his mobile and now supremely confident, dialled Stafford's number. After four or five rings Stafford answered. After a short, mainly one-sided conversation, Runihura threw the phone to the floor and stamped on it time and time again, until it was broken into a thousand pieces.

'Fuck you, Stafford, fuck you. You're a fucking dead man, Stafford,' Runihura screamed.

'Fuck's up with you?' asked Winstone.

'Just drive the fucking van, Winstone,' said Runihura. Winstone turned off the motorway and headed to Andover and their factory. Runihura used one of his other mobiles to call ahead to Eric.

Winstone drove through the opened gates and reversed the van up to the second mobile home. Runihura clambered out after Kapusniak, pulled his canvas bag from under the seat, removed his pistol and gave the bag to Eric who had closed the gates and walked up behind them.

'Yow bredda, my man, you don't look happy, bruv. Wah Gwaan?' he said in his awful Jamaicanize.

'Fuck off, Eric,' said Runihura.

'Bumboclaat!' (arse wipe) said Eric as he walked across the yard to the lab with the canvas bag of drugs slung over his shoulder. Runihura bounded up the steps and unlocked the door to his mobile home. On the top step he turned, looked at Kapusniak and Winstone then pointed at the neighbouring mobile home, and shouted, 'You two, get those women in there and cleaned up.' He looked around the yard, then shouted at Eric, 'Has Brandon been in with another load of WEEE?'

'No, boss, I ain't seen him today, but we are almost running out in the workshop, so we're gonna need some, and soon.'

Runihura searched in his pockets and pulled out a few loose dog treats. He moved down the steps and walked across to the dog pound. Immediately the three lean Alsatians rushed over to him, tails wagging. He petted each one and threw in the dog treats. He talked to them for a minute or two before returning to his mobile home.

--------------- **II** ---------------

Winstone unlocked and opened the doors of the Mercedes van. Immediately he was hit by the stench of piss. At least two of the women had wet themselves during the journey and the back of the van was awash. Kapusniak, who had readied himself to jump into the back, screwed up his face in disgust. He hesitated, then wandered over to the covered area at the front of the factory and picked up a long-handled hook, normally used for pulling wheeled stillages. He walked back to the rear of the van, unclipped the rope that linked the women together then reached in with the hook. When it was between the nearest woman's ankles, he pulled it on to the gaffer tape and roughly dragged her across the sopping wet floor. When her feet were overhanging the back of the van, he pulled a knife from a sheath on his belt. The woman flinched, but made no sound. Kapusniak grinned at her, then cut through the gaffer tape. With her arms still bound behind her back, he pulled her off the van and pushed her across to Winstone. Winstone half dragged, half walked her through the door of the mobile home. Kapusniak dragged the rest of the women out in the same way, across the rivers of urine that now covered most of the floor. Then, with a look of disdain at their smell, shoved six of the women over to Winstone. The seventh he half dragged into the mobile home, through the hall and into the kitchen.

Winstone had pushed the women through the narrow hallway into the living room and cut off the cable ties. There was a lot of wrist rubbing, mumbling and groaning as the circulation returned to their hands.

'Anyone speak English?' he asked.

One woman, who looked no older than eighteen or nineteen, said meekly, 'I can, a little.'

Winstone pulled her out of the group and into the kitchen. 'You all take off your clothes, put into washing machine,' he said, then grabbed her by the arm and pulled her to a shower room.

'You wash here.' He pushed her along the hallway to a small bedroom. It had two sets of bunk beds and the bottom beds were piled high with clean, second-hand clothes.

'Put clothes on and when you've done that there's food in the kitchen cupboards,' he said. She returned to the living room and explained to the other women what they were to do. Winstone left them to it.

'This one,' Kapusniak said to Winstone on his way past, 'can wash out the back of the motor so we can use it this afternoon for the deliveries.' He cut the cable ties from her wrists, pulled out a bucket from under the sink and thrust it into her hands. He dumped a scrubbing brush and a box of soap powder into the bucket. The circulation hadn't properly returned to her hands and she dropped the bucket to the floor. Kapusniak slapped her across the face with the back of his hand.

'Bitch, now pick it the fuck up, fill with water and clean fucking van.'

When the van's load space had been cleaned to Kapusniak's satisfaction he took the woman by the arm and ushered her to the front door of the mobile home. The door was locked and as he fumbled for his key, she dropped the cleaning stuff and made a dash for the main gate. Kapusniak watched her go, a look of mild amusement on his thin face. He walked towards the dog pound, opened the gate and let just one of the dogs out. He said one word, 'Fetch.'

The dog raced across the yard and reached the woman yards before she got to the gate. With teeth bared the dog sprang at her and hit her mid back. She crashed to the ground with the dog straddling her, savaging the back of her head. The dogs in the pound barked angrily, frustrated they weren't in on the action.

Kapusniak whistled once and the dog returned to him. He patted it, said, 'Good dog,' and let it back into the pound. Winstone, who had driven the van across the yard to the laboratory, walked to the woman, took hold of her right arm, rolled her over then pulled her to her feet. He half dragged the terrified, weeping female back to Kapusniak, who punched her full in the face. The blood from the rips in her scalp mingled with the blood from her nose as he pushed her roughly into the mobile home.

Wordlessly Kapusniak and Winstone walked back to the van and finished sticking the Southern Washroom Services signs on it.

They loaded the van with bins of various drugs and two bins of Eric's latest DVD. A "snuff" film, showing in not very glorious technicolor, George Saunders's multiple rape, beheading and dismemberment. Eric came out of the lab and said to Kapusniak, 'That's your lot, mate, give me a sec and I'll open up the gates for you.' Kapusniak and Winstone climbed into the van and drove out to start their deliveries.

II

Though Runihura had showered and changed his clothes, his mood was no better. He poured himself a drink, sat down in the tiny kitchen and thought about what Stafford had said. He had to admit there was a lot of truth in it. Fair enough, he earned plenty of money, but he did all the dirty work and took all the risk. But he knew he'd come too far to stop. He had to finish what he had started. Get control of Stafford's company one way or another, even if it meant killing the bastard. Then he remembered that Fisher had given him the postcode of the safe house in Portsmouth. Maybe he should check it out. *Maybe use the black bitch or one of her kids for leverage,* he mused.

CHAPTER 43

As Nicole drove into Shamrock Quay, the horror of seeing Lewis's damaged body being pulled out of the river, flashed into her mind. She battled hard to put the terrible images to one side so she could concentrate on finding the perpetrator. She began to think out loud, 'I'm going to drive down to "F" pontoon and if we don't see Lee and Ryan, I'll come back round and park facing the entrance.'

'Can't see them anywhere yet,' said Stafford, as he peered out and looked around the quay. Nicole completed the circuit, chose a spot where two cars could park next to each other and rolled to a stop.

Moments later the Vauxhall Vectra driven by Peters parked alongside. Ryan and Lee got into the Volvo.

Stafford asked, 'So what's the situation now with Mr Bockus?'

'Looks like they're gonna pull the plug any day now. From what the doctors were saying, the chances of him waking up are minimal. They're keeping him on life support for a bit longer, hoping for a miracle, but no one seems to think it will happen,' said Peters.

'So that's the end of him doing any deal then, except maybe with the Devil,' said Stafford.

'Guess he's already done that,' said Nicole.

'Anyway, the better news is, we now know, or think we know, where Runihura's lorries were working from. The transfer notes show the address as Southampton Metal Recycling, just round the corner from here, but it also shows SMR as the receiving depot,' said Stafford.

'Yeah, we think that's a bit odd, because their website shows them dealing with bigger items, you know, like cars, trucks and washing machines, stuff like that,' said Nicole.

'So it looks as though they are keeping the smaller stuff specifically for Runihura. Anyway, we need to work out a surveillance rota to see what goes on,' said Stafford.

'Do you want to use both cars?' asked Peters.

'Yes, we looked on Google Maps and there's plenty of places to park close by, so if you follow us round I'll show you the area where I want you to check, and we'll shoot off to the other side of SMR and check that out,' said Stafford.

'The satellite view shows that one and a half sides of SMR's yard is on the river, so there's ample room to park a boat,' said Nicole as she fired up the Volvo.

As Ryan and Lee returned to the Vectra, she drove towards SMR and found a couple of spaces in a Chinese supermarket parking lot. Peters drew up alongside and they both got out of the car. Stafford joined them and said, 'If you walk down this street as far as you can, you'll see SMR at the end there. See what's going on, take pictures if you see anything interesting. We'll come back to this place when we've done our recce, OK?' Ryan and Lee nodded. Peters locked the Vectra and they wandered off in the direction of SMR. Stafford and Nicole drove the two minutes to Saxon Wharf, and parked up.

As soon as she stepped out of the car she could hardly contain her excitement. The road continued through the wharf past a long modern "shed" that housed a number of maritime businesses, right down to the water's edge. She bounced up and down, exasperated, as she waited for Stafford to join her at the side of the car.

'Yes,' he said grinning, 'I can see where you're looking and it looks very much like there's a motor launch moored right alongside the fence of SMR. We'll walk down to the end of this row of businesses and see what we can see from that far corner, without going past the yard.' They walked, well, Stafford almost had to run to keep up with her, past the six or seven businesses. At the last one they peered around the corner of the building. Clearly visible were the rear gates to SMR's yard. A high chainlink fence ran from the gates to the end of the compound, some seventy-five yards away. The last twenty-five yards or so of the fence were half hidden by scrubby bushes. Between the fence and the river was a narrow grassy bank, with a well-trodden footpath leading to the boat moored alongside. Parked a few yards inside the compound was a hook loader lorry with "Metal Recycling" and a mobile number on the door. Other similar lorries were moving in the yard, emptying their bins into the various bays. These lorries all had the SMR logo, landline number and website details. Stafford pulled out his mobile and took a picture of the gates and the stationary lone vehicle. Further down on the opposite side of the road, was a slipway going down to the river and a wooden pontoon alongside it.

Land side, and a little to the left of the slipway, a motor launch rested on supports, the boat obviously in the process of being restored. Stafford pointed to this and said, 'If we get down to that pontoon and stand facing the boat being repaired as if we were talking about it, we could take some pictures of the boat moored up by the yard.'

'Yeah, let's go for it.' She grabbed his arm and started to walk him down towards the pontoon. Stafford still had his mobile phone out and as they got closer, clicked off a couple of pictures. He walked on to the pontoon, turned and pointed his mobile at the motor launch tied up to capstans by SMR's fence.

'Jesus! That looks like the boat on George's computer, but it's called the *Cleopatra*. I'll zoom in on the name plate, see if that'll show us anything.'

He had taken a number of shots when he heard a loud voice say, 'Can I help you people?'

Nicole turned and gave the man who the voice belonged to a beaming smile and said, 'Yes, sorry, we got a bit carried away there, my dad owns a boat rather like this one you're fixing up, and his needs a lot of work doing to it, so I thought we'd come and take some pictures to show him the good work you do.' The ruddy-faced man appeared to be in his early sixties. He was wearing a carpenter's apron over baggy jeans and a tee shirt. He thought for a moment, then said, 'Why don't you come into the office and I'll give you one of our brochures explaining what we can do.'

'That would be great, thank you,' she said, then turning to Stafford, 'I won't be a moment, darling.' Stafford smiled and followed them back to the office. Ten minutes later Nicole shook hands with the ruddy-faced man and promised she would give her father all the information and persuade him to contact them. It seemed to Stafford that she had gained a new fan. As they walked back to the car, he said, 'Well done you, that sounded like a very convincing spiel.' Nicole stopped in her tracks, Stafford walked on a pace or two before he realised she wasn't alongside.

'What makes you think it was just a spiel then, Major Stafford?' she asked straight-faced. Stafford, unable to come up with a sensible answer, shrugged and with ears starting to go red, continued to walk to the car. Nicole drove them back to the Chinese supermarket, where Peters and Gibson were already waiting, leaning against the side of the Vectra. As Nicole pulled up, they climbed into the back of the Volvo.

'What's up, lads? You don't look too happy,' said Stafford.

'Not much to report at all, boss, I'm afraid. It all looked pretty normal to us. Though we did spot a bay where they appeared to be dumping all the smaller electrical and electronic items. I took a few pictures, not sure if it tells us much though,' said Peters.

'Oh, I don't know, I think it tells us quite a lot. It tells us that Runihura still has a supply of the goods he's after. Albeit a smaller quantity than when he had the tips, but add that to what we've seen over the other side of the yard and I think we're beginning to make some headway.'

Stafford and Nicole outlined what they had seen and showed the pictures they had taken. Stafford had already used his mobile to send the pictures to his computer. Later they would make prints and enlarge the images to examine them in greater detail.

'So what's our next move?' asked Gibson.

'Hmm, I'd like to get on board that boat and have a look around. There's a couple of ways we could do that without getting a warrant. We could call in customs or the border force. To be honest, I'm so tempted just to go and do it, but I think we need to proceed with all caution and do it by the book. And we really need to do it when all these businesses are closed. So, Lee, you and me are going to head back to Eastleigh nick and organise search warrants. I'd prefer to go back to Aldershot, but we need a DI and a magistrate to sign it, so timewise Eastleigh's best.'

'And you've got DCI Talbot there, he knows about Runihura and was pretty pissed off that Fisher let him off the hook, so he'd be sure to sign off on it,' said Nicole.

'Me and Nic'll keep watch from Saxon Wharf, and if anything moves in or out we'll do whatever we can to keep it under surveillance,' said Peters.

'Yep, I guess that's about the size of it for now. I'll come back and give you a bit of a break when we've got the search warrants in hand,' said Stafford. Gibson was about to say something when Stafford jumped in, 'And you, Gibbo, when we've done this warrant, you are going home for an early night, and no argument. And I said no argument,' he said with a grin as Gibson began to object.

'OK, boss, whatever you say,' he said not looking best pleased.

Even with the help of another police sergeant, it took Stafford and Gibson over an hour to complete the search warrant and application form before DCI Talbot was satisfied enough to sign off on it.

They presented the documents and their case details to a Justice of the Peace taking a lunch break at Winchester magistrates' court and twenty-five minutes later they arrived back at the Eastleigh nick with a "live" warrant. Stafford had spoken earlier to the DCI about sending forensic techs down to the boat once the documents had been made official. When they returned to Talbot's office, he read through the warrants carefully and said, 'OK, Major, leave it with me. You say Acting DS Martin and Captain Peters are down there now?'

'Yes; I'll jot down Captain Peters's mobile number for your men. They're on Saxon Wharf in a Vauxhall Vectra, but ideally I'd like the search done this evening, when all the local businesses are closed.' He paused for a moment then said, 'I appreciate your help, DCI Talbot, I will of course keep you up to date with our progress.'

As the two men shook hands, Talbot said, 'You're going to need more men at some stage if you're planning 24/7 surveillance, and when you need to take further action. So at that stage call me on this number.' Stafford took the offered card and put it in his wallet.

'That's good to know, and again, thanks,' he said.

Once they were back in the Volvo, Stafford called Peters. 'Any movement down there?'

'No, all quiet at present, boss,' said Peters.

'Good, well, we've got the warrants, I've left them with the DCI. He's organising a couple of forensic techs to come down and help with the search. They'll have your number if they can't find you. Tell them it's imperative we leave the boat as we find it, we don't want to leave any sign we've been in, OK?'

'Yep, point taken, I'll make sure of that.'

'Right, I'm gonna take Gibbo' back to Aldershot and I've told him to be back down with you at 07:30 tomorrow. I've got to sort out a few things up there and I'll be down with you in a couple of hours. Keep me up to speed meanwhile.'

'Roger, rog,' said Peters ending the call.

Parked up at the Aldershot nick, Stafford left Gibson in the car park after again telling him to go home. He went straight into the squad room and fired up the nearest computer. Getting up the pictures from Saxon Wharf, he printed a number of copies of the *Cleopatra*, then enlarged the name plate and printed off a couple more. In the enlarged picture, it was obvious that the name *Cleopatra* was on a computer-generated plastic stick-on sign. The left-hand end with the letter "C" sat cleanly just below the top edge of the hull. Protruding from underneath the sign on the right-hand side, were two parallel lines about five inches apart, joined at the end by another line at right angles. Exactly halfway between the lines and inside the end line was what appeared to be a screw hole. It looked to Stafford as though something had been removed and the *Cleopatra* sign stuck in the same spot, without the dirt being cleaned away first. Next he brought up on screen the pictures of the boat from George Saunders's computers and printed off copies. The boats seemed identical, except for the name. There were identical scuff marks in what appeared to be the same places along the hull. The position, quantity, shape and colour of the fenders on both boats were exactly the same. He enlarged the *Whitelines* name plate. This appeared to be a block of white-painted, chamfered wood, neatly sign-written in gold copperplate lettering. He made a print of this and it seemed as though this sign would fit exactly into the marks left underneath the plastic *Cleopatra* sign. Stafford was convinced the *Cleopatra* and *Whitelines* were the same boat. Stafford called Peters again. 'Any movement?'

'No, still quiet down here, boss.'

'No one's moved the hook loader with that mobile number on it, then?'

'No, the yard itself seems pretty busy, but nothing happening to the bits we're interested in.'

'OK, look, when the techs arrive, can you get them to check out the *Cleopatra* signs, because from the pictures it looks like they've taken the original ones off and stuck plastic ones over the site of the others; see what they make of it?'

'Yeah, no worries, Staf, so over and out.'

'Oh, before you go, I'm going to call into the tips before I come down to you They've all sounded positive when I've spoken to them, but I think it's time I showed my face again. But I'll be down asap.'

'Roger, rog,' said Peters.

It was a couple of hours before Stafford returned to Saxon Wharf. The metal recycling yard had closed for the day. The car park had emptied as the other businesses had shut up shop.

Nicole and Peters were now desperate for a pee and the coffees Stafford brought with him.

Two forensic techs arrived in a small unmarked white van. Both had been part of the team involved in the Shamrock Quay search. After greetings all round, Stafford took the search warrant from them and said, 'There's no one here for us to present this to, so I'll hang on to it until I can give it to the right person.'

Knowing Peters's skill for picking locks would be needed, Stafford decided to stay with Nicole and keep watch from where the Vauxhall Vectra was parked. He turned to the two techs and said, 'OK, guys, I guess you have a video cam in your kit, can you video the whole search, starting with a close-up of the search warrant. Then of Ry… er, er, Captain Peters opening the cockpit padlocks and then the complete interior, before you start doing your fingerprint stuff?' The way they responded was enough for Stafford to register they meant, we know what we're doing, mate.

Stafford and Nicole left them to it and withdrew to the parking area.

──────────── **II** ────────────

The techs donned their protective suits, gloves and booties and found a set for Peters. The cockpit had padlocks on both sides of the stern, but it took Peters no more than twenty seconds to open each of them. The tech with the digital video camera went in alone, after shouting a cursory, 'POLICE, COMING ABOARD.' Ten or twelve minutes later he came back into the cockpit and waved for Peters and the other tech to join him. It was obvious to Peters as he stepped aboard that this was a quality boat. The well-appointed cockpit had fitted, plush leather seating. The hand rails were brass and the high gloss surfaces were, Peters thought, polished walnut.

The first tech pointed out to Peters a pile of screwed up, thick blue-polythene sheeting and waxed brown paper pushed out of the way under the dashboard. He said, 'This looks like the sort of wrapping we see around blocks of compressed cocaine and heroin. We'll pull it out, take some swabs and a small sample piece of each; they'll never know we've moved it.'

They found lots of areas that had good retrievable fingerprints. Below deck they also found a locked, fitted, metal security box. The waterproof sort, used to store items such as distress flares. Peters asked the tech to film him opening the box's two locks. These locks were more of a challenge, but he still managed to open them in less than four minutes. As he swung the door open, he was not surprised to see an opened pack of twelve-gauge Orion distress flares and lying next to them was a bright orange-plastic Heckler and Koch signal pistol. Peters pulled out his mobile and took a number of pictures of the items in place.

'God, I hope you can get some decent prints off those two items,' said Peters.

'We'll do our very best,' said the second technician with a grin.

'Well, it could be that's the pistol used to kill our mate over on Shamrock Quay, so I can't tell you how much we want a result off it.'

Peters sent a picture to Stafford, with a caption saying, "Keeping everything crossed for prints, can't believe they left it here, let alone kept the bloody thing."

The tech said, 'We should be able to compare these flares to the one taken from your colleague. I'll take pictures of the flares and the box, at the very least we'll be able to compare batch numbers.' Peters nodded and went below deck, to stay out of their way as they worked in the confined space.

He walked into a cabin and sat on the lower bunk. The bedding was grubby and wet. The cabin didn't smell of urine or mould. He stood up, took off one of his forensic gloves and patted the bottom sheet, duvet and pillow. They were all wet. Not sodden, but more than damp. He reached up to the top bunk; it too was wet. He walked into the other cabins and found those with bunk beds all had wet linen. Two other cabins with beds had cleaner and dry bed linen. As there were no obvious signs of a leak in the ceilings above the beds, it was, Peters thought, safe to assume that the beds had been used by people in wet clothes. He explained what he'd found to the techs and they came to the same conclusion. In the larger of the two dry-bed cabins, tech number two opened a storage cabinet and found two white wooden boards, two and a half feet long by five inches wide, neatly sign-written *Whitelines*, in gold copperplate lettering. Peters pulled out his mobile phone and sent pictures to Stafford, his excitement palpable as he texted the caption "no doubt now!".

Shortly after this they concluded their search. The three of them replaced everything exactly as it had been, using video playback where necessary. Every surface they had tested for fingerprints was wiped clean. Peters walked slowly through the boat one last time to make sure everything was just as they found it. The technicians packed up their equipment and disembarked while Peters closed and re-padlocked both sides of the cockpit canopy. They returned to the car park where Stafford and Nicole had got out of the car to meet them. Even Peters, who had seen it all before, was buoyed up, excited.

'Bloody hell, Staf, I never expected to get such brilliant confirmation,' he said as he pulled out his mobile and clicked on to the picture of the polythene wrapping and waxed brown paper. He gave the phone to Stafford who showed it to Nicole.

'The lads here say that's the type of packaging used for wrapping compressed blocks of heroin and cocaine. If it can be confirmed, then they've used the boat for transporting, probably even smuggling drugs.'

'OK, Major Stafford, we'll get this stuff down to the labs and check it out. We'll get back to you as soon as we get results. I'll email the video to you as well. We've got some good fingerprints, so let's hope we can find some match-ups,' said tech number one. They put their gear in the van and left.

'What's next on the agenda?' asked Peters.

'I don't think much is going to happen down here tonight, so Nicole, if you take the Volvo and shoot off. Get your head down for a few hours, and get back here 07:30 tomorrow, OK?'

'Yep, fine by me, but Ryan, do you want me to pick you up a pizza and a coffee before I disappear?' she asked.

'Bloody good idea, girl,' said Peters pulling out his wallet.

'Nah, this one's on me, so what do you fancy?'

CHAPTER 44

Unable to settle, Runihura had paced around his mobile home most of the night. He couldn't sleep. *Why the fuck won't they listen?* he thought. *I told them it was stupid to expect Stafford to roll over and work with us. Stafford's fucked though, making me lose face like that.*

'Bastard's gotta die,' he said out loud. But he knew it was no good just killing Stafford, he would have to bury that posh twat, Peters, and anyone else working with him. But he knew with Stafford's contacts and blue-eyed-boy status at HCC, it would be so much better to have him alive and working with the syndicate. In the back of his brain he could feel the germ of an idea. He wandered through to the living room and switched on his laptop computer. Finding the note with the postcode DI Fisher had given him earlier, he entered it into Google Maps. Fisher had seemed certain that the black guy Lewis's wife and kids were there. Using the satellite image, Runihura zoomed in on the house. *Maybe*, he thought, *just maybe he could snatch one of the kids. That surely would be enough to focus Stafford's mind.* He knew he couldn't do it alone. He would need a couple of men and some weapons.

—————————— ❚❚ ——————————

Over the last few months, since he began to have doubts about "urban fucking mining", he'd managed to buy a considerable number of weapons and ammo. Ten machine pistols, half a dozen rifles, a number of revolvers and even half a dozen hand grenades. He'd smuggled them in alongside the immigrants and drugs. Kapusniak, Winstone and Bockus, and his "lieutenants" who had proved their worth, knew how to use the weapons. The cooks, club doormen, lab staff, drivers and even the yard guys, he had selected because they were ex-military or mercenary and knew weapons. He bustled into the living room, closed the door behind him, walked across to the windows and closed the curtains.

Kneeling down on the floor behind the door he reached into the far corner and lifted the edge of the carpet. He pulled it back far enough to clear a three-foot-square trapdoor. He opened it, revealing the cavity created to hide the mobile home's wheels and chassis. He laid down on the floor, peered inside and with some pride, looked at the half a dozen wooden boxes stored there. Khaki with white stencilled signs, grey with black markings. Boxes from America, Bosnia and Yugoslavia, all containing weapons or ammunition.

'I think we're gonna be needing you soon, my little beauties,' he said out loud. He closed the trapdoor, smoothed the carpet back down, sat there for a few minutes with his back against the wall, and decided that he needed to get down to Portsmouth and do a recce... Then he thought, *why is it, when I think about killing someone, I always get horny? Well, at least I can do something about that.* Grinning he clambered up from the floor and wandered through the narrow hallway to the front door. Making sure he had his keys, he left his mobile home and walked the few yards across to the adjacent one. Finding the key in his bunch, he let himself in.

As he stood inside the front door he could hear sounds of despair. Someone was crying quietly, somebody else was snoring and two girls were murmuring quietly to each other in a language he couldn't make out. He looked into both bedrooms. It went silent as he walked in. Most of the women pretended to be asleep, some were huddled together, maybe for warmth, maybe for comfort. In one bedroom he pointed at what he considered to be the two most attractive women.

'You two, come with me,' he said as he pulled the bed covers off. They were both still fully clothed, but their feet were bare. They looked frightened and bewildered as they climbed slowly down from the bunk beds. He grabbed the nearest girl by the arm and frogmarched her down the hallway. The other girl followed. The three of them stepped outside. He locked the front door behind them and they walked the few paces across the yard to his unit. He ushered them into the hallway and down the little corridor to his bedroom. He closed and locked the door, then turned to the older girl and said, 'Undress her.' Not understanding, she looked at him, her brown eyes wide with fear and she shrugged her shoulders. He reached out and the girl flinched as he undid the top button of her shirt. He put the other girl's hands on the buttons.

'Undo, undo, take clothes off, comprenday?' he said. He sat down on the bed and kicked off his shoes. He lay back and watched the girl slowly being undressed. By the time she was naked, he was rock hard. He pulled his prick out of his trousers, grabbed the naked girl's arm and dragged her on to the bed. He pushed her head down to his genitals. She knew what she was supposed to do, and she did it with only a moment's hesitation. The other girl began to undress. Runihura lay back and watched. Their training had begun.

This part of their training lasted two hours. The girls had done all that he had demanded. The tears, blood and bruises bore testament to their initial reluctance to carry out some of his demands. When he had finished, he picked up some of their clothes and threw them at them.

'Get dressed,' he said. Tears streamed down their faces as they hurriedly complied. They followed him back to the second unit. He opened the door and they ran inside, weeping. He locked up and returned to his own place. Now he was tired, he lay on the bed and said out loud, 'Fuck it, Tony can do the boat run tomorrow night, I'll be too fucking knackered, I'll just take the women up to Whitelines, then drive down to Portsmouth.' With that he slept the sleep of the dead.

CHAPTER 45

The following morning Nicole and Gibson arrived at Saxon Wharf within minutes of each other. They found parking spaces and ambled over to the Vauxhall Vectra. Nicole was carrying a Tesco's "bag for life" and four Starbucks cardboard coffee cups in a little cardboard tray. She opened the Vectra's driver door and handed Stafford and Peters a coffee, then slid into a rear seat as Gibson climbed in the other side.

'Ah, well done you. Good grief we needed this. What a goddamned boring night. All that moved was bloody Ryan in the back there, fidgeting and farting around.'

'I wasn't fidgeting,' protested Ryan. 'So where are the donuts?'

'As it happens, in my shopping bag,' she said pulling out a brown paper bag with five jam donuts.

'Oh, by the way, Nicky, did I tell you how particularly lovely you look this morning, even at this early hour, unlike your scruffy friend alongside you, who obviously got dressed in the dark,' said Stafford.

'Creep,' she said with a grin, hoping maybe he meant it more than a joke. She took a donut out and passed the bag to Stafford. Gibson gave a rueful smile, said nothing and absentmindedly rubbed his stubbly chin.

The car park was already almost full, as workers in the retail and industrial units nearby arrived to start their daily grind.

'So all's been quiet in Saxon Wharf then?' asked Nicole.

'Yep,' said Stafford, 'and I refuse to say anymore until I finish this donut, or I'll have jam and sugar all over my shirt.'

'Anyway, what's up with you, Gibbo; kids keep you up all night?' asked Peters.

'Hmmn, something like that,' Gibson replied through a mouthful of donut.

'Well, must have been some night, Lee, you look even worse than those two in the front, and they've been on watch all night,' said Nicole.

After washing down the last bite of his donut with a swig of coffee, Gibson said with a half smile, 'Don't have to worry about me, I'll be right as rain when the caffeine and sugar kick in.'

'So you're OK if me and Ryan disappear for a few hours kip and a clean up?' asked Stafford. Receiving a couple of yeses, Stafford said, 'Let's have the keys to the Volvo then, Nic, you hang on to the Vectra for now.' They exchanged keys, seats, cars and goodbyes, then Stafford and Peters headed for the M3.

'D'you wanna get your head down in the back for a while?' asked Nicole.

'No, I said I'll be OK,' snapped Gibson.

'Suit yourself, I was only asking.' They sat in silence,

heads facing front, eyes fixed on the boat and rear gates of the scrap yard. Ten minutes passed.

'You gonna eat that last donut?' asked Gibson sheepishly. Nicole couldn't help but grin as a naughty schoolboy image flashed through her mind.

'No, you have it if you want.'

'I didn't have time for breakfast.'

'Lee, you can have it, you don't need to explain.' The donut disappeared in three bites.

As Gibson was wiping the sugar from his hands on to his jeans, a black Mercedes pickup pulled up alongside the hook loader lorry in the metal recycling yard. Nicole hit the camera button on her phone and with two fingers enlarged the image so the number plate was readable, then fired off a number of shots. As the driver got out and walked around the front of the Mercedes, Nicole managed to get a number of pictures, including one or two good head shots. Neither she nor Gibson recognised the blonde-haired IC1 male, who looked to be in his thirties. He was wearing jeans and what Gibson insisted was the Southampton FC, home football shirt. They watched as he climbed into the hook loader lorry. After a few moments settling in he fired up the engine. Gibson decided to take a closer look. He got out of the car and with mobile to his ear, walked slowly towards the rear gates. He stopped and waved his free hand around as though he was explaining something to a particularly dumb caller. The lorry driver reversed up to a twenty-foot-long metal bin and expertly manoeuvred the vehicle and hook into place. In one smooth movement he pulled the bin on to the back of the lorry and continued across the yard to a bay where a pile of small electrical and electronic equipment had been dumped. As he rolled to a halt, a mechanical shovel scooped up around a third of the pile and tipped it into the lorry's bin. Two more scoops cleared the lot.

Gibson had managed to take pictures of the action. The driver of the shovel gave a single blast on his horn to indicate job done, then drove away to load other lorries. Gibson hurried back to the car. As he climbed in he said, 'Quick, Nicky, I think he's gonna drive on to the weighbridge, pick up his transfer notes and be off.' She started the motor, rolled out of Saxon Wharf, and turned right heading for the junction. She pulled into the forecourt of a motorcycle business, where they could watch for the lorry to pass. Gibson said, 'It's no good, girl, we can't just leave the boat. You follow the lorry, I'll watch the boat from my car.'

'Good thinking. Christ, here's the lorry now. Talk soon,' she said as Gibson bailed out.

She waited a couple of heartbeats, then pulled out behind it. She knew to stay at least five or six cars behind the lorry. It was still before 9 a.m and traffic was heavy. She guessed he was aiming for the M3. She was right, but eventually the lorry left the motorway and joined the A34.

This was unfamiliar territory to her. She saw a sign saying Andover, but the lorry rolled on past it. They continued on through a little hamlet and the lorry took the first exit on a mini roundabout at the end of the village. Traffic now was very sparse and Nicole had to hang back, first 150 yards, then 200 yards. A mile or so further, on the lorry indicated a right turn and seemed to disappear into the front garden of a brick bungalow almost hidden behind a tall hedgerow. Nicole slowed and peered in through the front entrance. She caught a glimpse of the bungalow, but no lorry. She continued on past and after a few hundred yards came to a T-junction. She pulled out, did a U-turn and headed back towards where the lorry had disappeared. She approached the gates cautiously and peered to her left. All she could see was the side of the bungalow and a long concrete drive ending at a high brick wall. She drove on for a half mile or so, then turned left into a little service road. She rolled to a halt and pulled out her mobile, she called Stafford and tried to explain where she was, but he cut her short and said, 'Look, Nic, drive back into Andover, and find the tip. I'll meet you there in about forty-five minutes. OK?'

'Yep, no problem, boss, see you shortly.' She followed the signs back to Andover and found the tip without too much bother. She didn't know any of the people working there. After parking up she wandered down to the Portakabin office and introduced herself to the Polish manager and explained she was meeting Stafford there.

It took Stafford a little over fifty minutes to get there. He parked next to the Vectra, and waved hello to a couple of workers as he walked to the office. Tomasz Lewandowski, the manager, brought Stafford up to date with the business of the tip.

'He must make a fortune you know, this Jan Kapusniak,' he said.

'In this game, Tomasz, nothing unusual in that,' said Stafford with a grin.

'No, but we get lots of people, not all in car. Some walking, some on bikes. All want to see Kapusniak. All want to find him. They say, "need to score", I find out it means drugs, they all want drugs, sometimes ask for DVD,' he explained in his accented English.

'Hmm, we guessed he and the other ones we got rid of were into drug dealing. It is pretty good cover, much less risk than street corners or nightclubs. Most people assume we're council workers, never even think about drug dealers, so that would work in their favour,' said Stafford. Then turning to Nicole, he said 'Right, d'you reckon you can drive us to this place you found?'

'Yeah, I got the postcode from Google Maps, so if we get lost I can always find it again.'

They left the tip in the Vectra and drove out of the industrial estate to the ring road. It took just ten minutes to the little hamlet. At the mini roundabout, Nicole took the first exit and said, 'When you see the garden centre on the left we'll have about half a mile to go. Then if you look to the right, you'll see a long run of very tall hedges and then a large entrance. All I could see was a bit of the bungalow and a long concrete drive, up to a brick wall.'

They cruised slowly down the incline towards the property. Stafford pulled out his mobile.

'Don't worry, I'll turn round at the bottom of the hill and you'll be able to see it better on the way back up.'

'And you're sure that's where the lorry turned in?'

'Can't see another place with an entrance big enough, can you?' she said curtly.

Stafford looked at her and grinned, 'I didn't mean it quite like it came out.'

'So how did you mean it then?' Stafford pretended to check his phone's camera, thinking, *why do I end up tying myself in knots around her?*

Nicole turned the car around and drove slowly back up the hill. Stafford held up his phone and videoed the property as they drove by. At the top of the hill, Nicole pulled into the service road she had used earlier.

'So what do you think, boss?'

'What I think is, we sit here, well out of the way for a while and see if the lorry comes back out. I'm gonna give Talbot in Eastleigh a ring, see if he can galvanise his troops to pull our man over on the motorway, and arrest him on suspicion of breaking some law or other, we're bound to be able to find one,' said Stafford as he pulled out his mobile.

'But he may have left already.'

'Yeah, but no matter, the sooner I phone it in the better, we have his registration number, we know he comes out of the depot in Southampton, so we'll get him sooner rather than later.' As he spoke, he was keying in the DCI's number. Talbot answered and Stafford outlined what he needed, 'Oh yes, if they can't find anything wrong with the lorry or driver, then there are any number of ways they could use the Environment Agency's regs to muddy the waters,' he said, then, 'Yeah, get them to look up "false or misleading information", from, I think it's *The Hazardous Waste Regs 2005*, section 10; something in there should do it,' said Stafford laughing. 'Well, you might even be able to get one of the EA patrol vans to help in the stop, they have the power to confiscate the vehicle and their assistance would be invaluable. OK, DCI Talbot, that's great, we're going on to the Andover tip now, to check out Google Satellite pictures of the compound, and we'll try to get some surveillance pictures we can use to see how best to gain access... oh, hang on just a minute... yep, here it is, the lorry has just this minute gone past us, so I guess he'll be on the motorway in about forty minutes,' said Stafford ending the call.

'I hope that's enough time for him to put wheels in motion.'

'With the the finest police force in the world, of course it is!' she said with a laugh. 'So, where to now, boss?'

'I think we'll go back to the recycling centre, get Tomasz's laptop fired up and check the place out on Google Maps. If we use the satellite image, that'll give us a good idea of what's behind that wall and then I reckon, it's time we used another of Ryan's talents.'

'And what talent would that be?'

'Well, I'm surprised no one has told you, Captain Ryan Peters not only has his army pilot's wings, he has a PPL, in brackets "H", in other words a private pilot's licence, with an H for helicopter. And he has a part share in a helicopter parked not a million miles from here, at Popham Airfield by the A303.'

'Is there no end to the man's talents?'

'You don't know the half of it, Nic.'

'But won't they get suspicious of a helicopter flying over?'

'I guess there is a small risk, but what's good about that location is, Thruxton Airfield is just a stone's throw away, so there's light aircraft and choppers flying over all the time. I doubt they'll even notice.'

Ten minutes later they were in Tomasz Lewandowski's office looking at the satellite image of Runihura's compound.

'That's absolutely amazing. You can't see the compound at all from the road. Let alone how huge it is,' said Stafford.

'I know, it's incredible, it looks like there's a huge

warehouse, two residential mobile homes and eight caravans,' said Nicole.

'And these look like black pickup trucks, and there's two hook loader lorries with what looks like five bins next to them,' said Stafford.

'Jeez, we knew it had to be a pretty big operation to have trucks that size and space to work on the electronic scrap,' said Nicole.

'I wonder how old these satellite pictures are?' said Stafford.

'I can help with that,' said Tomasz pointing at the map. 'Garden centre there along road, only open short time. I remember all papers in door, and loads here in tip,' he ended with a laugh.

'Brilliant, there's plenty of cars in the car park so the place is open, so the picture must be fairly current,' said Nicole.

'OK, time to wake up Ryan, and get him to meet us at Popham Airfield. Then we'll get our own close-up pictures.'

It took Stafford and Nicole twenty minutes to get to Popham Airfield. They had taken both cars and were leaning up against the bonnet of the Volvo. Stafford had retrieved his binoculars from the boot and they were draped on a strap around his neck. They watched the comings and goings of the aircraft. Twenty-five minutes later Peters rolled up. He parked, pulled out a khaki canvas bag from the rear seat, slung it over his shoulder and ambled across the field to Nicole and Stafford. He grinned as he approached them.

'Gotta say, this is an unexpected pleasure, a chance to take the old bird out for the afternoon,' he said.

'Hope you're not referring to me, Captain Peters?' said Nicole with a laugh.

'Of course not, besides you're much older than my bird. That's her over there, she's called the Raven... So, come fly with me the pair of you,' he said as he walked with them across the grassy field to a shiny black helicopter, with the call sign G-BIGS painted on the fuselage near the tail rotor.

'Woah! It looks so small,' said Nicole.

'Yeah, I hear that a lot, but it's powerful,' said Peters with a wry grin.

'Have you flown in one of these before?' asked Stafford.

'No, never, but I'm really looking forward to it, I think,' she said.

'I've spoken to the ground crew and they've unhitched her and say she's ready to go,' said Stafford to Peters.

'Right, let's get you both aboard and strapped in then. I've gotta do the preflight checks, then we'll be away,' said Peters. Stafford took off his binoculars, opened up the front door and put them on the floor in front of the passenger seat.

'Nicole, you climb in the back for today. Sitting next to the pilot with just glass in front of you can be a bit scary at first,' said Stafford, without mentioning the full-view side doors were just as scary. Stafford supported her elbow as she climbed in through the starboard rear door, then helped her fasten the safety straps.

'There's a pair of binoculars in the little compartment between the seats,' he said. He checked her straps again. Satisfied, he clambered into the front passenger seat and fastened himself in. He reached down for the binoculars and looped the leather strap around his neck. Peters completed his mandatory preflight checks, rechecked Stafford's and Nicole's straps, then climbed into the pilot's seat and strapped himself in.

'OK, folks, put your headsets on,' he said. He turned the key for the electrics, and watched carefully as the dials lit up and reached their required settings.

'Popham tower, Golf, Bravo, India, Golf, Sierra, request engine start,' said Peters.

Seconds later came the response,

'Golf, Bravo, India, Golf, Sierra, Popham tower, start approved.' Peters pushed the start button and the rotors began to move slowly. Gradually they increased speed as Peters throttled up. He let it run, warming up for a minute. The noise, even with the headset on amazed, Nicole.

'Popham tower, Golf BIGS, readied for take-off,' said Peters .

Nicole, eyes shut tight, face screwed up in terror, gripped the sides of her seat with both hands, her knuckles white.

'Golf BIGS cleared for take-off,' came back the response. Peters increased the rotor speed and the little craft rocked in time with the rotors. Slowly he pulled the control lever and the Raven rose. When she was at tree height, Peters pushed the second control lever forward, the Raven dipped its nose and Nicole nearly threw up.

'All right in the back there?' Peters asked as the little aircraft flew high and west towards their target. Stafford turned to look at her; she was rigid, ashen-faced-looking dead ahead.

'Whiskey, Tango, Foxtrot,' was all she managed to say.

'There are sick bags under the binoculars if you need one,' said Stafford with an evil grin. But Nicole didn't see it, she just nodded, eyes still firmly on the back of Peter's head. Peters turned to Stafford and said, 'I'll keep a distance from the compound until we get close to Thruxton Airfield, then I'll turn and fly directly over it. See how the land lies, then do a second, lower pass. It'd be good if I can hover so we can take some decent pictures.'

When Nicole realised the aircraft had settled into constant forward flight, she risked a quick turn of her head to look out of the full-view door. Her hands gripped her seat even harder.

'Wow!' she said, 'that's bloody amazing.' Stafford turned and grinned at her.

'Welcome back,' he said.

'OK, brace yourself, Nicole,' came Peter's voice on the headsets. 'Thruxton Airfield is coming up, so I'm gonna swing round to starboard, then dip the nose as we fly over the compound, so Staf can take pictures.'

'Do your worst, Captain,' she said with an attempt at a grin. But she still braced herself for the change of direction. Stafford had his camera at the ready, and used his binoculars to pinpoint the target. As they flew over, he clicked away, occasionally checking the screen to see he had the pictures they needed.

'Good grief, this place is bloody massive, how many people have they got working there?' said Peters.

'I guess we'll be finding out soon,' said Stafford, 'one way or another.'

CHAPTER 46

Ayman Runihura was sitting on the top step to the front door of his mobile home. He was smoking a cigarette and talking to Eric Potter.

'You're looking bloody pissed off, Ayman, what's your problem, mate?'

'Gotta tell ya my first thought was to pack up and fuck off somewhere warm, but the syndicate has a huge network of contacts. That's how we bring in all these illegals. Y'know, partners in Iraq, Syria, Turkey and throughout Europe. And with our Russian mob contacts, I doubt I'd last a month. My details and pictures would be flashed around the world in seconds, mate, I'd have no chance,' said Runihura. He stopped talking for a couple of minutes. Then he took a last drag on his cigarette, flicked it across the yard and said, 'No two ways about it, Eric, Stafford and his lot are gonna have to die. They ain't gonna suddenly give up, but there's still one angle I'll try.' Eric looked at him quizzically.

'Well, before that dickhead DI fried himself, he gave me the address of the safe house in Portsmouth where Stafford stashed the black woman and her kids. I'm gonna go down there later, see if I can get a bargaining chip or two.'

Eric's mobile bleeped. He looked at it and said, 'Floyd

and Jan are about to drive in, I'll get the gates.' He got up and walked away.

Runihura yawned, stretched his arms above his head, got to his feet and wandered across the yard to where Tony Amos was sitting at a bench in the factory, eating a sandwich and drinking coffee from a plastic mug.

'Right, Tony, I know it's a bit short notice but I need you to do tonight's trip with Jan and Floyd.'

'Fucking hell, guv', a bit short notice? That's taking the fucking piss,' said Amos.

'Yeah, but I got no choice, mate. And when I've got no choice, you've got no choice, comprenday?' With a mouthful of sausage and egg sandwich, the only reply Amos could make was a sullen nod of the head.

'So when you've finished your grub, go and help Kapusniak and Winstone get the women ready for the trip to Basingstoke. Get them locked in the Mercedes van. Then take the other van and fuck off to Southampton. You got ten to pick up, and the usual package.' With that he walked across the yard to the dog pound. The three Alsatians bounded over eager for him to pat them. After a few moments talking to the dogs he went to where Kapusniak and Winstone were offloading the empty bins and taking them back to the lab.

'I've got stuff to do this afternoon and later on, so Tony's going with you tonight. When you've finished offloading, get the women on board, I'll be taking them to Basingstoke. You use the other van and get down to the boat,' Runihura said.

'No problem, boss,' said Kapusniak. The compound became a hive of activity. Brandon Miller's recent load of scrap electronics was being carried into the factory building.

The fearful workforce wincing visibly each time one of the cable-wielding "supervisors" walked by or issued a shouted instruction.

Kapusniak, Winstone and Amos had taken the eight women from the mobile home, cable-tied their hands behind their backs and herded them into the load space of the Mercedes van. Once inside, they again bound their ankles together with gaffer tape. Kapusniak locked the van and gave the key to Runihura.

'I'll be gone maybe three hours. So, Floyd, sort out the fishing gear you're taking. Tony, the pick-up time is at 01:00 hours, earlier than previous trips because of tides their side. And the pick-up coordinates are logged into the GPS system,' said Runihura, 'and make sure there are no fuck-ups.' Amos glared at him, but said nothing.

'Fuck, boss, we hav…' started Kapusniak only to be cut off by Runihura.

'Shut it, Jan, no fuck-ups, comprenday?' Kapusniak looked like a scolded schoolboy as he slowly nodded his head.

'Eric, you got enough gear to keep 'em working in the lab?' Runihura asked.

'Yeah, yeah, we can even keep the factory busy with that last load,' said Eric.

'OK, then keep a watchful eye on the CCTV, we don't need any surprise visits,' said Runihura as he climbed into the van.

'Don't fret, boss, systems up and running,' said Potter as he wandered across the yard to open up the gates for his boss.

Half an hour later, Kapusniak and Winstone and a well pissed-off Tony Amos left the compound and headed towards Southampton and Saxon Wharf.

CHAPTER 47

Stafford decided they had seen enough and taken enough photographs to give them all the information they needed to put a plan of action together. He told Peters to head back to Popham Airfield. Once on the ground they headed for Stafford's Volvo and piled into it. Nicole was trying hard to be professional and hide her excitement and anxiety caused by the helicopter flight. After a brief discussion it was obvious that they needed to get some prints of the pictures Stafford had taken.

They knew it would be suicide to simply wander in the front gates and try to arrest them. They needed a plan. And they still had to find out where the boat fitted into Runihura's operation. Stafford decided to send Nicole back down to Lee Gibson at Saxon Wharf and asked her to keep watch until the bad guys turned up to do whatever they were going to do. He phoned Gibson to keep him in the loop, and Gibson reported no change in the situation down there. Peters and Stafford arranged to meet up at Eastleigh Police HQ. He anticipated that DCI Talbot would, now they appeared to be making progress, allow them access and offer help if required in formulating a plan of attack.

They parked in the multistorey car park and walked to the police station. The front desk person dialled Talbot's number and after a moment or two she handed the phone to Stafford, who explained to the DCI what they needed. Talbot readily agreed, and asked to speak to the call handler. She promptly issued them with visitors' passes. They made their way to the DCI's office. Talbot said, 'I guess you'll be pleased to know that we have your driver chappie, one Brandon Miller, safely in custody.'

'Bloody hell, that's brilliant, how did it go?' asked Stafford.

'Much easier than expected really; as soon as the blues and twos were flashed at him, he pulled over. Must have thought it was just a brake light out or something. He was amazed when we asked for his transfer notes; denied having them at first,' said Talbot.

'Good, we'll let him stew for a bit before we have a chat with him, but have a look at where he made his delivery,' said Stafford and he showed the DCI the pictures of Runihura's compound on the small screen of his digital camera.

'Well, I have to say I'm pretty impressed with Mr Runihura. Always had him down as a petty crook, but with a set-up like this, he's got to have money behind him,' said the DCI.

'Yeah, we felt the same, always seemed like a tinpot operation, but it looks like the precious metals in electronics thing was a new venture. Probably trying to diversify in an area that is beginning to grow, not only here but worldwide. We reckon he's being backed by a very silent and clever partner or group. One who keeps well away from the action,' said Stafford.

'So you'll be working on a plan of action?' said Talbot.

'Yes, now we've found the boat and that sort of led us to this compound. The boat's under surveillance now, trying to find out where it actually fits in. But we need to get some blow-ups of these pictures to see what sort of access there is to the site,' said Stafford.

'Then we can determine what size team we need to breach it,' said Peters.

'You know where the squad room is, so just make yourself at home, but make sure you keep me up to date,' said Talbot. Stafford and Peters thanked him and made their way to the squad room. There were a couple of other uniformed officers working there. They looked up and nodded a noncommittal response to Peters's "Afternoon, lads," then went back to their own work. Stafford pulled the memory card out of his camera and slotted it into the nearest computer. He hit a couple of keys, eventually found the pictures and sent them to the printer. Seconds later the unmistakable sound of a printer in action pinpointed where they would find the finished items. Peters wandered across the room and pulled out a dozen or so full colour A4 prints. They were certainly fit for purpose. Peters walked back to the desk Stafford had selected and spread out the pictures. Neither man spoke as they examined them, then Stafford said, 'That's bloody ridiculous, it looks like the front gate is the only way in. Surely they must have thought to put in an escape route?'

'Can't see one from these pics, Staf, but if you count the number of cars and buildings there, it adds up to a bloody big workforce.'

'So someone must have thought about what happens if they get raided? For Christ's sake.'

'We need to be on the safe side, so I guess a bit of close-quarter surveillance is called for.'

'Yeah, if you believe the rumours, and Special Branch info, Runihura was in Sa'ka Force, the Egyptian Military Commando Unit, so surely he wouldn't miss something as obvious as that. I know they were a bit gung-ho, but that was where the public or hostages were concerned; he must have set up an exit strategy,' said Stafford. 'So you're right, we need to get up close and personal.'

'We could do it tonight. I guess you've got the bag in the car?' said Peters. The bag was a sort of survival kit, kept in the boot of a car, or under a bed, or in a hotel wardrobe, where they could grab it and be on their way at moment's notice.

'Yep, you?'

'Yep. Right, let's go and get something to eat. Then we'll have our little chat with the driver and get ready for a bit of night ops,' said Peters with a grin, feeling that they were on the move at long last.

'Sounds like a plan, but I want to check out the ownership of the compound before we go,' said Stafford. After a few failed attempts, he finally found what he was looking for.

'Yes, look, here we are, bloody place is owned by Whitelines International Ltd, that's so bloody annoying, you need to be a magician to sort out the tangle of companies that's mixed up with.' Then after a few more clicks, 'But that's interesting, it's been leased lock, stock and smoking barrels to... Runihura Enterprises. So that's bloody good news. Now I'm gonna phone Gibbo, see if he's awake and if Nicole has turned up yet.' He was and she had. They left the police station to find something to eat.

—————————— ‖ ——————————

While Stafford and Peters were eating, Stafford received a text from one of the forensic techs who had been at the boat earlier. The message said, "Sent emails to Eastleigh. Full reports. Lots of good prints, few matches. Flare same batch, traces of heroin and cocaine on wrapping."

'Looks like they're using the boat for drug smuggling then,' said Stafford as he showed the text to Peters.

'That's brilliant, can't wait to see what the details are.' They finished their food in a hurry, left their hot drinks and raced back to the nick. They dashed into the incident room and Stafford fired up the computer they had used previously. He found the emails, the first one giving details of the flare and the flare gun, stating the flare that killed Garfield Lewis was from the same batch and identical to the others found in the secure cabinet on the boat. Further emails showed they'd found masses of fingerprints, but had only found three matches. One print taken from the outside of the secure cabinet was shown to be that of Ayman Runihura. Another match was a fingerprint found inside a cabinet in one of the cabins, and was linked to a conviction for possession of a class A drug to a Mr Brandon Miller. It seemed Brandon Miller had been represented in court by a solicitor called Howard Neilson.

'Bloody bingo!' shouted Peters as he punched the air.

'Hang on a bit though, Ryan, this next email is even better. Listen to this,' and he read aloud, 'A series of fingerprints were lifted from the under side of an overhead locker in the master stateroom. These proved to be the middle and index finger from the left hand of George Saunders. Matching exactly (15 points) prints taken posthumously from George Saunders's severed left arm.'

'So it would seem that our new friend Brandon Miller has quite a lot of explaining to do. Christ, I can't wait to get started on this interview,' said Peters, rubbing his hands together.

'Hold your horses, Ryan, there's still one more email.' The final email outlined tests made on the blue plastic and waxed brown paper wrapping found on the boat. The tests showed the presence of heroin and cocaine, and concluded that both materials had been used to wrap quantities of the drugs for transportation.

'So I guess it's pretty much conclusive that Runihura used that boat for smuggling drugs,' said Stafford. 'OK, I think we're about ready to meet Mr Miller.' He printed off a couple of copies of each of the emails, and walked a set through to DCI Talbot.

'I think we are now ready to have a chat with Brandon Miller, if that's OK with you, Detective Chief Inspector?' said Stafford.

'Excellent,' said Talbot, and he picked up his phone, punched in a short number, and after a second said, 'Major Stafford is ready to talk to Miller now, can you set it up please?' He listened for a second or two then said, 'Thank you, sergeant,' and replaced the phone. He turned to Stafford and said, 'The sergeant is setting up in Interview Room Five. If you return to the ground floor, the desk sergeant will point you in the right direction.'

When they reached the interview room the fair-haired

Brandon Miller was already there, seated on the far side of a Formica-topped table. Stafford and Peters took the two chairs facing Miller. A uniformed constable closed the door behind them and stood with his back against the door watching the proceedings. Peters leaned across the table and switched on the audio recorder. The interview would be recorded on audio and video. Peters stated the day, date, time and place, then introduced himself as Captain Peters of the Security Forces. He asked Stafford and the constable to identify themselves, then stated that they were there to interview Brandon Miller. Peters then asked Miller to identify himself for the benefit of the tape. Miller stated his name, date of birth and address.

'You realise you are still under caution and you have the right to have a solicitor present, are you sure you don't want legal representation?' asked Peters.

'No, I just want to answer your stupid bloody questions and get out of here,' said Miller.

'You can stop whenever you want and ask for a solicitor, it's your right and it's free,' said Peters.

'Just get on with it,' said Miller.

'This interview is being recorded and the recordings may be used in a court of law if charges are brought against you. I will explain how you or your legal representative can get a copy at...,'

'For fuck's sake, just ask your bleeding questions,' said Miller.

'OK, let's get started then,' said Peters.

'Hoo fucking ray,' came the response.

'Are you self-employed or do you work for Southampton Metal Recycling?'

Peters noticed a slight hesitation and a fractional

narrowing of the eyes at the mention of SMR before Miller replied, 'Self-employed.'

'So how often do you deliver scrap WEEE to Ayman Runihura's compound? Yes, Brandon, we know about SMR, so think carefully before you answer,' said Peters.

'Well, at the moment it's only about once a week, just can't get enough of it to do anymore.'

'So that's not even gonna keep you in beer and fags for the week, what else do you do to survive?'

'I get other work with the lorry,' said Miller defensively.

'So who else do you work for then, Brandon?' asked Stafford.

The change of inquisitor seemed to throw Miller somewhat. He looked from one to the other before saying, 'Well, I do lots of odd jobs for Ayman.'

'Is that with the lorry then?' asked Peters.

'Sometimes, yeah.'

'So why do you keep your lorry at SMR?' asked Stafford.

'Cos it's near where I live, and my front garden ain't big enough,' said Miller with a laugh.

'How come SMR let you do that?' asked Stafford.

'Ayman's mates with Frank down there, so he does it as a favour to Ayman,' said Miller.

'So what does Frank do?' asked Peters.

'For fuck's sake, this is a load of bollocks. Just charge me with whatever you wanna charge me with, I'll put my hand up to it, and be on my way,' said Miller rising and pushing his chair back forcefully.

'Sit down, Brandon,' said Peters leaning forward across the table. Miller looked defiantly at Peters for a second or two then sank back into the chair.

'Trust me on this, Brandon, you've got a lot more to worry about than a load of dodgy scrap. We're investigating five deaths here and a drug smuggling operation,' said Peters. Miller leaned back in his chair, mouth open in horror. He threw his arms out wide, 'Don't be fucking silly, what do I know about five deaths?' he asked.

'OK, let's start with the drug smuggling then,' said Peters.

'That's not what I meant,' said Miller.

'Brandon, look, do yourself a favour, lose the aggression and talk to us. We can probably help you sort this out. But so far the people who have fucked up in your little band of brothers, have ended up dead, or in a coma,' said Stafford.

'I ain't telling you nothing,' said Miller.

'Shame that, cos if George had talked to us, maybe he'd still be alive. Same with Matis. Oh no, he is still alive... just in a coma. What say we turn him loose, Staf? They'll probably think he talked anyway,' said Peters standing up and preparing to turn off the tape machine.

'We could add some more offences, like being an accessory to murder, then we could keep him safely locked up though,' said Stafford.

'But they might still get to him, I mean, just ask Matis Bockus. Oh no, you can't, he's still in a coma,' said Peters. There was complete silence in the room for a moment or two, then Miller spoke.

'I want a solicitor,' he said.

'I guess your solicitor will be Howard Neilson then,' said Stafford looking across at Peters, who laughed out loud. Stafford couldn't help but join in for a few seconds, then he turned to Miller and said, 'Good luck with that then, Brandon.'

Miller had an extremely puzzled look on his face as he was escorted back to the cells.

CHAPTER 48

Nicole had stopped off at a burger van parked near Saxon Wharf and purchased a couple of cheeseburgers, fries and coffees. She parked close to Gibson's car and nearly frightened the life out of him as she pulled open the passenger door and thrust the bag of food at him and said very loudly, 'Wakey, wakey, here, grab this while I get sat… Jeeez, Lee, it smells like a fucking farmyard in here, can we open a window or two while we eat this?'

'I wasn't asleep, I was concentrating hard on looking out of the windscreen. And it smells in here cos it's been warm, and I've had the windows shut listening to Radio One to keep me awake.'

'Yeah, yeah,' said Nicole as she settled into the passenger's seat. 'Hope you like cheeseburgers?'

'I do as it happens, but I'm so bloody ravenous I'd eat anything, so thanks for this,' he said as he buzzed down the two front windows. They sorted out the bag of food and began to eat.

'So what's been happening down here then? Any action at all?'

'Nothing happened at all, except the boat bobbed up and down a bit, nearly put me in a trance; up, down, up;

down, up and fucking down,' he said with a grin. 'But what about you? Stafford told me a bit, said you'd made good progress, but never went into detail.' Nicole outlined what had happened since she'd left the wharf earlier. She included the bit about the helicopter flight, but left out the bit about her being terrified, telling it as though it was just part of her daily routine.

'Bloody hell, that's really great, that's the first time for ages I've felt we're getting somewhere.'

'Yeah, I know what you mean, but then I've been thinking, you don't get to pull strings like Stafford does. Y'know, like he did to get us on board, and other stuff like the car, unless you've got a decent track record. So I've always kind of felt he was a safe pair of hands.' Then quickly added, 'Anyway do you want to get out and stretch your legs for a while, or are you gonna have a kip in the back?'

'I'll get out and have a wander for half an hour or so, I think, if you're OK with that. I hear what you're saying about Stafford though, and from what I gather, underneath the boyish good looks and calm demeanour, beats a heart of pure steel.'

Nicole stayed silent, facing the front for a long moment thinking about the boyish good looks… and warm brown eyes and nice pecs…

'Nic?' said Gibson.

'Oh yeah, yeah, go for your walk, mate,' she said waving him off.

<hr>

‖

Gibson returned from his walk about and had climbed into the passenger seat when Nicole slid further down in her seat.

'Quick, Lee, get down, get down,' she hissed.

'Why, what's up?'

'Transit van coming down behind us,' she said. The van rolled to a stop a few feet away from the rear gates of the metal recycling compound.

'Christ, that's Floyd Winstone driving, but I don't recognise the tall blonde-haired geezer opening the gates,' said Gibson. The unknown man, wearing jeans and a black leather jacket opened the gates wide enough to let the van inside. Winstone parked alongside the fence, got out and reached into the back doors pulling out fishing rods and what looked like a tackle box. As he relocked the rear doors, Jan Kapusniak climbed out of the van and joined them while the unknown man closed and locked the gates.

'Fuck, it's that bastard Kapusniak,' said Gibson pulling out his mobile and taking pictures of the three of them as they made their way down the little footpath to the boat.

'Hmmm, the guy in the chandlery certainly got his description spot on, if that's Kapusniak.'

'Oh yeah, that's him all right. Look, I'm gonna phone Stafford, see what he wants us to do.' He called Stafford's mobile.

'Bloody hell, Staf, Kapusniak, Winstone and another guy we don't know have just turned up. They've parked their van in SMR's yard and they've taken a load of fishing gear down on to the boat.'

'Bloody brilliant, can you get a picture of the unknown guy?'

'Yeah, already got one, I'll send it after this phone call. But what do you want us to do if they set off in the boat?' Stafford thought for a moment then said, 'I don't think you need do anything, just stay there. If they go out, they will either be fishing or picking up a consignment of some sort, so I reckon they'll come back anyway. But whatever happens don't attempt to approach them. Any sign of trouble get the fuck out of there. Do you hear? Make sure Nicole understands that too. I don't want anyone else dying.'

'No worries, boss, we'll keep a low profile.'

'OK mate, well, send me the pictures and I'll get back to you soon with some more info, hopefully.'

'Roger, rog,' said Gibson as he ended the call. He selected the pictures of the unknown man and shipped them to Stafford's phone, then repeated what Stafford had said to Nicole.

CHAPTER 49

Stafford and Peters were sitting in the incident room discussing the layout of Runihura's compound, when the desk phone rang. Stafford picked it up. It was the custody sergeant, who said, 'Miller has just asked if he could have a word. He wouldn't tell me what about. Any chance you could come down here and see what he wants?' Stafford agreed and with Peters, walked down through the building to the ground floor where the custody sergeant took them through to Miller's cell.

'I'll leave the door open. I'll be down at the desk, holler if you need anything.'

The cell was small, ten feet by eight feet. Miller was seated on the built-in concrete ledge, covered with a two-inch thick foam mattress.

'So, Brandon, what can we do for you?' asked Stafford.

'What did you mean when you said "best of luck with that then," earlier about Neilson?' he asked.

'Look, everyone has the right to free legal advice when they're being questioned. Mr Neilson may well be a brilliant lawyer, but if Runihura's paying him, does he have to report back to him? Who knows? Brandon, who knows? But what would you think? We reckon it'll be in your best interest to get a solicitor with no ties, with no axe to grind.'

'This'll get very nasty, very quickly, Brandon. Your problems with dodgy scrap electronics is small beer in our overall investigation. You need to think about yourself, your future, mate,' said Peters.

'So if I talk to you, what are you gonna do for me?'

'Brandon, we can't give you any guarantees, but we'll do what we can to fight your corner. And when this comes to court we'll make sure the judge is aware of any help you give us,' said Stafford.

Miller's head and shoulders drooped. He stayed hunched forward for a moment or two. He sat upright, leaned against the wall, sighed heavily and said, 'OK, get your duty solicitor in, I'll talk to you.'

'For what it's worth, I think you're doing the right thing and I'll do the best I can for you,' said Stafford and he patted him on the shoulder as they walked away. Miller closed his eyes and nodded. Peters walked down to the custody sergeant, who returned to lock Miller's cell. Stafford asked the sergeant to call for the duty solicitor and set up another interview as soon as possible.

II

Anne Borley was an up and coming lawyer. Attractive as well as smart, the thirty-two-year-old brunette worked for a well-established firm of solicitors settled in Eastleigh High Street. She loved the random nature of the on-call duty solicitor's roll. Whenever her mobile's display showed the local nick's number she never knew if she would be dealing with a teenage multiple offender suffering with ADHD, or a drunk fifty-year-old charged with GBH. When the call came asking her to represent Brandon Miller, she was pleasantly surprised to find he was neither drunk, nor apparently suffering from a mental disorder or trauma. She was well known at the local nick and the custody sergeant took her through to Brandon Miller's cell. He gave her details of the arrest and outlined the involvement of Major Paul Stafford and the security forces. Ms Borley shook hands with Miller and said, 'Hmm, on the face of it this looks pretty straightforward... Is it, or isn't it, transporting hazardous waste illegally? Then enter the security forces and now it doesn't seem so straightforward. I think you'd better start at the beginning, Brandon, and tell me what's going on.'

Miller looked at her mournfully. 'What I want is for you to fight my bloody corner here. There's some really heavy shit gonna go down shortly. I'm sat on the edge of it, I need some protection, some guarantees here,' he said.

'Brandon, Brandon, you should know I can't give you guarantees, no one can. Tell me your story and I'll say what I think you need to do for the best.' Neither one said anything for a while, then with a sigh Brandon Miller started.

It took almost an hour. Anne Borley had been, for most of the time, simply sitting quietly, trying to look composed and professional. But inside she was in turmoil, switching from euphoria at how big this was going to be, to horror at the almost unbelievable level of violence and inhumanity being described by such a normal looking bloke, in such an everyday manner. Miller ended by saying, 'I'm telling you this because the police and the geezers from the security forces have obviously been watching me. They know the yard I work out of. They know where I take the stuff to. Once they bust the site at Weyhill, we're all fucked. The shit will really hit the wotzit, there'll be a fucking war, believe me, a fucking shootin' war. I need protection here, woman, I need protection if I talk to them.'

'You've got to know that you're going to jail for this. By covering up and not reporting the crimes you've outlined, you could be charged as an accessory to God knows how many offences. So the fact is, you've got to keep cooperating with them and I will fight my hardest to get you the best deal possible. Brandon, that's all I can promise.'

'OK, let's get it done,' said Miller after just a moment's thought. Ms Borley called for the custody sergeant and leaving Miller locked in his cell, she asked the sergeant if Stafford was ready to start the interview. The sergeant assured her everything was ready to go, and walked with her to Interview Room Five.

‖

Stafford and Peters made their way to the interview room. The custody sergeant had set it up ready to roll. He made the introductions and then disappeared to collect Brandon Miller.

Stafford, Peters and Ms Borley seated themselves around the Formica-topped table. The sergeant and a uniformed constable returned with Miller, who sat next to Ms Borley. As the sergeant left, the constable closed the door and stood with his back to it, facing the proceedings. Peters checked that the audio and video recorders were working, then started the interview, introducing himself. Everyone in the room did likewise, but before Stafford could ask his first question Anne Borley said, 'My client has been stopped and brought here on fairly minor and straightforward charges. The likelihood of you following up with a visit to the Weyhill premises has prompted my client to offer to talk about the activities and personnel involved there. My client initially became involved whilst innocently trying to find work for his waste carrying business. Having carried out a number of jobs for,' she hesitated and looked through her notes, 'a Mr Ayman Runihura, he realised that this was not a normal place of work. When Mr Miller broached the subject with Mr Runihura, it was made clear to my client that his life would be in jeopardy if he ever talked to anyone about what he had seen. It was then my client decided in order to stay alive and keep food on the table, so to speak, he would simply do the work. Fearful for his own safety, he was too frightened to report the wrongdoing to the authorities.'

'We all need to put food on our tables, Ms Borley, but most of us do it legally,' said Peters.

'But you don't have the threat of death, for seeing too much, hanging over you, do you, Captain Peters?' Peters's mouth twitched, the start of a smile as Borley blushed, realising that a captain from the security forces would often have the threat of death hanging over him.

'Well, Mr Miller is prepared to answer all your questions, and more, as it's likely you only know a very small part of the set-up. But he will only do so, if we can come to an agreement about his subsequent treatment.'

'So for being a good citizen and doing the right thing at last, your client thinks he deserves rewarding?' asked Stafford.

'Not at all, it's not a question of reward, my client is going to need protection. Mr Miller knows too much about this organisation. He would be dead now, if he had reported this before. My client has been between a rock and a hard place. In fact he still is; just by being arrested it's likely they will take action against him to protect themselves.'

'Ms Borley, I've been between lots of rocks and lots of hard places...' started Stafford.

'And you've always managed to extract yourself within the law, Major Stafford?' asked Ms Borley with the hint of a smile. 'If he goes to prison he'll be a target. You know that. Do you want his death on your conscience too?' The room was quiet, all eyes on Stafford, waiting for his response.

'Ms Borley, your client doesn't have a leg to stand on pushing for a deal. Let's face it, we know where he keeps his lorry. We know where the boat is and we know where the illegal work on the waste electronics is being carried out. We'll just raid the factory and sort it out from there,' he said with a shrug.

'You're right,' said Miller, speaking for the first time, 'you could do that, but trust me on this, if you just bust the yard, a lot of people, innocent people, are gonna die. Mark my words, these people don't fuck about; guilty or innocent, people will die. Listen to what I have to say and you'll save lives, believe me.'

'If it's as bad as you say, how come there are innocent people in there? And what makes you think we couldn't go in mob-handed and sort it before they knew what hit them?' asked Peters.

'You obviously don't know Runihura and Kapusniak.

351

These guys aren't just tinpot petty crooks, these guy are pros, the real deal, mate,' said Miller, 'and the innocents are the immigrants.'

'What do you mean, immigrants?' asked Stafford. By now Brandon Miller's Southampton FC shirt was soaking wet. Dark patches of sweat showed not only under his armpits, but spread across his chest, down to his belly.

'Don't answer that question, Brandon,' said Ms Borley slapping her hand on the table in front of Miller. Startled, Miller flinched and the rapid movement seemed to unleash the stench of sweat from him. Stafford looked at Peters, who gave an almost imperceptible nod.

'OK, Ms Borley, Mr Miller, we'll listen to what you've got to say. We'll take what you give us to our bosses and persuade them you need protection,' said Stafford.

'Look, Major, I need a couple of moments alone with my client to discuss this.'

'You got it,' said Stafford as he and Peters got up and left the room. Two moments later Borley called them back in.

'Right, Major Stafford, we're going to trust you on this… don't let my client down,' she said.

'Don't worry, Ms Borley, if we get good stuff, we'll do our best for him. Now let's get started,' said Stafford. Stafford took out the A4 aerial prints of the Weyhill compound and laid them on the table.

'These pictures are right up to date, Brandon, so talk us through them,' he said.

Miller didn't even bother to turn the prints to face him, he started with the largest building first.

'This is the factory. I dump my electronics under that

front awning. The illegals take it into the factory and take out all the preci…'

Peters interrupted, 'When you say illegals, what exactly do you mean?' he asked.

'The people we bring in on the boat of course,' said Miller giving Peters a withering look.

'Here, look, they work in the factory and live in there,' he said pointing to the eight caravans.

'So how many people are you talking about?' asked Stafford.

'I guess actually in the factory, about a dozen men, but in all there's got to be twenty-five or thirty people on site most of the time,' said Miller.

'And all these have been brought in by boat?' asked Stafford.

'Not all. Seven or eight are English. Well, you know, not all English, some like Runihura and Kapusniak. They're the ones that run it,' said Miller.

'So how often do you bring in a boatload of people?' asked Stafford.

'Not really sure, but I think it's four or five times a month, sometimes more.'

'That seems unlikely if there's only thirty or so on site,' said Peters.

Miller looked at him as though he were the weakest link and said, 'They're not all kept there, most of the women are shipped out by van as soon as they're cleaned up; don't really know where they're sent to. But I guess it's to earn money for the syndicate.'

'So Runihura's not the top man then?' asked Stafford.

'Would you run a tip if you were the top man?' said

Miller. Stafford smiled inwardly at that, as the obvious answer was yes, Stafford would and had. Miller continued, 'Well, he tries to make out he is, but I think all the immigrants and drugs are set up over the Internet and I don't think Ayman does that. And he's always moaning about the electronics stuff, saying we should never have started doing it. I think he'd stop that if he was the boss. But I think he organises the guns.'

'You think Runihura's bringing in guns?' asked Stafford.

'Jesus, you don't know fuck all, do you?' said Miller shaking his head. 'Yeah, he's getting guns, grenades and I've even seen some packs of Semtex, so if you do bust the place you'd better go in massively tooled up.'

It took over an hour and a half to cover all of Miller's information. But it also removed the need for them to go on a recce of the compound as they had planned to do. By now Miller's body odour was beginning to affect everyone.

'I wonder, Major Stafford, could we perhaps have the constable open the door for a while and maybe organise a drink, tea or something?' asked Ms Borley.

Stafford grinned, 'Bloody good idea, miss.' They took a break when the tea arrived.

Then Miller talked about the virtually hidden double gates in the rear wall, the CCTV coverage of only the front gates. He had explained about the drug laboratory and how the workforce were controlled by getting them addicted to crack cocaine or MDMA, and how they worked simply to get their next fix. He outlined the set-up in the bungalow, where he said they made films of some of the immigrants being raped or tortured. He added that he'd never seen or witnessed it himself, but he knew it happened because

Kapusniak and the other "supervisors" would laugh and joke about it. And they would occasionally offer him a DVD to watch; he said he never accepted.

Miller told of immigrants that had died. Mainly, he said, from drug overdoses' and were buried there, but again he denied being involved or even knowing where the graves were.

As he outlined the whole operation, he slumped forward in his chair, his lips trembled as he spoke, and he constantly wiped away the sweat that ran down his forehead and cheeks. It was as though he too, had only just opened his eyes to the enormity of what he had described; the level of violence and debauchery used in their quest for money.

Hunched over and weeping uncontrollably he was led back to his cell.

Stafford, Peters and Ms Borley sat in stunned silence as they tried to assimilate what they'd just heard.

CHAPTER 50

Ayman Runihura had delivered his cargo of eight women to their new place of work, in the care of Third-Floor Sheila. He was back on the M3 heading south when he received a phone call. The screen showed "FRANK" and he accepted the call.

'Frank, what can I do for you?'

'Not sure really, mate, just wondered if you've heard from Brandon in the last few hours?'

'Well, he dumped a load of electronics up at my place earlier this morning, I thought he left just after. Why? What's up?'

'Probably nothing, guess he's just off skiving in a lay-by somewhere. He was gonna do another trip for me, but the wanker's not answering his phone.'

'You tried phoning my place?'

'Yeah, I spoke to Eric; said he left ages ago.'

'OK, well, I was thinking of heading for Portsmouth, but I'll go back to Weyhill, see what I can find out from the lads there. And I'll give you a bell later,' said Runihura as he ended the call. After a moment's thought he hit the speed dial button for Brandon Miller. The dialling tone ended with a request to leave a message; he chose not to.

The trouble with driving alone, thought Runihura, *is that your mind goes in directions it's best not to go.* He shook his head and tried to concentrate on just driving. Then on the traffic, then the two women he'd shagged yesterday. That brought a smile to his face, but not for long. His mind kept returning to the same question, where the fuck was Brandon Miller?

Five minutes out he called Eric at Weyhill, 'I'm just coming in, Eric, get the gates ...ummm, by the way, has Brandon been back there today?'

'Nah, mate, he left here ages ago. Anyway, what is it with everyone today? Everyone wants to find Brandon.'

Runihura drove in through the gates, parked up outside his mobile home and wandered across the yard to Eric.

'Gotta tell ya, Eric, I got a bad feeling about Brandon. He knew he had another job to do for Frank this afternoon, but he ain't turned up or phoned anyone. And the bastard's not answering his mobile either.'

'You're worrying too much, boss, give it a couple of hours, you'll see, it'll work itself out,' said Eric.

'Yep, it's about all I can do for the moment, but with Matis out of the picture and the other three down at the boat, it leaves us a bit short-handed if we get a problem up here.'

'Why would we get a problem? You know he's a lazy bastard, he's probably kipping in a lay-by somewhere.' Runihura turned away, nodding his head.

'I hope you're fucking right,' he said almost to himself. He walked across the yard to the dog pound. The three dogs came to him immediately. He unlatched the gate to the pound and walked inside. He sat down on an upturned wooden crate and the German Shepherd dogs sat silently, one each side of him, with the lead dog directly in front. He patted them in their perceived pecking order and said, 'Well, boys, you might be getting some more action tonight for a change.' After five minutes he left the dogs and went inside his mobile home. He walked through to the living room, closed the door, rolled back the carpet and lifted the trap-door. He began to pull out the crates of weapons and ammunition. Experience had taught him when you get a gut feeling, prepare for the worst… and he had a gut feeling.

When Kapusniak and Co arrived back there in the morning they could go to the Portsmouth safe house, tooled up and mob-handed. That way, they should be able to snatch one of the black kids to use as a bargaining chip. Or at least scare the crap out of them.

CHAPTER 51

S tafford and Peters said goodbye to Anne Borley and made their way back to DCI Talbot's office. Talbot waved them in and pointed them to the seats in front of his desk. Peters sat whilst Stafford laid out the pictures of the Weyhill compound on the DCI's desk, then outlined the details of the operation as Miller had explained. The DCI seemed stunned at the scope and audacity of the set-up. After a few moments thought, he said, 'At first you think, why can't people see what's going on under their noses. Then you see the aerial views and you realise the nearest neighbours are some distance away. And it's an agricultural area so no one bothers about heavy trucks moving around every now and then. So it really is a good spot for this operation. Makes you wonder why Fisher wasn't able to spot it, when he had Runihura under surveillance?'

'Well, far be it from me to speak ill of the dead, but we reckoned that Fisher was connected to this group. When we tried to flush him out, I think he realised we were on to him and decided he didn't want to end up like George Saunders. I'm sure we'll investigate Fisher's death more closely, further down the line,' said Stafford.

Stafford, Peters and the DCI spent the next forty-five minutes working out a plan of action to bring down the whole set-up. They all agreed that tackling the boat was the best starting point.

Miller had spelled out in detail their method of operating; how they docked the boat in the early hours, then immigrants, with hands bound, were transferred to the back of the van in the metal recycling compound. Once in the van their feet would be bound and they would be locked in. The crew would return to the boat, where with one lookout, they would sleep until the morning rush hour were well and truly underway. They would then take the van to Weyhill, knowing the chances of being stopped in the rush hour was minimal.

Miller had also named three of the men that he knew worked at the Weyhill compound. And this enabled them to identify the unknown man at the boat as Tony Amos, a thirty-six-year-old ex-military man who had previously appeared on the police radar a number of times. Until he seemed to have disappeared some eighteen months ago.

———————— **||** ————————

With a plan of action in place, DCI Talbot and Stafford made a number of phone calls, putting men and systems on alert, needing them to be ready at a moment's notice.

"Trashed" was the code name chosen for the boat bust. The take-down at Weyhill, was "Trojan Horse". The double operation would start the moment the boat crew made a move.

'Without doubt,' said Talbot, 'these men are bloody monsters, but we'll mobilise our own sea monster. See how the bad guys like to battle against Kraken.' Stafford and Peters looked at him blankly. Talbot grinned and explained how project Kraken (a mythical sea monster) had been set up to enable better communication with stakeholders concerning coastal crime. He added, 'Mind you, we'll wheel in... ah, perhaps I should say, sail in, SB's own marine unit to watch the *Cleopatra* as she goes out to the Channel.'

'Brilliant,' said Stafford, 'sounds ideal for this op.'

With planning complete, Talbot agreed to talk to the Armed Response Units and outline the plan of attack. Stafford phoned Gibson to get an update on the situation at Saxon Wharf and to give him the identity of the unknown man. He added that they would be joining them in around fifty minutes.

They took both cars. Stafford arrived a little later than Peters; he'd stopped off to buy cheeseburgers and four coffees. He clambered into the Vectra next to Peters, handed out the fodder and said, 'What's occurring then, folks?'

'Absolutely bugger all,' came the mumbled response from Gibson through a mouthful of burger.

'Reckon that's all about to change, but I'm nervous about all of us just sitting around in the car once the businesses around here close up. Four people in a car's a bit obvious, so I'll try and sort something else out,' said Stafford.

He then recounted Brandon Miller's story.

'Bloody hell,' said Nicole, 'we thought it was big, but that's ridiculous. I hope you've got contingency plans. Seems like four of us against that lot won't be enough.'

'You haven't seen Peters in action yet, have you?' laughed Stafford. 'No, don't worry, down here we'll be fine, apparently they only post one lookout and he usually stays inside the cockpit. We've worked out a plan of attack with Talbot. We've got Special Branch's marine unit, Immigration Enforcement and a police tactical firearms support unit on standby. The bomb squad will be on hand when we go into Weyhill, and another firearms unit. So as soon as things start happening we should have all the backup we need.'

'I hope the marine crew won't tackle the *Cleopatra* out at sea,' said Nicole.

'No way, that's ours; unless something goes really badly wrong…Their job will simply be to monitor the *Cleopatra* from a safe distance and make sure whatever they're collecting comes safely back to shore,' said Stafford.

'So we'll get the chance to take down Kapusniak?' she asked.

'That's the plan,' said Stafford with a grin, as he noted the look of grim determination on her face.

Stafford said, 'Anyway, listen up, this operation is code, named Trashed, we're unit one, so when we're in radio coms we use initially, trashed unit one, then revert to TU1 when received, OK? The marine unit is TU2, firearm support, TU3 and Immigration Enforcement, TU4, OK?' Getting nods all round he continued. 'So we think Trojan Horse, the Weyhill operation, should happen around 09:30 hours tomorrow, but it's flexible, really depends on how successful we are here. The operation is code-named Trojan Horse as a nod to the fact that we'll be using their van to gain access. We'll lose the marine unit for that one and DCI Talbot will put a team of officers in to close off both ends of the old Amesbury road, when we give him the sign. All clear?' He received nods of agreement all round.

Nothing was said as they finished their coffees, then Gibson and Nicole got out of the car to stretch their legs and get some much needed fresh air. For them it had been a long, boring day, but they knew tonight and for the next twelve hours or so, they would need all their wits about them.

Stafford and Peters climbed out of the car and walked over to the boat restoration unit opposite the metal compound's gates. Wandering into the little office area they were met by the elderly ruddy-faced gentleman Nicole had spoken to some days earlier. Stafford and Peters showed their Security Forces ID and explained that they were conducting surveillance on a suspected drug and people-smuggling gang. Stafford asked simply, 'We'd like to use your premises during the rest of the day and night as a base for our surveillance team.'

'You were with that lovely young lady the other day, weren't you?' he asked. 'So I guess her dad didn't want a boat fixed after all.'

'No, sorry about that, but she'll be over here in a minute so you can have a go at her yourself about that,' said Stafford grinning.

The old boy laughed and winked as he said, 'It'll be worth letting you use the place to see her again.'

Details agreed, they shook hands. Stafford phoned Nicole and asked her and Gibson to join them in the boat restorer's unit. They set up in an office with two windows overlooking the scrapyard where they could observe the *Cleopatra*.

Afternoon dragged into evening. All that moved outside was the *Cleopatra*, gently up and down, up and down, relentlessly up and down. By now the four of them were on their own. The old boy, having chastised Nicole good-humouredly about her deception, had gone home.

When night had settled in, Peters noticed movement on the boat. Kapusniak and the man they now knew as Tony Amos began to take down the cockpit cover. When it was stowed away, they were joined in the cockpit by Winstone. The three of them sat around drinking beers and smoking.

'Hmm,' said Nicole, 'bit cold for that I'd have thought.'

'I think you'll find this means they'll be off in about forty or forty-five minutes,' said Peters. 'This is a sign that they've done a lot of this before. They're getting their eyes acclimatised to the dark. Getting their best night vision so they can steer safely down river.'

'According to Miller they pick up just a few miles off the coast of Cherbourg, so it'll be a few more hours before we see any action ourselves,' said Stafford.

'I'll get back to sleep then, boss,' said Gibson. 'Wake me when the fun starts.'

Forty minutes later Kapusniak and Amos clambered across the side of the boat and on to the little footpath. They unhitched the ropes, coiled them carefully and getting back on board, stowed them away. Winstone made his way to the bow. Tony Amos turned on the "be seen" lights, fired up the motors and skilfully navigated his way into the River Itchen. Stafford pulled out his mobile and called DCI Talbot.

'Operation Trashed is underway, the *Cleopatra* is heading out. I'll revert to radio coms and alert the marine unit. I'll keep you informed,' said Stafford and he ended the call.

Once the *Cleopatra* was out of sight, Stafford and Peters went to the back of their cars and pulled out their "to go" bags. They took out their combat radios and night-vision monoculars. They clipped the radios to their belts, connected the lightweight headsets and stuffed the "D" shaped earpiece into place. They adjusted their microphones accordingly. Carrying the depleted bags back to the office, Stafford turned on his radio. 'Come in trashed unit 2, come in trashed unit 2.'

Within seconds he heard, 'Trashed unit 2 responding.'

'Target *Cleopatra* is under way, over,' said Stafford.

'TU2 received and understood, over,' came back the reply. Stafford settled back on his seat.

'So what happens now?' asked Nicole.

'Nothing, we do nothing till they come back, but TU2 will make their way down towards the Solent and just wait for and observe the *Cleopatra*. They won't intercept unless there's a major problem. And they'll notify us when they have her in sight,' said Stafford.

It was an hour before Stafford's earpiece told him TU2 had visual contact with the *Cleopatra*.

It was some hours before Stafford's radio burst into life again. It was the marine unit commander, who said, 'Target *Cleopatra* picked up eight people, target returning. ETA 04:00 hours, over.'

Using their call sign, Stafford said, 'Message received, over and out.' He radioed TU4, the Immigration Enforcement team, and gave them the details, then to his crew, 'As you've just heard they've picked up eight people and they're due back here at around 04:00 hours, there's nothing more we can do but wait.'

———————— ‖ ————————

Within the next hour, two garishly marked Immigration Enforcement cell vans arrived, each carrying three officers. One of them was a chief immigration officer, who seemed a little embarrassed that on an undercover operation they would turn up in vehicles with sky blue and navy blue Battenburg markings, red and yellow rear door chevrons and "Immigration Enforcement" emblazoned on a yellow strip down both sides. He obviously realised it was not conducive to a low-key operation as the first thing he asked when he shook hands with Stafford was, 'Where can we hide the vans?'

Peters took them to an area close to the main gates at the other side of the SMR yard, far enough away not to be spotted from the boat. While there, Peters used his lock picks to open the padlocks on the front gates and said to the CIO, 'When we take custody of the immigrants, we'll bring them across the yard to this gate and get them aboard your motors. Once that's done, that's your lot here, you can take them on to the immigration centres.' He walked with the immigration team through the scrapyard to the rear gates, where he used his set of picks to unlock the padlocks there. He gave the padlocks to the CIO and explained the procedures he thought the bad guys would use, according to Brandon Miller's recent outlines. Before he returned to their new base, he said to the CIO, 'The padlock needs to be locked when you set up in the yard. So the lock-up man may need to stay on the outside.'

The CIO looked at him for a moment, then said, 'Ah yeah, I see what you mean, good point, thank you.'

The six immigration officers were kitted out in stab vests underneath their black boiler suits. The only weapons they carried were extendable batons. They wore protective helmets fitted with radio earpieces and mic's connected to radios on their belts.

While his men set up in the scrapyard, the CIO met up with Stafford in their newly commandeered office. Stafford was relieved the immigration teams weren't wearing hi-viz tabards. *At least they would be difficult to spot in the dark*, he thought.

'I'd like to get the immigrants into your custody and away without a battle, so we'll let Kapusniak and his crew bring them from the boat to their van. Then let Kapusniak's guys return to the boat and settle down again before we go in,' said Stafford.

'But won't they lock the van?' asked the CIO.

'Yeah, but Ryan... Captain Peters will take care of that, as he has with the gates,' said Stafford. They shook hands and the CIO left to organise his teams.

Stafford and his crew settled in for another long wait. Time dragged. Everyone was keyed up, ready for action. The temperature in the office had gone up a few degrees and the atmosphere had changed from a homely smell of sawn wood to a more earthy aroma, perspiration.

At 03:30 hours, Stafford and Peters went to the two bags they'd brought in earlier and took out their pistol cases. They checked the weapons, Glock 17s, ensured they were operational and the magazines were full. Slipping the loaded pistols into shoulder holsters and each selecting another full magazine, they too were fully operational.

As Stafford returned to the window, a sudden movement against the fence of the metal recycling yard caught his eye. Instinctively he raised the pistol in his right hand and moved to the door. Opening the door quietly, he watched as the shadowy figure disappeared into the untidy bushes at the end of the little footpath alongside the mooring. Stafford grinned to himself and thought, *not a bad place for the CIO to position one of his men.* He closed the door gently and returned to the window.

———————————— ll ————————————

At 03:45 the radio burst into life again, the marine unit calling Stafford and TU4. Stafford responded and seconds later so did the CIO of TU4.

'Target *Cleopatra*, ETA at mooring fifteen minutes, over and out.'

Just moments after 04:00 hours the thin layer of mist rising from the river parted and the *Cleopatra* gently nosed its way up to the mooring. Kapusniak and Amos jumped ashore and tied up fore and aft. The tension in the office rose considerably, each of them wanting to see what was happening, yet trying to keep still and out of eyeline. Stafford spoke quietly into his radio mic, 'Target docked TU4.'

'Roger that,' came the immediate response. Kapusniak and Amos clambered back on board and disappeared below decks. All that moved for what seemed to Stafford, forever, was the boat, repeating its up down, up down motion again and again…

Then Kapusniak returned to the cockpit. As he turned to step on to the footpath, Stafford raised his right hand, made a pistol shape and mouthed a silent 'Bang.' Peters, Gibson and Martin nodded their heads in quiet approval.

Winstone came up next, dragging by the arm, one of the female immigrants. Her hands were bound behind her back. He stood with one foot on terra firma, the other on the boat and pushed the woman across the divide. She stood by the fence, looking bewildered, soaked to the skin and shaking with cold. Kapusniak had opened the gates to the compound and the rear doors of the van. As each person was put into the van, their ankles were bound together with gaffer tape. Six women and two men were bundled, crying and groaning, into the load space. All, it seemed, were too exhausted, terrified and cold to do anything other than comply. Winstone closed and locked the van doors, then reversed it so the back doors were tight up against the fence. He jumped out, locked up and the three of them returned to the boat.

They began to set up the cockpit canopy and once in place, with the interior light on, they could be seen through the plastic windows, drinking beer and smoking. Twenty minutes later the light was turned out and all became quiet. Stafford waited a further twenty minutes before saying over the radio, 'TU4 time to move, over.' The message came back, 'Underway TU1.'

Peters slipped out of the office. The door was closed quietly behind him. Bent double and dodging between parked cars, he ran as swiftly as he could to the metal yard's back gates. The padlock was undone, he entered the compound and within seconds had opened the driver's door of the van. Joined by the Immigration Enforcement team, he released the handbrake and between them they rolled the van forward a hundred yards or so. They could now open the rear doors with less danger of being heard or spotted from the boat. When the doors were opened, the immigrants began to murmur and chatter, noisily, nervously. Unable to sit up, they began to wriggle and squirm around, trying to see what was happening. Peters hissed, 'Shhhh, for fuck's sake, anyone speak English?'

A female responded, 'I can, a little.'

'OK, we are here to help. To get you outa here, but you gotta stay silent. Shhh. Make no noise, understand?' whispered Peters.

'Yes, yes, I understand,' the voice whispered urgently back. Then with a little more confidence, translated for her companions what Peters had said. Silence descended and the wriggling stopped.

Two immigration officers climbed into the back of the van and began to cut through the gaffer tape and the cable-tie bonds. Gently they helped the shivering immigrants out and gave each one a hypothermia foil blanket. The officers walked the group across the yard, out through the front gates and into their waiting vehicles.

Once the vans had gone, Peters started back to the rear gates. In his earpiece he heard, 'TU4 to TU1, all away safely, nice job, Major, see you at Trojan Horse, over and out.'

Stafford said, 'Roger that, and thanks for your help TU4.'

Peters, dodging and ducking in between parked cars, returned to the office. The anticipation and tension was palpable, everyone keen to end this. As Peters returned to look out of the window, he said, 'You know, when I came out of the yard, I stopped to check before coming out of the gates. I couldn't see any lookout or sign of movement on the boat. I think the lookout's dozed off, or they're so cocky they haven't bothered.'

'Well, whatever the situation,' said Stafford turning to Gibson and Nicole, 'I promised Sergeant Hawkins I wouldn't put you two in harm's way, so Ryan and me will take the lead on this. I've got two Kevlar vests and helmets in the bag so let's get that on you...'

Stafford, interrupted by Peters's shout of, 'What the fuck?' turned to look out of the windows. A hooded, dark shadowy figure was standing next to the boat. Stafford's immediate thought was that it was Kapusniak's lookout. They watched for a second, then scrambled out of the office, too late to stop the figure splashing liquid from what looked like a petrol can on to the cockpit canopy.

'Christ, that's petrol, I can smell it from here,' shouted Stafford as he dashed towards the footpath. Unable to reach the hooded figure in time, he watched in horror as it reached out and dropped a blazing lighter on to the canopy. The canopy erupted. Blazing liquid ran into the cockpit, setting fire to the seats, then down the stairs below deck. Within seconds the whole back end of the boat was ablaze. Stafford took a flying leap and ripping through the blazing cockpit cover landed in the centre deck. He grabbed the little fire extinguisher he'd spotted and hitting the handle, aimed it at the stairwell. He shouted,

'Kapusniak, for fuck's sake, get up here, your boat's on fire, get up here.'

The shadowy assailant, who had seemed rooted to the spot, screamed, 'That's for George, you bastards, I hope you burn in hell.' Then ran down past the gates of the yard trying to escape. Peters, with gun drawn, and Gibson dashed to the side of the boat and shouted at Stafford to get off. Peters called for the emergency services. Nicole had seen the assailant make a run for it and gave chase. Within a couple of hundred yards the assailant came to a full stop, leaned backwards and gasped for breath. Then leaned forward, hands on knees, gasping and sobbing uncontrollably. Nicole caught up, grabbed an arm and said, 'You're bloody nicked.' She turned the assailant round to face her and pulled off the hood. A mess of blonde hair tumbled across the attacker's face. Pushing the hair roughly aside, Nicole was astounded to see the face of a wild-eyed, but triumphant Eileen Saunders.

'Fuck's sake, Eileen, what the hell do you think you're doing?' she said.

———————————— ‖ ————————————

The fire had now taken hold of the stairwell, and the steps and door were ablaze. Stafford realised the fire extinguisher was useless. He shouted once more, 'Kapusniak, for Christ's sake, get out here, the boat's gonna blow up, get the fuck up here!' It was then he saw the new man, Tony Amos, lying across the leather bench seats, apparently unconscious. He threw the fire extinguisher ashore, grabbed Amos by one arm and pulled him into an almost upright position.

With an arm between his legs he hoisted Amos across his back. The boat rocked furiously from side to side seemingly determined to tip him over, but somehow Stafford managed to stagger across to the footpath. He took a dozen or so paces forward before dumping Amos flat on his back on to the ground. Then he could see that Amos was clutching a bottle of vodka.

Winstone was the first to emerge from below deck. He burst through the door, gasping and spluttering for air. He dashed up the stairs, stumbling as his eyes streamed from the smoke and acrid fumes.

'Get your hands in the air,' yelled Peters as he pointed his pistol at him. Coughing violently Winstone struggled to keep his balance. He used his good hand trying to carry a package wrapped in blue plastic. When he saw Peters and Stafford on the footpath he dropped the package, put his hands in the air and made to jump ashore.

'Bring the package, Mr Winstone, or you can burn with it,' snarled Peters. Winstone stopped in his tracks and stared wide-eyed at Peters.

'Yeah, we know who you are, now pick up the package.' Winstone reached down and with his good hand picked it up. He screamed as the melting plastic stuck to his hands. He seemed about to dump it again, then changed his mind as Peters raised the pistol and aimed it at his face. He leapt ashore, tried to dump the parcel on the footpath but the plastic was now welded to his hands. Peters gave a grin of satisfaction at the extended scream Winstone let out as he wrenched the parcel out of his grasp.

Gibson, having already handcuffed Amos, made Winstone help him get Amos to his feet. And with Winstone wailing about his busted and burnt hands, Gibson patted them down and locked them into the Vectra, having first removed their mobile phones and Winstone's van keys. When he returned, the boat was an inferno. Fumes from burning plastic and fibreglass stung their eyes, smoke made it impossible to see more than a few feet and extremely difficult to breathe. Every breath seared their lungs with acrid fumes. Their eyes streamed and their throats rasped. Stafford shouted once more, 'Kapusniak, get out here, you docile bastard, this boat's gonna blow. You gotta get out here now!'

Kapusniak, eyes wide, scarf around his nose and mouth, charged from the cabins, up through the blazing stairwell and into the cockpit inferno.

Stafford couldn't resist a grin at the thought that he was seeing the Devil himself rising from the fires of hell. The thought instantly disappeared as he dived to one side when Kapusniak levelled a pump-action shotgun at him. Peters didn't hesitate, he fired his pistol, double tap, hitting Kapusniak close together high in the right side of his chest. Kapusniak's eyes opened even wider as he staggered backwards. His shotgun blasted harmlessly into the smoky black sky as he crashed into the river. Gibson peered through the smoke into the water. He could see by the light from the inferno that Kapusniak was floating on his back, shotgun still in his arms. *How the fuck did we not seen him bring the shotgun aboard?* flashed into his mind as he pulled off his jacket and shoes and dived into the water. He reached Kapusniak in a few strokes, grabbed him by the collar of his jacket and pulled him to the riverbank. Gibson pulled the shotgun from Kapusniak's grasp and dumped it on the footpath. Stafford hauled Gibson out and together they managed to get the still breathing Kapusniak ashore. Peters, Gibson and Stafford carried the moaning, soaking wet figure of Kapusniak along the riverbank and laid him down in the car parking area. Gibson told Stafford that he had a bag of spare clothes in his car and would take just a few moments to dry off and change into dry clothes. Stafford gave him a surprised look and Gibson said quietly, 'I'll explain later, boss.'

The ambulance took eight minutes to arrive. The paramedics immediately began working to keep Kapusniak alive. The fire tenders and police turned up seconds later. Within moments the police had cordoned off Saxon Wharf and the fire brigade had the blaze under control.

As Nicole Martin returned with Eileen Saunders, so the dried out Gibson walked back from his car. Eileen saw him, broke away from Nicole and ran over to him. 'I'm sorry, Lee, I'm sorry… Stephanie; I found out. I had to do it. I did it for George,' she shouted incoherently.

Gibson, not sure what to say, nodded, looked sheepishly at Stafford and the others and said, 'I'll explain later, boss.' Stafford nodded and walked away.

'We'll have to arrest you, Mrs Saunders, got no choice,' said Gibson as he handed her over to the newly arrived police officers. Nicole looked at Gibson, shook her head despairingly, then walked over to Eileen and the other coppers and said, 'I need to ask her a couple of questions before you take her, OK?' The officers nodded.

'Eileen, how the hell did you find us? The boat?' she asked.

Eileen looked at her defiantly and said, 'I went to George's office, they said they knew nothing, wouldn't help.

They didn't care, just wanted me to go. I sat at her desk, Stephanie's desk, said I wouldn't go till they told me. Then I saw her name and address on the blotter. I remembered it, and went to see her. He was there too, the policeman, that Lee, she told me quick enough. They wanted shot of me too.' Finished, she got into the police car, stone-faced and defiant as they drove her away.

‖

Nicole saw the paramedics wheeling Kapusniak handcuffed to a gurney, towards the ambulance. She walked across and saw that he was conscious. 'Have you given him any pain relief?' she asked one of the medics.

'Yeah, but it will take a while to help,' he said.

'Good,' she said, then made a fist and rose to her full height on her toes. She smashed it on to the bandage that covered Kapusniak's wounds. Kapusniak's whole body jerked violently. His screams were muffled by the oxygen mask. Not satisfied, she raised her fist again. This time the paramedics were too quick for her and managed to move the trolley a yard or so and the blow landed on his crotch. Kapusniak convulsed again, tore off the mask, let out an anguished scream. Satisfied, Nicole said quietly in his ear, 'That's for Garfield Lewis,' and walked away smiling. A second paramedic had attended to the whinging Winstone's burned and busted hands, and wearing plastic "mittens" he was bundled into the back of a police car alongside a drunken Tony Amos.

By now the area was a heaving, seething mass of people, flashing red and blue lights, headlights from the emergency vehicles creating intricate patterns in the swirling mist and smoke. Local media had got wind of an incident at Saxon Wharf and were turning up in their droves. TV trucks, radio and newspaper reporters gathered noisily at the police cordons, clamouring for details. Stafford realised they would have to act quickly before news of the incident reached Runihura. He called DCI Talbot and explained what had happened. 'We can't take a chance with "Trojan Horse", we need to go in asap, will you arrange for the two armed response vehicles to meet us in the service road at Weyhill, and get the teams ready to cordon off the road? I'll mobilise the Immigration Enforcement units to meet us there,' he said. Talbot agreed to put wheels into motion immediately.

Stafford called his crew together. 'We can't wait until the morning rush hour, we've gotta go now, before Runihura becomes aware of what's happened here. So into the Vectra. Ryan, you're driving.' They piled into the car. Peters fired it up, turned on the blues and twos and headed for the M3. Gibson started to speak, 'Stafford, look I...' but Stafford cut him short, 'Not now, Lee, time for that later. Just concentrate on getting this done. OK?' Gibson nodded silently.

Stafford spoke into his radio mic, 'TU1 to TU4, over.' When TU4 responded, Stafford told the CIO that the plan had changed. That operation "Trojan Horse" was no more and TU4 should meet with them at the service road in Weyhill. He asked them to bring breaching explosives as well as their "enforcer" battering ram. TU4 responded, 'Roger that TU1, over and out.'

CHAPTER 52

The thirty-four-mile drive took Peters twenty-eight minutes. The two ARVs were already there. A few moments later the two garish Immigration Enforcement vehicles rolled up.

It was already getting light when Stafford gathered the leaders of each team around the bonnet of the Vectra and laid out the aerial pictures of the compound.

'Now I know your bosses have been through this with you already, but I need to know that we're all on the same page here,' said Stafford. It took him ten minutes to outline the plan of attack.

'Is that all clear? Are there any questions?' Receiving murmurs of approval he continued, 'TU 3-1, roll out now, park up 150 yards away from the compound. Silent approach: radio when you're in position.' The five-man team climbed into their ARV and headed to the compound. Stafford and the others piled into their vehicles and waited.

It was thirty minutes before TU 3-1 radioed in. 'TU1 received, over,' said Stafford, then, 'Roll out, roll out, over.' As planned the Immigration Enforcement vans rolled out first, followed by the second ARV. Stafford, with his team, brought up the rear in the Vectra.

A hundred yards from the target, all vehicles hit their switches, headlights blazed, blues and twos, red and blues flashed and with a cacophony of sirens they swept into the front drive of the compound. The immigration team dashed from their vehicles and prepared a line of three mini breaching explosives and attached it to the centre join of the two gates.

The second armed response unit swiftly disembarked. Three men ran to the front door of the bungalow, two men to the rear. Stafford and Nicole ran to the front door, Stafford carrying the "enforcer". It took him three hits before the door folded. He stood back and the three armed response officers burst through shouting, 'Armed police, armed police, come out with you, hands in the air.'

Stafford put down the enforcer and pulled out his pistol. He stepped carefully over the busted door, Nicole close behind him. As they moved from room to room they could hear the other officers shouting their warnings, then, 'All clear', numerous times.

Peters, Gibson and the two armed response officers who had broken through the rear door, met no resistance either. The place was obviously being used, but no one, it appeared, was home. Stafford told Gibson and Nicole to stay in the bungalow and search the place. To take pictures and collect evidence.

Stafford and Peters with TU 3-2, stepped over the broken rear door and joined the immigration team at the front gates to the compound proper. Even above the noise of the sirens they could hear ferocious barking.

'Fucking Miller never mentioned dogs to us,' said Peters with a chuckle. Stafford grinned at him, raised his hand and using the call signs, said into his radio, 'Ready to breach compound, counting down, over.' The CIO looked for the hand signal as Stafford counted down '5, 4, 3, 2, 1, fire,' he shouted and he slapped his hand against his thigh. The CIO hit the switch and the breaching explosives blew the gates apart. Almost immediately a second explosion ripped through the air behind them. Diving for cover, they turned to face the bungalow and had to shield themselves as splintered roof tiles, wood and brick debris from a gaping hole in the side of the bungalow rained down on them. Realising they had to go forward Stafford signalled the CIO to throw in the smoke grenades. Two of the immigration team moved to the gap in the gates and lobbed in the grenades then withdrew. Within seconds the acrid grey smoke billowed out in front of them. Stafford led the armed response team in through the gates. Hidden by the smoke, they spread out across the compound, taking cover behind vehicles and the building they knew was the drug manufacturing laboratory.

One of the dogs had been hit by a gate and was lying twitching on the ground. Another had run yelping back to its pound and was licking a badly wounded paw. TU 3-1 had successfully breached the rear gate and had shot and killed the third dog.

As they moved further into the yard the sirens stopped. For a second or two the silence was deafening. Peters looked at Stafford who nodded his understanding; either Lee or Nicole were still in action.

Stafford and the five firearms officers spread out slowly. Stafford said into the radio, 'TU 4, stay behind the wall.' Then, 'TU 3-1, find cover behind the dog pound and those five bins.'

'Roger that,' came back the responses. Peters slipped his pistol back into its holster. He walked across to the unconscious German Shepherd dog, bent down, lifted it up and carried it across the yard to the dog pound. He walked inside; the injured dog already there, snarled but made no move to attack as Peters laid its mate down beside it. He withdrew, closed the gate behind him and joined TU 3-1 at the far end of the yard.

Stafford had begun to suspect that Runihura and his men had somehow got wind of the attack and fled the compound, when Runihura stepped out of his front door holding a mobile phone high in his left hand.

'So you've decided to pay us a visit then, Major? Sadly we have no work for you at present. But then you know that cos it was you that fucked it up for us,' he said with a sneer.

'Well, Ayman, I see you've got your phone with you, I reckon it'd be a good idea if you phoned Neilson right now.'

Runihura kept the phone high as he walked slowly down the steps and over towards the dog pound. He paused as he came to the body of the dead German Shepherd, he knelt alongside it and stroked its head. He stayed there for a long moment, then continued into the pound. The two dogs wandered unsteadily across to him and whimpered quietly as he patted them. He turned back to Stafford and shouted, 'I saw what Captain Peters did, that may just have saved his life, but the bastard who shot my other dog will die for that.' Stafford made to move forward.

Runihura waved the phone at him. 'Do you want me to blow up another building, Major? One press and those caravans will blow sky high.'

'What have you done with the workers, Ayman? The immigrants?'

'Fuck me, you are stupid, aren't you? They're in the caravans of course,' he said laughing.

'They've done nothing to you, why don't you let us take them out of here; it would go in your favour?'

'And that's your trouble, Major, too much of a bleeding heart.'

'So where are Whitlock and Potter and the others? Did they fuck off, and leave you to hide behind innocent immigrants?'

Runihura's eyes widened slightly. 'Ah, so you've met our Mr Miller then, Major.' While they had been talking, Runihura had moved out of the dog pound and Stafford had been moving slowly forward.

His earpiece crackled into life.

'If you can keep him talking, we'll take out the mobile homes with stun grenades,' said Peters.

The smoke had almost dispersed when one of the armed response officers spoke, 'I've got a sight on Runihura, do you want me to take the shot?'

Stafford said quietly into the radio, 'Go Ryan, hold fire...' Before he could say TU 3-1, from the rear of the site came the crash of windows breaking, followed almost immediately by two muffled explosions. At the same time a shot rang out from Stafford's left. Startled, Runihura turned to the noise behind him so quickly he dropped his mobile phone. The bullet whistled harmlessly past him, but the phone broke apart as it bounced across the concrete floor. Stafford ran forward and with a flying tackle hit Runihura in the midriff. The speed and force of the attack took them both to the floor, Stafford landing on top. Runihura's grunt as he hit the ground echoed around the compound. Stafford took advantage and managed to land a couple of punches that splattered Runihura's nose across his face. As Stafford climbed to his feet and reached for his pistol, the door to one of the mobile homes burst open. Eric Potter ran out, followed by two other men. All were obviously disorientated and, in panic, they sprayed the compound with fire from their semi-automatic assault rifles. Stafford and others fired off a couple of shots in their direction as they dived for cover. Runihura was quick to take advantage and with blood streaming from his nose, ran to the hook loader lorry. He ripped open the door and leapt into the cab. Bullets ricocheted off the grill and bonnet, and the windscreen shattered. He fired up the engine and drove through the yard scattering armed officers as he went. He slowed to negotiate the gate and tight right-hand turn. This gave Stafford the chance to get to the vehicle's rear end. He lunged for the nearside rear double mudguard.

Pulled off balance, arms almost wrenched from their sockets, and with his face inches from the rear wheels he tried desperately to haul himself on board. With his legs and feet bouncing crazily on the ground he managed to grab the net cover arm and pulled himself on to the chassis. He steadied himself against the arm and began to inch his way along the narrow chassis members towards the cab. As he crossed to the centre his foot slipped, he fell sideways smashing his hip into the offside rail. Stretching out his left arm he managed to grasp the upright hook. Wincing with pain he paused to catch his breath before pulling himself upright and reaching for his pistol.

He saw Nicole, hair matted with dust and blood, grab something from the rear of the immigration team's van. He watched as she ran along the nearside of the lorry and pulled a pin from the item she carried. She jumped on to the passenger door step, threw the item through the busted window, and leapt off, landing in an untidy heap on the concrete driveway. Winded, she stayed there momentarily before climbing to her feet, then she pulled out her mobile and called in the waiting ambulances.

Seconds later a huge bang and searing flash came from the hook loader's cab. Runihura stunned senseless and blinded, albeit temporarily, slumped in the driver's seat. The lorry careered down the driveway, crunching, scraping and bouncing off the vehicles parked there. It thundered on to the road and lurched crazily as its nearside wheel hit the far kerb. Stafford still managed to hang on to the hook, though he'd lost his footing a number of times and his legs were badly torn and grazed as he struggled to stay on board. The lorry bounced back on to the carriageway, heading downhill towards the T-junction.

Two police patrol cars had been positioned there to close off public access to the hill. Police officers directed traffic behind the cars, and two others patrolled the front looking up the hill. The lorry's front wheels kept bouncing into and back off the nearside kerb, throwing Stafford backwards and forwards across the chassis members. His legs crashed on the solid metal bars and his feet slipped through to the road rushing by underneath. Yet somehow he managed to stay on board. The police officers dived for safety as the lorry, with smoke pouring from the broken windscreen and steam spewing from the grill and bonnet, hit the left-hand patrol car, trapping it like a toy under its huge bumper. The lorry forced it across the junction, ripping off both front wheels, where it careered into the hedgerow, finally unseating Stafford, throwing him headlong into one of the bushes.

It took him three or four minutes to compose himself, then he climbed gingerly down from his perch, clambered around to the driver's door and dragged the semi-conscious Runihura out of the cab.

Nicole caught up with them and helped Stafford get Runihura back to the compound. The ambulances had been waiting in the service road and took only two minutes to arrive. Paramedics began to work on Runihura who was now handcuffed to a gurney.

Though gunfire could still be heard from the yard Stafford gave Nicole a hug and said, 'Christ, girl, I'm glad you're safe. I was worried there for a bit, I don't know what I'd have said to Sergeant Hawkins if you'd really been hurt.' She gave him a hard thump on the arm, which made him wince. 'Serves you right,' she said, then gave him another hug and added, 'Now can we go and see if we can get Lee out in one piece?'

Back in the compound, Peters and the armed response unit had managed to disarm Eric Potter and the other two men, when the door to the second mobile home had opened. Mark Whitlock stumbled out with his hands in the air. In his left hand he held an assault rifle, but he was in no condition to fight; he'd breathed in the fumes from the stun grenade for too long. As Whitlock was taken into custody, Peters called in the bomb squad and the Black Marias. Without warning one of the officers leading Whitlock away was hit in the shoulder by bullets fired from the drug lab. Peters and the rest of the armed response team turned their guns on the lab. Peters grabbed a stun grenade from one of the officers, pulled the pin and hurled it at a window. The window shattered and instantly a five million or so candela flash and a 175 dB bang silenced the guns inside. Peters held up his arm to stop the armed officers going straight in. He walked to the side of the shattered window, and peered inside. As he strolled back and found cover behind a black Mercedes 4 x 4, he said into his radio mic, 'Fire in the hole! Take cover NOW! Fire in the hole!' Flames licked around the sides of the window. The grenade flash had set alight flammable material inside the lab and within minutes the room was an inferno. Then the whole building blew apart. Blazing shards of timber, chunks of bricks and mortar and roof tiles flew into the air and across the yard. The compound's perimeter wall behind the lab seemed to propel debris forwards. As it rained down on them Peters said into his radio mic, 'What a bummer, I forgot they used dangerous chemicals to make this stuff.'

Peters turned his attention to the largest building in the yard, the factory. Access was through a wicket door in the main roller shutter. The wicket door was unlocked and he pushed it wide open. It was dark inside. He stood to one side and listened; he heard nothing. Gun in his right hand, he dived through the door to one side. Left arm outstretched he went into a forward roll, came back on to his feet into a crouch. He held the gun out in front with both hands and moved towards the nearest workbench for cover. It was too dark to see the full length of the space. Peters turned back to the wicket door. He saw the light switches on the wall and the two button switches that controlled the roller shutter. He switched on the lights, closed the little door and hit the up button for the shutter. The gate rose slowly and clanged to a stop at the top. The armed response boys walked in weapons at the ready, but the place was clear of bad guys.

Peters wandered out into the yard and said into his radio mic, 'All buildings clear, need bomb squad to sort IEDs under caravans, over and out.' He wandered out to the bungalow to find Stafford and the other two.

Stafford and Nicole with the help of a couple of Immigration Enforcement officers had managed to lift heavy timbers and brick debris from Lee Gibson's broken legs.

He was conscious when they handed him over to the paramedics. As they put him on the gurney and wheeled him towards the ambulance, he told Stafford how he had stayed two or three nights with Stephanie Turnbull. And one time while he was there, Eileen had turned up. Stephanie had told Eileen they were close to catching the killers because the police were watching their boat. Then Eileen had become aggressive, demanding to know where the boat was. Desperate to get rid of her, Stephanie had blurted out, Saxon Wharf.

Stunned, Stafford stood and watched as the medics closed the ambulance doors and drove away.

When the bomb squad had removed and dismantled two IEDs from underneath the caravans, the Immigration Enforcement team moved in and found eighteen male and two female foreign nationals living in the dilapidated caravans. After being checked over by the paramedics, thirteen men were sent directly to immigration centres, five were taken to hospital suffering with old untreated injuries. Both women were taken taken to hospital suffering from injuries thought to have been caused by vicious sexual abuse. All twenty appeared to be suffering with severe drug withdrawal symptoms and psychological damage.

Peters had called the RSPCA and they had collected the two German Shepherd dogs, and removed the carcass of the third.

Stafford called DCI Talbot and Sergeant Hawkins and gave them a brief outline of the successful end to operation TRASHED.

Once Nicole and Stafford had been patched up by the paramedics they found Peters.

'Fuck, I've been looking for you two, I thought you'd gone home and left me to sort it,' he said laughing out loud. He raised his arms and they came together in a group hug. They stayed that way for a very long moment, and said nothing.

When they pulled apart, Stafford said almost to himself, 'I guess I'd better contact the safe house now and tell 'em that it's OK, safe for us all to go back home.'

Nicole looked at him, her big brown eyes wide, she opened her mouth to speak. In the end she said nothing.